After the King

After the King

Stories in Honor of J. R. R. Tolkien

Edited by Martin H. Greenberg
Introduction by Jane Yolen

TOR
fantasy

A TOM DOHERTY ASSOCIATES BOOK
NEW YORK

AFTER THE KING: Stories in Honor of J. R. R. Tolkien

Copyright © 1992 by Martin H. Greenberg

This anthology has not been authorized by the estate of J. R. R. Tolkien, Christopher Tolkien or Unwin Hyman, Ltd. Nothing in its publication is meant to imply such authorization or approval.

"Reave the Just" copyright © 1992 by Stephen R. Donaldson. "Troll Bridge" copyright © 1992 by Terry and Lyn Pratchett. "A Long Night's Vigil at the Temple" copyright © 1992 by Agberg, Ltd. "The Dragon of Tollin" copyright © 1992 by Elizabeth Ann Scarborough. "Faith" copyright © 1992 by Poul and Karen Anderson. "In the Season of the Dressing of the Wells" copyright © 1992 by Brunner Fact & Fiction Ltd. "The Fellowship of the Dragon" copyright © 1992 by Patricia A. McKillip. "The Decoy Duck" copyright © 1992 by Harry Turtledove. "Nine Threads of Gold" copyright © 1992 by Andre Norton. "The Conjure Man" copyright © 1992 by Charles de Lint. "The Halfling House" copyright © 1992 by Dennis L. McKiernan. "Silver or Gold" copyright © 1992 by Emma Bull. "Up the Side of the Air" copyright © 1992 by Karen Haber. "The Naga" copyright © 1992 by Peter S. Beagle. "Revolt of the Sugar Plum Fairies" copyright © 1992 by Mike Resnick. "Winter's King" copyright © 1992 by Jane Yolen. "Götterdämmerung" copyright © 1992 by Barry N. Malzberg. "Down the River Road" copyright © 1992 by Abbenford Associates. "Death and the Lady" copyright © 1992 by Judith Tarr.

This book is printed on acid-free paper.

A Tor Book
Published by Tom Doherty Associates, Inc.
175 Fifth Avenue
New York, N.Y. 10010

Library of Congress Cataloging-in-Publication Data

After the king : stories in honor of J. R. R. Tolkien / edited by Martin H. Greenberg : introduction by Jane Yolen.
    p. cm.
"A Tom Doherty Associates book."
ISBN 0-312-85175-8
1. Fantastic fiction, American. I. Greenberg, Martin Harry.
II. Tolkien, J. R. R. (John Ronald Reuel), 1892–1973.
PS648.F3A46 1992
813′.0876608—dc20   91-34382
                                         CIP

First edition: January 1992

Book design by Maura Fadden Rosenthal

Printed in the United States of America

0 9 8 7 6 5 4 3 2 1

Contents

Introduction

Jane Yolen

ometimes it is difficult to remember that there were fantasy books written before J. R. R. Tolkien's work burst onto the literary scene. Yet there *were* landmark volumes, stories of childhood, such as *The Wind in the Willows* and *The Jungle Books*. There were adult books of mythic proportion such as *The Well at the World's End* and of Gothic proportion such as *Dracula* and the delicious anachronisms of *A Connecticut Yankee in King Arthur's Court*. There were family fantasy books to be shared at the hearthside by well-known writers like Charles Dickens and unknown mathematicians such as the Reverend Charles Dodgson.

The history of literature is a mindfield of fantasy books.

But what John Ronald Reuel Tolkien created at his typewriter in his garage study, this "great but dilatory and unmethodical man" as his friend C. S. Lewis called him, was the phenomenon of fantasy as market genre.

He thought that he was only making up a world, peopling it, chronicling its lineages and laws. Middle-earth, he always insisted, was not an allegory. In fact he loathed allegory. And though he was a critic and a professor, he abhorred the symbol-hunting that went on about his books. He came down firmly and finally on the side of pure storytelling. What he forgot was that, as a god, he might create a universe, but then that universe would, clockworklike, go on without him.

I am too old to have read Tolkien as a child, but I first heard about his books from a British friend. And then I read *about* them in Peter Beagle's delightful book about his ride across America on a motorcycle— *I See By My Outfit*. When my husband and I decided to camp across Europe and the Middle East for as long as our money held out in 1965 and 1966, I got hold of a hardcover British edition of *The Lord of the Rings* and read it as we sailed to England on the *Castel Felice*. While the other passengers danced to the music of "Anastasio E Sui Happy Boys," I devoured the books. Ten days later, when we docked in Southampton, it did not surprise me in the slightest that the houses all looked like hobbit holes and I restrained myself—but barely—from asking a publican to take off his shoes so I might examine the tops of his feet for hair.

As changed as I was by my first reading of Tolkien, I was only a microcosm of the changes wrought on writers in general and fantasy writers in particular, for after the success of *The Lord of the Rings,* there was a rush to profit. Publishers and booksellers together invented the market for fantasy *as a genre.* Fantasy writers became—like it or not (and it must be admitted that there are some fantasy writers who despise Tolkien and vociferously distance themselves from his influence)—a Post-Tolkien Fellowship. We wrote books whose very natures proclaimed them to be Tolkienesque: books marked by the mythic quality of the stories, the background of saga and folklore, the often pastoral and/or pseudo-medieval setting, and the underlying assumption that magic has consequences as surely as the ring carried to the dark mountain wore down its wearer. And whether or not the influences went well beyond Tolkien, back to the misty dark ages of myth, folktale, legend and the like, the books all carried apothegms (printed or assumed) declaring "In the style of J. R. R. Tolkien."

Of course given such parameters, what began in grace and power easily degenerated into a kind of mythic silliness—elves in fur loincloths, pastel unicorns, coy talking swords, and a paint-by-number medieval setting with the requisite number of dirty inns, evil wizards, and gentle hairy-footed beings of various sexual persuasions. Tolkien would not have been amused.

Amused? He would have been horrified.

Still, amidst the post-1960s flood of Post-Tolkien fantasy writing, a few authors stand out, writing the kinds of stories that Tolkien himself might have looked favorably on and enjoyed. Writers like Andre Norton, the queen of the fantasy adventure novel; and Poul Anderson who set his own thumbprints on the mythic North; and Robert Silverberg that protean storyteller; and Peter S. Beagle whose debt to Tolkien was so unabashedly limned in his nonfiction book and the splendid few—too few—novels that followed. They, and the other wonderful authors in this volume, were asked specifically to write a Tolkienesque story, not in imitation of the master—for none of us are imitators—but in honor of his work. A birthday volume, a *festschrift*, a present for the 100th anniversary of his birth—and for his many readers.

We hope those same readers will feel about these stories as did the electrician at Oxford who was called to repair some wiring in the English Faculty Library. Noticing the bust of Tolkien, he put down his tools and walked over to it and clapped an arm companionably around the bronze shoulder. Then, speaking to it unembarrassed, as if talking to a dear old friend, he said, "Well done, Professor! You've written a smashing good yarn."

—Jane Yolen
Phoenix Farm
April 1991

Reave the Just

Stephen R. Donaldson

f all the strange, unrelenting stories which surrounded Reave the Just, none expressed his particular oddness of character better than that concerning his kinsman, Jillet of Forebridge.

Part of the oddness was this—that Reave and Jillet were so unlike each other that the whole idea of their kinship became difficult to credit.

Let it be said without prejudice that Jillet was an amiable fool. No one who was not amiable would have been loved by the cautious people of Forebridge—and Jillet was loved, of that there could be no doubt. Otherwise the townsfolk would never have risked the unpredictable and often spectacular consequences of sending for Reave, merely to inform him that Jillet had disappeared. And no one who was not a fool would have gotten himself into so much trouble with Kelven Divestulata that Kelven felt compelled to dispose of him.

In contrast, neither Reave's enemies—of which his exploits had attracted a considerable number—nor his friends would have described him as amiable.

Doubtless there were villages across the North Counties, towns perhaps, possibly a city or two, where Reave the Just was admired, even adulated: Forebridge was not among them. His decisions were too wild, his actions too unremitting, to meet the chary approval of the farmers and farriers, millers and masons who had known Jillet from birth.

Like a force of nature, he was so far beyond explanation that people had ceased trying to account for him. Instead of wondering why he did what he did—or how he got away with it—the men and women of Forebridge asked themselves how such an implausible individual chanced to be kinsman to Jillet, who was himself only implausible in the degree to which likable character was combined with unreliable judgment.

In fact, no one knew for certain that Reave and Jillet were related. Just recently, Jillet had upon occasion referred to Reave as, "Reave the Just, my kinsman." That was the true extent of the information available in Forebridge. Nothing more was revealed on the subject. In an effort to supply the lack, rumor or gossip suggested that Jillet's mother's sister, a woman of another town altogether, had fallen under the seduction of a carnival clown with delusions of grandeur—or, alternatively, of a knight errant incognito—and had given Reave a bastard birth under some pitiful hedgerow, or perhaps in some nameless nunnery, or conceivably in some lord's private bedchamber. But how the strains of blood which could produce Reave had been so entirely suppressed in Jillet, neither rumor nor gossip knew.

Still it must have been true that Reave and Jillet were related. When Reave was summoned in Jillet's name, he came.

By the time Reave arrived, however, Jillet was beyond knowing whether anyone valued him enough to tell his kinsman what had become of him.

How he first began to make his way along the road to Kelven's enmity was never clearly known. Very well, he was a fool, as all men knew— but how had he become enmeshed in folly on this scale? A few bad bargains with usurers were conceivable. A few visits to the alchemists and mages who fed on the fringes of towns like Forebridge throughout the North Counties were conceivable, in fact hardly to be wondered at, especially when Jillet was at the painful age where he was old enough to want a woman's love but too young to know how to get it. A few minor and ultimately forgettable feuds born of competition for trade or passion were not only conceivable but normal. Had not men and women been such small and harmless fools always? The folk of Forebridge might talk of such matters endlessly, seeking to persuade themselves that they were wiser. But who among them would have hazarded himself against Kelven Divestulata? Indeed, who among them had not at one time or another suspected that Kelven was Satan Himself, thinly disguised by swarthy flesh and knotted muscle and wiry beard?

What in the name of all the saints had possessed Jillet to fling himself into such deep waters?

The truth—which no one in Forebridge ever divined—was that Jillet brought his doom down on his own head by the simple expedient of naming himself Reave's kinsman.

It came about in this fashion. In his early manhood, Jillet fell victim to an amiable, foolish, and quite understandable passion for the widow Huchette. Before his death, Rudolph Huchette had brought his new bride—foreign, succulent, and young—to live in the manor-house now occupied by Kelven Divestulata, thinking that by keeping her far from the taints and sophistication of the cities he could keep her pure. Sadly for him, he did not live long enough after settling in Forebridge to learn that his wife was pure by nature and needed no special protection. And of course the young men of the town knew nothing of her purity. They only knew that she was foreign, young, and bereaved, imponderably delicious. Jillet's passion was only one among many, ardent and doomed. The widow Huchette asked only of the God who watched over innocence that she be left alone.

Needless to say, she was not.

Realistically considered, the only one of her admirers truly capable of disturbing her was dour Kelven. When she spurned his advances, he laid siege to her with all the cunning bitterness of his nature. Over the course of many months, he contrived to install himself in the manor-house which Rudolph had intended as her lifelong home; he cut off her avenues of escape so that her only recourse was to accept the drudgery of being his housekeeper since she steadfastly refused the grim honor of being his wife. And even there he probably had the best of her, since he was no doubt perfectly capable of binding and raping her to satisfy his admiration.

However, Jillet and the other men enamored of the widow did not consider her circumstances—and their own—realistically. As men in passion will, they chose to believe that they themselves were the gravest threat to her detachment. Blind to Kelven's intentions, Jillet and his fellow fools went about in a fog of schemes, dreaming of ways to persuade her to reveal her inevitable preference for themselves.

However, Jillet carried this scheming further than most—but by no means all—of his peers.

Perhaps because of his amiability—or perhaps because he was foolish—he was not ordinarily successful in competitions over women. His
face and form were goodly enough, and his brown eyes showed pleasure
as openly as any man's. His kindness and cheery temper endeared him
throughout Forebridge. But he lacked forthrightness, self-assertion; he
lacked the qualities which inspired passion. As with women everywhere,
those of Forebridge valued kindness; they were fond of it; but they did
not surrender their virtue to it. They preferred heroes—or rogues.

So when Jillet first conceived his passion for the widow Huchette, he
was already accustomed to the likelihood that he would not succeed.

Like Kelven Divestulata after the first year or so of the widow's bereavement—although no one in Forebridge knew at the time what Kelven was doing—Jillet prepared a siege. He was not wise enough to ask
himself, Why am I not favored in the beds of women? What must I learn
in order to make myself desirable? How may I rise above the limitations
which nature has placed upon me? Instead, he asked, Who can help me
with this woman?

His answer had already occurred to a handful of his brighter, but no
less foolish, fellows. In consequence, he was no better than the fifth or
sixth man of Forebridge to approach the best-known hedgerow alchemist
in the County, seeking a love-potion.

According to some authorities, the chief distinction between alchemists and mages was that the former had more opportunities for charlatanism, at less hazard. Squires and earls consulted mages: plowmen
and cotters, alchemists. Certainly, the man whom Jillet approached was
a charlatan. He admitted as much freely in the company of folk who
were wise enough not to want anything from him. But he would never
have revealed the truth about himself to one such as Jillet.

Charlatan or not, however, he was growing weary of this seemingly
endless sequence of men demanding love-potions against the widow
Huchette. One heartsick swain by the six-month or so may be profitably
bilked. Three may be a source of amusement. But five or six in a season
was plainly tedious. And worrisome as well: even Forebridge was capable
of recognizing charlatanism when five or six love-potions failed consec-
utively.

"Go home," the alchemist snapped when he had been told what Jillet
wanted. "The ingredients for the magick you require are arduous and
expensive to obtain. I cannot satisfy you."

But Jillet, who could not have put his hand on five farthings at that moment, replied, "I care nothing for the price. I will pay whatever is needed." The dilemma of cost had never entered his head, but he was certain it could be resolved. The widow Huchette had gold enough, after all.

His confidence presented an entirely different dilemma to the alchemist. It was not in the nature of charlatans to refuse money. And yet too many love-potions had already been dispensed. If Providence did not inspire the widow to favor one of the first four or five men, the alchemist's reputation—and therefore his income—would be endangered. Perhaps even his person would be endangered.

Seeking to protect himself, the alchemist named a sum which should have stunned any son of a cotter.

Jillet was not stunned. Any sum was acceptable, since he had no prospect of ever paying it himself. "Very well," he said comfortably. Then, because he wished to believe in his own cleverness, he added, "But if the potion does not succeed, you will return that sum with interest."

"Oh, assuredly," replied the alchemist, who found that he could not after all refuse money. "All of my magicks succeed, or I will know the reason why. Return tomorrow. Bring your gold then."

He closed his door so that Jillet would not have a chance to change his mind.

Jillet walked home musing to himself. Now that he had time to consider the matter, he found that he had placed himself in an awkward position. True, the love of the widow Huchette promised to be a valuable investment—but it was an investment only, not coin. The alchemist would require coin. In fact, the coin was required in order to obtain the investment. And Jillet had no coin, not on the scale the alchemist had mentioned. The truth was that he had never laid mortal eyes on that scale of coin.

And he had no prospects which might be stretched to that scale, no skills which could earn it, no property which could be sold for it.

Where could a man like Jillet of Forebridge get so much money? Where else?

Congratulating himself on his clarity of wit, Jillet went to the usurers.

He had had no dealings with usurers heretofore. But he had heard rumors. Some such "lenders" were said to be more forgiving than others, less stringent in their demands. Well, Jillet had no need of anyone's forgiveness; but he felt a natural preference for men with amiable reputations. From the honest alchemist, he went in search of an amiable usurer.

Unfortunately, amiable, forgiving usurers had so much kindness in their natures because they could afford it; and they could afford it because their investments were scantly at risk: they demanded collateral before hazarding coin. This baffled Jillet more than a little. The concept of collateral he could understand—just—but he could not understand why the widow Huchette did not constitute collateral. He would use the money to pay the alchemist; the alchemist would give him a love-potion; the potion would win the widow; and from the widow's holdings the usurer would be paid. Where was the fallacy in all this?

The usurer himself had no difficulty detecting the fallacy. More in sorrow than in scorn, he sent Jillet away.

Other "lenders" were similarly inclined. Only their pity varied, not their rejection.

Well, thought Jillet, I will never gain the widow without assistance. I must have the potion.

So he abandoned his search for an amiable usurer and committed himself, like a lost fish, to swim in murkier waters. He went to do business with the kind of moneylender who despised the world because he feared it. This moneylender feared the world because his substance was always at risk; and his substance was always at risk because he required no collateral. All he required was a fatal return on his investment.

"One fifth!" Jillet protested. The interest sounded high, even to him. "No other lender in Forebridge asks so much."

"No other lender in Forebridge," wheezed the individual whose coin was endangered, "risks so much."

True, thought Jillet, giving the man his due. And after all one fifth was only a number. It would not amount to much, if the widow were won swiftly. "Very well," he replied calmly. "As you say, you ask no collateral. And my prospects cannot fail. One fifth in a year is not too much to pay for what I will gain, especially"—he cleared his throat in a dignified fashion, for emphasis—"since I will only need the use of your money for a fortnight at most."

"A *year*?" The usurer nearly burst a vessel. "You will return me one fifth *a week* on my risk, or you can beg coin of fools like yourself, for you will get none from me!"

One fifth in a week. Perhaps for a moment Jillet was indeed stunned. Perhaps he went so far as to reconsider the course he had chosen. One fifth in a week, each and every week— And what if the potion failed? Or if it was merely slow? He would never be able to pay that first one fifth, not to mention the second or the third—and certainly not the original sum itself. Why, it was ruinous.

But then it occurred to him that one fifth, or two fifths, or twenty would make no difference to the wealth of the widow Huchette. And he would be happy besides, basking in the knowledge of a passion virtuously satisfied.

On that comfortable assumption, he agreed to the usurer's terms.

The next day, laden with a purse containing more gold than he had ever seen in his life, Jillet of Forebridge returned to the alchemist.

By this time, the alchemist was ready for him. The essence of charlatanism was cunning, and the alchemist was nothing if not an essential charlatan. He had taken the measure of his man—as well as of his own circumstances—and had determined his response. First, of course, he counted out Jillet's gold, testing the coins with spurious powders and honest teeth. He produced a few small fires and explosions, purely for effect: like most of his ilk, he could be impressive when he wished. Then he spoke.

"Young man, you are not the first to approach me for a potion in this matter. You are merely the first"—he hefted the purse—"to place such value on your object. Therefore I must give you a magick able to supersede all others—a magick not only capable of attaining its end, but in fact of doing so against the opposition of a—number—of intervening magicks. This is a rare and dangerous enterprise. For it to succeed, you must not only trust it entirely, but also be bold in support of it.

"Behold!"

The alchemist flourished his arms to induce more fires and explosions. When an especially noxious fume had cleared, he held in his palm a leather pouch on a thong.

"I will be plain," said the alchemist, "for it will displease me gravely if magick of such cost and purity fails because you do not do your part. This periapt must be worn about your neck, concealed under your"— he was about to say "linen," but Jillet's skin clearly had no acquaintance with finery of that kind—"jerkin. As needed, it must be invoked in the following secret yet efficacious fashion." He glared at Jillet through his eyebrows. "You must make reference to 'my kinsman, Reave the Just.' And you must be as unscrupulous as Reave the Just in pursuing your aim. You must falter at nothing."

This was the alchemist's inspiration, his cunning at work. Naturally, the pouch contained only a malodorous dirt. The magick lay in the words, "my kinsman, Reave the Just." Any man willing to make that astonishing claim could be sure of one thing: he would receive opportunities which would otherwise be impossible for him. Doors would be opened, audiences granted, attention paid anywhere in the North Counties, regardless of Jillet's apparent lineage, or his lack of linen. In that sense, the magick the alchemist offered was truer than any of his previous potions. It would open the doors of houses. And conceivably, if the widow Huchette was impressionable enough, it would open the door of her heart; for what innocent and moony young female could resist the enchantment of Reave's reputation?

So, of course, Jillet protested. Precisely because he lacked the wit to understand the alchemist's chicanery, he failed to understand its use. Staring at his benefactor, he objected, "But Reave the Just is no kinsman of mine. My family is known in Forebridge. No one will believe me."

Simpleton, thought the alchemist. *Idiot.* "They will," he replied with a barely concealed exasperation born of fear that Jillet would demand the return of his gold, "if you are bold enough, *confident* enough in your actions. The words do not need to be true. They are simply a private incantation, a way of invoking the periapt without betraying what you do. The magick will succeed if you but *trust* it."

Still Jillet hesitated. Despite the strength which the mere idea of the widow Huchette exercised in his thinking, he had no comprehension of the power of ideas: he could not grasp what he might gain from the idea that he was related to Reave. "How can that be?" he asked the air more than the alchemist. No doubt deliberately, the alchemist had challenged his understanding of the world; and it was the world which should have answered him. Striving to articulate his doubt, he continued, "I want a love potion to change the way she looks at me. What will I gain by saying or acting a thing that is untrue?"

Perhaps this innocence explained some part of the affection Forebridge felt for him; but it did not endear him to the alchemist. "Now hear me," *clod, buffoon, half-wit,* said the alchemist. "This magick is precious, and if you do not value it I will offer it elsewhere. The object of your desire does not desire you. You wish her to desire you. Therefore something must be altered. Either she must be made to"—*stifle her natural revulsion for a clod like you*—"feel a desire she lacks. Or you must be made more desirable to her. I offer both. Properly invoked, the periapt will instill desire in her. And bold action and a reputation as Reave the Just's kinsman will make you desirable.

"What more do you require?"

Jillet was growing fuddled: he was unaccustomed to such abstract discourse. Fortunately for the alchemist's purse, however, what filled Jillet's head was not an idea but an image—the image of a usurer who demanded repayment at the rate of one fifth in a week, and who appeared capable of dining on Jillet's giblets if his demands were thwarted.

Considering his situation from the perspective not of ideas but of images, Jillet found that he could not move in any direction except forward. Behind him lurked exigencies too acute to be confronted: ahead stood the widow Huchette and passion.

"Very well," he said, making his first attempt to emulate Reave's legendary decisiveness. "Give me the pouch."

Gravely, the alchemist set the pouch in Jillet's hand.

In similar fashion, Jillet hung the thong about his neck and concealed the periapt under his jerkin.

Then he returned to Forebridge, armed with magick and cunning—and completely unshielded by any idea of what to do with his new weaponry.

The words *trust* and *bold* and *unscrupulous* rang in his mind. What did they mean? *Trust* came to him naturally; *bold* was incomprehensible; *unscrupulous* conveyed a note of dishonesty. Taken together, they seemed as queer as a hog with a chicken's head—or an amiable usurer. Jillet was altogether at sea.

In that state, he chanced to encounter one of his fellow pretenders to the widow Huchette's bed, a stout, hairy, and frequently besotted fletcher named Slup. Not many days ago, Slup had viewed Jillet as a rival, perhaps even as a foe; he had behaved toward Jillet in a surly way which had baffled Jillet's amiable nature. Since that time, however, Slup had obtained his own alchemick potion, and new confidence restored his good will. Hailing Jillet cheerfully, he asked where his old friend had been hiding for the past day or so.

Trust, Jillet thought. *Bold. Unscrupulous.* It was natural, was it not, that magick made no sense to ordinary men? If an ordinary man, therefore, wished to benefit from magick, he must require himself to behave in ways which made no sense.

Summoning his resolve, he replied, "Speaking with my kinsman, Reave the Just," and strode past Slup without further explanation.

He did not know it, of course, but he had done enough. With those few words, he had invoked the power, not of the periapt, but of ideas. Slup told what he had heard to others, who repeated it to still others. Within hours, discussion had ranged from one end of the village to the other. The absence of explanation—when had Jillet come upon such a relation? why had he never mentioned it before? how had *Reave the Just*, of all men, contrived to visit Forebridge without attracting notice?—far from proving a hindrance, actually enhanced the efficacy of Jillet's utterance. When he went to his favorite tavern that evening, hoping to meet with some hearty friend who would stand him a tankard of ale, he found that every man he knew had been transformed—or he himself had.

He entered the tavern in what was, for him, a state of some anxiety. The more he had thought about it, the more he had realized that the gamble he took with Slup was one which he did not comprehend. After all, what experience had he ever had with alchemy? How could he be sure of its effectiveness? He knew about such things only by reputation, by the stories men told concerning alchemists and mages, witches and warlocks. The interval between his encounter with Slup and the evening taught him more self-doubt than did the more practical matter of his debt to the usurer. When he went to the tavern, he went half in fear that he would be greeted by a roar of laughter.

He had invoked the power of an idea, however, and part of its magick was this—that a kinship with Reave the Just was not something into which any man or woman of the world would inquire directly. No one asked of Jillet, "What sort of clap-brained tale are you telling today?" The consequences might prove dire if the tale were true. Many things were said about Reave, and some were dark: enemies filleted like fish; entire houses exterminated; laws and magistrates overthrown. No one credited Jillet's claim of kinship—and no one took the risk of challenging it.

When he entered the tavern, he was not greeted with laughter. Instead, the place became instantly still, as though Reave himself were present. All eyes turned on Jillet, some in suspicion, some in speculation—and no small number in excitement. Then someone shouted a welcome; the room filled with a hubbub which seemed unnaturally loud because of the silence that had preceded it; and Jillet was swept up by the conviviality of his friends and acquaintances.

Ale flowed ungrudgingly, although he had no coin to pay for it. His jests were met with uproarious mirth and hearty backslappings, despite the fact that he was more accustomed to appreciating humor than to venturing it. Men clustered about him to hear his opinions—and he discovered, somewhat to his own surprise, that he had an uncommon number of opinions. The faces around him grew ruddy with ale and firelight and pleasure, and he had never felt so loved.

Warmed by such unprecedented good cheer, he had reason to congratulate himself that he was able to refrain from any mention of alchemists or widows. That much good sense remained to him, at any rate. On the other hand, he was unable to resist a few strategic references to *my kinsman, Reave the Just*—experiments regarding the potency of ideas.

Because of those references, the serving wench, a buxom and lusty girl who had always liked him and refused to sleep with him, seemed to linger at his elbow when she refreshed his tankard. Her hands made occasion to touch his arm repeatedly; again and again, she found herself jostled by the crowd so that her body pressed against his side; looking up at him, her eyes shone. To his amazement, he discovered that when he put his arm around her shoulders she did not shrug it away. Instead, she used it to move him by slow degrees out from among the men and toward the passageway which led to her quarters.

That evening was the most successful Jillet of Forebridge had ever known. In her bed and her body, he seemed to meet himself as the man he had always wished to be. And by morning, his doubts had disappeared; what passed for common sense with him had been drowned in the murky waters of magick, cunning, and necessity.

Eager despite a throbbing head and thick tongue, Jillet of Forebridge commenced his siege upon the manor-house and fortune and virtue of the widow Huchette.

This he did by the straightforward, if unimaginative, expedient of approaching the gatehouse of the manor and asking to speak with her.

When he did so, however, he encountered an unexpected obstacle. Like most of the townsfolk—except, perhaps, some among his more recent acquaintance, the usurers, who had told him nothing on the subject—he was unaware of Kelven Divestulata's preemptive claim on Rudolph's widow. He had no knowledge that the Divestulata had recently made himself master of the widow Huchette's inheritance, possessions, and person. In all probability, Jillet would have found it impossible to imagine that any man could do such a thing.

Jillet of Forebridge had no experience with men like Kelven Divestulata.

For example, Jillet knew nothing which would have led him to guess that Kelven never made any attempt to woo the widow. Surely to woo was the natural action of passion? Perhaps for other men; not in Kelven's case. From the moment when he first conceived his desire to the moment when he gained the position which enabled him to satisfy it, he had spoken to the object of his affections only once.

Standing before her—entirely without gifts or graces—he had said bluntly, "Be my wife."

She had hardly dared glance at him before hiding her face. Barely audible, she had replied, "My husband is dead. I will not marry again." The truth was that she had loved Rudolph as ardently as her innocence and inexperience permitted, and she had no wish whatsoever to replace him.

However, if she had dared look at Kelven, she would have seen his jaws clenched and a vein pulsing inexorably at his temple. "I do not brook refusal," he announced in a voice like an echo of doom. "And I do not ask twice."

Sadly, she was too innocent—or perhaps too ignorant—to fear doom. "Then," she said to him gravely, "you must be the unhappiest of men."

Thus her sole interchange with her only enemy began and ended.

Just as Jillet could not have imagined this conversation, he could never have dreamed the Divestulata's response.

In a sense, it would have been accurate to say that all Forebridge knew more of Reave the Just, who had never set foot in the town, than of Kelven Divestulata, whose ancestral home was less than an hour's ride away. Reave was a fit subject for tales and gossip on any occasion: neither wise men nor fools discussed Kelven.

So few folk—least of all Jillet—knew of the brutal and impassioned marriage of Kelven's parents, or of his father's death in an apoplectic fury, or of the acid bitterness which his mother directed at him when her chief antagonist was lost. Fewer still knew of the circumstances surrounding her harsh, untimely end. And none at all knew that Kelven himself had secretly arranged their deaths for them, not because of their treatment of him—which in fact he understood and to some extent ap-

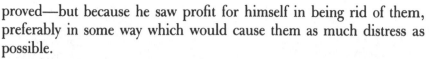

proved—but because he saw profit for himself in being rid of them, preferably in some way which would cause them as much distress as possible.

It might have been expected that the servants and retainers of the family would know or guess the truth, and that at least one of them would say something on the subject to someone; but within a few months of his mother's demise Kelven had contrived to dispense with every member of his parents' establishment, and had replaced them with cooks and maids and grooms who knew nothing and said less. In this way, he made himself as safe from gossip as he could ever hope to be.

As a result, the few stories told of him had a certain legendary quality, as if they concerned another Divestulata who had lived long ago. In the main, these tales involved either sums of money or young women that came to his notice and then disappeared. It was known—purportedly for a fact—that a usurer or three had been driven out of Forebridge, cursing Kelven's name. And it was undeniable that the occasional young woman had vanished. Unfortunately, the world was a chancy place, especially for young women, and their fate was never clearly known. The one magistrate of Forebridge who had pursued the matter far enough to question Kelven himself had afterward been so overtaken by chagrin that he had ended his own life.

Unquestionably, Kelven's mode of existence was secure.

However, for reasons known only to himself, he desired a wife. And he was accustomed to obtaining what he desired. When the widow Huchette spurned him, he was not daunted. He simply set about attaining his goal by less direct means.

He began by buying out the investments which had been made to secure the widow's future. These he did not need, so he allowed them to go to ruin. Then he purchased the widow's deceased husband's debts from the usurer who held them. They were few, but they gave him a small claim on the importing merchantry from which Rudolph Huchette's wealth derived. His claim provided him with access to the merchantry's ledgers and contacts and partners, and that knowledge enabled him to apply pressure to the sources of the merchantry's goods. In a relatively short time, as such things are measured, he became the owner of the merchantry itself.

He subsequently found it child's play to reveal—in the presence of a magistrate, of course—that Rudolph Huchette had acquired his personal fortune by despoiling the assets of the merchantry. In due course, that fortune passed to Kelven, and he became, in effect, the widow Huchette's landlord—the master of every tangible or monetary resource on which her marriage had made her dependent.

Naturally, he did not turn her out of her former home. Where could she have gone? Instead, he kept her with him and closed the doors to the manor-house. If she made any protest, it was unheard through the stout walls.

Of all this, Jillet was perfectly innocent as he knocked on the door of the manor's gatehouse and requested an audience with the widow. In consequence, he was taken aback when he was admitted, not to the sitting room of the widow, but to the study of her new lord, the Divestulata.

The study itself was impressive enough to a man like Jillet. He had never before seen so much polished oak and mahogany, so much brass and fine leather. Were it not for his unprecedented successes the previous evening, his aching head, which dulled his responses, and his new warrant for audacity, he might have been cowed by the mere room. However, he recited the litany which the alchemist had given him, and the words *trust, bold,* and *unscrupulous* enabled him to bear the air of the place well enough to observe that Kelven himself was more impressive, not because of any greatness of stature or girth, but because of the malign and unanswerable glower with which he regarded everything in front of him. His study was ill-lit, and the red echo of candles in his eyes suggested the flames of Satan and hell.

It was fortunate, therefore, that Kelven did not immediately turn his attention upon Jillet. Instead, he continued to peruse the document gripped in his heavy hands. This may have been a ploy intended to express his disdain for his visitor; but it gave Jillet a few moments in which to press his hand against his hidden pouch of magick, rehearse the counsel of the alchemist, and marshal his resolve.

When Kelven was done with his reading or his ploy, he raised his grim head and demanded without preamble, "What is your business with my wife?"

At any former time, this would have stopped Jillet dead. *Wife?* The widow had already become Kelven Divestulata's *wife?* But Jillet was possessed by his magick and his incantation, and they gave him a new extravagance. It was impossible that Kelven had married the widow. Why? Because such a disappointment could not conceivably befall the man who had just earned with honest gold and courage the right to name himself the kinsman of Reave the Just. To consider the widow Huchette Kelven's wife made a mockery of both justice and alchemy.

"Sir," Jillet began. Armed with virtue and magick, he could afford to be polite. "My 'business' is with the widow. If she is truly your wife, she will tell me so herself. Permit me to say frankly, however, that I cannot understand why you would stoop to a false claim of marriage. Without the sanction of the priests, no marriage can be valid—and no sanction is possible until the banns have been published. This you have not done."

There Jillet paused to congratulate himself. The alchemist's magick was indisputably efficacious. It had already made him *bolder* than he had ever been in his life.

In fact, it made him so *bold* that he took no notice of the narrowing of Kelven's eyes, the tightening of his hands. Jillet was inured to peril. He smiled blandly as the Divestulata stood to make his reply.

"She is my wife," Kelven announced distinctly, "*because* I have claimed her. I need no other sanction."

Jillet blinked a time or two. "Do I understand you, sir? Do you call her your wife—and still admit that you have not been wed?"

Kelven studied his visitor and said nothing.

"Then this is a matter for the magistrates." In a sense, Jillet did not hear his own words. Certainly, he did not pause to consider whether they would be pleasing to the Divestulata. His attention was focused, rather, on alchemy and incantations. Enjoying his new boldness, he wondered how far he could carry it before he felt the need to make reference to his kinsman. "The sacrament of marriage exists to protect women from those who are stronger, so that they will not be bound to any man against their will." This fine assertion was not one which he had conceived for himself. It was quoted almost directly from the school lessons of the priests. "If you have not wed the widow Huchette, I can only conclude that she does not choose to wed you. In that case"—Jillet was becoming positively giddy—"you are not her husband, sir. You are her enslaver.

"You would be well advised to let me speak to her."

Having said this, Jillet bowed to Kelven, not out of courtesy, but in secret delight. The Divestulata was his only audience for his performance: like an actor who knew he had done well, he bowed to his audience. All things considered, he may still have been under the influence of the previous evening's ale.

Naturally, Kelven saw the matter in another light. Expressionless except for his habitual glower, he regarded Jillet. After a moment, he said, "You mentioned the magistrates." He did not sound like a man who had been threatened. He sounded like a man who disavowed responsibility for what came next. Having made his decision, he rang a small bell which stood on his desk. Then he continued, "You will speak to my wife."

The servant who had conducted Jillet to the Divestulata's study appeared. To the servant, Kelven said, "Inform my wife that she will receive us."

The servant bowed and departed.

Jillet had begun to glow inwardly. This was a triumph! Even such a man as Kelven Divestulata could not resist his alchemy—and he had not yet made any reference to Reave the Just. Surely his success with the widow was assured. She would succumb to his magick; Kelven would withdraw under threat of the magistrates; and all would be just as Jillet had dreamed it. Smiling happily at his host, he made no effort to resist as Kelven took him by his arm.

However, allowing Kelven to take hold of him may have been a mistake. The Divestulata's grip was hard—brutally hard—and the crush of his fingers upon Jillet's arm quickly dispelled the smile from Jillet's lips. Jillet was strong himself, having been born to a life of labor, but Kelven's strength turned him pale. Only pride and surprise enabled him to swallow his protest.

Without speaking—and without haste—Kelven steered Jillet to the chamber where he had instructed his wife to receive visitors.

Unlike Kelven's study, the widow's sitting room was brightly lit, not by lamps and candles, but by sunshine. Perhaps simply because she loved the sun, or perhaps because she wished herself to be seen plainly, she immersed herself in light. This made immediately obvious the fact that she remained clad in her widow's weeds, despite her new status as the Divestulata's *wife*. It also made obvious the drawn pallor of her face, the hollowness of her cheeks, the dark anguish under her eyes. She did nothing to conceal the way she flinched when Kelven's gaze fell upon her.

Kelven still did not release Jillet's arm. "This impudent sot," he announced to the widow as though Jillet were not present, "believes that we are not wed."

The widow may have been hurt and even terrified, but she remained honest. In a small, thin voice, she said, "I am wed to Rudolph Huchette, body and life." Her hands were folded about each other in her lap. She did not lift her gaze from them. "I will never marry again."

Jillet hardly heard her. He had to grind his teeth to prevent himself from groaning at Kelven's grip.

"He believes," Kelven continued, still addressing the widow, "that the magistrates should be informed we are not wed."

That made the widow raise her head. Sunlight illuminated the spark of hope which flared in her eyes—flared, and then died when she saw Jillet clearly.

In defeat, she lowered her gaze again.

Kelven was not satisfied. "What is your answer?" he demanded.

The widow's tone made it plain that she had not yet had time to become accustomed to defeat. "I hope he will inform the magistrates," she said, "but I believe he was a fool to let you know of his intentions."

"Madam—my lady." Jillet spoke in an involuntary gasp. His triumph was gone—even his hope was gone. His arm was being crushed. "Make him let go of me."

"Paugh!" With a flick of his hand, Kelven flung Jillet to the floor. "It is offensive to be threatened by a clod like you." Then he turned to the widow. "What do you believe I should do when I am threatened in this fashion for your sake?"

Despite her own distress, Rudolph's widow was still able to pity fools. Her voice became smaller, thinner, but it remained clear. "Let him go. Let him tell as many magistrates as he wishes. Who will believe him? Who will accept the word of a laborer when it is contradicted by Kelven Divestulata? Perhaps he is too shamed to tell anyone."

"And what if he is not shamed?" Kelven retorted instantly. "What if a magistrate hears him—and believes him enough to question you? What would you say?"

The widow did not raise her eyes. She had no need to gaze upon her *husband* again. "I would say that I am the prisoner of your malice and the plaything of your lusts, and I would thank God for His mercy if He would allow me to die."

"That is why I will not let him go." Kelven sounded oddly satisfied, as though an obscure desire had been vindicated. "Perhaps instead I will put his life in your power. I wish to see you rut with him. If you do it for my amusement, I will let him live."

Jillet did not hear what answer the widow would have made to this suggestion. Perhaps he did not properly hear anything which the Divestulata and his *wife* said to each other. His shame was intense, and the pain in his arm caused his head to throb as though it might burst; and, in truth, he was too busy cursing himself for not invoking the power of alchemy sooner to give much heed to what was said over him. He was a fool, and he knew it—a fool for thinking, however briefly, that he might accomplish for himself victories which only magick could achieve.

Therefore he struggled to his feet between Kelven and the widow. Hugging his arm to his side, he panted, "This is intolerable. My kinsman, Reave the Just, will be outraged when he learns of it."

Despite their many differences, Kelven Divestulata and the widow Huchette were identical in their reactions: they both became completely still, as though they had been turned to stone by the magick of the name, *Reave the Just*.

"My kinsman is not forgiving," Jillet continued, driven by shame and pain and his new awareness of the power of ideas. "All the world knows it. He has no patience for injustice or tyranny, or for the abuse of the helpless, and when he is outraged he lets nothing stand in his way." Perhaps because he was a fool, he was able to speak with perfect conviction. Any man who was not a fool would have known that he had already said too much. "You will be wiser to come with me to the magistrate yourself and confess the wrong you have done this woman. He will be kinder to you than Reave the Just."

Still united by the influence of that name, the widow and Kelven said together, "You fool. You have doomed yourself."

But she said, "Now he will surely kill you."

His words were, "Now I will surely let you live."

Hearing Kelven, Jillet was momentarily confused, misled by the impression that he had succeeded—that he had saved the widow and himself, that he had defeated the Divestulata. Then Kelven struck him down, and the misconception was lost.

When he awakened—more head-sore, bone-weak, and thirst-tormented than he had ever been in his life—he was in a chamber from which no one except Kelven himself and his own workmen had ever emerged. He had a room just like it in his ancestral home and knew its value. Shortly, therefore, after his acquisition of the manor-house he had had this chamber dug into the rock beneath the foundations of the building. All Forebridge was quite ignorant of its existence. The excavated dirt and rock had been concealed by being used in other construction about the manor-house—primarily in making the kennels where Kelven housed the mastiffs he bred for hunting and similar duties. And the workmen had been sent to serve the Divestulata in other enterprises in other Counties, far from Forebridge. So when Jillet awakened he was not simply in a room where no one would ever hear him scream. He was in a room where no one would ever look for him.

In any case, however, he felt too sick and piteous to scream. Kelven's blow had nearly cracked his skull, and the fetters on his wrists held his arms at an angle which nearly dislocated his shoulders. He was not surprised by the presence of light—by the single candle stuck in its tallow on a bench a few feet away. His general amazement was already too great, and his particular discomfort too acute, to allow him the luxury of surprise about the presence or absence of light.

On the bench beside the candle, hulking in the gloom like the condensed darkness of a demon, sat Kelven Divestulata.

"Ah," breathed Kelven softly, "your eyes open. You raise your head. The pain begins. Tell me about your *kinship* with Reave the Just."

Well, Jillet was a fool. Alchemy had failed him, and the power of ideas was a small thing compared to the power of Kelven's fist. To speak frankly, he had lived all his life at the mercy of events—or at the dictates of the decisions or needs or even whims of others. He was not a fit opponent for a man like the Divestulata.

Nevertheless he was loved in Forebridge for a reason. That reason went by the name of *amiability,* but it might equally well have been called *kindness* or *open-heartedness.* He did not answer Kelven's question. Instead, through his own hurt, he replied, "This is wrong. She does not deserve it."

" 'She'? Do you refer to my wife?" Kelven was mildly surprised. "We are not speaking of her. We are speaking of your kinsman, Reave the Just."

"She is weak and you are strong," Jillet persisted. "It is wrong to victimize her simply because she is unable to oppose you. You damn yourself by doing so. But I think you do not care about damnation." This was an unusual insight for him. "Even so, you should care that you demean yourself by using your strength against a woman who cannot oppose you."

As though Jillet had not spoken, Kelven continued, "He has a reputation for meddling in other men's affairs. In fact, his reputation for meddling is extensive. I find that I would like to put a stop to it. No doubt his reputation is only gossip, after all—but such gossip offends me. I *will* put a stop to it."

"It is no wonder that she refuses to wed you." Jillet's voice began to crack, and he required an effort to restrain tears. "The wonder is that she has not killed herself rather than suffer your touch."

"Simpleton!" spat Kelven, momentarily vexed. "She does not kill herself because I do not permit it:" He promptly regained his composure, however. "Yet you have said one thing which is not foolish. A strong man who exerts his strength only upon the weak eventually becomes weak himself. I have decided on a more useful exercise. I will rid the world of this 'Reave the Just.'

"Tell me how you propose to involve your *kinsman* in my affairs. Perhaps I will allow you to summon him"—the Divestulata laughed harshly—"and then both you and my wife will be rescued."

There Jillet collapsed. He was weeping with helplessness and folly, and he had no understanding of the fact that Kelven intended to keep him alive when the widow Huchette had predicted that Kelven would kill him. Through a battle of tears and self-recrimination and appeals for pity, he told the Divestulata the truth.

"I am no kinsman of Reave the Just. That is impossible. I claimed kinship with him because an alchemist told me to do so. All I desired was a love-potion to win the widow's heart, but he persuaded me otherwise."

At that time, Jillet was incapable of grasping that he remained alive only because Kelven did not believe him.

Because Kelven did not believe him, their conversation became increasingly arduous. Kelven demanded; Jillet denied. Kelven insisted; Jillet protested. Kelven struck; Jillet wailed. Ultimately Jillet lost consciousness, and Kelven went away.

The candle was left burning.

It was replaced by another, and by yet another, and by still others, so that Jillet was not left entirely in darkness; but he never saw the old ones gutter and die, or the new ones set. For some reason, he was always unconscious when that happened. The old stumps were not removed from the bench; he was left with some measure for his imprisonment. However, since he did not know how long the candles burned he could only conclude from the growing row of stumps that his imprisonment was long. He was fed at intervals which he could not predict. At times Kelven fed him. At times the widow fed him. At times she removed her garments and fondled his cold flesh with tears streaming from her eyes. At times he fouled himself. But only the candles provided a measure for his existence, and he could not interpret them.

How are you related to Reave?

How do you contact him?

Why does he meddle in other men's affairs?

What is the source of his power?

What *is* he?

Poor Jillet knew no answer to any of these questions.

His ignorance was the source of his torment, and the most immediate threat to his life; but it may also have saved him. It kept Kelven's attention focused upon him—and upon the perverse pleasures which he and the widow provided. In effect, it blinded Kelven to the power of ideas: Jillet's ignorance of anything remotely useful concerning Reave the Just preserved Kelven's ignorance of the fact that the townspeople of Forebridge, in their cautious and undemonstrative way, had summoned Reave in Jillet's name.

Quite honestly, most of them could not have said that they knew Reave had been summoned—or that they knew how he had been summoned. He was not a magistrate to whom public appeal could be made; not an official of the County to whom a letter could be written; not a lord of the realm from whom justice might be demanded. As far as anyone in Forebridge could have said for certain, he was not a man at all: he was only a story from places far away, a persistent legend blowing on its own queer winds across the North Counties. Can the wind be summoned? No? Then can Reave the Just?

In truth, Reave was summoned by the simple, almost nameless expedient of telling the tale. To every man or woman, herder or minstrel, merchant or soldier, mendicant or charlatan who passed through Forebridge, someone sooner or later mentioned that "Reave the Just has a kinsman here who has recently disappeared." Those folk followed their own roads away from Forebridge, and when they met with the occasion to do so they told the tale themselves; and so the tale spread.

In the end, such a summons can never be denied. Inevitably, Reave the Just heard it and came to Forebridge.

Like a breeze or a story, he appeared to come without having come *from* anywhere: one day, not so long after Jillet's disappearance, he was simply *there,* in Forebridge. Like a breeze or a story, he was not secretive about his coming: he did not lurk into town, or send in spies, or travel incognito. Still it was true that he came entirely unheralded, unannounced—and yet most folk who saw him knew immediately who he was, just as they knew immediately why he was there.

From a certain distance, of course, he was unrecognizable: his clothing was only a plain brown traveler's shirt over leather pants which had seen considerable wear and thick, dusty boots; his equally dusty hair was cropped to a convenient length; his strides were direct and self-assured, but no more so than those of other men who knew where they were going and why. In fact, the single detail which distinguished him from any number of farmers and cotters and wagoneers was that he wore no hat against the sun. Only when he drew closer did his strangeness make itself felt.

The dust showed that he had walked a long way, but he betrayed no fatigue, no hunger or thirst. His clothing had been exposed to the elements a great deal, but he carried no pack or satchel for food or spare garments or other necessities. Under the prolonged pressure of the sun, he might have developed a squint or a way of lowering his head; but his chin was up, and his eyes were open and vivid, like pieces of the deep sky. And he had no knife at his belt, no staff in his hand, no quiver over his shoulder—nothing with which to defend himself against hedgerow robbers or hungry beasts or outraged opponents. His only weapon, as far as any of the townspeople could see, was that he simply appeared *clearer* than any of his surroundings, better focused, as though he improved the vision of those who looked at him. Those who did look at him found it almost impossible to look away.

The people who first saw him closely enough to identify him were not surprised when he began asking questions about "his kinsman, Jillet of Forebridge." They were only surprised that his voice was so kind and quiet—considering his reputation for harsh decisions and extreme actions—and that he acknowledged the implausible relation which Jillet had claimed for the first time scarcely a week ago.

Unfortunately, none of the people questioned by Reave the Just had any idea what had become of Jillet.

It was characteristic of the folk of Forebridge that they avoided ostentation and public display. Reave had the effect, however, of causing them to forget their normal chariness. In consequence, he did not need to go searching for people to question: they came to him. Standing in the open road which served Forebridge as both public square and auctioneer's market, he asked his questions once, perhaps twice, then waited quietly while the slowly growing crowd around him attracted more people and his questions were repeated for him to the latecomers until a thick fellow with the strength of timber and a mind to match asked, "What's he look like, then, this Jillet?"

The descriptions provided around him were confusing at first; but under Reave's influence they gradually became clear enough to be serviceable.

"Hmm," rumbled the fellow. "Man like that visited my master 'tother day."

People who knew the fellow quickly revealed that he served as a guard for one of the less hated usurers in Forebridge. They also indicated where this usurer might be found.

Reave the Just nodded once, gravely.

Smiling as though they were sure of his gratitude, and knew they had earned it, the people crowding around him began to disperse. Reave walked away among them. In a short time, he had gained admittance to the usurer's place of business, and was speaking to the usurer himself.

The usurer supplied Reave with the name of the widow Huchette. After all, Jillet had offered her wealth as collateral in his attempt to obtain gold. Despite his acknowledged relation to Jillet, however, Reave was not satisfied by the information which the usurer was able to give him. Their conversation sent him searching for alchemists until he located the one he needed.

The alchemist who had conceived Jillet's stratagem against the widow did not find Reave's clarity of appearance and quietness of manner reassuring: quite the reverse. In fact, he was barely able to restrain himself from hurling smoke in Reave's face and attempting to escape through the window. In his wildest frights and fancies, he had never considered that Reave the Just himself might task him for the advice he had sold to Jillet. Nevertheless, something in the open, vivid gaze which Reave fixed upon him convinced him that he could not hope for escape. Smoke would not blind Reave; and when the alchemist dove out the window, Reave would be there ahead of him, waiting.

Mumbling like a shamed child—and inwardly cursing Reave for having this effect upon him—the alchemist revealed the nature of his transaction with Jillet. Then, in a spasm of defensive self-abnegation, attempting to deflect Reave's notorious extravagance, he produced the gold which he had received from Jillet and offered it to Jillet's "kinsman."

Reave considered the offer briefly before accepting it. His tone was quiet, but perfectly distinct, as he said, "Jillet must be held accountable for his folly. However, you do not deserve to profit from it." As soon as he left the alchemist's dwelling, he flung the coins so far across the hedgerows that the alchemist had no hope of ever recovering them.

In the secrecy of his heart, the alchemist wailed as though he had been bereft. But he permitted himself no sound, either of grief or of protest, until Reave the Just was safely out of hearing.

Alone, unannounced, and without any discernible weapons or defenses, Reave made his way to the manor-house of the deceased Rudolph Huchette.

Part of his power, of course, was that he never revealed to anyone precisely how the strange deeds for which he was known were accomplished. As far as the world, or the stories about him which filled the world, were concerned, he simply did what he did. So neither Jillet nor the widow—and certainly not Kelven Divestulata—were ever able to explain the events which took place within the manor-house after Reave's arrival. Beginning with that arrival itself, they all saw the events as entirely mysterious.

The first mystery was that the mastiffs patrolling within the walls of the manor-house did not bark. The Divestulata's servants were not alerted; no one demanded admittance at the gatehouse, or at any of the doors of the manor. Furthermore, the room in which Jillet was held prisoner was guarded, not merely by dogs and men and bolted doors, but by ignorance: no one in Forebridge knew that the chamber existed. Nevertheless, after Jillet's imprisonment had been measured by a dozen or perhaps fifteen thick candles, and his understanding of his circumstances had passed beyond ordinary fuddlement and pain into an awareness of doom so complete that it seemed actively desirable, he prised open his eyelids enough to see a man standing before him in the gloom, a man who was not Kelven Divestulata—a man, indeed, who was not anyone Jillet recognized.

Smiling gravely, this man lifted water to Jillet's lips. And when Jillet had drunk what he could, the man put a morsel or two of honeycomb in his mouth.

After that, the man waited for Jillet to speak.

Water and honey gave Jillet a bit of strength which he had forgotten existed. Trying harder to focus his gaze upon the strange figure smiling soberly before him, he asked, "Have you come to kill me? I thought he

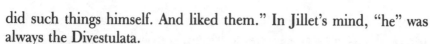

did such things himself. And liked them." In Jillet's mind, "he" was always the Divestulata.

The man shook his head. "I am Reave." His voice was firm despite its quietness. "I am here to learn why you have claimed kinship with me."

Under other conditions, Jillet would have found it frightening to be confronted by Reave the Just. As an amiable man himself, he trusted the amiability of others, and so he would not have broadly assumed that Reave meant him ill. Nevertheless, he was vulnerable on the point which Reave mentioned. For several reasons, Jillet was not a deceptive man: one of them was that he did not like to be *found out*—and he was always so easily *found out*. Being discovered in a dishonest act disturbed and shamed him.

At present, however, thoughts of shame and distress were too trivial to be considered. In any case, Kelven had long since bereft him of any instinct for self-concealment he may have possessed. To Reave's inquiry, he replied as well as his sense of doom allowed, "I wanted the widow."

"For her wealth?" Reave asked.

Jillet shook his head. "Wealth seems pleasant, but I do not understand it." Certainly, wealth did not appear to have given either the widow or Kelven any particular satisfaction. "I wanted her."

"Why?"

This question was harder. Jillet might have mentioned her beauty, her youth, her foreignness; he might have mentioned her tragedy. But Reave's clear gaze made those answers inadequate. Finally, Jillet replied, "It would mean something. To be loved by her."

Reave nodded. "You wanted to be loved by a woman whose love was valuable." Then he asked, "Why did you think her love could be gained by alchemy? Love worth having does not deserve to be tricked. And she would never truly love you if you obtained her love falsely."

Jillet considered this question easy. Many candles ago—almost from the beginning—the pain in his arms had given him the feeling that his chest had been torn open, exposing everything. He said, "She would not love me. She would not notice me. I do not know the trick of getting women to give me their love."

"The 'trick,'" Reave mused. "That is inadequate, Jillet. You must be honest with me."

Honey or desperation gave Jillet a moment of strength. "I have been honest since he put me in this place. I think it must be hell, and I am already dead. How else is it possible for you to be here? You are no kinsman of mine, Reave the Just. Some men are like the widow. Their love is worth having. I do not understand it, but I can see that women notice such men. They give themselves to such men.

"I am not among them. I have nothing to offer that any woman would want. I must gain love by alchemy. If magick does not win it for me, I will never know love at all."

Reave raised fresh water to Jillet's lips. He set new morsels of honeycomb in Jillet's mouth.

Then he turned away.

From the door of the chamber, he said, "In one thing, you are wrong, Jillet of Forebridge. You and I are kinsmen. All men are of common blood, and I am bound to any man who claims me willingly." As he left, he added, "You are imprisoned here by your own folly. You must rescue yourself."

Behind him, the door closed, and he was gone.

The door was stout, and the chamber had been dug deep: no one heard Jillet's wail of abandonment.

Certainly the widow did not hear it. In truth, she was not inclined to listen for such things. They gave her nightmares—and her life was already nightmare enough. When Reave found her, she was in her bedchamber, huddled upon the bed, sobbing uselessly. About her shoulders she wore the tatters of her night-dress, and her lips and breasts were red with the pressure of Kelven's admiration.

"Madam," said Reave courteously. He appeared to regard her nakedness in the same way he had regarded Jillet's torment. "You are the widow Huchette?"

She stared at him, too numb with horror to speak. In strict honesty, however, her horror had nothing to do with him. It was a natural consequence of the Divestulata's love-making. Now that he was done with her, he had perhaps sent one of his grooms or servingmen or business associates to enjoy her similarly.

"You have nothing to fear from me," her visitor informed her in a kindly tone. "I am Reave. Men call me 'Reave the Just.'"

The widow was young, foreign, and ignorant of the world; but none of those hindrances had sufficed to block her from hearing the stories which surrounded him. He was the chief legend of the North Counties:

he had been discussed in her presence ever since Rudolph had brought her to Forebridge. On that basis, she had understood the danger of Jillet's claim when she had first met him; and on that same basis she now uttered a small gasp of surprise. Then she became instantly wild with hope. Before he could speak again, she began to sob, "Oh, sir, bless Heaven that you have come! You must help me, you must! My life is anguish, and I can bear no more! He rapes me and rapes me, he forces me to do the most vile things at his whim, we are not wed, do not believe him if he says that we are wed, my husband is dead, and I desire no other, oh, sir! You must help me!"

"I will consider that, madam," Reave responded as though he were unmoved. "You must consider, however, that there are many kinds of help. Why have you not helped yourself?"

Opening her mouth to pour out a torrent of protest, the widow stopped suddenly, and a deathly pallor blanched her face. "Help myself?" she whispered. "Help myself?"

Reave fixed his clear gaze upon her and waited.

"Are you mad?" she asked, still whispering.

"Perhaps." He shrugged. "But I have not been raped by Kelven Divestulata. I do not beg succor. Why have you not helped yourself?"

"Because I am a woman!" she protested, not in scorn, but piteously. "I am helpless. I have no strength of arm, no skill with weapons, no knowledge of the world, no friends. He has made himself master of everything which might once have aided me. It would be a simpler matter for me to tear apart these walls than to defend myself against him."

Again, Reave shrugged. "Still he is rapist—and likely a murderer. And I see that you are not bruised. Madam, why do you not resist him? Why do you not cut his throat while he sleeps? Why do you not cut your own, if his touch is so loathsome to you?"

The look of horror which she now turned on him was unquestionably personal, caused by his questions, but he was not deterred by it. Instead, he took a step closer to her.

"I offend you, madam. But I am Reave the Just, and I do not regard who is offended. I will search you further." His eyes replied to her horror with a flame which she had not seen in them before, a burning of clear rage. "Why have you done nothing to help Jillet? He came to you in innocence and ignorance as great as your own. His torment is as terrible as yours. Yet you crouch there on your soft bed and beg for rescue from an oppressor you do not oppose, and you care nothing what becomes of him."

The widow may have feared that he would step closer to her still and strike her, but he did not. Instead, he turned away.

At the door, he paused to remark, "As I have said, there are many kinds of help. Which do you merit, madam?"

He departed her bedchamber as silently as he had entered it, leaving her alone.

The time now was near the end of the day, and still neither Kelven himself nor his dogs nor his servingmen knew that Reave the Just moved freely through the manor-house. They had no reason to know, for he approached no one, addressed no one, was seen by no one. Instead, he waited until night came and grew deep over Forebridge, until grooms and breeders, cooks and scullions, servingmen and secretaries had retired to their quarters, until only the hungry mastiffs were awake within the walls because the guards who should have tended them had lost interest in their duties. He waited until Kelven, alone in his study, had finished readying his plans to ruin an ally who aided him loyally during a recent trading war, and had poured himself a glass of fine brandy so that he would have something to drink while he amused himself with Jillet. Only then did Reave approach the Divestulata's desk in order to study him through the dim light of the lamps.

Kelven was not easily taken aback, but Reave's unexpected appearance came as a shock. "Satan's balls!" he growled shamelessly. "Who in hell are *you*?"

His visitor replied with a smile which was not at all kindly. "I am grieved," he admitted, "that you did not believe I would come. I am not as well known as I had thought—or men such as you do not sufficiently credit my reputation. I am Reave the Just."

If Reave anticipated shock, distress, or alarm in response to this announcement, he was disappointed. Kelven took a moment to consider the situation, as though to assure himself that he had heard rightly. Then he leaned back in his chair and laughed like one of his mastiffs.

"So he spoke the truth. What an amazing thing. But you are slow, Reave the Just. That purported kinsman of yours has been dead for days. I doubt that you will ever find his grave."

"In point of fact," Reave replied in an undisturbed voice, "we are not kinsmen. I came to Forebridge to discover why a man of no relation would claim me as he did. Is he truly dead? Then I will not learn the truth from him. That"—in the lamplight, Reave's eyes glittered like chips of mica—"will displease me greatly, Kelven Divestulata."

Before Kelven could respond, Reave asked, "How did he die?"

"How?" Kelven mulled the question. "As most men do. He came to the end of himself." The muscles of his jaw bunched. "You will encounter the same fate yourself—eventually. Indeed, I find it difficult to imagine why you have not done so already. Your precious reputation"— he pursed his lips—"is old enough for death."

Reave ignored this remark. "You are disingenuous, Kelven. My question was less philosophical. How did Jillet die? Did you kill him?"

"I? Never!" Kelven's protest was sincere. "I believe he brought it upon himself. He is a fool, and he died of a broken heart."

"Pining, no doubt," Reave offered by way of explanation, "for the widow Huchette—"

A flicker of uncertainty crossed Kelven's gaze. "No doubt."

"—whom you pretend to have married, but who is in fact your prisoner and your victim in her own house."

"She is my *wife!*" Kelven snapped before he could stop himself. "I have claimed her. I do not need public approval, or the petty sanctions of the law, for my desires. I have claimed her, and she is *mine.*"

The lines of Reave's mouth and the tightening about his eyes suggested a variety of retorts which he did not utter. Instead, he replied mildly, "I observe that you find no fault with my assertion that this house is hers."

Kelven spat. "Paugh! Do they call you 'Reave the Just' because you are honest, or because you are 'just a fool'? This house was awarded to me publicly, by a *magistrate,* in compensation for harm done to my interests by that dead thief, Rudolph Huchette."

The Divestulata's intentions against Reave, which he had announced to Jillet, grew clearer with every passing moment. For some years now, upon occasions during the darkest hours of the night, and in the deepest privacy of his heart, he had considered himself to be the natural antagonist of men like Reave—self-righteous meddlers whose notions of virtue cost themselves nothing and their foes everything. In part, this perception of himself arose from his own native and organic malice: in part, it sprang from his awareness that most of his victories over lesser men—men such as Jillet—were too easy, that for his own well-being he required greater challenges.

Nevertheless, this conversation with his natural antagonist was not what he would have wished it to be. His plans did not include any defense of himself: he meant to attack. Seeking to capture the initiative, he countered, "However, my ownership of this house—like my ownership of Rudolph's relict—is not your concern. If you have any legitimate concern here, it involves Jillet, not me. By what honest right do you sneak into my house and my study at this hour of the night in order to insult me with questions and innuendos?"

Reave permitted himself a rather ominous smile. As though he were ignoring what Kelven had just asked, he replied, "My epithet, 'the Just,' derives from coinage. It concerns both the measure and the refinement of gold. When a coin contains the exact weight and purity of gold which it should contain, it is said to be 'just.' You may not be aware, Kelven Divestulata, that the honesty of any man is revealed by the coin with which he pays his debts."

"*Debts?*" Involuntarily, Kelven sprang to his feet. He could not contain his anger sitting. "Are you here to annoy me with *debts?*"

"Did you not kill Jillet?" Reave countered.

"I did *not*! I have done many things to many men, but I did not kill that insufferable clod. *You,*" he shouted so that Reave would not stop him, "have insulted me enough. Now you will tell me why you are here—how you *justify* your actions—or I will hurl you to the ground outside my window and let my dogs feed on you, and *no one* will dare criticize me for doing so to an intruder in my study in the dead of night!"

"You do not need to attack me with threats." Reave's self-assurance was maddening. "Honest men have nothing to fear from me, and you are threat enough just as you stand. I will tell you why I am here.

"I am Reave the Just. I have come as I have always come, for blood—the blood of kinship and retribution. Blood is the coin in which I pay my debts, and it is the coin in which I exact restitution.

"I have come for your blood, Kelven Divestulata."

The certainty of Reave's manner inspired in Kelven an emotion he did not recognize—and because he did not recognize it, it made him wild. "*For what?*" he raged at his visitor. "What have I done? Why do you want my blood? I tell you, *I did not kill your damnable Jillet!*"

"Can you prove that?"

"Yes!"

"How?"

Shaken by the fear he did not recognize, Kelven shouted, "He is still alive!"

Reave's eyes no longer reflected the lamplight. They were dark now, as deep as wells. Quietly, he asked, "What *have* you done to him?"

Kelven was confused. One part of him felt that he had gained a victory. Another knew that he was being defeated. "He amuses me," the Divestulata answered harshly. "I have made him a toy. As long as he continues to amuse me, I will continue to play with him."

When he heard those words, Reave stepped back from the desk. In a voice as implacable as a sentence of death, he said, "You have confessed to the unlawful imprisonment and torture of an innocent man. I will go now and summon a magistrate. You will repeat your confession to him. Perhaps that act of honesty will inspire you to confess as well the crimes you have committed upon the person of the widow Huchette.

"Do not attempt to escape, Kelven Divestulata. I will hunt you from the vault of Heaven to the pit of Hell, if I must. You have spent blood, and you will pay for it with blood."

For a moment longer, Reave the Just searched Kelven with his bottomless gaze. Then he turned and strode toward the door.

An inarticulate howl rose in Kelven's throat. He snatched up the first heavy object he could find, a brass paper-weight thick enough to crush a man's skull, and hurled it at Reave.

It struck Reave at the base of his neck so hard that he stumbled to his knees.

At once, Kelven flung himself past his desk and attacked his visitor. Catching one fist in Reave's hair, he jerked Reave upright: with the other, he gave Reave a blow which might have killed any lesser man.

Blood burst from Reave's mouth. He staggered away on legs that appeared spongy, too weak to hold him. His arms dangled at his sides as though he had no muscle or sinew with which to defend himself.

Transported by triumph and rage and stark terror, the Divestulata pursued his attack.

Blow after blow he rained upon Reave's head: blow after blow he drove into Reave's body. Pinned against one of the great bookcases which Rudolph Huchette had lovingly provided for the study, Reave flopped and lurched whenever he was struck, but he could not escape. He did not fight back; he made no effort to ward Kelven away. In moments, his face became a bleeding mass; his ribs cracked; his heart must surely have faltered.

But he did not fall.

The utter darkness in his eyes never wavered. It held Kelven and compromised nothing.

In the end, Reave's undamaged and undaunted gaze seemed to drive Kelven past rage into madness. Immersed in ecstasy or delirium, he did not hear the door of the study slam open.

His victims were beyond stealth. In truth, neither the widow Huchette nor Jillet could have opened the door quietly. They lacked the strength. Every measure of will and force she possessed, she used to support him, to bear him forward when he clearly could not move or stand on his own. And every bit of resolve and desire that remained to him, he used to hold aloft the decorative halberd which was the only weapon he and the widow had been able to find in the halls of the manor-house.

As weak as cripples, nearly dying from the strain of their exertions, they crossed the study behind Kelven's back.

They were slow, desperate, and unsteady in their approach. Nevertheless, Reave stood patiently and let his antagonist hammer him until Jillet brought the halberd down upon Kelven Divestulata's skull and killed him.

Then through the blood which drenched his face from a dozen wounds, Reave the Just smiled.

Unceremoniously, both Jillet and the widow collapsed.

Reave stooped and pulled a handkerchief from Kelven's sleeve. Dabbing at his face, he went to the desk, where he found Kelven's glass and the decanter of brandy. When he had discovered another glass, he filled it as well; then he carried the glasses to the man and woman who had rescued him. First one and then the other, he raised their heads and helped them to drink until they were able to sit and clutch the glasses and swallow without his support.

After that, he located a bell-pull and rang for the Divestulata's steward.

When the man arrived—flustered by the late summons, and astonished by the scene in the study—Reave announced, "I am Reave the Just. Before his death, Kelven Divestulata confessed his crimes to me, in particular that he obtained possession of this house by false means, that he exercised his lusts in violent and unlawful fashion upon the person of the widow Huchette, and that he imprisoned and tortured my kinsman, Jillet of Forebridge, without cause. I will state before the magistrates that I heard the Divestulata's confession, and that he was slain in my aid, while he was attempting to kill me. From this moment, the widow is once again mistress of her house, with all its possessions and retainers. If you and all those under you do not serve her honorably, you will answer both to the magistrates and to me.

"Do you understand me?"

The steward understood. Kelven's servants were silent and crafty men, and perhaps some of them were despicable; but none were stupid. When Reave left the widow and Jillet there in the study, they were safe.

They never saw him again.

As he had promised, he spoke to the magistrates. When they arrived at the manor-house shortly after dawn, supported by a platoon of County pikemen and any number of writs, they confirmed that they had received Reave's testimony. Their subsequent researches into Kelven's ledgers enabled them to validate much of what Reave had said; Jillet and the widow confirmed the rest. But Reave himself did not appear again in Forebridge. Like the story that brought him, he was gone. A new story took his place.

This also was entirely characteristic.

Once the researches and hearings of the magistrates were done, the widow Huchette passed out of Jillet's life as well. She had released him from his bonds and the chamber where he was imprisoned; she had half carried him to the one clear deed he had ever performed. But after Rudolph Huchette she had never wanted another husband; and after Kelven Divestulata she never wanted another man. She did one thing to express her gratitude toward Jillet: she repaid his debt to the usurer. Then she closed her doors to him, just as she did to all other men with love-potions and aspirations for her. In time, the manor-house became a kind of nunnery, where lost or damaged women could go for succor, and no one else was welcome.

Jillet himself, who probably believed that he would love the widow Huchette to the end of his days, found he did not miss her. Nor, in all candor, did he miss Reave. After all, he had nothing in common with them: she was too wealthy; he was too stringent. No, Jillet was quite content without such things. And he had gained something which he prized more highly—the story; the idea.

The story that he had struck the blow which brought down Kelven Divestulata.

The idea that he was kinsman to Reave the Just.

Troll Bridge

Terry Pratchett

he wind blew off the mountains, filling the air with fine ice crystals.

It was too cold to snow. In weather like this wolves came down into villages, trees in the heart of the forest exploded when they froze.

In weather like this right-thinking people were indoors, in front of the fire, telling stories about heroes.

It was an old horse. It was an old rider. The horse looked like a shrink-wrapped toast rack; the man looked as though the only reason he wasn't falling off was because he couldn't muster the energy. Despite the bitterly cold wind, he was wearing nothing but a tiny leather kilt and a dirty bandage on one knee.

He took the soggy remnant of a cigarette out of his mouth and stubbed it out on his hand.

"Right," he said, "let's do it."

"That's all very well for you to say," said the horse. "But what if you have one of your dizzy spells? And your back is playing up. How shall I feel, being eaten because your back's played you up at the wrong moment?"

"It'll never happen," said the man. He lowered himself onto the chilly stones, and blew on his fingers. Then, from the horse's pack, he took a sword with an edge like a badly-maintained saw and gave a few half-hearted thrusts at the air.

"Still got the old knackcaroony," he said. He winced, and leaned against a tree.

"I'll swear this bloody sword gets heavier every day."

"You ought to pack it in, you know," said the horse. "Call it a day. This sort of thing at your time of life. It's not right."

The man rolled his eyes.

"Blast that damn distress auction. This is what comes of buying something that belonged to a wizard," he said, to the cold world in general. "I looked at your teeth, I looked at your hooves, it never occurred to me to *listen*."

"Who did you think was bidding against you?" said the horse.

Cohen the Barbarian stayed leaning against the tree. He was not entirely sure that he could pull himself upright again.

"You must have plenty of treasure stashed away," said the horse. "We could go Rimwards. How about it? Nice and warm. Get a nice warm place by a beach somewhere, what do you say?"

"No treasure," said Cohen. "Spent it all. Drank it all. Gave it all away. Lost it."

"You should have saved some for your old age."

"Never thought I'd *have* an old age."

"One day you're going to die," said the horse. "It might be today."

"I know. Why do you think I've come here?"

The horse turned and looked down towards the gorge. The road here was pitted and cracked. Young trees were pushing up between the stones. The forest crowded in on either side. In a few years, no one would know there'd even been a road here. By the look òf it, no one knew now.

"You've come here to *die*?"

"No. But there's something I've always been meaning to do. Ever since I was a lad."

"Yeah?"

Cohen tried easing himself upright again. Tendons twanged their red-hot messages down his legs.

"My dad," he squeaked. He got control again. "My dad," he said, "said to me—" He fought for breath.

"Son," said the horse, helpfully.

"What?"

"Son," said the horse. "No father ever calls his boy 'son' unless he's about to impart wisdom. Well-known fact."

"It's *my* reminiscence."

"Sorry."

"He said . . . Son . . . yes, okay . . . Son, when you can face down a troll in single combat, then you can do anything."

The horse blinked at him. Then it turned and looked down, again, through the tree-jostled road to the gloom of the gorge. There was a stone bridge down there.

A horrible feeling stole over it.

Its hooves jiggled nervously on the ruined road.

"Rimwards," it said. "Nice and warm."

"No."

"What's the good of killing a troll? What've you got when you've killed a troll?"

"A dead troll. That's the point. Anyway, I don't have to kill it. Just defeat it. One on one. Mano a . . . troll. And if I didn't try my father would turn in his mound."

"You told *me* he drove you out of the tribe when you were eleven."

"Best day's work he ever did. Taught me to stand on other people's feet. Come over here, will you?"

The horse sidled over. Cohen got a grip on the saddle and heaved himself fully upright.

"And you're going to fight a troll today," said the horse.

Cohen fumbled in the saddlebag and pulled out his tobacco pouch. The wind whipped at the shreds as he rolled another skinny cigarette in the cup of his hands.

"Yeah," he said.

"And you've come all the way out here to do it."

"Got to," said Cohen. "When did you last see a bridge with a troll under it? There were hundreds of 'em when I was a lad. Now there's more trolls in the cities than there are in the mountains. Fat as butter, most of 'em. What did we fight all those wars for? Now . . . cross that bridge."

It was a lonely bridge across a shallow, white and treacherous river in a deep valley. The sort of place where you got—

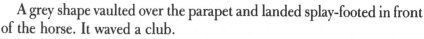

A grey shape vaulted over the parapet and landed splay-footed in front of the horse. It waved a club.

"All *right*," it growled.

"Oh—" the horse began.

The troll blinked. Even the cold and cloudy winter skies seriously reduced the conductivity of a troll's silicon brain, and it had taken it this long to realise that the saddle was unoccupied.

It blinked again, because it could suddenly feel a knife point resting on the back of its neck.

"Hello," said a voice by its ear.

The troll swallowed. But very carefully.

"Look," it said desperately, "it's tradition, okay? A bridge like this, people ort to *expect* a troll.

"'Ere," it added, as another thought crawled past, "'ow come I never 'eard you creepin' up on me?"

"Because I'm *good* at it," said the old man.

"That's right," said the horse. "He's crept up on more people than you've had frightened dinners."

The troll risked a sideways glance.

"Bloody hell," it whispered. "You think you're Cohen the Barbarian, do you?"

"What do *you* think?" said Cohen the Barbarian.

"Listen," said the horse, "if he hadn't wrapped sacks round his knees you could have told by the clicking."

It took the troll some time to work this out.

"Oh, *wow*," it breathed. "On *my* bridge! Wow!"

"What?" said Cohen.

The troll ducked out of his grip and waved his hands frantically. "It's all right! It's all right!" it shouted, as Cohen advanced. "You've got me! You've got me! I'm not arguing! I just want to call the family up, all right? Otherwise no one'll ever believe me. *Cohen the Barbarian!* On *my* bridge!"

Its huge stony chest swelled further. "My bloody brother-in-law's always swanking about his huge bloody wooden bridge, that's all my wife ever talks about. Hah! I'd like to see the look on his face . . . Oh, no! What can you think of me?"

"Good question," said Cohen.

The troll dropped its club and seized one of Cohen's hands.

"Mica's the name," it said. "You don't know what an honour this is!"

He leaned over the parapet. "Beryl! Get up here! Bring the kids!"

He turned back to Cohen, his face glowing with happiness and pride.

"Beryl's always sayin' we ought to move out, get something better, but I tell her, this bridge has been in our family for generations, there's always been a troll under Death Bridge. It's tradition."

A huge female troll carrying two babies shuffled up the bank, followed by a tail of smaller trolls. They lined up behind their father, watching Cohen owlishly.

"This is Beryl," said the troll. His wife glowered at Cohen. "And this"—he propelled forward a scowling smaller edition of himself, clutching a junior version of his club—"is my lad Scree. A real chip off the old block. Going to take on the bridge when I'm gone, ain't you, Scree. Look lad, this is Cohen the Barbarian! What d'you think o' that, eh? On *our* bridge! We don't just have rich fat soft ole merchants like your Uncle Pyrites gets," said the troll, still talking to his son but smirking past him to his wife, "we 'ave proper heroes like they used to in the old days."

The troll's wife looked Cohen up and down.

"Rich, is he?" she said.

"Rich has got nothing to do with it," said the troll.

"Are you going to kill our dad?" said Scree suspiciously.

" '*Course* he is," said Mica severely. "It's his job. An' then I'll get famed in song an' story. This is Cohen the Barbarian, right, not some bugger from the village with a pitchfork. 'E's a famous hero come all this way to see us, so just you show 'im some respect.

"Sorry about that, sir," he said to Cohen. "Kids today. You know how it is."

The horse started to snigger.

"Now look—" Cohen began.

"I remember my dad tellin' me about you when I was a pebble," said Mica. " ' 'E bestrides the world like a clossus,' he said."

There was silence. Cohen wondered what a clossus was, and felt Beryl's stony gaze fixed upon him.

"He's just a little old man," she said. "He don't look very heroic to me. If he's so good, why ain't he *rich*?"

"Now you listen to me—" Mica began.

"This is what we've been waiting for, is it?" said his wife. "Sitting under a leaky bridge the whole time? Waiting for people that never come? Waiting for little old bandy-legged old men? I should have lis-

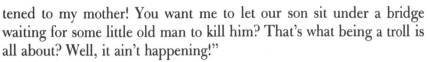

tened to my mother! You want me to let our son sit under a bridge waiting for some little old man to kill him? That's what being a troll is all about? Well, it ain't happening!"

"Now you just—"

"Hah! Pyrites doesn't get little old men! He gets big fat merchants! He's *someone*. You should have gone in with him when you had the chance!"

"I'd rather eat worms!"

"Worms? Hah? Since when could we afford to eat worms?"

"Can we have a word?" said Cohen.

He strolled towards the far end of the bridge, swinging his sword from one hand. The troll padded after him.

Cohen fumbled for his tobacco pouch. He looked up at the troll, and held out the bag.

"Smoke?" he said.

"That stuff can kill you," said the troll.

"Yes. But not today."

"Don't you hang about talking to your no-good friends!" bellowed Beryl, from her end of the bridge. "Today's your day for going down to the sawmill! You know Chert said he couldn't go on holding the job open if you weren't taking it seriously!"

Mica gave Cohen a sorrowful little smirk.

"She's very supportive," he said.

"I'm not climbing all the way down to the river to pull you out again!" Beryl roared. "You tell him about the billy goats, Mr. Big Troll!"

"Billy goats?" said Cohen.

"I don't know *anything* about billy goats," said Mica. "She's always going on about billy goats. I have no knowledge whatsoever about billy goats." He winced.

They watched Beryl usher the young trolls down the bank and into the darkness under the bridge.

"The thing is," said Cohen, when they were alone, "I wasn't intending to kill you."

The troll's face fell.

"You weren't?"

"Just throw you over the bridge and steal whatever treasure you've got."

"You were?"

Cohen patted him on the back. "Besides," he said, "I like to see people with . . . good memories. That's what the land needs. Good memories."

The troll stood to attention.

"I try to do my best, sir," it said. "My lad wants to go off to work in the city. I've tole him, there's bin a troll under this bridge for nigh on five hundred years—"

"So if you just hand over the treasure," said Cohen, "I'll be getting along."

The troll's face creased in sudden panic.

"Treasure? Haven't got any," it said.

"Oh, come *on*," said Cohen. "Well-set-up bridge like this?"

"Yeah, but no one uses this road any more," said Mica. "You're the first one along in months, and that's a fact. Beryl says I ought to have gone in with her brother when they built that new road over his bridge, but"—he raised his voice—"I said, there's been trolls under this bridge—"

"Yeah," said Cohen.

"The trouble is, the stones keep on falling out," said the troll. "And you'd never believe what those masons charge. Bloody dwarfs. You can't trust 'em." He leaned towards Cohen. "To tell you the truth, I'm having to work three days a week down at my brother-in-law's lumber mill just to make ends meet."

"I thought your brother-in-law had a bridge?" said Cohen.

"One of 'em has. But my wife's got brothers like dogs have fleas," said the troll. He looked gloomily into the torrent. "One of 'em's a lumber merchant down in Sour Water, one of 'em runs the bridge, and the big fat one is a merchant over on Bitter Pike. Call that a proper job for a troll?"

"One of them's in the bridge business, though," said Cohen.

"Bridge business? Sitting in a box all day charging people a silver piece to walk across? Half the time he ain't even there! He just pays some dwarf to take the money. And he calls himself a troll! You can't tell him from a human 'til you're right up close!"

Cohen nodded understandingly.

"D'you know," said the troll, "I have to go over and have dinner with them every week? All three of 'em? And listen to 'em go on about moving with the times . . ."

He turned a big, sad face to Cohen.

"What's wrong with being a troll under a bridge?" he said. "I was brought up to be a troll under a bridge. I want young Scree to be a troll under a bridge after I'm gone. What's wrong with that? You've got to have trolls under bridges. Otherwise, what's it all about? What's it all *for?*"

They leaned morosely on the parapet, looking down into the white water.

"You know," said Cohen slowly, "I can remember when a man could ride all the way from here to the Blade Mountains and never see another living thing." He fingered his sword. "At least, not for very long."

He threw the butt of his cigarette into the water. "It's all farms now. All little farms, run by little people. And *fences* everywhere. Everywhere you look, farms and fences and little people."

"She's right, of course," said the troll, continuing some interior conversation. "There's no future in just jumping out from under a bridge."

"I mean," said Cohen, "I've nothing against farms. Or farmers. You've got to have them. It's just that they used to be a long way off, around the edges. Now *this* is the edge."

"Pushed back all the time," said the troll. "Changing all the time. Like my brother-in-law Chert. A lumber mill! A *troll* running a lumber mill! And you should see the mess he's making of Cutshade Forest!"

Cohen looked up, surprised.

"What, the one with the giant spiders in it?"

"Spiders? There ain't no spiders now. Just stumps."

"Stumps? *Stumps?* I used to like that forest. It was . . . well, it was darksome. You don't get proper darksome any more. You really knew what terror was, in a forest like that."

"You want darksome? He's replanting with spruce," said Mica.

"Spruce!"

"It's not his idea. He wouldn't know one tree from another. That's all down to Clay. He put him up to it."

Cohen felt dizzy. "Who's Clay?"

"I said I'd got *three* brothers-in-law, right? He's the merchant. So he said replanting would make the land easier to sell."

There was a long pause while Cohen digested this.

Then he said, "You can't sell Cutshade Forest. It doesn't belong to anyone."

"Yeah. He says that's why you can sell it."

Cohen brought his fist down on the parapet. A piece of stone detached itself and tumbled down into the gorge.

"Sorry," he said.

"That's all right. Bits fall off all the time, like I said."

Cohen turned. "What's happening? I remember all the big old wars. Don't you? You must have fought."

"I carried a club, yeah."

"It was supposed to be for a bright new future and law and stuff. That's what people said."

"Well, I fought because a big troll with a whip told me to," said Mica, cautiously. "But I know what you mean."

"I mean it wasn't for farms and spruce trees. Was it?"

Mica hung his head. "And here's me with this apology for a bridge. I feel really bad about it," he said. "You coming all this way and every-thing—"

"And there was some king or other," said Cohen, vaguely, looking at the water. "And I think there were some wizards. But there was a king. I'm pretty certain there was a king. Never met him. You know?" He grinned at the troll. "I can't remember his name. Don't think they ever told me his name."

About half an hour later Cohen's horse emerged from the gloomy woods onto a bleak, windswept moorland. It plodded on for a while before saying, "All right . . . how much did you give him?"

"Twelve gold pieces," said Cohen.

"Why'd you give him twelve gold pieces?"

"I didn't have more than twelve."

"You must be mad."

"When I was just starting out in the barbarian hero business," said Cohen, "every bridge had a troll under it. And you couldn't go through a forest like we've just gone through without a dozen goblins trying to chop your head off." He sighed. "I wonder what happened to 'em all?"

"You," said the horse.

"Well, yes. But I always thought there'd be some more. I always thought there'd be some more edges."

"How old are you?" said the horse.

"Dunno."

"Old enough to know better, then."

"Yeah. Right." Cohen lit another cigarette and coughed until his eyes watered.

"Going soft in the head!"

"Yeah."

"Giving your last dollar to a troll!"

"Yeah." Cohen wheezed a stream of smoke at the sunset.

"Why?"

Cohen stared at the sky. The red glow was as cold as the slopes of hell. An icy wind blew across the steppes, whipping at what remained of his hair.

"For the sake of the way things should be," he said.

"Hah!"

"For the sake of things that were."

"Hah!"

Cohen looked down.

He grinned.

"And for three addresses. One day I'm going to die," he said, "but not, I think, today."

The wind blew off the mountains, filling the air with fine ice crystals. It was too cold to snow. In weather like this wolves came down into villages, trees in the heart of the forest exploded when they froze. Except there were fewer and fewer wolves these days, and less and less forest.

In weather like this right-thinking people were indoors, in front of the fire.

Telling stories about heroes.

A Long Night's Vigil at the Temple

Robert Silverberg

he moment of total darkness was about to arrive. The Warder Diriente stepped forward onto the portico of the temple, as he had done every night for the past thirty years, to perform the evening invocation. He was wearing, as always, his bright crimson warder's cassock and the tall double-peaked hat of his office, which had seemed so comical to him when he had first seen his father wearing it long ago, but which he now regarded, when he thought of it at all, as simply an article of clothing. There was a bronze thurible in his left hand and in the right he held a tapering, narrow-necked green vessel, sleek and satisfying to the touch, the fine celadon ware that only the craftsmen of Murrha Island were capable of producing.

The night was clear and mild, a gentle summer evening, with the high, sharp sound of tree-frogs in the air and the occasional bright flash of golden light from the lantern of a glitterfly. Far below, in the valley where the sprawling imperial city of Citherione lay, the myriad lights of the far-off residential districts were starting to come on, and they looked like glitterfly gleams also, wavering and winking, an illusion born of great distance.

It was half an hour's journey by groundwagon from the closest districts of the city to the temple. The Warder had not been down there in months. Once he had gone there more frequently, but now that he was old the city had become an alien place to him, dirty, strange-smelling, discordant. The big stone temple, massive and solid in its niche on the hillside, with the great tawny mountain wall rising steeply behind it, was all that he needed these days: the daily round of prayer and observance and study, the company of good friends, a little work in the garden, a decent bottle of wine with dinner, perhaps some quiet music late at night. A comfortable, amiably reclusive life, untroubled by anguished questions of philosophy or urgent challenges of professional struggle.

His profession had been decided for him before his birth: the post of temple warder was hereditary. It had been in his family for twelve generations. He was the eldest son; his elevation to the wardership was a certainty throughout all his childhood, and Diriente had prepared himself unquestioningly for the post from the first. Of course, somewhere along the way he had lost whatever faith he might once have had in the tenets of the creed he served, and that had been a problem for him for a time, but he had come to terms with that a long while back.

The temple portico was a broad marble slab running the entire length of the building along its western face, the face that looked toward the city. Below the portico's high rim, extending outward from it like a fan, was a sloping lawn thick as green velvet—a hundred centuries of dedicated gardeners had tended it with love—bordered by groves of ornamental flowering shrubs. Along the north side of the temple garden was a stream that sprang from some point high up on the mountain and flowed swiftly downward into the far-off valley. There were service areas just alongside and behind the temple—a garbage dump, a little cemetery, cottages for the temple staff—and back of those lay a tangle of wilderness forming a transitional zone between the open sloping flank of the mountain on which the temple had been constructed and the high wall of rock that rose to the rear of the site.

Warders were supposed to be in some semblance of a state of grace, that receptivity to the infinite which irreverent novices speak of as "cosmic connection," when they performed the evening invocation. Diriente doubted that he really did achieve the full degree of rapport, or even that such rapport was possible; but he did manage a certain degree of concentration that seemed acceptable enough to him. His technique of attaining it was to focus his attention on the ancient scarred face of the moon, if it was a night when the moon was visible, and otherwise to look toward the Pole Star. Moon or stars, either would do: the essential thing was to turn his spirit outward toward the realm where the great powers of the Upper World resided. It usually took him only a moment or two to attune himself properly for the rite. He had had plenty of practice, after all.

This night as he looked starward—there was no moon—and began to feel the familiar, faintly prickly sensation of contact awakening in him, the giddy feeling that he was climbing his own spinal column and gliding through his forehead into space, he was startled by an unusual interruption. A husky figure came jogging up out of the garden toward the temple and planted itself right below him at the portico's edge.

"Diriente?" he called. "Listen, Diriente, you have to come and look at something that I've found."

It was Mericalis, the temple custodian. The Warder, his concentration shattered, felt a sharp jolt of anger and surprise. Mericalis should have had more sense than that.

Testily the Warder indicated the thurible and the celadon vessel.

"Oh," Mericalis said, sounding unrepentant. "You aren't finished yet, then?"

"No, I'm not. I was only just starting, as a matter of fact. And you shouldn't be bothering me just this minute."

"Yes, yes, I know that. But this is important. Look, I'm sorry I broke in on you, but I had a damned good reason for it. Get your ceremony done with quickly, will you, Diriente? And then I want you to come with me. Right away."

Mericalis offered no other explanation. The Warder demanded none. It would only be a further distraction, and he was distracted enough as it was.

He attempted with no more than partial success to regain some measure of calmness.

"I'll finish as soon as you let me," he told the custodian irritably.

"Yes. Do. I'll wait for you down here."

The Warder nodded brusquely. Mericalis disappeared back into the shadows below the portico.

So. Then. Starting over from the beginning. The Warder drew his breath in deeply and closed his eyes a moment and waited until the effects of the intrusion had begun to ebb. After a time the jangling in his mind eased. Then once more he turned his attention to his task, looking up, finding the Pole Star with practiced ease and fixing his eyes upon it. From that direction, ten thousand years ago, the three Visitants had come to Earth to rescue mankind from great peril; or so the Scriptures maintained. Perhaps it actually had happened. There was no reason to think that it hadn't and some to think that it had.

He focused the entire intensity of his being on the Upper World, casting his soul skyward into the dark terrible gulfs between the galaxies. It was a willed feat of the imagination for him: with conscious effort he pictured himself roving the stars, a disembodied attenuated intelligence gliding like a bright needle through the black airless infinities.

The Warder often felt as though there once had been a time when making that leap had not required an effort of will: that in the days when he was new to his priestly office he had simply stepped forth and looked upward, and everything else had followed as a matter of course. The light of the Pole Star had penetrated his soul and he had gone out easily, effortlessly, on a direct course toward the star of the Three. Was it so? He couldn't remember. He had been Warder for so long. He had performed the evening invocation some ten thousand times at least. Everything was formula and rote by now. It was difficult now to believe that his mind had ever been capable of ascending in one joyous bound into those blazing depths of endless night, or that he had ever seriously thought that looking at the stars and dumping good wine into a stone channel might have some real and undeniable redemptive power. The best he could hope for these days was some flicker—some quivering little stab—of the old ecstasy, while he stood each night beneath the heavens in all their glory. And even that flicker, that tiny stab, was suspect, a probable counterfeit, an act of willful self-delusion.

The stars were beautiful, at any rate. He was grateful for that one blessing. His faith in the literal existence of the Visitants and their one-time presence on the Earth might be gone, but not his awareness of the immensity of the universe, the smallness of Man, the majesty of the great vault of night.

Standing poised and steady, head thrust back, face turned toward the heavens, he began to swing the thurible, sending a cloud of pungent incense swirling into the sky. He elevated the sleek green porcelain vessel, offering it to the three cardinal points, east and west and zenith. The reflexes of his professionalism had hold of him now: he was fully into the ceremony, as deeply as his skepticism would allow him ever to get.

In the grasp of the moment he would let no doubts intrude. They would come back to him quickly enough, just afterward.

Solemnly now he spoke the Holy Names:

"Oberith . . . Aulimiath . . . Vonubius."

He allowed himself to believe that he had made contact.

He summoned up the image of the Three before him, the angular alien figures shimmering with spectral light. He told them, as he had told them so many times before, how grateful the world was for all that they had done for the people of Earth long ago, and how eager Earth was for their swift return from their present sojourn in the distant heavens.

For the moment the Warder's mind actually did seem free of all questions of belief and unbelief. Had the Three in fact existed? Had they truly come to Earth in its time of need? Did they rise up to the stars again in a fiery chariot when their work was done, vowing to return some day and gather up all the peoples of the world in their great benevolence? The Warder had no idea. When he was young he believed every word of the Scriptures, like everyone else; then, he was not sure exactly when, he stopped believing. But that made no conspicuous difference to the daily conduct of his life. He was the Warder of the high temple; he had certain functions to perform; he was a servant of the people. That was all that mattered.

The ritual was the same every evening. According to generally accepted belief it hadn't changed in thousands of years, going back to the very night of the Visitants' departure from Earth, though the Warder was privately skeptical of that, as he was of so many other matters. Things change with time; distortions enter any system of belief; of that he was certain. Even so, he outwardly maintained the fiction that there had been no alterations in any aspect of the liturgy, because he was aware that the people preferred to think that that was the case. The people were profoundly conservative in their ways; and he was here to serve the people. That was the family tradition: we are Warders, and that means we serve.

The invocation was at its climax, the moment of the offering. Softly the Warder spoke the prayer of the Second Advent, the point of the entire exercise, expressing the hope that the Three would not long delay their return to the world. The words rolled from him quickly, perfunctorily, as though they were syllables in some lost language, holding no meaning for him. Then he called the Names a second time, with the same theatrical solemnity as before. He lifted the porcelain vessel high, inverted it, and allowed the golden wine that it contained to pour into the stone channel that ran down the hill toward the temple pond. That was the last of it, the finale of the rite. Behind him, at that moment, the temple's hydraulus-player, a thin hatchet-faced man sitting patiently in the darkness beside the stream, struck from his instrument the three great thunderous chords that concluded the service.

At this point any worshipers who had happened to have remained at the temple this late would have fallen to their knees and cried out in joy and hope while making the sign of the Second Advent. But there were no worshipers on hand this evening, only a few members of the temple staff, who, like the Warder, were going about the business of shutting the place down for the night. In the moment of the breaking of the contact the Warder stood by himself, very much conscious of the solitude of his spirit and the futility of his profession as he felt the crashing wave of his unbelief come sweeping back in upon him. The pain lasted only an instant; and then he was himself again.

Out of the shadows then came Mericalis once more, broad-shouldered, insistent, rising before the Warder like a specter he had conjured up himself.

"You're done? Ready to go?"

The Warder glared at him. "Why are you in such a hurry? Do you mind if I put the sacred implements away first?"

"Go right ahead," the custodian said, shrugging. "Take all the time you want, Diriente." There was an unfamiliar edge on his voice.

The Warder chose to ignore it. He re-entered the temple and placed the thurible and the porcelain wine-vessel in their niche just within the door. He closed the wrought-iron grillwork cover of the niche and locked it, and quickly muttered the prayer that ended his day's duties. He put aside his tall hat and hung his cassock on its peg. Underneath it he wore a simple linen surplice, belted with a worn strip of leather.

He stepped back outside. The members of the temple staff were drifting off into the night, heading down by torchlight to their cottages along the temple's northern side. Their laughter rose on the soft air. The Warder envied them their youth, their gaiety, their assurance that the world was as they thought it was.

Mericalis, still waiting for him beside a flowering bayerno bush just below the thick marble rim of the portico, beckoned to him.

"Where are we going?" The Warder asked, as they set out briskly together across the lawn.

"You'll see."

"You're being very damned mysterious."

"Yes. I suppose I am."

Mericalis was leading him around the temple's northwestern corner to the back of the building, where the rough road began that by a series of steep switchbacks ascended the face of the hill against which the temple had been built. He carried a small automatic torch, a mere wand of amber light. On this moonless evening the torch seemed more powerful than it really was.

As they went past the garbage dump Mericalis said, "I really am sorry I broke in on you just as you were about to do the invocation. I did actually think you were done with it already."

"That doesn't make any difference now."

"I felt bad, though. I know how important that rite is to you."

"Do you?" the Warder said, not knowing what to make of the custodian's remark.

The Warder had never discussed his loss of faith with anyone, not even Mericalis, who over the years had become perhaps his closest friend, closer to him than any of the temple's priests. But he doubted that it was much of a secret. Faith shines in a man's face like the full moon breaking through the mists on a winter night. The Warder was able to see it in others, that special glow. He suspected that they were unable to see it in him.

The custodian was a purely secular man. His task was to maintain the structural integrity of the temple, which, after all, had been in constant service for ten thousand years and by now was perpetually in precarious condition, massive and sturdy though it was. Mericalis knew all the weak places in the walls, the subtle flaws in the buttresses, the shifting slabs in the floor, the defects of the drains. He was something of an archaeologist as well, and could discourse learnedly on the various stages of the ancient building's complex history, the details of the different reconstructions, the stratigraphic boundaries marking one configuration of the temple off from another, showing how it had been built and rebuilt over the centuries. Of religious feeling, Mericalis seemed to have none at all: it was the temple that he loved, not the creed that it served.

They were well beyond the garbage dump now, moving along the narrow unpaved road that ran up toward the summit of the mountain. The Warder found his breath coming short as the grade grew more steep.

He had rarely had occasion to use this road. There were old altars higher up on the mountain, remnants of a primitive fire-rite that had become obsolete many hundreds of years before, during the Samtharid Interregnum. But they held no interest for him. Mericalis, pursuing his antiquarian studies, probably went up there frequently, the Warder supposed, and now he must have made some startling discovery amidst the charred ancient stones, something bizarre and troublesome enough to justify breaking in on him during the invocation. A scene of human sacrifice? The tomb of some prehistoric king? This mountain had been holy land a long time, going back, so it was said, even into the days before the old civilization of machines and miracles had collapsed. What strangeness had Mericalis found?

But their goal didn't seem to lie above them on the mountain. Instead of continuing to ascend, the custodian turned abruptly off the road when they were still only a fairly short distance behind the temple and began pushing his way vigorously into a tangle of underbrush. The Warder, frowning, followed. By this time he knew better than to waste his breath asking questions. He stumbled onward, devoting all his energy to the job of maintaining his footing. In the deep darkness of the night, with Mericalis' little torch the only illumination, he was hard pressed to keep from tripping over hidden roots or vines.

After about twenty paces of tough going they came to a place where a second road—a crude little path, really—unexpectedly presented itself. This one, to the Warder's surprise, curved back down the slope in the direction of the temple, but instead of returning them to the service area on the northern side it carried them around toward the opposite end of the building, into a zone which the Warder long had thought was inaccessible because of the thickness of the vegetation. They were behind the temple's southeastern corner now, perhaps a hundred paces from the rear wall of the building itself. In all his years here the Warder had never seen the temple from this angle. Its great oblong bulk reared up against the sky, black on black, a zone of intense starless darkness against a star-speckled black backdrop.

There was a clearing here in the scrub. A roughly circular pit lay in the center of it, about as wide across as the length of a man's arm. It seemed recently dug, from the fresh look of the mound of tailings behind it.

Mericalis walked over to the opening and poked the head of his torch into it. The Warder, coming up alongside him, stared downward. Despite the inadequacy of the light he was able to see that the pit was actually the mouth of a subterranean passageway which sloped off at a sharp angle, heading toward the temple.

"What's all this?" the Warder asked.

"An unauthorized excavation. Some treasure-hunters have been at work back here."

The Warder's eyes opened wide. "Trying to tunnel into the temple, you mean?"

"Apparently so," said Mericalis. "Looking for a back way into the vaults." He stepped down a little way into the pit, paused, and looked back, beckoning impatiently to the Warder. "Come on, Diriente. You need to see what's here."

The Warder stayed where he was.

"You seriously want me to go down there? The two of us crawling around in an underground tunnel in the dark?"

"Yes. Absolutely."

"I'm an old man, Mericalis."

"Not all that old. And it's a very capably built little passageway. You can manage it."

Still the Warder held back. "And what if the men who dug it come back and find us while we're in there?"

"They won't," said Mericalis. "I promise you that."

"How can you be so sure?"

"Trust me, Diriente."

"I'd feel better if we had a couple of the younger priests with us, all the same."

The custodian shook his head. "Once you've seen what I'm going to show you, you'll be glad that there's no one here but you and me to see it. Come on, now. Are you going to follow me or aren't you?"

Uneasily the Warder entered the opening. The newly broken ground was soft and moist beneath his sandaled feet. The smell of the earth rose to his nostrils, rich, loamy, powerful. Mericalis was five or six paces ahead of him and moving quickly along without glancing back. The Warder found that he had to crouch and shuffle to keep from hitting his head on the narrow tunnel's low roof. And yet the tunnel was well made, just as the custodian had said. It descended at a sharp angle until it was perhaps twice the height of a man below the ground, and then leveled out. It was nicely squared off at the sides and bolstered every ten paces by timbers. Months of painstaking work must have been required for all this. The Warder felt a sickly sense of violation. To think that thieves had managed to work back here undisturbed all this time! And had they reached the vaults? The temple wasn't actually a single building, but many, of different eras, each built upon the foundation of its predecessor. Layer beneath layer of inaccessible chambers, some of them thousands of years old, were believed to occupy the area underneath the main ceremonial hall of the present-day temple. The temple possessed considerable treasure, precious stones, ingots of rare metals, works of art: gifts of forgotten monarchs, hidden away down there in those old vaults long ago and scarcely if ever looked at since. It was believed that there were tombs in the building's depths, too, the burial places of ancient kings, priests, heroes. But no one ever tried to explore the deeper vaults. The stairs leading down to them were hopelessly blocked with debris, so that not even Mericalis could distinguish between what might once have been a staircase and what was part of the building's foundation. Getting down to the lower strata would be impossible without ripping up the present-day floors and driving broad shafts through the upper basements, and no one dared to try that: such excavation might weaken the entire structure and bring the building crashing down. As for tunneling into the deep levels from outside—well, no one in the Warder's memory had ever proposed doing that, either, and he doubted that the Grand Assize of the Temple would permit such a project to be carried out even if application were made. There was no imaginable spiritual benefit to be gained from rooting about in the foundations of the holy building, and not much scientific value in it either, considering how many other relics of Earth's former civilizations, still unexcavated after all this time, were on hand everywhere to keep the archaeologists busy.

But if the diggers had been thieves, not archaeologists—

No wonder Mericalis had come running up to him in the midst of the invocation!

"How did you find this?" the Warder asked, as they moved farther in. The air here was dank and close, and the going was very slow.

"It was one of the priests that found it, actually. One of the younger ones, and no, I won't tell you his name, Diriente. He came around back here a few days ago with a certain young priestess to enjoy a little moment or two of privacy and they practically fell right into it. They explored it to a point about as far as we are now and realized it was something highly suspicious, and they came and told me about it."

"But you didn't tell me."

"No," Mericalis said. "I didn't. It seemed purely a custodial affair then. There was no need to get you involved in it. Someone had been digging around behind the temple, yes. Very likely for quite some time. Coming in by night, maybe, working very, very patiently, hauling away the tailings and dumping them in the woods, pushing closer and closer to the wall of the building, no doubt with the intent of smashing through into one of the deep chambers and carrying off the vast wealth that's supposedly stored down there. My plan was to investigate the tunnel myself, find out just what had been going on here, and then to bring the city police in to deal with it. You would have been notified at that point, of course."

"So you haven't taken it to the police yet, then?"

"No," said Mericalis. "I haven't."

"But why not?"

"I don't think there's anyone for them to arrest, that's why. Look here, Diriente."

He took the Warder by the arm and tugged him forward so that the Warder was standing in front of him. Then he reached his arm under the Warder's and flashed the torch into the passageway just ahead of them.

The Warder gasped.

Two men in rough work clothes were sprawled on the tunnel floor, half buried beneath debris that had fallen from overhead. The Warder could see shovels and picks jutting out from the mound of fallen earth beside them. A third man—no, this one was a woman—lay a short distance away. A sickening odor of decay rose from the scene.

"Are they dead?" the Warder asked quietly.

"Do you need to ask?"

"Killed by a rockfall, you think?"

"That's how it looks, doesn't it? These two were the diggers. The girl was their lookout, I suspect, posted at the mouth of the tunnel. She's armed: you see? Two guns and a dagger. They must have called her in here to see something unusual, and just then the roof fell in on them all." Mericalis stepped over the slender body and picked his way through the rubble beyond it, going a few paces deeper into the passageway. "Come over here and I'll show you what I think happened."

"What if the roof collapses again?"

"I don't think it will," Mericalis said.

"If it can collapse once, it can collapse again," said the Warder, shivering a little now despite the muggy warmth of the tunnel. "Right on our heads. Shouldn't we get out of here while we can?"

The custodian ignored him. "Look here, now: what do you make of this?" He aimed the torch to one side, holding it at a ninety-degree angle to the direction of the tunnel. The Warder squinted into the darkness. He saw what looked like a thick stone lintel which had fallen from the tunnel vault and was lying tipped up on end. There were archaic-looking inscriptions carved in it, runes of some sort. Behind it was an opening, a gaping oval of darkness in the darkness, that appeared to be the mouth of a second tunnel running crosswise to the one they were in. Mericalis leaned over the fallen lintel and flashed his beam beyond it. A tunnel, yes. But constructed in a manner very different from that of the one they had been following. The walls were of narrow stone blocks, carefully laid edge to edge; the roof of the tunnel was a long stone vault, supported by pointed arches. The craftsmanship was very fine. The joints had an archaic look.

"How old is this?" the Warder asked.

"Old. Do you recognize those runes on the lintel? They're proterohistoric stuff. This tunnel's as ancient as the temple itself, most likely. Part of the original sacred complex. The thieves couldn't have known it was here. As they were digging their way toward the temple they intersected it by accident. They yelled for the girl to come in and look—or maybe they wanted her to help them pull the lintel loose. Which they proceeded to do, and the weak place where the two tunnels met gave way, and the roof of their own tunnel came crashing down on them. For which I for one feel no great sorrow, I have to admit."

"Do you have any idea where this other tunnel goes?"

"To the temple," said Mericalis. "Or under it, rather, into the earliest foundation. It leads straight toward the deepest vaults."

"Are you sure?"

"I've been inside already. Come."

There was no question now of retreating. The Warder, following close along behind Mericalis, stared at the finely crafted masonry of the tunnel in awe. Now and again he saw runic inscriptions, unreadable, mysterious, carved in the stone floor. When they had gone about twenty paces yet another stone-vaulted passageway presented itself, forking off to the left. The custodian went past it without a glance. "There are all sorts of tunnels down here," Mericalis said. "But this is the one we want. So far as I've been able to determine at this point, it's the only one that enters the temple." The Warder saw that Mericalis had left a marker that glowed by the reflected light of his torch, high up on the wall of the passage they were following, and he supposed that there were other markers farther on to serve as guides for them. "We're in a processional hypogeum," the custodian explained. "Probably it was just about at ground level, ten thousand years ago, but over the centuries it was buried by construction debris from the later temples, and other trash of various sorts. There was a whole maze of other stone-walled processional chambers around it, leading originally to sacrificial sites and open-air altars. The tunnel we just passed was one of them. It's blocked a little way onward. I spent two days in here going down one false trail after another. Until I came through this way, and—behold, Diriente!"

Mericalis waved his torch grandly about. By the pale splash of light that came from its tip the Warder saw that the sides of the tunnel expanded outward here, spreading to the right and the left to form a great looming wall of superbly dressed stone, with one small dark aperture down at the lower left side. They had reached the rear face of the temple. The Warder trembled. He had an oppressive sense of the thickness of the soil above him, the vast weight pressing down, the temple itself rising in all its intricacy of strata above him. He was at the foundation of foundations. Once all this had been in the open: ten thousand years ago, when the Visitants still walked the Earth.

"You've been inside?" the Warder asked hoarsely.

"Of course," said Mericalis. "You have to crawl the first part of the way. Take care to breathe shallowly: there's plenty of dust."

The air here was hot and musty and dry, ancient air, lifeless air. The Warder choked and gagged on it. On hands and knees, head down, he crept along behind Mericalis. Several times, overcome by he knew not what, he closed his eyes and waited until a spasm of dizziness had passed.

"You can stand now," the custodian told him.

They were in a large square stone chamber. The walls were rough-hewn and totally without ornament. The room was empty except for three long, narrow coffers of unpolished white marble side by side at the far end.

"Steady yourself, old friend," Mericalis said. "And then come and see who we have here."

They crossed the room. The coffers were covered with a thick sheet of some transparent yellowish material that looked much like glass, but in fact was some other substance that the Warder could not identify.

An icy shiver ran through the Warder as he peered through the coverings.

There was a skeleton in each coffer, lying face upward: the glistening fleshless bones of some strange long-shanked creature, manlike in size and general outline, but different in every detail. Their heads bore curving bony crests; their shoulders were crested also; their knees were double ones; they had spikelike protrusions at their ankles. Ribs, pelvises, fingers, toes—everything strange, everything unfamiliar. These were the bodies of alien beings.

Mericalis said, "My guess is that the very tall one in the center is Vonubius. That's probably Aulimiath on the right and the other one has to be Oberith, then."

The Warder looked up at him sharply. "What are you saying?"

"This is obviously a sepulcher. Those are sarcophagi. These are three skeletons of aliens that we're looking at here. They've been very carefully preserved and buried in a large and obviously significant chamber on the deepest and therefore oldest level of the Temple of the Visitants, in a room that once was reached by a grand processional passageway. Who else do you think they would be?"

"The Visitants went up into the heavens when their work on Earth was done," said the Warder hollowly. "They ascended on a ship of fire and returned to their star."

"You believe that?" Mericalis asked, chuckling.

"It says so in the Scriptures."

"I know that it does. Do you believe it, though?"

"What does it matter what I believe?" The Warder stared again at the three elongated alien skeletons. "The historical outlines aren't questioned by anybody. The world was in a crisis—in collapse. There was war everywhere. In the midst of it all, three ambassadors from another solar system arrived and saw what was going on, and they used their superior abilities to put things to rights. Once a stable new world order had emerged, they took off for the stars again. The story turns up in approximately the same form in every society's myths and folk-tales, all over the Earth. There's got to be some truth to it."

"I don't doubt that there is," said Mericalis. "And there they are, the three wise men from afar. The Scriptures have the story a little garbled, apparently. Instead of going back to their native star, promising to return and redeem us at some new time of trouble, they died while still on Earth and were buried underneath the temple of the cult that sprang up around them. So there isn't going to be any Second Advent, I'd tend to think. And if there ever is, it may not be a friendly one. They didn't die natural deaths, you'll notice. If you'll take a careful look you'll see that the heads of all three were severed violently from their trunks."

"What?"

"Look closely," Mericalis said.

"There's a break in the vertebrae, yes. But that could have been—"

"It's the same sort of break in all three. I've seen the skeletons of executed men before, Diriente. We've dug up dozens of them around the old gibbet down the hill. These three were decapitated. Believe me."

"No."

"They were martyrs. They were put to death by their loving admirers and devoted worshipers, the citizens of Earth."

"No. No. No. No."

"Why are you so stunned, Diriente? Does it shock you, that such a dreadful thing could have happened on our lovely green planet? Have you been squirreled up in your nest on this hillside so long that you've forgotten everything you once knew about human nature? Or is it the unfortunate evidence that the Scriptural story is wrong that bothers you? You don't believe in the Second Advent anyway, do you?"

"How do you know I don't?"

"Please, Diriente."

The Warder was silent. His mind was aswirl with confusions.

After a time he said, "These could be any three aliens at all."

"Yes. I suppose they could. But we know of only three beings from space that ever came to this planet: the ones who we call the Visitants. This is the temple of the faith that sprang up around them. Somebody went to great trouble to bury these three underneath it. I have difficulty believing that these would be three *different* alien beings."

Stubbornly the Warder said, "How do you know that these things are genuine skeletons? They might be idols of some sort."

"Idols in the form of skeletons? *Decapitated* skeletons, at that?" Mericalis laughed. "I suppose we could test them chemically to see if they're real, if you like. But they look real enough to me."

"The Visitants were like gods. They *were* gods, compared with us. Certainly they were regarded as divine—or at least as the ministers and ambassadors of the Divine Being—when they were here. Why would they have been killed? Who would have dared to lay a hand on them?"

"Who can say? Maybe they didn't seem as divine as all that in the days when they walked among us," Mericalis suggested.

"But the Scriptures say—"

"The Scriptures, yes. Written how long after the fact? The Visitants may not have been so readily recognized as holy beings originally. They might simply have seemed threatening, maybe—dangerous—tyrannical. A menace to free will, to man's innate right to make trouble for himself. It was a time of anarchy, remember. Maybe there were those who didn't *want* order restored. I don't know. Even if they *were* seen as godly, Diriente: remember that there's an ancient tradition on this planet of killing one's gods. It goes back a long, long way. Study your prehistoric cults. You dig down deep enough, you find a murdered god somewhere at the bottom of almost all of them."

The Warder fell into silence again. He was unable to take his eyes from those bony-crested skulls, those strange-angled empty eye sockets.

"Well," Mericalis said, "there you have them, at any rate: three skeletons of what appear to be beings from another world that somebody just happened to bury underneath your temple a very long time ago. I thought you ought to know about them."

"Yes. Thank you."

"You have to decide what to do about them, now."

"Yes," the Warder said. "I know that."

"We could always seal the passageway up again, I suppose, and not say a word about this to anyone. Which would avoid all sorts of uncomfortable complications, wouldn't it? It strikes me as a real crime against knowledge, doing something like that, but if you thought that we should—"

"Who knows about this so far?"

"You. Me. No one else."

"What about the priest and priestess who found the excavation pit?"

"They came right to me and told me about it. They hadn't gone very far inside, no more than five or six paces. Why should they have gone any farther?"

"They might have," the Warder said.

"They didn't. They had no torch and they had their minds on other things. All they did was look a little way in, just far enough to see that something unusual was going on. They hadn't even gone far enough to find the thieves. But they didn't say a thing about dead bodies in the tunnel. They'd certainly have told me about them, if they had come upon them. And they'd have looked a whole lot shakier, too."

"The thieves didn't come in here either?"

"It doesn't seem that way to me. I don't think they got any farther than the place where they pulled that lintel out of the passage wall. They're dead, in any case."

"But what if they did get this far? And what if there was someone else with them, someone who managed to escape when the tunnel caved in? Someone who might be out there right now telling all his friends what he saw in this room?"

Mericalis shook his head. "There's no reason to think that. And I could see, when I first came down this passage and into the sepulchral chamber, that nobody had been through here in more years than we can imagine. There'd have been tracks in the dust, and there weren't any. This place has gone undisturbed a very long time. Long enough for the whole story of how the Visitants died to be forgotten and covered over with a nice pretty myth about their ascent into the heavens on a pillar of fire."

The Warder considered that for a moment.

"All right," he said finally. "Go back outside, Mericalis."

"And leave you here alone?"

"Leave me here alone, yes."

Uneasily Mericalis said, "What are you up to, Diriente?"

"I want to sit here all by myself and think and pray, that's all."

"Do I have to believe that?"

"Yes. You do."

"If you go wandering around down here you'll end up trapped in some unknown passageway and most likely we'll never be able to find you again."

"I'm not going to wander around anywhere. I told you what I'm going to do. I'm going to sit right here, in this very room. You've brought me face to face with the dead bodies of the murdered gods of the religion that I'm supposed to serve, and I need to think about what that means. That's all. Go away, Mericalis. This is something I have to do all by myself. You'll only be a distraction. Come back for me at dawn and I promise you that you'll find me sitting exactly where I am now."

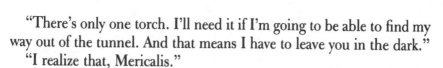

"There's only one torch. I'll need it if I'm going to be able to find my way out of the tunnel. And that means I have to leave you in the dark."

"I realize that, Mericalis."

"But—"

"Go," the Warder said. "Don't worry about me. I can stand a few hours of darkness. I'm not a child. Go," he said again. "Just go, will you? Now."

He couldn't deny that he was frightened. He was well along in years; by temperament he was a sedentary man; it was totally against his nature to be spending a night in a place like this, far beneath the ground, where the air managed to seem both dusty-dry and sticky-moist at the same time, and the sharp, pungent odor of immense antiquity jabbed painfully at his nostrils. How different it was from his pleasant little room, sur- rounded by his books, his jug of wine, his familiar furnishings! In the total darkness he was free to imagine the presence of all manner of dis- agreeable creatures of the depths creeping about him, white eyeless toads and fleshless chittering lizards and slow, contemplative spiders lowering themselves silently on thick silken cords from invisible recesses of the stone ceiling. He stood in the center of the room and it seemed to him that he saw a sleek fat serpent, pallid and gleaming, with blind blue eyes bright as sapphires, issue from a pit in the floor and rise up before him, hissing and bobbing and swaying as it made ready to strike. But the Warder knew that it was only a trick of the darkness. There was no pit; there was no serpent.

He perspired freely. His light robe was drenched and clung to him like a shroud. With every breath it seemed to him that he was pulling clusters of cobwebs into his lungs. The darkness was so intense it ham- mered at his fixed, rigidly staring eyes until he was forced to shut them. He heard inexplicable sounds coming from the walls, a grinding hum and a steady unhurried ticking and a trickling sound, as of sand tumbling through hidden inner spaces. There were menacing vibrations and trem- ors, and strange twanging hums, making him fear that the temple itself, angered by this intrusion into its bowels, was preparing to bring itself down upon him. What I hear is only the echoes of Maricalis' footfalls, the Warder told himself. The sounds that he makes as he retraces his way down the tunnel toward the exit.

After a time he arose and felt his way across the room toward the coffers in the corner, clinging to the rough stones of the wall to guide himself. Somehow he missed his direction, for the corner was empty when he reached it, and as he continued past it his inquiring fingers found themselves pressing into what surely was the opening that led to the tunnel. He stood quietly for a moment in the utter darkness, trying to remember the layout of the funeral chamber, certain that the coffers must have been in the corner he had gone to and unable to understand why he had not found them. He thought of doubling back his path and looking again. But perhaps he was disoriented; perhaps he had gone in precisely the opposite direction from the one he supposed he had taken. He kept going, past the opening, along the wall on the other side. To the other corner. No coffers here. He turned right, still clinging to the wall. A step at a time, imagining yawning pits opening beneath his feet. His knee bumped into something. He had reached the coffers, yes.

He knelt. Grasped the rim of the nearest one, leaned forward, looked down into it.

To his surprise he was able to see a little now, to make out the harsh, angular lines of the skeleton it contained. How was that possible? Perhaps his eyes were growing accustomed to the darkness. No, that wasn't it. A nimbus of light seemed to surround the coffer. A faint reddish glow had begun to rise from it and with the aid of that unexpected illumination he could actually see the outlines of the elongated shape within.

An illusion? Probably. Hallucination, even. This was the strangest moment of his life, and anything was to be expected, anything at all. There is magic here, the Warder found himself thinking, and then he caught himself up in amazement and wonder that he should have so quickly tumbled into the abyss of the irrational. He was a prosaic man. He had no belief in magic. And yet—and yet—

The glow grew more intense. The skeleton blazed in the darkness. With eerie clarity he saw the alien crests and spines, the gnarled alien vertebrae, everything sending up a strange crimson fire to make its aspect plain to him. The empty eye sockets seemed alive with fierce intelligence.

"Who are you?" the Warder asked, almost belligerently. "Where did you come from? Why did you ever poke your noses into our affairs? Did you even *have* noses?" He felt strangely giddy. The closeness of the air, perhaps. Not enough oxygen. He laughed, too loudly, too long. "Oberith, is that who you are? Aulimiath? And that's Vonubius in the center box, yes? The tallest one, the leader of the mission."

His body shook with sudden anguish. Waves of fear and bewilderment swept over him. His own crude joking had frightened him. He began to sob.

The thought that he might be in the presence of the actual remains of the actual Three filled him with confusion and dismay. He had come over the years to think of the tale of the Advent as no more than a myth— the gods who came from the stars—and now he was stunned by this evidence that they had been real, that they once were tangible creatures who had walked and eaten and breathed and made water—and had been capable of dying, of being killed. He had reached a point long ago of not believing that. This discovery required him to reevaluate everything. Did it trivialize the religion he served into mere history? No—no, he thought; the existence here in this room of these bones elevated history into miracle, into myth. They truly had come. And had served, and had departed: not to the stars, but to the realm of death. From which they would return in the due course of time, and in their resurrection would bring the redemption that had been promised, the forgiveness for the crime that had been committed against them.

Was that it? Was that the proper way to interpret the things this room held?

He didn't know. He realized that he knew nothing at all.

The Warder shivered and trembled. He wrapped his arms around himself and held himself tight.

He fought to regain some measure of control over himself.

"No," he said sternly. "It can't be. You aren't them. I don't believe that those are your names."

From the coffers no answer came.

"You could be any three aliens at all," the Warder told them fiercely. "Who just happened to come to Earth, just dropped in one afternoon to see what might be here. And lived to regret it. Am I right?"

Still silence. The Warder, crouching down against the nearest coffer with his cheek pressed against the dry cold stone, shivered and trembled.

"Speak to me," he begged. "What do I have to do to get you to speak to me? Do you want me to pray? All right, then, I'll pray, if that's what you want."

In the special voice that he used for the evening invocation he intoned the three Holy Names:

"Oberith . . . Aulimiath . . . Vonubius."

There was no reply.

Bitterly he said, "You don't know your names, do you? Or are you just too stubborn to answer to them?"

He glowered into the darkness.

"Why are you here?" he asked them, furious now. "Why did Mericalis have to discover you? Oh, damn him, why did he ever have to tell me about you?"

Again there was no answer; but now he felt a strange thing beginning to occur. Serpentine columns of light were rising from the three coffers. They flickered and danced like tongues of cold fire before him, commanding him to be still and pay heed. The Warder pressed his hands against his forehead and bowed his head and let everything drain from his mind, so that he was no more than an empty shell crouching in the darkness of the room. And as he knelt there things began to change around him, the walls of the chamber melted and dropped away, and he found himself transported upward and outward until he was standing outside, in the clear sweet air, under the golden warmth of the sun.

The day was bright, warm, springlike, a splendid day, a day to cherish. But there were ugly dissonances. The Warder heard shouts to his right, to his left—harsh voices everywhere, angry outcries.

"There they are! Get them! Get them!"

Three slender grotesque figures came into view, half again as tall as a man, big-eyed, long-limbed, strange of shape, moving swiftly but with somber dignity, as though they were floating rather than striding, keeping just ahead of their pursuers. The Warder understood that these were the Three in their final moments, that they have been harried and hunted all this lovely day across the sweet meadows of this lush green valley. Now there is nowhere further for them to go, they are trapped in a cul-de-sac against the flank of the mountain, the army of their enemies is closing in and all hope of escape is impossible.

Now the Warder heard savage triumphant screams. Saw reddened, swollen, wrathful faces. Weapons bristling in the air, clubs, truncheons, pitchforks, hatchets. Wild eyes, distended lips, clenched fists furiously shaken. And on a little mound facing their attackers are the Three, standing close together, offering no resistance, seemingly at peace. They appear perplexed by what is happening, perhaps, or perhaps not—how can he tell? What do their alien expressions mean? But almost certainly they are not angry. Anger is not an emotion that can pertain to them in any way. They have a look about them that seems to indicate that they had expected this. *Forgive them, for they know not what they do.* A moment of hesitation: the mob suddenly uneasy at the last, frightened, even, uncertain of the risks in what they are doing. Then the hesitation was overcome, the people surged forward like a single berserk creature, there was the flash of steel in the sunlight—

The vision abruptly ended. He was within the stone chamber again. The light was gone. The air about him was dry and stale, not sweet and mild. The tomb was dark and empty.

The Warder felt stunned by what he has seen, and shamed. A sense of almost suicidal guilt overwhelmed him. Blindly he rushed back and forth across the dark room, frenzied, manic, buffeting himself against the unseen walls. Then, exhausted, he paused for a moment to gasp for breath and stared into the darkness at the place where he thought the coffers were situated. He would break through those transparent coverings, he told himself, and snatch up the three strange skulls and carry them out into the bright light of day, and he would call the people together and show them what he has brought forth from the depths of the Earth, brandishing the skulls in their faces, and he would cry out to them, "Here are your gods. This is what you did to them. All your beliefs were founded on a lie." And then he would hurl himself from the mountain.

No.

He will not. How can he crush their hopes that way? And having done it, what good would his death achieve?

And yet—to allow the lie to endure and persist—

"What am I going to do about you?" the Warder asked the skeletons in their coffers. "What am I going to tell the people?" His voice rose to a wild screech. It echoed and reechoed from the stone walls of the room, reverberating in his throbbing skull. "The *people!* The *people!* The *people!*"

"Speak to me!" the Warder cried. "Tell me what I'm supposed to do!"

Silence. Silence. Silence. They would give him no answers.

He laughed at his own helplessness. Then he wept for a time, until his eyes were raw and his throat ached from his sobbing. He fell to his knees once more beside one of the coffers. "Who are you?" he asked, in nothing more than a whisper. "Can you really be Vonubius?"

And this time imagines that he hears a mocking answer: *I am who I am. Go in peace, my son.*

Peace? Where? How?

At last, a long while later, he began to grow calm once more, and thought that this time he might be able to remain that way. He saw that he was being ridiculous—the old Warder, running to and fro in a stone chamber underground, crying out like a lunatic, praying to gods in whom he didn't believe, holding conversations with skeletons. Gradually his churning soul moved away from the desperate turbulence into which it had fallen, the manic frenzy, the childish anger. There was no reddish glow, no. His overwrought mind had conjured up some tormented fantasy for him. Darkness still prevailed in the chamber. He was unable to see a thing. Before him, he knew, were three ancient stone boxes containing age-old dry bones, the earthly remains of unearthly creatures long dead.

He was calm, yes. But there seemed no way even now to hide from his despair. These relics, he knew, called his whole life into question. The whole ugly truth of it stood unanswerably revealed. He had served a false creed, knowingly offering people the empty hope that they would be redeemed by benevolent gods. Night after night standing up there on the portico, invoking the Three, praying for their swift return to this troubled planet. Whereas in truth they had never left Earth at all. Had perished, in fact, at the hands of the very people they had come here— so he supposed—to redeem.

What now? the Warder asked himself. Reveal the truth? Display the bodies of the Three to the dismayed, astounded faithful, as he had imagined himself doing just a short time ago? Would he do any such thing? Could he? *Your beliefs were founded on a lie,* he pictured himself telling them. How could he do that? But it was the truth. Small wonder that I lost my own faith long ago, he thought. He had known the truth before he ever knew he knew it. It was the truth that he had sworn to serve, first and always. Was that not so? But there was so much that he did not understand—could not understand, perhaps.

He looked in the direction of the skeletons, and a host of new questions formed in his mind.

"Why did you want to come to us?" he asked, not angrily now, but in a curious tranquillity of spirit. "Why did you choose to serve us as you did? Why did you allow us to destroy you, since surely it was in your power to prevent it?"

Powerful questions. The Warder had no answers to them. But yet who knew what miracles might grow from the asking of them. Yes. Yes.

Miracles! True faiths can arise from the ruined fragments of false ones, was that not so?

He was so very tired. It had been such a long night.

Gradually he slipped downward until he was lying completely prone, face pillowed in his arms. It seemed to him that the gentle light of morning was entering the chamber, that the long vigil was over at last. How could that be, light reaching him underground? He chose not to pursue the question. He lay quietly, waiting. And then he heard footsteps. Mericalis was returning. The night was over indeed.

"Diriente? Diriente, are you all right?"

"Help me up," the Warder says. "I'm not accustomed to spending my nights lying on stone floors."

The custodian flashes his torch around the room as if he expects it to have changed in some fashion since he last saw it.

"Well?" he says, finally.

"Let's get out of here, shall we?"

"You're all right?"

"Yes, yes, I'm all right!"

"I was very worried. I know you said you wanted to be alone, but I couldn't help thinking—"

"Thinking can be very dangerous," says the Warder coolly. "I don't recommend it."

"I want to tell you, Diriente, that I've decided that what I suggested last night is the best idea. The evidence in this room could blow the Church to pieces. We ought to seal the place up and forget we ever were in here."

"No," says the Warder.

"We aren't required to reveal what we've found to anybody. My job is simply to keep the temple building from falling down. Yours is to perform the rituals of the faith."

"And if the faith is a false one, Mericalis?"

"We don't know that it is."

"We have our suspicions, don't we?"

"To say that the Three never returned safely to the stars is heresy, isn't it, Diriente? Do you want to be responsible for spreading heresy?"

"My responsibility is to promote the truth," says the Warder. "It always has been."

"Poor Diriente. What have I done to you?"

"Don't waste your pity on me, Mericalis. I don't need it. Just help me find my way out of here, all right? All right?"

"Yes," the custodian says. "Whatever you say."

The passageway is much shorter and less intricate on the way out than it seemed to be when they entered. Neither of them speaks a word as they traverse it. Mericalis trudges quickly forward, never once looking back. The Warder, following briskly along behind, moves with a vigor he hasn't felt in years. His mind is hard at work: he occupies himself with what he will say later in the day, first to the temple staff, then to the worshipers who come that day, and then, perhaps, to the emperor and all his court, down in the great city below the mountain. His words will fall upon their ears like the crack of thunder at the mountaintop; and then let whatever happen that may. *Brothers and Sisters, I announce unto you a great joy,* is how he intends to begin. *The Second Advent is upon us. For behold, I can show you the Three themselves. They are with us now, nor have they ever left us—*

The Dragon of Tollin

Elizabeth Ann Scarborough

The emissary flew for many days until he at last came to a spot cool enough for his feet to touch the surface without harm. The High Queen should have sent an ifrit instead of one of the Sky-Fey, the emissary thought. Ifrits flew by magic and thus could be wherever they desired in the twinkling of an eye, whereas the Sky-Feys' wings took them no further in each mote of time than those of a bird of comparable size. Of course, speed was the only advantage ifrits possessed as emissaries. Their chancy dispositions made them otherwise useless for that purpose. But on this mission, speed would have sufficed, for nowhere in all of these blasted lands had the emissary found a living spirit with whom to converse.

The first hint the emissary had seen of the ruination was that a pall of black and gray boiling smoke hung over the shoreline of the southernmost reaches of Northworld. Here and there the sky would crack open to reveal streaks of angry orange or the clouds would suddenly bloom with fiery color within. An appalling stink assailed the emissary's nose, and all during the subsequent flight he had had to cover his nostrils with a piece of his robe to filter the air.

Where the bustling port cities had been, black ooze trickled into the sea, scoring with deep gullies of blistering and popping magma the mountainous rim that had protected these prosperous lands from invasion for so many years. Where sentinel castles had guarded the coast smoldered piles of fused rubble. No ship or even the wreck of a ship wallowed in the fouled harbors. No man, woman or creature of any race walked the earth. No sea being within miles of the shore lifted its body from the waves to greet him. The sea creatures were the ones who had brought word of the disaster. The trading ships that normally plied the seas between this side of the world and the emissary's side of the world had not been seen for some months. Finally, a selkie left word with a fisherman that she was concerned for relatives who had not made their yearly migration from the Northworld seas to those in the south and the fisherman took word to his lord, who sent word to the King, whose responsibility it was to report such matters to the Queen. A caravan took the weekly report to the highest mountain pass in Southworld where the High Queen presided from her castle of ice (which was believed to impart to her cool judgment) over the disputes and concerns of the lands and peoples below her.

She dispatched the emissary. The emissary had traveled to Northworld once, as a youngling, with his father on matters of state. The coastline of this landmass beneath his wings now and its location told the emissary that it was indeed the continent known as Northworld, but as to other clues, they were all erased.

Where he remembered great seas of billowing green forest there were now jagged charred stumps sticking up like the ruined teeth from the skull of some long-dead crone. The emissary thought he might find some answers in Tollinlund, that greatest city of all Northworld, whose boundaries annexed what was once an entire independent country.

The emissary had thought to stop on the way to rest his wings, to have a bite to eat, to sleep perhaps, for it was necessary to cross the borders of six other countries and the Great Inland Sea, the Hungry Desert and the vast Ogrebones mountain range before reaching Bellgarten, the land of which Tollin was the capital city.

The inland seas heaved like a dying man with black sludge from shore to shore, and the mountains were mightily scored on the southernmost side, though less so on the northern side. The emissary began to have some hope as he saw that the Hungry Desert, aside from sporting a new collection of still partially-clad bleached bones, looked much as it ever had, although the once-sparse vegetation was now nonexistent. Beyond the desert, however, where the northern loop of the Ogrebones guarded the fertile fields and populous towns of Bellgarten, the changes, though more subtle, were nonetheless evident. Bellgarten, as was well known, was the guardian country of Northworld, as the High Queen guarded Southworld. Bellgarten had this distinction and its enviable prosperity because it possessed a dragon, whose favor made it mighty and powerful, as well as wealthy.

Now the corpses of Bellgart houses gaped through yawning doors and broken windows, the crops were torn from the fields as if by giant claws and no person or beast moved on the face of the land. Here the emissary could have rested for a spell, and he did check several of the houses for habitation but, finding none, flew on to the city, where the devastation, though not as dramatic as that in the outlying lands, nonetheless appeared to have been as fatal.

No spires or towers stood to mark the skyline he remembered from his childhood. Where the markets had roared with animals and vehicles of all descriptions, the clink of coins, the brilliance of lines full of freshly dyed yarns draped between buildings, the patchwork of laundry spread on the rooftops to dry, the pleasant smell of well-washed, well-fed people who had discovered the magic of a well-engineered sewage system, now there was nothing. Or rather, there were many things but so thoroughly digested by whatever great calamity had overtaken Northworld that it was impossible to say what was cloth and what was wood or metal or what any item or being had been. The pleasant smell had been succeeded by the stench of death and rot and over all, the choking miasma of smoke that darkened the skies and blotted out the sun.

Wind whipped the rubble around the emissary's feet as he landed on the stonework of what must have once been the palace. He folded his wings and sat upon the remnants of a wall, and wept himself to sleep.

He awoke, shivering, later, to a sound distinguished from the wind by its rhythm, a little jiggling, rattling sound that seemed to be coming from debris trembling beneath his feet.

Though his hands were cold and his pin feathers fluffed with the chill of the sun-bereft land, he dug into the debris. Maybe he would find a survivor, someone, anyone, to explain what had befallen half of the world.

The warmth reached him first; warmth, vibration, and, as he cleared away more layers of filth, light. A soft, golden light humming with a heat like beach sand in summer.

As he uncovered its opalescent top, the object vibrated more strongly, working its way up from the ashes and filth toward him, a flower opening to the day.

The object was smooth, rounded, golden in hue but fired with flashes of red, blue and green and swirled with pearl. He thought it must be a rare treasure from the King's hoard. He thought it must be the priceless offering of some great artisan. He thought it must be—an egg. A very large egg, as large as a buckler, nesting in the ruins around it, vibrating expectantly.

An egg, of course. The dragon's egg. The dragon had died defending it from—what? Some monstrous attack? The dragon and the city and all of these lands had perished in the battle and only this egg remained.

The emissary laid his cheek against the glowing shell and said softly, "I understand, little orphan. Never fear. I will carry you back with me to the High Queen and there you will be cared for so that you may warm and protect our lands as once you protected—"

"H-hold," croaked a voice as rusty as unoiled chain. The emissary looked up from the egg, though he did not unhand it, and saw that the rubble a few feet away, where the debris had slid down the opening blasted in the wall, also stirred. Perhaps there was more than one survivor after all.

The emissary steadied the egg and scrambled down the welter of cloth and metal, bone and splintered wood, to where the mess moved, and again began to dig his way to what lay below.

His hand was grasped suddenly by what seemed to be a clawed band of iron and the whole mountain of debris slipped further down as a section of rubble an arm's length from him rose and faced him, a hole opening in it to plead, "Drink?"

From the top of the pile the vibrating grew louder and the egg teetered. The emissary fluttered his wings and swooped under the egg just as it started to roll, then carried it to the bottom of the pile. He set the egg down carefully before returning to the creature still unearthing itself. The warmth of the egg at his back comforted him as he unstrapped his pack and drew forth his flask to slake the creature's thirst.

"Easy, friend," he said as the survivor gulped half his flask. "This must last us until we find an unsullied atoll with fresh water and that may be days from here."

The survivor shook its head and rasped, "Can't leave. Egg. Must find the egg."

"Don't worry, my friend. It's safe," the emissary assured him and felt the egg purr at his back.

"Ah," the survivor said and wiped its mouth with its wrist. It had only one wrist on one very long arm, the emissary saw, and its legs were quite short. A dwarf then? "The—others?"

"I'm sorry. There don't seem to be any others. I am Dolhal, Emissary of the High Queen of Southworld. I must rest for a time, and then if you will ride between my wings, I can carry the egg and thus bear us both back to Her Majesty."

"Southworld?" asked the halfling.

"Onlyworld, perhaps I should say," Dolhal answered him. "I fear the north is all dead."

The halfling nodded and, crawling forward on his knees and one elbow, found the egg and curled against it and slept. Perhaps he had more right, Dolhal thought, but he, Dolhal, had found the egg first and he experienced an unaccustomed spasm of revulsion at the idea of lying in the muck next to such a foul-visaged creature. But there was the egg, beautiful and warm despite its burial and disinterment, despite the filth below it and around it, promising, somehow, safety and comfort if only Dolhal would cherish it and keep it whole until it hatched.

He noticed before he slept that the halfling's stump seemed to have been cauterized, and that a flat red scar covered it and one side of the creature's face so that the ear, neck and jaw were all one line and the coarse black hair burned away.

Dolhal awoke suddenly, immediately alert, as if a shock had gone through him. He rose to see the halfling drop a large rock. Surely the creature couldn't have meant to harm him? His wings were the only escape from this place.

The halfling grimaced painfully from the whole side of his face and laid his hand palm up on his knee. He looked somewhat cleaner and stronger than he had when they fell asleep. Dolhal, who felt completely refreshed himself, said aloud, "I feel much improved and you look it. Are you well enough to travel while our supplies last?"

A melodious voice welled up from that ruined face like fresh water from rock. "Soon. Give the dragon magic a little more time and we'll both feel ready to dance all night."

"I think not," said Dolhal, feeling the cold wind billow from the roiling clouds. "I think after seeing this I will never feel like dancing again."

"Ah, well. I suppose it could take a body like that, if you hadn't time to get used to it. But from my viewpoint, it makes me feel like dancing just to be able to see this, you understand."

"Who are you and how did you survive?" asked Dolhal.

"Someone had to be last," the halfling answered, grimacing again. "And since I was first, in a manner of speaking, it's fitting I suppose that I'm the last. Except for the egg, of course. I was called Sulinin the Halfling Harper until I found the first egg and thereafter I was Sulinin Dragonkeeper. I brought my discovery to the King shortly after the egg hatched into the dragonet and began to display its powers. The King was not so grateful for my loyalty in presenting him with the dragonet as to step down or give me his daughter and half his lands, you understand. That happens only in my stories. But he made my position permanent and I never had to wander again and saved my songs to cheer the dragon or to lull it to sleep as it grew."

"My condolences," the emissary said. "For everything."

"Very sensitive of you, I'm sure," said Sulinin.

"When the egg hatches its new dragon, perhaps the High Queen will grant that you retain your old position," Dolhal suggested, though he hoped not. He, Dolhal, had rescued the egg, after all.

"Do you think she would?" asked Sulinin. "That would be—convenient. I do think we'd better start soon, don't you? If the egg hatches here, we'll have to delay until the dragonet's wings grow strong enough to support its body and by that time—by that time it will have bonded with this place and will not leave it."

Dolhal sensed a lie in that explanation somewhere but he was too unfamiliar with this being and with dragonets to know where the lie might lay. "Then the mother—the dragon—is dead? You're certain?"

"Certain," Sulinin said. "I—you might say as how I was personally involved when she exploded."

"How painful for you."

"Friend," said Sulinin, "you don't know the half of it." This time Dolhal knew that the halfling spoke the truth, for the grim humor twisted from his mouth and his eyes teared up with anguish.

"Perhaps it would help if you would care to talk about it," Dolhal suggested. Emissaries were trained to be excellent listeners, and were trained to read the nuances of meaning behind what was said. He no longer felt tired or hungry or thirsty but he also felt disinclined to leave this spot for the moment. The egg, he felt, would be happier nesting here too. "I heard when I was very young about the Dragon of Tollin.

They say it was like no other dragon in the history of the world and that it was the reason for the prosperity of Bellgarten and because of it, Bellgarten gained its hegemony over Northworld."

"True, all true," the former harper said. "The dragons in tales of old are ugly and fearsome, greedy and foul—"

"Nothing like that could ever come from this egg," said Dolhal, stroking the shell.

"Yes—hmm, well, I felt much the same when I first beheld the egg. I found it in the Ogrebones the summer Doomspewer erupted. Do you have volcanoes in the south?"

"Oh, yes."

"Then you'll know that when they spew, not only the mountain changes but the landscape all around—lakes are filled in with ash and refill themselves miles away, rivers change their courses. I had never seen such change for myself and traveled to the Ogrebones with my harp to make songs of the eruption and the people who lived through it and who died in it. It seemed at the time to herald the ruin of Bellgarten, for the heat had seared the crops and the ash, as it does now, blotted out the sun so that winter came early and people sickened and died from breathing the thick air. I was a young, healthy fellow then, however, and hungry for novelty, which is part of why I took up the harp and followed the minstrel's road. I confess I had grown heartily weary of it by that time, however. I hoped with these songs to winter somewhere comfortable, where my voice, my fortune, would be safe from sickness and my belly would be full.

"The road ended long before it reached the place where it once led to the easiest pass through the mountains. I set out upon land as different as if it had been reborn then. As different as—as different as this land is from the Bellgarten of my youth. As different as this land was from the face of the moon. I thought in my ignorance that I would simply find the Bellgard River and follow its parallel course to the range until I reached its mouth. When I reached the place where the river had once been, however, I was amazed to see that that mighty flood, so wide and deep in some places that it had seemed to be the sea, had completely disappeared. Molten rock cooled in the dry bed and to my surprise, I saw stonework, cut and formed into what looked like the tops of towers, and in one place, the ruins of a great door. I sat right down to write a song about the lost city beneath the Bellgard but as I was debating between 'giver' and 'liver' as a rhyme for 'river,' I became aware that a third rhyme—'quiver'—was even more appropriate, for that was what the ground near my feet was doing."

"The egg worked its way to the surface for you too, then?" Dolhal said. "What an extraordinary creature to be so intelligent even in the shell!"

"Quite," said the halfling, biting off the end of the word with his ruined teeth.

"And was the mother's shell as beautiful as this one?" Sulinin asked.

"Yes, and I was as smitten with it as you are with this one. When the shell cracked, I thought my heart would break, but then the dragonet bumped her jewel-like head through the shell and into the air, her pudgy baby features and legs as engaging as those of any youngling. I had to carry her in my arms most of the way to Tollin since her wings were still too weak to hold her and she wobbled when she walked. Furthermore, she was hungrier than anything I had ever seen before when she was born and I hunted for her time and again before she was full enough to allow us to proceed. This, of course, made her staggeringly heavy but her appetite, once slaked, needed only a little maintenance for most of the rest of the journey and she charmed me by contenting herself with grass and flower buds.

"More charming still, wherever we traveled, her breath warmed the fields around us so that they grew fertile once more. I barely noted this at the time, so enchanted was I with my new companion, but we always slept warm and dry whatever the weather and I thought my music was better. I was—comfortable."

"Yes, yes I see. That's how I feel too. Mind you this is a long way from the High Queen's court and yet the egg is, as you say, comforting." Dolhal shuddered to the tips of his wings. "What a terrible tragedy for you to lose her," he added, wondering why he felt so much more truly the tragedy of losing the dragon than the tragedy of losing a continent and all of its other creatures.

"Her appetite grew as we traveled until she could eat the produce of whole fields and was looking longingly at the sheep and cows and I realized that I would not be able to keep her fed by my own efforts. That forced me to the difficult decision of presenting her to King Horhay. He was charmed, even when she ate the entire fifty-course banquet he had prepared for his daughter's ninth birthday. He was a wealthy man so he merely ordered another banquet prepared. The dragon seemed a bit ashamed of her appetite, and hunted and cooked to perfection all of the animals she had gobbled before and then, by order of the king, we were given our quarters in the royal zoo and I sang her to sleep, while she hummed in her soothing way.

"As she grew, her appetite increased but I persuaded the king that he should give over to her her own fields and her own livestock for her nurturing. In order to do this, he levied a small tax on the people, and in return we made flights together and she warmed the fields so that they yielded more than ever and blew away the ash. In the winter, she kept the palace warm and eventually conduits were sent from her den to burrow under all of the houses in the town so that she might warm them. Later, it was found that her breath could be confined in clay stoves that heated without wood for days at a time. But though she more than earned her keep, as her appetite increased, the people grew fearful. Some remembered the stories of dragons of old, who devoured virgins regularly, although our dragon had shown no signs of desiring any such fare.

"There were those, in fact, who wanted her to be put to death so that they would no longer have to pay for her maintenance. The invasion of Bellgarten by the armies of Orbdon stopped that talk."

"What happened?"

"What do you think happened? My beauty drove their troops back to their own borders and with one short raid on their nearest town, a roar and a single blast of fire, the enemy was decimated, destroyed, and thereafter followed our ways and paid tribute to our king. He wisely used much of it for the maintenance of the dragon, who seemed to take pity on the Orbdonese and, using her great strength and fire judiciously, rebuilt their city and helped them prosper as we had."

"What a marvelous creature!" Dolhal said and thought that the High Queen's reign would be much easier if she had such assistance—firm but benign, expensive but in part paying its own fee—to aid her.

"Yes," said Sulinin, "and only half-grown!"

"What wonders she must have worked when she reached maturity," Dolhal mused softly.

"And what an appetite she had," Sulinin said. "The people loved her, of course, and they loved me and they loved the king for her sake, for she brought them comfort and good crops—her warming of the ground made three plantings feasible and her scat was the most wonderful fertilizer imaginable. Then too, she brought prosperity to the kingdom. For fear of her, all the neighboring kingdoms paid tribute to Bellgarten and we in exchange settled their disputes. This worked very well until the dragon grew so large and her appetite so prodigious that all of the food stores and livestock in the neighboring kingdoms were reduced to starvation rations. The king was reluctant to tax our people further, though in time he had to. Rather than becoming angry at the dragon, people grew angry at the king and there was a rebellion, aided and abetted by subject kingdoms. Of course, my girl and I rapidly put it down and that was when the king decided, why pay an executioner? You understand that I did not like seeing my girl eating human beings—whole, mind you. She ate them whole. But the king was in no mood to listen to suggestions and might have found some other way to slay me."

"You could have then turned the dragon onto the king," the emissary suggested, surprised that Sulinin, who had been at court at least as long as the emissary, had failed to think of it himself.

Sulinin looked down at his clawed hand. "I might have but she knew the king nearly as well as she knew me and besides, he *was* the king and a man and if I asked her to murder him in order to save her from murdering those who had legally wronged the king, what would the point have been? The outcome would have been the same for the dragon. So I kept my peace. It was a mistake. News of the executions brought more insurrections and more border wars among the tribute countries and more executions. When full-scale war broke out, the king did not field soldiers. He simply sent the dragon out to do their job, thinking of the salaries he would save, no doubt.

"It didn't quite work out that way. As she flew her missions of destruction, she fed and as she fed she grew larger and needed even more feeding to enable her to fly. Soon all of the crops and livestock in Bellgarten were gone and then began—the draft."

Sulinin grew quiet. The egg was vibrating at greater speed and Dolhal thought he could hear a heartbeat through the shell, which shimmered expectantly.

"Go on," he told Sulinin, though he had begun to guess the end of the story—indeed, he had seen the end of the story and it was extremely disheartening. What a tragic waste of power and resources.

"As you may guess, the draft was not for soldiers for the field. Draftees were brought to the castle and fed through a doorway that led straight into my girl's enormous gullet. By now she was so big that a curious thing happened, however. Not all of the people who passed through her were digested or died. Some merely lost limbs or were somewhat scored or otherwise injured but came through her bowel whole and alive save for that. Others, the ones she ate just before sleeping, might emerge whole but completely mad from the process of passing through the dragon's stomach. But the majority, those who were fed to her before she flew into battle, were totally devoured and no one ever saw them again. I helped those who emerged from her belly alive escape back out into the city, but in time all of them were rounded up again, as were first the old people, then the women and children. By this time, there was no one left in all of the other lands for her to blast but still she kept feeding and still the king gave her the flesh and bones of his people.

"I suppose he had gone quite mad by then. Otherwise, how could he have shoved his own daughter into the dragon's maw? I heard the princess scream for her father and recognized her voice, for when she was a child she had often come to hear me sing the dragon to sleep. The dragon snapped her jaws shut but I pried them open and tried to wrest the princess from her. My girl never would have hurt me ordinarily, but she was still in her feeding frenzy and she was irritated with me so she let her jaws snap shut and a small flicker of her flame warn me away—which is how I came by these injuries you see." He touched his face and the stump of his arm. "I stumbled through the door with the roar of the dragon and the princess's screams echoing in my ears with the screams of all the other victims."

"I'm surprised the king didn't feed you to the dragon too."

"He tried. That's how he met his end. Even though by now the dragon was far too bulky to fly and there was nothing left for her to eat, she was hungry. She began thrashing about, and broke down the castle in her frenzy. She destroyed Tollin with her writhing and the flames she let forth as she bellowed in frustration and, I realized later, pain."

"Poor thing!" the emissary said. "I suppose she was starting to lay her egg then. I had no idea dragons had such a difficult time of it."

"Nor did I. All I knew was that there was nothing more for her to feed on save myself and that when I was gone she would starve to death so I made for her a loaf of explosives, hid, and when she came to feed at my call, lit the fuse. The lighted end was between her teeth before I saw the egg."

The emissary fixed him with a cold look but said, "I suppose you had to save yourself."

"Moreover, I didn't wish her to starve to death. I saw her explode and then—then I remember nothing until you found me."

The egg stretched and a tiny crack appeared at the top. "Did you not say I must take the egg away before it hatches if I wish it to adapt elsewhere?" Dolhal asked anxiously, stroking the shell and crooning to it.

"Better to let me crack it for you and slay the dragonet while it is still small enough to kill," Sulinin said, lifting in his one powerful hand the rock he had dropped earlier.

"Never! You've betrayed and slain the mother already. I will not let you have this little one."

"Did you hear none of what I said? The dragon becomes voracious as she grows and nothing can survive—"

"You allowed her to be corrupted. In a good and just land she will be an instrument for goodness and justice." Dolhal lifted the egg to his chest, shushing it as if hoping that his shushing would calm it and delay its hatching. Then, before the former dragonkeeper could rise to his feet, the emissary was airborne, the dragon egg cradled in his arms.

"Wait—you can't leave me here," Sulinin called to him. "Take me on your back as you promised."

"I must get the dragonet to the High Queen before it can fly," Dolhal called down to him. "Perhaps we'll return for you later. Perhaps." And with three great flaps of his wings he soared further aloft, disappearing from sight as he flew toward the Ogrebones.

Sulinin sighed and burrowed beneath the rubble again for warmth, to restore his strength with rest. Tomorrow he would pack up the rest of the rancid dragon meat and follow on foot in the direction the emissary had flown. Poor Dolhal. The emissary would find nowhere in all of this lifeless land the birds Sulinin's dragonet had so voluminously devoured upon hatching. Sulinin would travel as far as he could, looking for sign of the emissary and his burden—bits of shell and, the former dragonkeeper fervently hoped for the sake of the High Queen and all of Southworld, a few stray feathers.

Faith

Poul and Karen Anderson

ar northeast beyond the Storm Horse Mountains, Aeland
was the poorest of the shires, scantily peopled, so seldom
visited that it might almost have been a separate realm. Yet
it was happy enough. Farms prospered along the River Luta.
In places the sturdy, thatch-roofed earthen houses clustered
together to make a hamlet. Timbermen and charcoal burn-
ers worked Isung Wood south of them, while miners dug
metals in the Nar Hills on the northwest. Where Karumkill
flowed into the Luta, Yorun town had arisen. Most nations
would reckon it a village, but it had its halidom, assembly
hall, market, and busy little industries. Three taverns were
not too many.

North and east the fertile ground yielded to wasteland,
well-nigh treeless, begrown with ling, gorse, tussocky grass,
reeds around darkling pools. Flocks of wildfowl cruised its
winds, some deer cropped beneath, some wolves preyed on them, otherwise only hare, fox, and lesser game found dwelling. As for men, a
few shepherds grazed their beasts, a few hunters ranged about when they
were not in the forest or the hills. None ever fared more than two or
three days onward from the river valley: for yonder lay the marches of
the Twilight.

Too remote and humble to draw either bandits or conquerors, Aeland
provided modestly for itself, with a bit over to trade when a chapman

had crossed the mountains and followed Isung Road to Yorun. Sometimes folk bickered, once in a while they feuded bitterly, but for the main part they were friendly and helpful to each other. The priest led them in rites, hallowed whatever required it, and the rest of the time plied an ordinary trade. The reeve presided over shire meetings, arrested and punished the very rare felon, and judged between such disputants as chose to go before him. He also collected the taxes, most of which went off to the King. That was a service less gratefully received. However, people were resigned to government, as they were to sicknesses, blights, and the withering of their strength with age. On the whole, theirs were agreeable lives and gentle endings.

Then the goblins came.

The hunter Oric brought the first news to Yorun. Tracking a stag over Mimring Heath, he spied from a distance a thing so strange that he veered toward it. Soon his hounds would follow him no more, but milled about howling dismally, no matter how he whistled and cursed. With the recklessness of youth he pushed on alone.

What he reached was a black stone fortalice. Doorless and seemingly windowless, it sprawled across an acre in a repellently irregular outline. The walls lifted about thrice his height to a roof of jagged slates. Towers stood as high again at the angles and corners, with chimneys between. No two were alike, thin or squat, crenellated or coned or domed in different styles, but all of them lumpy and hideous.

Wind blew chill, snickering in the whins, driving a low gray wrack before it that mingled with smoke from the chimneys. Oric got a smell of something roasting, which somehow made him feel less hungry than sickened. His nerve failed him and he withdrew.

At his campfire that evening, for a night's sleep on the way home, he thought he glimpsed small misshapes running about at the flickery verge of sight, and thought he heard voices cackle and gabble. Certain was that his hounds whined and crowded around him, tails between legs. He slept only fitfully, ridden by nightmares.

"That is impossible," declared the reeve after Oric told him. "Workmen would have been seen. You say you did not even notice tracks left by wagons or stone boats."

"It is not impossible for such as come out of the Twilight," said the priest softly. "We must go look."

Led by these three, a band of the neighborhood's braver men went forth. Mostly they armed themselves with knives, wood axes, scythes, flails, and the like. Here and there was a sword or a bill that someone's great-grandsire had borne in the Margraves' War. They found the ugly castle out on the heath and stood shivering in a thin rain. The reeve hallooed, sounded his horn, rode around the walls and hammered on them. Nothing responded.

Oric felt need to show he had regained courage. He had comrades boost him onto the roof. The slates cut his leather breeks and scored his hands as he crept up the steep pitch to a chimney that was not smoking. When he looked down it, heat parched his eyeballs. Hell-deep below him, coals glowed white under wavery blue flames. He crept back to report, "None will get in by that way." His bloody palms became inflamed and took weeks to heal.

Nor could the rites of the priest do anything, then or ever.

The men returned to a sorrowful word. At several outlying farms, weanling infants had been stolen from their cradles. It appeared that although shutters were fastened on the inside, bolts had risen and an intruder that saw in the dark crawled through. Where ground was soft, it bore prints of small narrow feet with long talonlike toes. No hound would pursue those tracks, which presently lost themselves on the heath but pointed toward the castle.

The priest spent days and candlelit nights among his books. "I think that is a settlement of goblins," he announced at length. "What they want children for, it is not good to know."

During the months and years that followed, in dusk or by moonlight, folk fleetingly saw the creatures. Less often they heard gibbering or wicked laughter. The picture they fitted together piece by piece was of a thing upright, skinny-limbed, less than five feet tall. A big hairless head bore raggedy ears, monstrous nose, and eyes like glowing lanthorns. A flung stone, a cast spear, a shot arrow never struck.

The goblins did not attack grown humans. They stole grain from fields, fruit from orchards, young livestock from pastures, but such losses were bearable, no more than crows or wolves might take. What was cruel was the vanishing of babes. Parents could scarcely watch wakeful by turns every night, if they had a hard day's work to do. Older children were apt to drowse off, or fled screaming when shutters flew open and a horrible face in the window mouthed at them. Dogs seldom dared bark. Only well-to-do households could pay for guards. It took just a minute for a goblin to lift an infant and be gone.

In the first year the Aelanders strove. Twice they made battering rams and tried to smash a way into the castle; but they merely splintered the timber. They searched and dug for the tunnels that the goblins must use to pass in and out, but never found other than badgers' burrows, for no hound would sniff along goblin spoor and the wet parts of the heath broke any visible trails. They proclaimed aloud offers of gold, fine cloth, and similar wares, if the thieves would desist; raspy noises jeered reply. No trap or ambush caught a goblin, no horse ran one down before it had skipped from sight.

They sent messengers over the mountains to the King. In the second year, upon their third application, he dispatched a baron and men-at-arms. The baron had the folk build a mangonel and collect large stones before the castle. These missiles knocked hardly a chip loose; and at night the goblins gibed from beyond the firelight. "Men can no more cure this affliction than they can the plague," decided the baron, and took his party back. The King instituted a new tax in the shire, for defense.

The goblins grew more brazen, or else more numerous. Now and then they were seen in the streets of Yorun itself, by the yellow luminance out of homes. From the town also they plucked infants, as well as from everywhere else in Aeland.

To be sure, this spread the loss wider, so that no one neighborhood suffered worse than a single bereavement in a year or three. Sickness laid more than that in the earth. If the hours between sunset and sunrise were haunted, people could go in groups, swinging lanthorns and talking loudly, and perhaps starry summer nights no longer turned lad and lass too rashly loving. If there was no more wish to kindle midsummer bonfires and dance till dawn, services in the halidom remained safe and were decorous. Hunters, herders, and others whose work kept them in the open could walk with a certain swagger. The rest learned to keep any bitterness behind their teeth, save when a man and his wife stood alone by an empty cradle.

Best not speak of unpleasant matters. Best keep from your mind that nasty little castle on Mimring Heath. You must lead your life in sensible wise.

So did thirty years and three go by.

"You have been bad again," said Hork. He raised six inches of forefinger. The claw at the tip caught flamelight in the same ocherous shimmer as his eyes. "Do not compound the offense by denial." One of the few goblins fluent in a human tongue, he liked to show off his knowledge of its larger words. Perhaps he believed they outweighed his tittering accent—although the children had none other to compare. "This time you really must take your lesson to heart. Else we shall have to find different work for you, shall we not?"

Runt stiffened himself, fists knotted, to face his master. He tossed his head, throwing back the sandy shock-hair that had hedged sight for him. "Defiant, are you?" Hork hissed.

Runt thrust fear aside. He had had practice at that. His flesh stayed clammy with sweat and ashiver; but he could reply quietly: "No, lord. I only wonder what I may have done wrong." He was sure his latest raid on the pantry had gone unnoticed.

Hork sat straight in his chair made of bones. Gloom and chill seemed to move inward around him, then forward to enclose the boy. "You have blabbered in barracks," the goblin said. "You have let out what should never have been known to you at all. How much have you snooped? What else have you thieved of the Lore?"

"Nobody told me the Heartstone was secret!" Runt cried. "If you'd just told me, lord, I'd have kept still!"

Gray-blue skin flushed. "You were not told or shown anything," Hork said, "therefore it should have been clear to you that it was forbidden knowledge. How did you even hear of the Heartstone?"

Runt's courage stumbled. In truth he had been unaware this mattered greatly. "The, the lords Brumm and Ululu were talking—in the Arcane Chamber—they saw me, they never forbade, never warned—Please—"

"Ah." Hork's tone softened. "Tell me, what did you gather from this conversation?"

Faintly hopeful, Runt confessed. "It wasn't only that, lord. I can't help hearing things. Like the lord Drongg always swearing, 'By the doom of the Heartstone!' when he gets angry. And what Brumm—the lords Brumm and Ululu talked about—" His throat seized up.

"Go on, go on," Hork snapped. "What do you think you have deduced concerning the Heartstone?"

"It, it's down in the crypts and is—the life of the castle—"

"You slopped such information out?"

"Please, lord, what harm, I didn't know—"

"*I* didn't know how much of your masters' language you had gained, you sneak." Runt dared not protest that this had merely happened, had been going on longer than he could remember. All the children acquired a random handful of goblin words, though they were raised in their native speech and it was always used with them. Runt's work exposed him to the most. The quickness of mind that caused him to be posted in the Arcane Chamber uncovered many a meaning. "When your time comes," Hork went on, "can we release you to the Greenleaf World? I wonder."

Runt stood dazed by horror.

Dimly at first, he saw a smile bare fangs and heard: "I will miss you when you have reached the Measure. You are often ill-behaved, as your scars bear witness, but you are the best assistant we have ever had in the Arcana." The shrillness turned pensive. "In part because you have served the longest? It seems to me you have. . . ."

Runt could not tell. If the goblins kept no count of time, why should he?

"Well. It would doubtless impair you, were you to be denied your hope," Hork said. "Let us see how you conduct yourself after fresh instruction." He rose. The bracelets that were his clothing jangled. "Shall we to it?"

Almost gladly, Runt removed the tunic that children wore. For a moment, as Hork beheld him unclad, horny lids lifted above bulging eyes. Then the goblin shrugged indifferently and went to the instrument rack. Runt lay down on the lesson table. He clenched the dowel between his teeth, for he was not allowed to scream, gripped tight the handholds, and braced his feet in the stirrups.

At the end of the session, as usual, Hork sponged off blood, applied a salve that closed wounds and speeded healing, and gave Runt a remarkably strengthening drink. "Now go back and sleep," said the goblin. "Henceforward be discreet." He giggled. "And duly grateful, I trust."

"Thank you deeply, my lord," quavered Runt. He kissed the master's left big toe. Rising, he donned his garment and limped from the room.

Corridors twisted and intertwined. Sconces cast dull, uneasy light over walls otherwise bare. Sounds scuttled through the shadows, footfalls, whispers, noises less recognizable. Whenever a goblin went by, Runt stood aside, knees bent, head bowed.

That was rarely. Ageless and childless, the goblins are a pleasure-loving race who dash about hunting, stealing, inflicting minor torments on men, and consorting with such other beings of the Twilight as enjoy their company. At home they feast, frolic, devise elaborate entertainments, and do as little real work as possible. Except for a few necessary procedures learned by rote from witches and demons, they have no command of magic. When this band of them chose to settle in a human country, Baubo raised their stronghold for them. His payment is best forgotten.

Passing the Arcane Chamber, Runt paused to stare through its archway. Phosphorescence wavered over ovens, kettles, casks, alembics, wands, besoms, bones, moldering tomes, unholy relics. A vat seethed, slowly brewing a new goblin to replace one who had annoyed a troll. None was on hand at the moment. Ululu, who fancied himself a wizard, cast the occasional spell of maintenance. Brumm helped him. Slef and Khreeh experimented, under supervision, but this was for amusement. A boy fetched, carried, swept, washed, and did whatever else he was bidden, which included those tasks requiring patience and precision. Since Bandylegs reached the Measure and departed, Runt had had that post. By now his recollection of Bandylegs had blurred.

Curiosity flared afresh in him. What was yon silver spiderweb for? Whence came the dried herbs and pungent powders? What had grown such great branching horns? What were the moon and stars depicted in books and invoked in incantations? As much as he dared, especially when alone here, Runt searched, poked, pried, wondered. The mysteries and complexities filled his mind, beguiled him from despair, consoled him in pain.

Pain stitched through him yet. However, aided by the draught, his sturdy frame was already bouncing back from its chastisement. As he stood there, he felt more sense of hunger. How often he hungered! The rations in mess had ceased to suffice him, and he must filch what he could.

Regardless, he failed of the Measure. After a brief spurt, which brought him within an inch, his growth had slowed, perhaps to naught. Instead, perversely, bones thickened, muscles swelled. Changes more odd than that frightened him, shamed him, made him wash with his back to his roommates. Hair fuzzed out on face and body. His voice deepened, but would ridiculously crack just when he was speaking most earnestly. His dreams were different from of yore and his wakeful eyes strayed, as if of themselves, toward the girls.

Runt drew a breath and hastened on. He must not be seen idling. The worst thing he could imagine was to lose his station among the

Arcana before he got his release into the Greenleaf World—unless he never did. True, the carpentry shop or smithy would not be bad; weaving, sewing, and the like were for girls. The kitchens would be tolerable, and offer chances to steal food. Ordinary toil, scrubbing, drawing of water, shoveling of coal, that sort of thing he could endure, at least until the sameness of it wore away the fantasies that were his refuge. But the thought of personal service to a goblin knotted his throat, after what he had heard about it: especially the entertainment demanded at whim. Or he might be put to tending the loathly worms in their underground pens, in which case he would not likely live to reach the Measure. No, he thought, at all costs he must preserve what was his.

Then who had set it at hazard by tattling on him? Rage smoldered and spat in Runt's breast, like brands in a castle fireplace. The talebearing as such had not kindled it. When a child brought them news of rulebreaking, the goblins gave reward, sweetmeats or a toy or a span of leisure. When they learned that a child had had knowledge of transgression and failed to report it, that meant punishment. You learned early to keep your thoughts unspoken and to carry out your pilferings and neglectfulnesses unobserved. Runt had frequently been disciplined for infractions before he gained self-mastery. He accepted that as the natural order of things. Sometimes he bore to the masters his own tales of misdeeds detected.

This, though, was—was—he lacked a word for "unjust" but he felt the wrongness like an added pang. In full innocence had he blurted forth in barracks the amazing thing he had learned, that the castle possessed a heart. There had never been a ban on telling his fellows what he did and saw at work. Anything that gave their lives a bit of sparkle was welcome, helping them through their duties.

His inmost hope had been to impress Squeaky. He was not sure why, but her look upon him had become important. Now he was glad he had not drawn her aside for the tale, keeping it from the rest. He might have done so, were it less hard to find a private place. Then she too could well have received correction. That pain in him would never have stopped.

Somebody must have gone to the goblins out of malice, on the chance that Runt had broken a rule. Ignorance was an unacceptable excuse. He nursed his suspicion. Apples was his enemy of old. Both had suffered penalties for fighting, until Apples made a weapon of his tongue, swifter and sharper than Runt's. Lately Apples, too, had shot up in height and started favoring Squeaky's company. It led to more quarrels with Runt, over things that in themselves mattered not a glob of rat spit.

Thinking of this while he walked, Runt felt acridness rise in his gullet. To calm himself somewhat, he stopped again where a certain corridor crossed the one he trod.

The children generally did. His gaze traveled wistful down a vaulted length to the end. There he beheld a door, massive in iron-framed timber, full thirteen feet high. It gave on the outside.

So he had been told. No child ever saw any of its kind opened. Again and over again, waking and sleeping, Runt had dreamed of passing through. But a bar at the top held it fast. On the left side jutted a shelf. A goblin could easily leap to it and squat while he swung the bolt from its catch. A child could not, nor did anything exist in the castle which he might use for climbing.

Runt sighed and trudged onward. After a while his footsteps quickened. Squeaky should be in the barracks section.

He entered it and blinked. These three rooms and these solely knew sunlight, admitted by louvers in an attic and passed onward by mirrors. Though now fading rapidly into night, it was brighter than anyplace else. Goblins only came here when they must, preferably after dark, otherwise swathed in hooded cloaks.

The section had nothing to attract them. One chamber held a score of narrow bunks in double tiers, with scant space to spare. A second was for washing, laundry, storage, and suchlike needs. The largest served as mess hall and common room; you reached it first. Doors were lacking. Floors were wood, cracked, splintery, spotted with traces of old grease, bloodstains, and tears. Walls were unpainted plaster. Here and there, charcoal marks showed that someone had tried to keep track of days; but he or she always ceased caring after a few hundred.

Fragments of color relieved the mess hall. Toys and games lay sparsely about, bestowed by the goblins as rewards or fashioned by children from scraps. Manuscript pages to the number of seven, long ago torn out of a book, were nailed up. The children puzzled and puzzled over the inked words. Mainly they peered at the illuminations. Those tiny scenes—people, animals, fields, trees, blue overhead with a golden disc in the middle, marvels well-nigh beyond comprehension—showed the Greenleaf World. To it they would go when they reached the Measure, provided that they had faithfully served the kindly goblins who rescued them from the Terror and gave them shelter and nurture.

The children heard, moreover, that the pictures and fine playthings were of goblin make. Runt, who had never watched a goblin make any object, kept his doubts mute.

As he approached, he heard Squeaky: "No, dear, you must mend your tunic before that rip gets worse. Oh, and it needs washing too. I will show you how."

"I don't want to," said a small girl mutinously. "Why should I? The masters don't care."

"They will if they pick you to attend them," Squeaky answered. "Then you will have to be elegant. Meanwhile and forever, you owe it to your friends, and most of all to yourself, that you stay neat and clean. You are no roach or blowfly, you are a child. Someday you will go to live in the Greenleaf World where everything is beautiful."

Her voice had become soft and sweet while she gained in height, hips and bosom began to round, and the brown tresses fell to her waist. But the names that the children found for each other generally stayed with them. She sat on a bench at the table, spooning gruel into a newly arrived infant she held on her lap. Seeing how well she got on with the youngest, the goblins had appointed her their nurse and governess after Snubnose reached the Measure. It was duty she loved, even more than Runt liked his.

"Well, I will if you help me," said the little girl, Tummy. "An' will you tell us a story at sleepy time?"

" 'Bout the Birds," said Me Too, who was smaller yet. "An' the Flowers."

"What are Birds an' Flowers?" asked Tummy. She had chanced to be at the chores she could handle whenever they were spoken of.

"Naw," said Cockeye. "I want to hear 'bout . . . *Horses.*" Red-haired, freckled, snaggle-toothed, he had nonetheless lengthened to Runt's or Squeaky's shoulders. The goblins found reason to punish him oftenest, but his grin soon returned.

Squeaky smiled. "Let me think first," she said.

She was not sure. None of the children were. When the mood came on a goblin, he might relate this or that about the Greenleaf World. Then some, such as Runt, understood bits of overheard conversation. Hints like these, as well as the pictures on the wall, became ground for endless speculation and fabulation. As the generations of children passed, a wholy body of legend grew up among them, a cosmos in which many lived more than they did in the solid castle. But the tales were mostly vague, incomplete, and contradictory. Their single common theme was splendors and delights, peace and love, waiting beyond these walls in a land—nobody said this aloud—where there were no goblins.

"I'll ride a Horse when I'm big," said Cockeye, "an' I'll slay dragons an'—" He saw who had come. "Runt, you're back!"

Silence clapped down. They knew Runt had been summoned to woe. The very infant sensed misery and gaped big-eyed. Squeaky rose, laid him in his crib, and moved slowly toward the newcomer. The rest hung behind. Others were still at work. Each of these, beholding the red marks on arms and legs, felt wholly alone.

Runt halted. He forced a smile. "I'm back?" he mocked. "What a surprise! Tell me more."

Squeaky reached him. "Are you hurt badly?" she asked low.

"No, I'm hale," he blustered. "Hungry as a hellhound. Can't wait till supper."

Cockeye drew nearer. Worship shone in his blue gaze. "They'll never make you cry," he said. Yet it was Cockeye who last told the goblins when Runt thrashed Apples. Of course, he was a sprat then.

Runt paid no heed, for Squeaky offered her hands. He summoned his nerve and took them. How warm they were, delicate as Arcane glassware. Heat came and went in his face.

"I wish we could do something for you," she murmured unsteadily. He had no way to tell her what she had just done.

Fear wobbled through Tummy's voice: "Why'd they hurt you?"

Runt bit his lip. "I mustn't talk about that," he said.

"But I don't *know* what I mustn't," Tummy protested.

Squeaky left Runt standing and bent to console the girl. Resentment boiled high in him.

"*I* know," said Cockeye. "I'll keep quiet."

"Starting now, big mouth," Runt snapped. Cockeye caught his breath, returned glower for glower, and slunk aside. Runt wondered desperately what to do. Standing still like this was foolish. He wished he had somebody to hit. Somebody who deserved it.

The room was getting murky. It would soon be time to take a punk stick, ignite it at a flame in the hall outside, and bring it back to light the tallow candles here. But it wasn't his turn for that enjoyable task.

A noise brought everyone's attention around. Apples came in. He was the tallest of the children, and his work in the kitchens had given him the opportunity to wax plump. Mess hall rations were mostly fruit, grain, and roots, but included bits of meat or fish. Apples was never actually seen slipping an extra for himself from the pot, and the goblins didn't appear to notice his pudginess.

"You're early," exclaimed Cockeye. "What's the matter?"

"No food tonight?" wailed Me Too, aghast.

Apples beamed. He rubbed his hands. His cheeks shone ruddier than ever. "Don't fret, littling," he said. "The help will bring it when it's ready. And day after tomorrow, you'll feast."

The children stared. He kept them in suspense until he added: "When the masters have a banquet, you know, we get their leftovers. Not the flesh, no, that's for them, but nuts and sweets, remember? And they celebrate with a banquet whenever any of us has gone to the Greenleaf World. They've got such kind hearts."

"Are you going?" Squeaky gasped.

Apples nodded vigorously. "I am, I am," he crowed. "I've reached the Measure."

Red blew across Runt's vision. "You lie!" he yelled. "It can't be! You're no bigger than—less'n an inch over me, and—"

It was a ritual, when the goblins brought the oldest children to their council hall. Pulse thuttering, you stepped onto the dais and stood your straightest against the Rod. Lord Hork solemnly lowered the arm until it rested on your head. If its pointer then passed the crimson line—you were allowed to laugh and weep and dance before the helpless envy of your mates.

Apples smiled and smiled. "This was special," he said. "I'd done a proper deed, and when I went for my reward, I asked if that could be him reading my height, because I saw I'd gotten to the same as him and that's when— Well, he did, and I am big enough and I'm going!"

Runt understood quite well what that proper deed had been. He gripped himself with spirit fingers, lest he fly at yonder throat.

"Oh, Apples," Squeaky sang, "I'm so happy for you." She sprang to him, threw her arms about his neck, and kissed him.

He held her close. "I'll wait for you in the Greenleaf World," he vowed. Glancing past her head at Runt: "Looks like you'll never join us, growlguts."

Runt howled. He took a stiff-legged step forward, another, another. Apples released Squeaky and backed off. "I have to go," he said fast. "The masters are meeting me. I just wanted to tell you. Goodbye, goodbye." He wheeled and waddled down the corridor.

"You slime!" Runt screeched. "I'll—I'll kill—"

Squeaky caught his arm. "No, hold," she pleaded. "If you start a fight now— Please!"

He shook free of her. "Let me be," he raged. "All o' you." Her cry followed him out the doorway.

The flickery-lit dusk beyond breathed some of its chill into him. Indeed he could not afford to get into trouble again so soon. And yet, and yet. Apples was a whitish blob well ahead of him. It was as if an outside will settled into Runt's skull. He trailed after. When at length he must retreat, he would spit in Apples' tracks.

He kept to the shadows, though, close against the wall, taking advantage of every pillar, niche, and angle for concealment, then speeding to the next. Stealth was an art he had cultivated since the endless hunger came upon him. At the back of his mind he put together a story, in case a goblin spied him anyhow. He was sorry if he trespassed, he hadn't heeded whither he went, for he was meditating upon the salutary lesson the lord Hork had administered, he was firming his resolve to become a better boy.

Apples turned into a passage toward the council chamber. Abruptly Runt quailed. He heard piping voices and the *slither-click* of taloned feet. Flattened against stone, he listened to Hork: "Ah, there you are, my lad. No, no, don't beg our pardon. We're gathered to send you off in the way you have earned."

"What a handsome, stout fellow," said Khreeh. Like most goblins, he had a smattering of human speech. "Exactly to our taste."

"Thank you, thank you, masters," Apples blubbered. "I'll praise you to the people in the Greenleaf World."

"We understand how you feel," Brumm assured him. "We will think of you as sharing the banquet we hold in your honor."

"Come," said Drongg, "let us hurry you to your prize."

Again bitterness seared Runt's throat. He could not help himself, he had to risk a peek around the corner, to cast a final silent malediction.

Torch flames flapped and streamed. A score of goblins or more swarmed around Apples. Their ornaments jingled as they capered, chattered, and cackled. The boy walked like one in an enchanted dream.

Astonishment rammed through Runt. Where were they bound? He knew the castle well. Errands had taken him everywhere on the ground floor and numerous places on higher levels, even into the belfry of the Ghoul-Calling Bells. No door barred on top lay in this direction.

Then those doors couldn't really lead to freedom, he decided. The goblins had fooled the children, as a precaution. Runt gave a slight shrug. Lies were a part of life.

Excitement blazed. He could learn the true way out!

Crouched, heart athunder, he sidled onward.

Formerly he would not have been that reckless. On this day, he was driven half from his wits by pain, wrath, jealousy, heartbreak—Squeaky had kissed Apples— He gave scant thought to the likely consequences, were he seen. He scarcely cared. The possibility that he too might use that door seemed worth any hazard.

Yet his senses were strung wire-taut and he moved like another drift of torch smoke.

The hall went between rooms that stood open, deserted by those who thronged joyful Apples. It ended at a blank wall and a quite ordinary door. Runt had never ventured to glance behind it. Hitherto in this section, a goblin had always kept him in view. He had only vaguely wondered what lay there. All this while, the Greenleaf World?

He ducked into a chamber and lurked among grotesque tall vases. Peering around the entrance jamb, he saw Hork fling the door open with a flourish.

Apples jarred to a stop. "But," he stuttered. "But."

"You know we mislike bright light," Hork said. "We will escort you through this anteroom to where we bid you a tender farewell."

"I see. Thank you, lord." Apples trotted forward. The goblins pullulated with him. The last of them shut the door.

Runt waited. He thought he heard noises but could not be sure, for huge waves beat through his head and shook his bones.

It was forever and it was an eyeblink until the goblins returned. Runt hunkered as small as might be in his hiding place. If they found him here and now, maybe he would die. Maybe first he would tend the loathly worms. Certain it was that he would never go free.

The goblins passed by in a troop. They gibbered and gabbled. Runt understood some of it. "Ale for us, the best of Mother Carrion's brew," Drongg exulted. "Then a sound sleep, and then Smaga readies the feast, eh?"

"Ei-ya-a," they shrieked.

The last of their clamor had hardly died from hearing when Runt darted forth. Strange how steady his hands were as he laid hold of the latch. He drew the door aside just enough to let him past and immediately closed it anew. Wildly, he looked about for the portal beyond.

There was none. He stood in a bare brick chamber lit by a candelabrum whose nine arms twisted like limbs under torture. Their tallow tapers stank. A gutter ran between flagstones which glistened, freshly mopped. Implements for housekeeping stood against a wall. At the middle was a large, rough wooden table, blackly stained. Knives and cleavers lay on it. They too shone newly washed.

Runt screamed.

When he came to himself again, he lay on the floor in a puddle of his vomit. Cold gnawed into his marrow; his teeth clattered. He opened his eyes. They were aimed straight at the sight above the table—Apples, naked, blanched, hung by a hook from the ceiling.

The boy's mouth was open. His tongue stuck out, gray. His eyes were dry and unblinking. His belly was also open, empty. The goblins had piled his entrails in a bucket. Economical, they had caught most of the blood in another.

"I didn't mean it, Apples," sobbed a voice somewhere. "I didn't want this. Truly I didn't."

Runt crawled to his feet. He felt numb, as hollow as the corpse. Thought clanked slowly. Here was the end of service, for every child who ever dwelt in the castle. Tomorrow the goblins would strip off the flesh. They would bring it to their kitchen. Smaga, their chef, would supervise the children on his staff as they spiced and cooked it, sauced and served it. How natural that child waiters told their mates what jolly occasions the going-away feasts were.

If the goblins knew Runt knew, would they hold a second banquet at once? They might pickle him for snacks. They might consider it a jest to give the mess a share.

Well, they would not. A water bucket was still full. Runt carefully cleaned his tunic, his skin, and the floor. The scrubbing stung his injuries. They reminded him of the price of talking freely. This time he would keep silence. He would go about his work, make no further trouble, and—and—

What?

Why, when no Greenleaf World awaited him?

"Goodbye, Apples," he mumbled, and left.

Stunned as he was, he went with little caution. However, no goblins were present, and his path through the labyrinth avoided their festival salon. Noises of carousal echoed faint. Not many remained awake. He must have been in the butcher room a long while.

Entering familiar territory, he hastened his steps. At least his bunk was nigh. At least he could creep into it, pull the blankets over his head, and be alone. Tomorrow, when the alarm horns roused children to their labors—tomorrow, among the goblins, he would take care to look away from their mouths.

A light burned outside the quarters but none within. The entrance yawned black. Runt stopped. He cringed, remembering. "No," he whimpered. "Please no."

Pallor glimmered. He sprang back. Almost, he fell. His heart racketed.

Squeaky stepped out of the common room. The tunic she had thrown on was wanness and shifty shadows. Legs, arms, face shone white. A living white, though, he thought crazily. Blood beat in a fine blue vein beneath her throat. Wide eyes beheld him. Brilliances moved in them. "Runt," she breathed. "Where were you? I couldn't sleep, I was so afraid for you. Are you well?"

He stood slack.

She came to him and took his hands. "You're cold," she said. "Freezing cold. What's wrong? What happened, Runt?"

"Who cares?" he rasped. "What does it matter?"

"I care," she answered. Did that blood in her rise through the cheeks and over the brow? Warmth flowed from her into him.

She shivered. "Something terrible has happened," she knew.

He strove. Finally: "Yes," he got out. "Something terrible will."

"What is it?"

His wounds twinged. "I told you—earlier—"

"You daren't?" Her grasp tightened. She lifted her head. Light rippled down the loose hair. "I understand. No, don't say. I don't—" Tears gleamed on lashes. "I, I don't want them to hurt you, ever again."

"But they will hurt you!" shouted someone.

She let go. "Runt, are you sick?" she asked anxiously. "Come in with me. I saved your ration for you, and part of mine. You'll feel better when you've eaten."

"Eaten? Squeaky, Squeaky! The hook, the knives, the buckets!"

She glanced behind. Half wakened, a child made a sound. Her palm

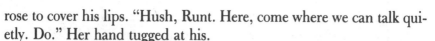

rose to cover his lips. "Hush, Runt. Here, come where we can talk quietly. Do." Her hand tugged at his.

He lurched after her. They found a niche. In darkness they sat, enfolding one another, and trembled. Soon his head dropped to her breast. He wept. She held him, stroked his hair, and crooned.

"No," he said at last. "They won't do that to you. I won't let them."

And he told her. Now she clung to him, in need of his strength. He knew not where he found it for her, but he did.

"What'll we do, what'll we do?" she stammered in sightlessness. Only the faintest unrestful flame-flicker hazed a stony corner.

He felt how she shivered. Beneath it felt the throb of her aliveness. His nostrils drank odors like sunshine, and thyme, and things for which he had no name. Confusion tumbled through him. It swept bewilderment away. Out of a sudden vast clarity, he said: "We'll escape. Those doors they tell us open on the Greenleaf World, they've got to go somewhere."

"No," she moaned. "I couldn't bear seeing—poor Apples—"

"Whatever we find, have we aught to lose?" Runt replied starkly. "This same night. Else the masters are bound to notice we've changed." Resolution set. "And, you know, it *could* be those doors give on the outside. We know the masters go away and come back. We know they bring things home—food, cloth, gold, yes, toys and games and—and babes, Squeaky. Where do we come from, if not from outside?"

His voice cracked, a silly squawk. Fury at that flogged weariness and weakness till they fled him.

Squeaky clutched his arm. "We can't go through." Her words wavered. "The Terror—"

"That the masters—the goblins saved us from?" Runt sneered. "Do you believe that anymore? I say they stole us from the Greenleaf World, same as they steal everything else."

"We can't open those doors. We can't reach the bolts."

His mind leaped. "I know how. Three of us together can do it. You and me and—" He faltered. "And—"

"Who?" she wondered desolately. "The little ones aren't strong or clever. The big ones, why should they believe you? Why shouldn't they run and tell the masters?" She was still a moment. "I don't know why I believe you, Runt. I truly don't know why."

It struck him hard: What an awful, stupid chance he had taken, speaking frankly to her. Nothing would be easier than for her to betray him, and the payment ought to be extra rich. Was she leading him on till she could sneak off? The thought flashed: If he killed her, nobody would know who'd done it. He had powerful hands. Laid around her neck—

"Maybe it's because you trust me," Squeaky said.

His arms dropped. He barked his knuckles on the floor. Horror rushed through him. He heard: "Or maybe it's because you are you, Runt. You were always good to me."

Had she forgotten his childhood teasing? Or had she put it aside, or even found a different meaning in it? He strangled on a sob.

She caught hold of him anew. "What's the matter, Runt? Tell me."

"We've *got* to escape," he groaned. Escape from more than death. "But who will help us? Who can we ask?"

Silence drove the hammering of pulses inward until she, now curiously calm, proposed, "What about Cockeye?"

In the midst of everything, Runt bridled. "Cockeye? That pest?"

"He'd think sunlight of you, if you'd let him," Squeaky said.

"No, he's loud and flighty and can't sit still a single minute. He'd bring the goblins straight down on us."

"Runt," she sighed, "if you say we must be three to open a door, I don't know what you are thinking about, but I believe you. Well, you have to believe in me, and we both have to trust Cockeye, or we'll never get anything done, will we?"

He sagged back against the wall, overwhelmed by thoughts altogether new. She stood up. "Wait here," she said, and padded back to the sleeping quarters.

Alone, Runt sat in a whirl. His fist pounded the flagstones. What to do, what to do? He could leave before Squeaky returned with Cockeye. Those two might well be afraid to approach the goblins. He, Runt, might manage to skulk about, evading capture, lifting food and water by night, until he saw a goblin open a door. He might thereupon dart past, too quick to be caught. No, goblins moved faster. But they weren't really so strong. He might kill that one and get away before others arrived.

Might, might, might, maybe!

And Squeaky would stand forsaken.

Runt stayed where he was.

He scrambled to his feet when the shadowy shapes came around the corner. His heartbeat slowed. The earlier clearness rallied. There was

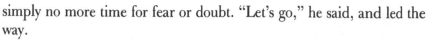

simply no more time for fear or doubt. "Let's go," he said, and led the way.

"What for, what for?" Cockeye demanded.

"Hush." Squeaky tightened her clasp on his hand. "You promised when I woke you, if we took you along on this adventure, you'd do what you were told and stay quiet. Runt and I trust you. Please don't fail us."

Cockeye sucked in a breath and held it as long as he could.

Squeaky plucked Runt's tunic. A flame showed tears on her cheekbones. "But the others," she begged. "What about them? I left them sleeping. We can't just go from them."

"We'd never control the whole lot," he replied. "Maybe later, when we're free, we can bring help. We'll try."

"We will? Honest?"

"I don't know, I can't tell— Yes, Squeaky, we will."

The nearest of the tall doors loomed before them. They heard the final shrill sounds of goblin revelry, echoing through the glooms. Squeaky looked up and up with dismay. "What we gonna do?" asked Cockeye. "Oh!" He laid palms over mouth and threw Runt a contrite glance.

"Listen," Runt said. "If I stand here by the jamb and brace my arms on the wall, can you climb and stand on my shoulders, Squeaky? My tunic'll give you a hold. And then can you get onto hers, Cockeye? From there, step off onto that shelf and swing the bolt free."

"Why?" the small boy wondered, carefully soft-voiced.

"Can't stop to explain. Will you do it, you both? Can you?" They had better be able to, Runt thought.

They were, barely. As Cockeye was swarming over Squeaky's back, she, precariously in the middle, started to fall sideways. Runt felt her weight shift, heard her gasp, and took a counterbalancing step. Agony jabbed into his back. He held fast and held silent. A minute afterward, he heard a thud as the bolt swiveled.

Sweat sprang forth all over him, more cold than the air. "C'mon down, quick," he wheezed. Cockeye scrambled to a safe jumping height. Runt's back could take no more. He and Squeaky toppled in a heap.

He clenched his teeth and clambered from her. Squeaky saw him lamed. "Lean on me," she said. Her left arm circled his waist, her right hand caught an iron knob and pulled. The door creaked open—loud enough to rouse Apples, thought Runt through the fog of pain.

No sunlight, no flowers, no moon or stars lay beyond. A chill breath wafted out of darkness. It smelled of damp and mould. Cockeye shrank back. "I'm scared," he said.

"Don't be," Runt gritted. Squeaky helped him hobble through. Cockeye gulped and followed.

They found themselves on the landing of a stair that plunged down into the murk. Flames, blue at intervals along rough stone walls, gave light to walk by. "This has got to go somewhere," Runt pushed between his lips. "You wouldn't expect the Greenleaf World right outside the castle, would you? Come on."

Squeaky closed the door. They couldn't very well lower the bolt that was on this side, but maybe the goblins hadn't heard anything, maybe they wouldn't soon notice the inner fastening loosened.

Deep the stairs went before they ended in a tunnel that reached beyond sight. Each step he took sent a knife through Runt's back. He tottered on, harshly breathing. How delicious it would be to curl on the wet stone, wrap sleep's blanket snug around him, and dream forever. But they were bound to the Greenleaf World, weren't they? And his friends might yet have need of him.

He heard Squeaky tell Cockeye the reason for their faring. The boy keened. "Naw, can't be, awful! I don't b'lieve you!"

"Well," said the girl wearily, "if you don't, you can turn around and go back to the masters. P'r'aps when they've caught us they'll give you a sweetmeat."

Cockeye swallowed hard, then clutched her free hand again. "I'm coming 'long," he told them, and stumped onward.

However toilsome for the children, wrung as they were, the tunnel was not much over three miles long. At the end—at the end!—they found a slanting door. Runt was past caution or hope or anything save pain. He fumbled at the handle. The door wouldn't budge for him. Squeaky tried. It swung heavily on noisy hinges.

The air that met their faces was fresh but nearly as cold as underground. Light also was as dim, gray light from no source in view, shadowless, veiled by countless little white flakes. Those dropped in silence to an earth they had already decked, a ground where shrubs were formless colorless masses within which lurked thorns and sharp twigs. It sloped, the children had emerged on a hillside, but they saw only a few yards before the white blindness overtook their eyes.

"What's this? No Greenleaf World?" cried Cockeye. It was the tone of a child struck for no known reason.

"I can't say," Runt grated. "We've got to keep going, that's all."

Squeaky shut the door. Its outer surface was a box of dirt in which grew dense heather, so that when it lay closed it was indistinguishable. She took note of a lean lichenous stone rising nearly—a menhir of the Ancients, though she did not know that. It must be a landmark for the goblins. Not that she meant to return, whatever laired ahead. Shuddering, she hurried to Runt's aid. His gait staggered.

The three went downhill because that was the least hard way. Their bare feet soon left blood spots behind. However, the falling white stuff swiftly covered every track. The goblins could not trail them. Belike that made scant difference. They would leave their bones here rather than traded off to the ghouls. Starving, hurting, on their last strength they covered several thousand paces. They reeled a bit longer on hope, before it too drained away.

"No use," Runt coughed. "I can't go on any more. Leave me."

"N-n-never," Squeaky answered. She hauled him onward while her gaze roved right and left. Yes, there, a dip in the slope, bushes clustered around, shelter of sorts. "This way. Please. Trust me."

He collapsed in it. She knelt beside him and felt how chilled he was, saw how lids drooped over eyes rolling back in his head. "You must get warmer, Runt," she said, wondering if he heard. "Here, Cockeye, you sit close on his left side and I'll be on his right."

"But I'm cold an' tired m'self," the younger boy objected.

"He gave us everything he had," Squeaky said. "It's our turn."

Cockeye shook his head at the baffling new idea but obeyed. After a time he noticed how the flakes melted on his skin. He scooped some off the ground, cautiously licked it, at length put it in his mouth. "Hey," he yelped, "this turns into water! We don't got to stay thirsty, anyhow."

"Maybe we'll find something more, if we keep trying," Squeaky said.

Light increased. The snowfall slackened until it was no more. Runt slept, huddled between his comrades. They looked across a rolling white landscape beneath a leaden sky which, at one point low above the horizon, was somewhat brighter. But they lacked words for what they saw, or understanding of it. When black wings flapped overhead and a hoarse caw drifted down to them, they cowered.

Distance and terrain hid the castle, not that they would have recognized it. Otherwise they felt themselves far indeed, illimitably far, from the Greenleaf World.

Abruptly Cockeye straightened. His finger jabbed the air. "Yonder, yonder!" he squealed. "See it?"

The girl squinted against the weird whiteness. Over a ridge a hundred yards away came a form walking, high and gaunt as the marker stone. Four lesser things loped after it, heads near the ground as though they sought what to devour. "A goblin?" she wondered. "No. But—"

"It's a people!" shouted Cockeye. He bounced up. Runt slumped back. A snore rattled in his gullet. "A people like in the pictures!"

"Get down," Squeaky told him frantically. "How do you know? We've heard about demons and trolls and, and everything horrible."

Cockeye stood where he was. His glance challenged hers. "I think it's a people," he said, "an' if we don't fetch it, it'll go by not knowin' an' we'll die. I . . . I *b'lieve* it."

Squeaky sat mute for a space. The crow jeered at her.

"You may be right," she said. "I suppose I have to believe too. What else? Can you run and meet . . . whatever that is?"

"Whoo-ee!" yelled Cockeye. Squeaky held Runt close and watched the short figure bound away over the snow.

Despite his years, Oric the hunter still ranged widely. Scornful of fears that spooked in the homes of men, he quested for deer onto Mimring Heath, alone but for his hounds. Thus it was that he saw a boy speed, stumbling and panting, across the waste toward him. "Hold, Grip," he ordered. "Down, Greedy. You, Loll and Noll, quiet." The dogs cut off their baying and stood by his spear.

The boy's red hair made a single splash of color in the winterscape. When he fell at Oric's feet, the hunter saw bruises and slashes on his shins, gooseflesh everywhere, for he wore merely a tunic of coarse weave, fouled by hard travel. "Well, well," Oric said. "What have we here?" He laid down his weapon and hunkered to help the boy rise.

The boy started. He squirmed aside, jerked onto all fours, scuttered off like an animal. His eyes shone enormous in the chalkiness beneath his freckles.

"Ascared, are you?" Oric drawled. "You galloped to me, but when you came nigh, I was too strange, eh? Or is it the hounds? They won't bite you, younker."

Smiling, he took a piece of cheese from his pocket and tossed it. The boy retreated farther. Oric rose. "I'll retrace your steps, slow-like," he said. The boy yammered. "Sorry, I don't follow you." Oric cupped hand to ear. "Repeat?"

"You a people?" he heard. The accent was so peculiar he must think before he knew what was meant. "Y-y-you won't eat me?"

Knowledge struck into Oric. His vision blurred. "No, kid," he answered most gently, "I won't. I'll bring you home."

He started along the tracks in the snow. A peek behind showed the boy squatted where the cheese had fallen, ravenously consuming it, before slinking after him.

As he neared the two others, he stuck his spear in the ground, bade the dogs sit, and advanced empty-handed. A girl looked up at him, terrified, but did not leave the half-conscious boy she hugged. "I guess you couldn't," Oric murmured, "and me, I'd better prove I'm harmless."

Under the wild stares he brushed a space clear, gathered wood, with flint and tinder started a fire. Eventually the younger boy ventured close and crouched by the coals. Later the girl half supported, half lugged the older boy there. Oric left food for them. He settled a ways off, unpacked his flute, and played the prettiest tunes he knew.

In due course he went to the bigger lad. Although the companions withdrew, they did not bolt. He laid down his cloak and blanket. "Wrap those around you," he told them. "Best I can do." He lifted the slumped body. "We're going home," he said to the girl. "You want to carry my spear for me? That thing with the shaft." He nodded at it. "Careful of the edge. But it's comforting to have a defense."

She did as he suggested. At first he moved cautiously, lest she panic and attack him. When she seemed more at ease, he lengthened his stride.

It was a slow journey, with frequent stops. The strength of Oric's youth was diminished, and Runt—the girl uttered the name—became a heavy burden. Camped at eventide, he had as much as he could do to make a new fire and cook supper. "You and Runt take my bedroll," he told the girl. He grinned wryly. "I don't suppose anything can happen that shouldn't. Uh, Cockeye, you and I'll bundle up in my cloak to keep warm, if possible."

The small boy hung back. "Suit yourself," Oric said. "Whenever you like, you're welcome."

The overcast parted. Stars glittered. The children cried out. It grew bitterly cold. Cockeye crept to lie with Oric among the hounds.

By morning Runt could walk, albeit painfully, and progress was easier. They reached farmland about noon, Yorun shortly after sunset.

Along the way, the children exclaimed at everything they saw. They kept aside, together. Often alarm sent them scuttling. But they would return to tag after their guide.

Dusk settled blue over the town. Snowclad roofs reached toward the earliest returning stars. Light spilled yellow through window glass. Oric led the children to the house of Guthlach the smith.

At a knock, that man opened the door. Limned against lamp-glow, he stood black and huge, sudden as the blow of a hammer. Cockeye shrieked and scampered back. Runt shoved Squeaky behind him and poised with fingers bent like claws, teeth bared, ready to fight.

"Slow, slow, friend," Oric urged the smith. "I've got company for you who're easily scared. They've been with the goblins, I think."

"What?" sounded from within. Guthlach's wife brushed him aside and sped forth. "Our Westmar come back?"

"I fear we'll never know for sure," Oric said. "A baker's dozen of years since you lost him, am I right? But I thought this is a home that'd give fostering."

"Gladly, gladly," she wept, knelt in the snow, and held her arms open to the half-seen children.

"They escaped?" rumbled Guthlach. "What can they tell us?" He hit fist on wall; it thundered. "How I've dreamed o' this!" he roared.

"Slow and easy, now," cautioned the hunter. "They've had a dreadful time, plain to see."

The wife waited on her knees, patient as the rising moon. Runt took a step toward her, and another. Squeaky went past him, hand in hand with Cockeye. They stood atremble, but they stood, while the wife rose to embrace them.

"Yes, let them heal," she said through her tears. "Let them talk to us when they're ready, when the leaves are green again."

> Hark! We have heard of Oric the hunter,
> Guthlach the great-thewed, and other goodmen
> Following far, fellowship vengeful,
> Over the heath, into the underground,
> Ramming their road through a rugged portal.
> Mighty on Mimring, men slew goblins,
> Cleansing that keep of accursedness,
> Saving their stolen sons and daughters.
> Yet well might the wicked still have won,

Had Guthlach not gained that grim deep cave
Where with his hammer he smashed the Heartstone.
Then crumbled the castle to dust and cloud,
Sunlight smote the spawn of evil,
Free were the folk. The wind blew fair.
Men will remember through many lives
Deeds that were done upon that day.

Thus begins "The Wrath of the Fathers," Aeland's epic.

In the Season of the Dressing of the Wells

John Brunner

ars numb with the thunder of exploding shells, eyes stinging and throat raw from poison gas, Ernest Peake forced himself to grope for the bell-pull alongside his bed. He had woken with his fists clenched and his heart pounding, and he felt so exhausted he might as well not have slept at all.

Better if I hadn't, perhaps . . .

The door opened. Tinkler, who had been his batman in France and Flanders, entered and drew the curtains. As daylight flooded in he said, "Another bad night, sir."

It wasn't a question. The tangled state of the bedclothes was evidence.

Among pillboxes on the bedside table stood a bottle of tincture of valerian, a glass, and a jug of water. Measuring out the prescribed dose, he diluted, stirred and offered it.

Resignedly Ernest gulped it down. It did seem to be helping, and Dr. Castle had shown him an article describing its success in other cases of shellshock . . .

Every one of them alone like me, inside the prison of his skull.

"Would you like your tea now, sir?" Tinkler inquired.

"Yes, and run my bath. And I'll take breakfast up here."

"Very good, sir. What shall I lay out?"

Rising with difficulty, silently cursing the bullet-shattered kneecap that made his left leg permanently stiff, Ernest gazed at the clear sky and shrugged.

"Looks like a day for blazer and flannels."

"With respect, sir, it is Sunday, and—"

"To hell with what day it is!" Ernest roared, and was instantly contrite. "I'm sorry. My nerves are on edge again. Bad dreams. You can go to church if you want."

"Yes, sir," Tinkler murmured. "Thank you, sir."

Waiting for his tea, Ernest stared glumly at the sunlit view from his window. The grounds of Welstock Hall had—like so many others— been turned over to vegetables during the War, and those parts which even his patriotic uncle Sir Roderick had been unwilling to see dug and trenched had been left to the weeds. But there were signs of a return to normal. Of course, staff was almost impossible to get, but one elderly man and two fifteen-year-old boys were doing their best. The tennis-court was not yet restored, but the lawn was neatly mown and set with croquet hoops, and a good half of the surrounding beds were bright with flowers. The tower of the church was visible from here, though its nave was hidden by dense-leaved trees and shrubs, as was all but a corner of the adjacent vicarage.

Normally it was an idyllic prospect, and one that had often made him wonder what it would have been like to spend his childhood here instead of in India, educated by tutors. Uncle Roderick and Aunt Aglaia, who were childless, had repeatedly suggested he be sent home to school and spend the holidays at Welstock. But his parents had always declined the offer, and at heart he wasn't sorry. So much more had changed in England than was ever likely to in that far-off, ancient, and slow-moving country a quarter of the world away, so he had far less to regret the passing of.

Today, though, sunk as he was in the recollected misery of nightmare, the very pleasure-dome of Kubla Khan could not have dispersed the clouds that shrouded his mind, wounded as surely by the War as his stiff leg.

Tinkler delivered the tea-tray. Before heading for the bathroom, he inquired, "Have you made any plans for today, sir?"

Ernest turned from the window with a sigh. His eye fell on the folding easel propped against a table that bore a large stiff-covered portfolio of paper, a box of water-colours, and other accoutrements proper to an artist.

Shall I ever become one? Even a bad one? They say I have a certain talent . . . But I can't seem to see any longer. I can't see what's there, only what's lying in ambush behind it. All the hidden horrors of the world . . .

"I'll probably go out sketching," he said at random.

"Should I ask Cook to prepare a lunch-basket?"

"I don't know!" Ernest barely prevented himself from snapping a second time. "I'll decide after breakfast."

"Very good, sir," Tinkler responded, and was gone.

Bathed, shaved, dressed, but having hardly touched his breakfast, Ernest made his slow way across the entrance hall. Every least action nowadays cost him vast mental effort, and as for making major decisions . . . Preoccupied with his bad manners towards Tinkler, who had stuck by him as loyally as any friend well could, he was within arm's reach of the door that led to the terrace and garden beyond when a harsh unwelcome voice bade him good morning.

Turning, across the parquet floor he confronted his Aunt Aglaia, clad in the unrelieved black she had adopted on her husband's death from influenza. That had been three years ago, so the customary time for mourning was long past, but she seemed determined to do as Queen Victoria had done for Albert. There was no resemblance in any other respect; the little monarch would barely have come up to her ample and efficiently-corseted bosom.

Worse still, her attitudes appeared to have become as rigid as her undergarments. On the few occasions he had met her when on leave from the Front, while Uncle Roderick was still alive, Ernest had thought of her as tolerably pleasant, if somewhat over-conscious of her status as wife of the Lord of the Manor. Now, however, she had taken to describing herself as the *châtelaine* of Welstock, hence the official guardian of not merely her estate but also the lives and behaviour of her tenants and dependants. Among whom, very much against his will, was Ernest.

Before he had time to return her greeting, she went on, "That is scarcely suitable attire for Divine Service!"

Morbid religiosity was among her new attributes. She had reinstituted "family" prayers, which Ernest resignedly attended on the grounds that

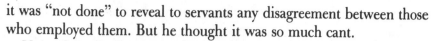

it was "not done" to reveal to servants any disagreement between those who employed them. But he thought it was so much cant.

Now, through the open door of the breakfast-room, he could see a maid clearing the table. Keeping his voice down in case the girl was in earshot, he said as civilly as possible, "I'm not coming to church, Aunt Aglaia."

She advanced on him. "Young man, I've put up with a great deal from you on account of your alleged ill-health! But you are beginning to try my patience. You've been here a month now, and Dr. Castle assures me you are making good progress. Perhaps one of these days you will choose to consider the hospitality I am extending you and even, as I sincerely hope, your duty towards your Creator!"

The blood drained from Ernest's face; he could feel the whiteness of his cheeks. Locking his fingers together for fear that otherwise he might strike this hypocritical old bitch, he grated between his teeth, "I owe nothing to the god that authorised such foulness as the War!"

And, before she could brand him a blasphemer, he tugged the door open and limped into blinding sunshine hatless and without his stick.

A single bell was chiming from the church. To his distorted perception it sounded like the tolling of a knell.

"Mr. Peake? Mr. Peake!"

A soft, inquiring voice. Ernest came to himself with a start. He was leaning on the wall dividing the grounds of the Hall from those of the vicarage. The bell had stopped. Facing him was a slender girl, face shaded by a broad-brimmed hat, wearing a plain dress of the same dark grey as her large, concerned eyes.

Even as he wondered frantically whether he had been crying out aloud—he knew he sometimes did—his hand rose automatically to lift a nonexistent hat.

"Good morning, Miss Pollock," he forced out. "I'm sorry if I disturbed you."

"Not at all. I was just taking a turn around the garden while Grandfather puts some final touches to his sermon."

Feverishly eager to counter any bad impression he might have made: "Well, as you've no doubt deduced I shan't be there to hear it, I'm afraid. You see, as I've been trying to explain to my aunt, I lost my faith when I saw what was allowed to happen over there. I couldn't believe any more in a loving, beneficent, all-wise—" Suddenly aware that he was virtually babbling, he broke off in mid-word.

To his surprise and relief, there was no sign that Miss Pollock had taken offence. Indeed, she was saying, "Yes, I can understand. Gerald—my fiancé—he said very similar things the last time he came home on leave."

Oh, yes. I heard about Gerald, didn't I? Bought his at—Cambrai, I think it was. Tanks.

While he was still fumbling around for something else to say, from the direction of the house came a grinding of carriage-wheels on gravel, the sign that Lady Peake was about to depart for church. She could have walked this way in half the time it took to go around by the drive, but of course that would never have done.

She could also have well afforded a motor-car, and indeed Uncle Roderick had owned one before the War, but she had never approved, and more than once had mentioned how glad she'd been when their chauffeur joined up and her husband told him to drive to London in it and turn it over to the Army.

Miss Pollock glanced past Ernest's shoulder. "Ah, there's your aunt coming out. I'd better go back and rouse Grandfather. He does tend to lose track of time nowadays. Oh, by the way, in fine weather we like to take afternoon tea in the garden. Perhaps you'd care to join us?"

"Why—why, that's very kind of you," Ernest stammered.

"There's no need to fix a date in advance. Any time you're free, just ask one of the maids to pop over and say you're coming. Now I really must rush. Good morning!"

And she was gone, leaving Ernest to wonder all over again whether he had been talking aloud to himself when she noticed him, and if so, what he had been saying.

As ever, his charming surroundings, aglow with the onset of summer, seemed permeated with menace, like the germs in fertile soil that could bloat and burst the human frame.

Gas gangrene. But what is gangrened in me is my mind . . .

The Hall, the vicarage and the church stood on the crest of a low hill, with the rest of the village scattered on level ground below and on the flank of another hill opposite. In olden days it had been a weary and toilsome climb to attend Divine Service, especially for children and the old, and many were content to proceed no further than a spring that formerly had gushed out near the bottom of the slope, for its waters were held to possess the power of cleansing and absolution.

Early in the last century, though, the incumbent Lord of the Manor had had the spring covered, and athwart its site had caused to be constructed a slanting paved track, rising from what was still called Old Well Road, that offered greater ease of access. He also had planted, either side of the lych-gate, a pair of magnificent chestnut trees. Beneath their shade, uncomfortable in their dark Sunday clothes on such a warm morning, were foregathered most of the inhabitants of Welstock, among whom, despite the fine weather, there were few smiles to be seen. Tragedy had struck the little community again, during the past week. Young George Gibson, who had been gassed in France and taken prisoner, and come home to cough his life away, had died at last, leaving his wife with three children.

As ever, the villagers had separated into two groups. To the left were the womenfolk and young children, ebbing and flowing around the schoolmistress, Miss Hicks. Apart from regrets at George Gibson's death, their talk was mainly of high prices, illness—every hint of fever might signal another outbreak of the dreaded influenza—cottages out of repair and, with little optimism for the bride and groom, a forthcoming marriage. It was not a good time, they all agreed, to think of bringing more children into the world.

To the right were the fathers and grandfathers, surrounded by single young men—few of those, for more and more of their age-group were drifting away from the countryside in search of the glamour, and the better wages, to be found in cities. Beyond them again hung about a bored fringe of boys old enough to work but not yet concerned with the matters that so preoccupied their elders.

At the focus of this group were to be found Hiram Stoddard, smith and farrier—and incidentally wicket-keeper for the village cricket-team—and his brother Jabez who kept the Plough Inn, exchanging news and views with the local farmers. Within this cluster, but not of it, was the most prosperous of the latter, Henry Ames. He had moved here from the next county. Having lived in the area a bare ten years, he was still regarded as a foreigner, and though people were civil to him and his family they kept their distance. He was the only one among them still invariably addressed as Mister.

The men too wore grave countenances as they chatted. At first their talk, like the women's, was of George Gibson and his bereaved family; soon, though, they moved on to more pressing subjects. They spoke of the shortage of labour—George had been a farmhand, living in a cottage on the Peake estate; they dismissed the theorists who argued that farming would soon become entirely mechanized, for none among them (always excepting Mr. Ames) could afford the expensive new machinery, and so many horses had been killed during the War that it was proving hard to breed up to former levels, while much the same applied to other kinds of livestock, vastly diminished because there had not been enough hands to tend them . . . No doubt of it: times were hard, if anything harder than in wartime. Someone mentioned the politicians' promise of "homes fit for heroes" and the sally was greeted with derisive chuckles, lacking mirth.

Attempting to divert the conversation into a more cheerful path, Hiram broached the early arrival of summer and the promise of a good hay-crop. Mention of grass led by natural stages to mowing, mowing to the need to prepare the cricket-pitch, and that in turn to further de-pressed bouts of silence, as they remembered the many former players who would not again turn out for the team.

At length Hiram said with feigned heartiness, "Well, 'tes time to wait on her ladyship and ask to borrow the three-gang mower. I'll go after service. Who'll come with me?"

There were four or five reluctant offers. In the days of Sir Roderick it would have been a pleasant prospect—he'd have consented at once, and more than likely seen them off with a mug of beer apiece. Dealing with her ladyship, on the other hand . . .

As though sensing their thoughts, Gaffer Tatton said in his creaky voice, "Bad times, bain't they? *Bad* times!"

The group parted to let him through to its heart. He was leaning on an oaken stick he had cut before the rheumatism sapped his limbs and bowed his back, and panting from his climb up the slope. In his day he had been a carpenter and wheelwright, and an accomplished carver. But that day was long past, and not again would skills like his be called for. As he was fond of saying, if it could all be done in factories in wartime, they'd stick to the same now there was peace, leaving no space for the craftsman on his own. His dismal predictions had certainly been borne out so far, and though some of the younger sort made mock of him behind his back, others were coming to heed his old man's wisdom.

Halting, he gazed about him with bleared eyes.

"These times be sent to try us, bain't they? And small wonder. *It's the year*. And last time we neglected un. So it's for two."

Understanding, the older men shifted uneasily from foot to foot, looking as though they would rather change the subject. When one of the boys from the outer ring, puzzled, asked for enlightenment, and Mr. Ames looked relieved at someone putting the question in his own mind, there was shifting of eyes as well as feet. Gaffer, however, was not to be diverted from his theme.

"Shoulda been in '15," he emphasised. "'Course, with the War and all . . . She'll 'uv forgiven it. But not this time. Bain't there warnings? Sir Roderick gone! 'Im as should be the rightful heir lying under a curse!"

Some of his listeners winced. Even to them, that was straining the description of Mr. Ernest's condition which they had teased out of his man Mr. Tinkler. He had taken to dropping in at the Plough on evenings off, and despite being "one o' they Lunnon folks" by birth had shown himself to be a square fellow with a fund of anecdotes and a remarkable capacity for the local cider.

Nonetheless, so long after the War, and still in such a pitiable state—!

"Fragile," Mr. Tinkler had once said, and repeated the word with approval. "Yes, fragile! To do with what they call 'the artistic temperament,' you know. For those who have it, it's often as much a curse as a blessing."

He had at least uttered the word, if not in the sense that Gaffer Tatton meant it . . .

But the old man was still in full spate. Now, charging ahead on the assumption that the person they had been arranging to wait on when he arrived must be the vicar, he was saying, "And rightly too! Bain't none too long until Ascensiontide! If we don't make him bless the wells—"

With a cough Hiram interrupted. "We were talking about borrowing the gang-mower from the Hall for the cricket-field. After service we're going to call on her ladyship and—"

Gaffer's cheeks purpled. "And I thought you were talking about the dressing! Bain't *she* one of our ills, and a warning?"

It was in the minds of not a few of his listeners to admit how completely they agreed with him, but they had no chance, for just at that moment up rolled her carriage. To a chorus of "Good morning, m'lady!"

she descended, nodding acknowledgment of raised hats and touched caps, and paraded up the path between the gravestones.

Dutifully, they fell in behind.

And paid scant attention to the service.

Bit late mowing the cricket-field, aren't they?

The thought emerged unexpectedly into Ernest's mind as he wandered around the grounds of the Hall dogged by phantoms. Giving up all intention of painting, he had let his feet carry him where they would. Fragments of memory from a wartime summer leave fell into place as he gazed at what might have been taken for an ordinary meadow; indeed, a crop of hay had lately been reaped from it, and its grass was barely longer than wheat-stubble. But still too long for a good square-cut to drive the ball to its boundary.

All of a sudden the view was overlain with images from the past. Surely the pavilion must be on his left . . . Yes, there it was, its green planks in need of fresh paint, its tallywag board hanging awry after the winter winds.

A terrible ache arose within him. Short of a batsman because someone had just been called up, they had asked him to play for the village, and he'd agreed, and he'd made forty—off pretty poor bowling, admittedly, but enough to tip the balance so that Welstock won by two wickets.

And it was my last game.

He turned his back and hobbled towards the house, trying not to weep.

On his way he passed the summerhouse where croquet gear was stored in a weatherproof chest. He had a vague recollection of saying, "Croquet's about the most strenuous game I'll ever be fit for again!" Alert as ever to an unspoken command, Tinkler had set out the hoops and pegs.

For want of any better way to pass the time until lunch, he opened the chest, picked up a mallet and a ball at random, and set to listlessly driving around the lawn. All the time, though, he was preoccupied by recollected sights and sounds. For once, blessedly, they did not all concern the hell of the trenches. But awareness of the service at the church brought to mind Hindu processions following idols smeared with *ghee* and hung with garlands, and from there it was a short mental leap to his father's bearer Gul Khan, who was such a demon bowler and such a patient coach. During the hot season, in Simla . . .

"What the hell, though, is the bloody *point*?" he whispered, and slammed his mallet down as though it were a golf club. Squarely hit, the ball struck one of the hoops and knocked it clear out of the turf. He threw the mallet after it and turned back towards the house.

And was, on the instant, very calm.

Here, walking up the gravel drive, were six men in black suits and hats. He recognized them, though he could not certify their names save one. At their head, brawny and stolid, that was surely Mr. Stoddard, captain and wicket-keeper of the last side he would ever play for . . .

Once again he must have spoken aloud without intention, for a quiet voice at his back said, "Yes, sir. Mr. Hiram Stoddard, that is. There's also Mr. Jabez Stoddard, but he keeps the Plough Inn and had to go and open up."

And, apologetically: "Catching sight of you as we left the church, I excused myself to her ladyship and took the short cut."

"Thank you, Tinkler." For the moment Ernest felt quite in control of himself. "Any idea what brings them here?"

"None at all, sir."

"Is my aunt coming straight back?"

"No, sir. She intends to call on Mr. Gibson's family."

"You mean the poor devil who just died? Hmm! One point to my aunt, then. I didn't think she was so charitably inclined, except insofar as she considers it an obligation . . . Tinkler, is something wrong?"

"It's not my place, sir, to—"

"Out with it!" Ernest realized he was panting. Why?

"Since you insist, sir," Tinkler said after a pause, "I'm not entirely convinced about the charitable motive for her visit. I"—a discreet cough—"I detected a certain what you might call *gleam* in her ladyship's eye."

Ernest came to a dead stop and rounded on his manservant. "You've noticed it too?" he burst out.

Meeting his gaze dead level, Tinkler said, "Where did you last see it?" There wasn't even the echo of a "sir" this time.

"In—in the mad eyes of that general who sent us over the top at . . ."

"Say it!" He was in command. "I don't want to remember any more than you do. He killed ten thousand of us with that order, didn't he? And you and me survived by a miracle . . . But *say it!*"

"Mal . . ." Ernest's tongue was like a monstrous sponge blocking the name. He gulped and swayed and ultimately forced it out:

"Malenchines!"

"Yes. It was there. And I hoped never to see it again, neither. But I have . . . Now, sir, I'll go and find out what they want."

"No, Tinkler. *We'll* go."

As though uttering the terrible name had lifted a burden from his soul, Ernest was able to greet Mr. Stoddard and his companions and refer to their last encounter with scarcely a qualm. When they explained their errand he said at once he was sure it would be all right, though he was by no means so convinced as he sounded, and went on to inquire about prospects for the coming season.

The villagers exchanged glances. At length Mr. Stoddard shrugged.

"We've done poorly since the War. But there are a few good players coming along. Could do with more practice, though, and more coaching."

Is that a hint?

Assuming it was, Ernest forced a smile. "Well, I might offer a bit of help there," he said. Against his will a trace of bitterness crept back into his voice as he added, "My playing days are over, though, I'm afraid. Croquet is about my limit now, and I can't even find partners for that . . ."

Struck by a sudden thought, he glanced around. "Don't suppose any of you play, do you?"

A worried expression came and went on Tinkler's face, but Ernest paid no attention.

"It can be quite a good game, you know. Not much exercise, but a lot of skill. If you can spare a few minutes I'll show you. Tinkler, would you replace that hoop and bring me a mallet and a couple of balls?"

Strangely excited for the first time in years, he proceeded to initiate them into the mysteries of running a hoop, making one's peg, croquet and roquet and becoming a rover, with such enthusiasm that the visitors' stiffness melted and the youngest said at length, "Tell 'ee what, Mr. Ernest, I wouldn't mind 'aving a go some time!"

"Good man!" Ernest exclaimed. "And I tell you what, as well. I just remembered something. I was wandering around while I was on leave here once, and I came across some nets in one of the outbuildings. They may still be there. Have you got enough nets for practice?"

"No, sir!" said Hiram Stoddard promptly.

"Then let's go and—"

A gentle cough interrupted him. It was Tinkler. Her ladyship's carriage was rolling towards the house.

"Ah, fine! We can arrange about the mower. Aunt! Aunt Aglaia!"

Descending with the assistance of her groom and coachman Roger, who had been too young for the Army, Lady Peake fixed her nephew with a stony gaze.

"You are profaning the Sabbath!" she barked.

"What? Oh, you mean this?" Ernest waved the croquet mallet. "Not at all. I was just showing these people the rudiments in the hope they might give me a game some day."

He might as well have been addressing the air. She went on as though he had not spoken.

"And what are these—persons—doing here?"

"Oh, they came to borrow the three-gang mower. For the cricket-field. Uncle Roderick always used to—"

"Your uncle is no longer among us! And when, pray, was this *implement* to be put to use?"

Hiram had removed his hat and not replaced it. Turning it around between his large callused hands, he muttered, "We thought we might make a start this afternoon, m'lady."

An expression of triumph crossed Lady Peake's face.

"So, like my nephew, you are a breaker of commandments. 'The seventh day is the Sabbath of the Lord Thy God. In it thou shalt do no manner of work!' You may not borrow my mower, today or any other day. Return to the bosom of your families and pray to be forgiven."

She waddled away towards the house.

"Sorry, Mr. Stoddard," said young Roger. "But you know what she's like. 'Course, it don't apply to people working for 'er, do it? Like to see the look on 'er face if I answered back the same way: 'No, m'lady, can't drive you to church, can I? It'd be working on the Lord's Day!'"

For a second it looked as though Hiram was about to tell him off for being over-forward, but he changed his mind.

"I'm awfully sorry," Ernest muttered. "Never expected her to react like that . . . What will you do now?"

"Go back to the old way, I suppose, sir. Turn out men with scythes. Aren't that many left, though, that can mow a good tidy outfield, let alone a proper pitch. One of them dying skills Gaffer Tatton always talks about. If you'll excuse us, sir, we'd best make for the Plough before the rest of 'em head home for dinner, see who we can round up for the job."

"Hang on! I'll come with you! Just let me get my hat and stick! Roger, warn Cook I'll be late for lunch!"

As he hobbled towards the house, they looked questions at Tinkler. He hesitated. At length he said, "It's not exactly *comeelfoh*, is it? But his heart's in the right place. Only his wits are astray. And a chance to stand up to her ladyship may be just what he needs. I'll be there to keep an eye on him."

At which they relaxed. But only a little.

Startled silence fell beneath the low timbered ceiling of the Plough's single bar as they recognized who had come to join the company, and conversation was slow to resume. Only Gaffer Tatton, in his usual seat in the chimney-corner, went on talking as though nothing out of the ordinary were happening.

Or, at least, nothing so trivial as the presence of gentry.

He had finally stopped grousing about the lack of a fire to warm his aching bones, and had drifted on to the other subject preoccupying his mind—and, if truth be told, not his alone: the neglect of an ancient ceremony, to which he attributed their continuing misfortune. Making a valiant attempt to distract the visitor's attention, Hiram led the way to the bar, re-introduced his brother Jabez the landlord and presented several of the others, even going so far as to include Mr. Ames.

Aware of the problem, Jabez said heartily, "Well, sir, since it's the first time you've honoured my premises, let me offer you a glass! What'll it be?"

Ernest looked about him uncertainly. For the past few minutes he had been out of touch with himself, anger at his aunt having taken control. Now, in this unfamiliar setting, among people who clearly were uneasy at his presence, he was at a loss. He glanced at Tinkler, who said suavely, "I can recommend Mr. Stoddard's cider, sir. He makes it himself."

"By all means," Ernest agreed.

"Well, thank you, Mr. Tinkler," the landlord said, reaching for mugs. "Allow me to offer you the same."

And, as he turned the tap on the barrel, everyone tried to pick up the talk where it had left off. Instead the bad news about the mower circulated, trailing gloom around the room, and renewed silence.

Hiram invited his companions to take seats at the one partly-vacant table. Belatedly noticing them, and plainly still under the impression that it was the vicar they had been to see, Gaffer demanded their news.

"She won't let us 'ave the mower," Hiram said loudly and clearly. "Got to use scythes!"

Confused, Gaffer countered, "Don't use scythes in well-dressing! Bain't nothing used bar what's natural!"

"I don't quite get the drift of this," Ernest ventured.

"Oh, don't concern yourself with it, sir," Hiram said. "Got a bit of a bee in 'is bonnet, Gaffer do."

"He seems very upset," Ernest persisted.

And indeed he was, even though someone had made haste to refill his mug. His voice rose to the pitch of a revival preacher, despite attempts to hush him, and at last there was nothing for it but to explain.

"The way of it, sir, you see," Hiram sighed, "is this. Back before the War, come Ascensiontide, we had a local—ah—"

"Custom?" supplied a voice from the background.

"Custom, yes, a very good term. Thank you—" He glanced around and finished in a tone of surprise, "Mr. Ames! Used to make up sort of decorations, pictures out of flowers and leaves and alder-cones and such, and put them to the wells."

"And the wall below the church," someone inserted.

"Yes, in Old Well Road too. Three places." Hiram ran a finger around his collar as though it were suddenly too tight. "Then we'd get vicar to come and speak a blessing on 'em."

Gaffer's attention was completely engaged now. Leaning forward, mug in both hands, he nodded vigorously. "Ah, an' every seventh year—"

"Every seventh year, yes," Hiram interrupted loudly, "we had a sort of feast, as well. We'd roast a sheep, or a pig, and share it out among everybody, making sure bits got taken to the old folk or those sick abed."

"It sounds like a fascinating tradition," Ernest said, staring. "Has it fallen into disuse?"

"Ha'n't been kept up since the War."

"But why?"

There was an awkward pause. Eventually Hiram found no one else was willing to answer, so it was up to him again.

"Vicar used to say it were truly a heathen custom made over. I wouldn't know about that. But I daresay he's not un'appy."

"An' what would 'er ladyship say?" called Jabez from behind the bar, forgetting himself for a moment.

His brother glowered at him, but by now the cider was having an effect on Ernest. Since falling ill he had seldom touched alcohol; besides, he had had almost no breakfast.

Draining his mug, he said, "You're right, Tinkler. It is good, this stuff. Here, bring me another. And for Mr. Stoddard too, and Mr.— Oh, drinks all round, why not? Here!" He pulled banknotes from his wallet.

Somewhat reluctantly Tinkler complied. Meantime Ernest turned to Hiram and continued.

"Well, I don't see what my aunt has to do with it, you know. How did Sir Roderick feel?"

"'E were in favour," Hiram grunted.

"That's the truth!" chimed in someone from the background. "Remember 'ow, if there were visitors, 'e'd bring 'em round along of us? Or come by later in the day with 'em, with their Kodaks and all?"

The older men uttered a chorus of confirmation.

Returning with the full mugs, Tinkler murmured, "Here you are, sir."

Ernest gulped a mouthful and set his aside. By now his attention was fully engaged.

"Well, if your major problem is with the vicar, I can put in a word, at least. Miss Pollock has invited me to tea at the vicarage, and I can bring up the matter then. Would you mind?"

It was clear from their faces that they wouldn't, and Hiram said, "That's very generous, sir. Here!"—loudly—"I think we should drink Mr. Ernest's health!"

"Hear hear!"

Absent-mindedly drinking along with them, Ernest wiped his lip and took up another point that particularly interested him.

"What kind of—of decorations, or pictures?"

"Always Bible stories," Hiram said.

"To do with water? Walking on the waves, Jonah and the whale, that kind of thing?"

Headshakes. By now everyone in the bar was crowding around the table, so that Gaffer complained about not being able to see. They ignored him.

"No, just any that came to mind. 'Course . . ."

"Yes?"

"They was mostly the work of one that's gone."

"You mean one particular person used to work out the designs for you?"

"That's right, sir. Mr. Faber it were. Taken off in the same way as your poor uncle, but the year before."

"Bain't no one left got 'is skill an' touch," came a doleful voice.

Ernest hesitated. He glanced at Tinkler for advice, as had become his habit. Surprisingly, this time he wore a completely blank expression—indeed, was elaborately pretending not to notice. Abruptly annoyed, Ernest drank half of what was left in his mug and reached a decision.

"If you don't think it's out of place," he said, "you may know . . . Tinkler!"·

"Yes, sir?"

"Talked about me in here at all, have you?"

"Well, sir"—looking pained—"no more than is called for by ordinary politeness, I assure you."

"Don't worry, man! I only wanted to find out if they know that I do a bit of drawing and painting."

"That, sir, of course."

"Well, then . . ." Ernest took a deep breath. "Would you mind if I proposed a few ideas?"

Mingled doubt and excitement showed on all faces. Gaffer complained again about not knowing what was going on, and someone bent to explain. Before the murmured debate reached a conclusion he cut it short, rising effortfully to his feet.

"Don't turn it down! Remember it's the seventh year, and if we don't do it right then *she*—"

A dozen voices drowned out the rest.

"That's very handsome of you, sir," Hiram declared, and it was settled.

Feeling a renewal of that particular excitement which had possessed him earlier, Ernest said, "Well, now! You mentioned people sometimes took photographs of the—do you say well-dressings?"

"That's right, sir."

"So if I could look at a few of those, get the general idea . . . Tinkler, is something wrong?"

"Sir, I've noticed people are starting to look at the clock. Perhaps we should ask if they're expected home for dinner."

There was a rustle of relief, and Ernest rose in embarrassment. "I'm sorry, I wasn't thinking about the time!"

"Not at all, sir, not at all," Hiram countered. "But—well, there are

some whose wives do be expecting 'em. As to the photographs, though
. . . Jabez!"

The landlord looked round.

"Weren't there an album some place, with pictures in?"

"Why, indeed there were. I'll hunt around for un!"

"Excellent!" Ernest cried. "And I'll talk to the vicar as I promised.
Tinkler, where did I put my hat . . . ? Ah, thanks. Well, good afternoon,
gentlemen!"

There was a long pause after the door swung shut. At last Jabez voiced
the feelings of them all.

"*Proper* gentleman, 'e be. Calling *us* gentlemen! That'd've been Sir
Roderick's way."

"But not," said his brother, "'er ladyship's!"

At which, amid cynical laughter, the company made to disperse, only
to be checked by an exclamation from Mr. Ames: "Just a moment!"

All heads turned.

Lapels aside, thumbs in the armholes of his waistcoat, wearing an
expression that bordered on defiance, he said, "If you'll accept the support of Mr. Ernest, I dare to hope you'll accept the like from me. I have
a porker I've been fattening for Mankley show. After living in the district
for so long, and knowing"—a glance at Gaffer—"what store you set by
the well-dressing feast, I hope you'll let me donate it for Ascensiontide
instead."

For a long moment there was a sense of uncertainty. Hiram resolved
the matter. Advancing on Ames, he offered his hand.

"Spoken as handsomely as Mr. Ernest!" he exclaimed. "Jabez! Before
we go, draw one more mug—*for Henry*!"

"What be they going on about?" Gaffer demanded crossly.

The offer was explained to him, and also that in accepting it Hiram
had addressed Mr. Ames by his Christian name.

Gaffer beamed.

"'Tes like I always say," he declared. "Do right by 'er and she'll do
right by us. Bain't it already begun?"

On returning to the Hall Tinkler insisted that his master eat something,
and brought him cold meat, bread and pickles in the summerhouse.
Lady Peake was taking her customary afternoon nap, so they were spared
recriminations about her nephew's absence from the lunch-table.

Talking feverishly with his mouth full, Ernest at first exclaimed over and over about the excitement of finding a pre-Christian ceremony in a modern English village, and gave Tinkler positive orders to call at the vicarage and tell Miss Pollock he proposed to take up her invitation this very afternoon. Little by little the food and cider combined to make him drowsy, and in the end he muttered something about taking forty winks. Satisfied he was indeed asleep, Tinkler returned the tray to the kitchen and undertook his errand.

When he came back less than half an hour later, however, he found his master awake again and plagued by his old uncertainties. On being told that he was engaged for tea at four o'clock, he lapsed into his usual despondency.

"It's no use, Tinkler," he muttered. "I'm not up to it. You'll have to go back and apologise. How can I face the vicar? I don't believe in his religion! I'm likely to insult him in an unguarded moment, aren't I?"

"No, sir."

"What?" Ernest glanced up, blinking. "But you know damn' well I don't give a farthing for his mumbo-jumbo!"

"Yes, sir. But as a result of what has transpired today I am also aware that you take great interest in the survival of old customs. So does Mr. Pollock."

"But Mr. Stoddard said—"

"He seems to be mistaken. While I was at the vicarage I took the liberty of mentioning the subject to Mrs. Kail the housekeeper. She's local. And a very affable person, I may say. It is her opinion that were it up entirely to the vicar there would be no objection to resuming the ceremony."

Slowly—sluggishly—Ernest worked it out. He said at last, "You mean my aunt is once again the fly in the ointment?"

"It would appear so, sir."

"Hmm . . ." He glanced towards the house, towards the drawn curtains of his aunt's room. "In that case . . . All right, Tinkler. I'll put a bold face on it. But you come too. Go and pump Mrs.—did you say Kail? Yes?—and if I make a mess of it maybe you can think of a better approach next time."

He turned his gaze in the direction of the few cottages visible from here.

"They seem like decent people," he muttered, half inaudibly. "I don't want to let them down . . ."

. . .

"Good afternoon, Mr. Peake," said the vicar. His bespectacled face was deeply lined and his movements were stiff from arthritis, but his voice remained firm and resonant. "So glad you could join us. Do sit down."

Awkwardly, Ernest took his place at the table that had been set out in a shady arbor. Miss Pollock smiled at him and inquired whether he preferred Indian or China tea, then proffered plates of cakes and dainty fish-paste sandwiches.

But her smile struck Ernest as forced, and once again he wondered whether he was doing the right thing. His nerve had almost failed him again at the last moment, and he had been half minded to turn back, but Tinkler had kept on going and at last he had stumbled to catch up.

"I'm especially pleased you've come," the vicar continued, wiping a trace of tea from his upper lip with a wide white napkin. "I—ah—I have been hoping for a little chat with you."

About what? Instantly Ernest was on edge. Was there, after all, to be an argument about his non-attendance at church? In that case, the best form of defence was certainly attack. He countered, "As a matter of fact, padre"—the colloquial military term for a chaplain sprang automatically to his lips—"there's something I'd like to discuss with you as well. Apparently the people in the village . . ."

But the words trailed away. Miss Pollock had leaned forward, her expression troubled.

"If you don't mind, Mr. Peake, Grandfather did broach his subject first. And it concerns your aunt."

"It would," Ernest muttered.

"Excuse me?" the vicar said, cupping a hand to his ear. "I'm becoming a little hard of hearing, I'm afraid."

Disregarding him, his granddaughter said fiercely, "Have you heard what she's decided to do now?"

This sounded alarming. Ernest shook his head. "I'm afraid not. To be candid, I'm rather avoiding her at the moment."

"It's a scandal and a shame!" Under the table she stamped her small foot on the grass. Her grandfather laid a restraining touch on her arm, but she shook it off.

"I'm sorry, Grandfather, but I will not be silenced! What she intends to do is—is downright un-Christian!"

The old man sighed.

"Uncharitable at least, I must concede . . . But Mr. Peake doesn't yet know what we are talking about, does he?"

The girl swung to face the visitor.

"You heard about poor George Gibson's death?"

"Yes, of course."

"You know he was a labourer on your aunt's estate—not that he could do much work after being gassed?"

This time, a nod.

"And that he left a wife and three children?"

Another nod.

"Well, Sir Roderick said in his will he could stay in his cottage for life because he'd been wounded in the War. Now he's gone, your aunt intends to throw the family out. She told Mrs. Gibson today. They have one week."

"But that's disgraceful!" Ernest exclaimed. "Why?"

The vicar gave a gentle cough. She ignored it.

"Mrs. Gibson's youngest was born in March 1919."

For a moment Ernest failed to make the connection. Then he realised what the date implied. Slowly he said, "I take it you mean the youngest child is not her husband's?"

"How could it be? He'd been a prisoner of war since '17!" She leaned forward, her eyes beseeching. "But he'd forgiven her! He treated the child as he did his own—I saw. Why can't your aunt do the same? What gives her the right to pass this kind of 'moral' judgment? One week for the poor wretch to find a new home, or else it'll be the bailiffs and eviction!"

She was almost panting with the force of her tirade. In passing Ernest marvelled at how lovely it made her look. Previously he had thought of her as a rather pallid girl, meekly content to exist in her grandfather's shadow, but now there was colour flaming in her cheeks and righteous anger in her voice.

At length he said, "Whoso shall offend one of these little ones . . ."

In a tone of unexpected cordiality the vicar said, "I gather from Alice that you are one of the unfortunates who lost his faith owing to the War, but I must say that is precisely the text that has been running through my own mind. An attitude such as your aunt's belongs to the old covenant which Our Lord came to replace with the gospel of love. We no longer think it proper that the sins of the ancestors should be visited on the children, and it is they who will suffer the worst."

Wasn't the War the visiting of our forebears' sins upon us, the young cannon-fodder?

But Ernest bit back the bitter comment. He said after a pause, "I have scant influence with my aunt, I'm afraid. What I can do, though, I certainly will."

"Thank you," Alice said, leaning forward and laying her slim hand on his. "Thank you very much. More tea? And now: what was it that you wanted to discuss with us?"

"Well, you see . . ." And clumsily he brought it out. By the time he was done the vicar had finished his tea and was sitting back with a reflective expression, polishing his glasses on his napkin.

"Ah yes. They do take the well-dressing very seriously, don't they? And indeed I myself see little harm in it. Of course one is aware that it began as a pagan custom, but then so did Christmas, being timed to coincide with the Roman Saturnalia."

"The tradition really is that ancient?"

"Oh, yes. And formerly very widespread, though Welstock is the only place in the West Country where it is, or was, kept up. The most notable survivals are in Derbyshire, where several villages adhere to the custom. Its nature is much altered, naturally. The 'feast' you referred to was originally a sacrifice, indeed a human sacrifice, to the patron spirit of water. The Romans knew her as Sabellia, but that was a corruption of an even earlier name. She was also an embodiment of springtime, associated, as one might expect, with the fertility of plants and animals. Including—ah—human animals."

"Yet you saw no objection to continuing the rite?" Ernest couldn't keep the puzzlement out of his voice.

"It's been efficiently disinfected, as it were," answered the vicar with a thin smile. "Indeed the villagers no longer know that there was a heathen spirit, or goddess, connected with the ceremony. At least I never heard any of them mention her name. They do still refer to 'she,' but pronouns in the local dialect tend to be somewhat interchangeable, and at worst they tend to identify her with the Virgin. That smacks of Mariolatry, of course, which I am professionally unable to countenance, but at least it lacks specifically pagan associations."

"And I think it's rather fun," Alice said. "I remember when I was a little girl, following the procession around from well to well. The pictures Mr. Faber used to make were so clever, too! And using such ordinary bits and pieces! Grandfather!" She turned to the vicar. "I think

Mr. Peake has had a wonderful idea! Let's put our feet down, and insist on reviving the well-dressing this year!"

"I'm absolutely on your side," Ernest said fervently. "If you'll forgive me saying so, despite her apparent devoutness I cannot regard my aunt as—"

"As a good advertisement for religion?" the vicar interpolated gently. "No more, alas, can I. To my mind, these simple souls who want to celebrate the miracle of water, even more than bread the staff of life, have a deeper faith than she will ever attain—save, of course," he added, as to reproach himself for lack of charity, "by the grace of God, which I trust will reveal to her the beam in her own eye . . . Mr. Peake, I believe you have convinced me!"

He gave the table an open-palmed slap that made the teacups rattle, and winced as though regretting the impulse.

"We'll strike a bargain, shall we? We shall both defy Lady Peake! I shall announce that the well-dressing is to be resumed; you, for your part, will do your best to save the Gibson family from eviction."

It's not going to be easy . . .

But the thought only flashed across Ernest's mind for a fraction of a second. At once he was extending his hand to the vicar.

"Agreed, padre! It's a deal!"

When tea was over, Alice offered to accompany him to the gate. He was about to protest that it wasn't necessary when he realised that she wanted to say something more, out of hearing of her grandfather.

And when she uttered it, he was astounded.

At the very last moment before they separated she caught him by the arm.

"Mr. Peake—or may I call you Ernest? My name is Alice, as you know."

"Please do," he stammered.

"Ernest, do your utmost for Mrs. Gibson, won't you? What happened to her is so—so understandable! It could have happened to anybody during the War. It could . . ." She withdrew a pace, standing bolt upright, and looked him straight in the eyes.

"It could have happened to me."

"You mean—"

"Yes. I was Gerald's mistress. And before you ask, I do not feel in the least like a Fallen Woman! I'm only glad that he had the chance to become a complete man before his life was cut short . . . Have I shocked you? I apologise if so."

Ernest looked at her as though for the first time. He read defiance in her face, noted that her small hands were clenched, remembered that her voice had trembled as she made her admission. To his amazement, he heard himself say, "No, Alice. You haven't shocked me, not at all. My only feeling is that your Gerald was a very lucky man."

"Thank you," she whispered, and darted forward and gave him a brief kiss on the cheek before hastening away.

"Wait!" Ernest cried.

"I can't!"

"But I forgot to send a message to Tinkler—my man! Tell him I'm returning to the Hall!"

"Yes! Yes, of course! Goodbye!"

All the way home Ernest's head was spinning in a maelström of confused impressions. But the strongest was this: that for the first time (and in how unexpected a setting!) he had met a girl with more courage than a man.

By sheer force of will he compelled himself to be polite to his aunt at the dinner-table, chatting—for so long as the maid was in the room— about his visit to the vicarage (which mellowed her a trifle), the beauty of the area, and his vague plans to paint several views of it. He was unable to resist a few indirect comments about the plight of rural communities nowadays, but managed to avoid any overt references to either the Gibson children or her refusal to lend her mower to the cricket-team. Not until coffee was served in the drawing-room, and they were alone, did he steer the talk around to the former of those two subjects.

Then, adopting his most reasonable tone, he observed that the vicar, and particularly Miss Pollock, seemed very worried about the fate hanging over Mrs. Gibson and especially her children.

But at the mere mention of the name Lady Peake's face froze as hard as marble.

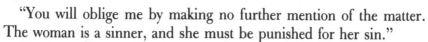

"You will oblige me by making no further mention of the matter. The woman is a sinner, and she must be punished for her sin."

"But, aunt, it's not the fault of the children that—"

"Be silent, sir! It is the duty of those in a position of authority to ensure that Christian values are upheld. That is what I am doing."

Oh, what's the use? But at least I tried . . .

"I see," he said after a pause. "Well, I must ask you to excuse me. I have some work to do."

"Work?"

"Yes"—setting aside his empty cup. "Among other things, I found out today about the well-dressing ceremony. It's to be revived this year, and I've offered to prepare some designs for it." He rose with a slight bow.

"You will do nothing of the kind!" his aunt thundered. "It's naked paganism!"

"You think so?" Ernest was very conscious of the way his heart was pounding, but he kept his voice steady. "The vicar doesn't. Indeed he said it has been completely Christianised with the passing of the years. And the designs I have in mind have an immaculately biblical basis. Good evening, aunt, and if I don't see you again before bedtime, good night."

He closed the door before she could erupt again.

Once in his room, however, staring at the first sheet from his portfolio, he suddenly found his mind as blank as the paper. He kept imagining what Mrs. Gibson's state of mind must be, alone in her isolated cottage, perhaps with the children crying, not knowing whether they would have a roof over their heads a week from now. He was still sitting, pencil in lax fingers, when Tinkler came in to turn down the bed, lay out his pyjamas, and mix his final draught of tincture of valerian. On his way to draw the curtains, he inquired sympathetically, "Shortage of inspiration, sir?"

Tossing the pencil angrily aside, Ernest rose and began to pace the room. "Yes," he muttered. "I thought I had a lot of ideas. I thought for instance I might base something on the story of the three wise men, and show scenes from various parts of the Empire where one might imagine them to have hailed from. My people once took me to a church in Goa, in India, where they claim to have originally been converted by the Apostle Thomas. And I've seen services in Singapore, too, and

Hong Kong. I was very young at the time, but I still remember a lot of details. But it seems—well—somehow wrong!" Slumping back into his chair, he concluded, "You've talked to the local folk much more than I have. Any suggestions?"

Tinkler hesitated for a moment. At length he said, "If I'm not presuming, sir—"

"Out with it!"

"Well, sir, are there not stories from the New Testament that would be more relevant to the present situation? For example, how about the woman taken in adultery?"

For an instant Ernest sat as though thunderstruck. Then he snapped his fingers.

"Of course! And Mary Magdalene—and the woman who met Jesus at the well! *That's* apt, if you like! There's a Bible under the night-table, isn't there? Pass it to me, there's a good chap."

Complying, Tinkler said, "Will there be anything else?"

"Hm? Oh—no, not tonight. You can turn in."

"Thank you, sir. Good night."

And he was gone, having uncharacteristically forgotten to draw the curtains.

By the time the church clock struck eleven-thirty Ernest was surrounded by a dozen rough sketches. Without seeing the promised photographs of Mr. Faber's creations he had no idea whether they would prove acceptable, but he had a subconscious conviction that they would, for into the background of each he had contrived to incorporate a haughty, self-righteous figure modelled on his aunt. At first he had considered portraying her full-face, but then bethought himself of the difficulty of showing fine detail using a mosaic of natural objects bedded in clay, and concluded it would be best to depict her turning her back on those in need of help. Was that not most appropriate?

Yawning, stretching, he set aside the drawings and rose. Turning to the window, meaning to close the curtains, he checked in mid-movement.

Beyond the trees that fringed the left side of the garden, there was a fitful red glow.

For a moment he thought his eyes were playing tricks. Then he whistled under his breath.

"That's a house on fire, or I'm a Dutchman . . . Tinkler! *Tinkler!*"
And, seizing the blazer he had hung on the back of his chair with one
hand, with the other he tugged frantically on the bell-pull.

He met his valet in a nightshirt on the landing, looking sleepily
puzzled, and explained in a rush.

"Get some clothes on! Rouse the coachman and tell him to wake
everyone he can! There isn't a fire-engine in Welstock, is there?"

"I believe it has to come from the next village, sir."

"Then tell them to bring buckets and ladders. Dr. Castle had better
be woken up, too; someone might be hurt."

"Where is the fire, sir?" Tinkler demanded.

"Over *that* way, but you can't miss it. I'll go via the vicarage and
have the bells rung . . . What's wrong?"

"There's only one cottage near the house on that side of the estate,
sir. And that's Mrs. Gibson's."

"What is this *infernal* row?" a stern voice demanded. Through her
partly-opened bedroom door his aunt was peering.

"There's a house on fire, and Tinkler says it must be the Gibsons'!"

He couldn't see his aunt's expression, but he could picture it. Because he heard her say, "It's a visitation, then."

"*What?*" Beside himself with rage, Ernest took a pace toward her.
But Tinkler caught his arm.

"The alarm, sir—the church bells! That's the important thing."

"Yes. Yes, you're right. The rest can wait. But not for long . . ."

And he was hobbling down the stairs, outside into the clear spring
night, across the garden towards the vicarage. From here the smoke
was already pungent, and he could hear faint cries.

By shouting and hammering on the oaken door, he managed to rouse
a middle-aged woman armed with a poker whom he took for Mrs. Kail.
He uttered instructions as though he were again briefing his men
against an enemy attack: *do this now, then do that, then come and help*.
And was off again, struggling through thorns and underbrush on the
straightest line to the burning cottage. Before he reached it a ragged
clang was sounding from the tower.

The fire had obviously begun in an ill-repaired chimney, for it was
still uttering most of the smoke. But by now the adjacent thatch was
well alight. Outside, weeping and terrified, were three scantily-clad
children. Where was their mother—? He glimpsed her through the
open door, striving to rescue her pitiful possessions. At that moment

she turned back with her arms full of oddments, coughing and choking and with tears streaming from her reddened eyes. She had on nothing but a soiled linen shift.

Limping forward, he shouted that she mustn't go inside again, but she seemed not to hear, and he had to hurry after and drag her away by force. She fought to break his grip, whimpering.

"I've raised the alarm! Help will be here soon! Look to your children!"

There was a crackling of trodden sticks behind him, and he turned gratefully to the first of the promised helpers, whom he took for a young man in the dimness.

"See if you can find a ladder! We'll need a bucket-chain until the engine comes! Where can we get water—? *Alice!*"

To his amazement, it was indeed. She had donned, practically enough, boots and trousers and an old jersey. Women in trousers or breeches had been a common enough sight during the War, but he hadn't seen one since and certainly had not expected to in Welstock. He was still at a loss when more half-glimpsed figures arrived at the double, laden with buckets and an invaluable ladder.

"I'll take care of her and the children," Alice said. "Take them to the vicarage and calm them down. You get things organised. There's a pump round the back."

Her coolness steadied his own racing thoughts. He issued brisk orders. By the time the fire-engine negotiated the rutted lane that was the only access to the cottage the unburnt portion of the thatch had been saturated and despite the mingled smoke and steam coachman Roger, who had been first to the top of the ladder, had begun to douse the glowing rafters.

Realising that hoses were playing on the roof, Ernest discovered his eyes were full of tears. Some were due to smoke, no doubt, but he felt that more stemmed from the sight of this small tragedy, one more burden inflicted on an innocent victim.

"You can come away now," a soft voice said at his side. "You've done wonders. Without you, the whole place would have been in ruins."

Blearily he looked at Alice. He wasn't the only one. Now they had been relieved, the volunteers were staring at her too, and one or two of their expressions were disapproving, as to say, "Her, in trousers? Shocking!"

He heard the imagined words in the voice of his aunt, and remembered what Tinkler had said about the glint in her eyes . . . Where was he, anyhow? Oh, over there, talking to the Stoddards.

"I don't want to go back under that woman's roof," he said without intention. "Know what she said when I told her Mrs. Gibson's house was burning down? She said it was a visitation on her!"

"You don't have to," Alice answered. "Not tonight. I can make up a bed at the vicarage. And I'll run you a bath, too. You need one."

For the first time Ernest realized he was grimy from head to toe with smoke.

And utterly exhausted.

"All right," he muttered. "Thanks. Let Tinkler know."

Oddly, during what was left of the night, for the first time in years his sleep was free from fearful dreams.

It was broad daylight. Opening his eyes, he discovered himself in a narrow bed, in a small room under the eaves, wearing—good heavens—his skin. Memory surged back. Alice had apologised for the fact that her grandfather had retired again and she didn't want to disturb him by creeping into his room in search of nightwear he could borrow, but produced a large towel that she said would do to cover him returning from his bath.

Someone, though, had stolen into this room while he was asleep. Neatly arranged on a chair were clean clothes, his own, and underneath a pair of shoes awaited him.

Bless you, Tinkler!

Abruptly he discovered he was ravenous. Rising, dressing hastily, he went downstairs, finding his way by guesswork. This was an old and rambling house, with many misleading passages and stairways, but eventually he located the entrance hall—and Mr. Pollock.

"Good morning, young fellow! I understand from Alice that you did sterling work last night!"

Embarrassed, Ernest shrugged. "I just happened to be the only person awake, I suppose. I spotted the fire by sheer chance."

"Professionally," the vicar murmured, "I tend not to think in terms of 'sheer chance' . . . The Gibsons, you'll be glad to know, are in reasonable spirits this morning; Mrs. Kail is looking after them. But we'll talk about that later. In the meantime, how about breakfast?"

"I'll get it for him," Alice said, appearing in one of the hall's many doorways. She looked amazingly fresh, considering the experiences of the night. Looking at her—she had put on a brown dress this morning, as plain as her usual grey—Ernest wondered how, even for a moment and in trousers, he could have mistaken her for a boy.

"There's no need," he protested. "Tinkler can—"

"Tinkler has gone to fetch the rest of your belongings."

He stared blankly. The vicar explained.

"I hope you won't be upset, Mr. Peake, but—well, you did say, I believe, that you couldn't face another night under your aunt's roof?"

"I . . . Well, yes, actually I did."

"It would appear that the feeling is mutual. First thing this morning, I received a note from her ladyship to the effect that if I proceed with plans to revive the well-dressing she will report me to my bishop and invoke ecclesiastical discipline. Apparently I am embroiling you, who are already a soul in danger of damnation, in pagan rites that will doom you past redemption. Fortunately"—his usual thin smile—"I happen to know that my bishop is, like myself, something of an antiquary, and had taken the precaution of notifying him of my intentions. I confidently predict that he will cast his vote in my favour."

"You must forgive us, Ernest," Alice said. "But we have taken the liberty of temporarily re-planning your life. We consulted Mr. Tinkler, and it was his view as well as ours that you might be better able to concentrate on your designs for the well-dressings here rather than at the Hall. Do you mind very much?"

"Do I mind?" Ernest blurted. "I'd give anything to be out of that— that gorgon's lair! I can't say how grateful I am!"

"There are," the vicar said sententiously, "many in Welstock this morning who are equally grateful to yourself . . . Alice, my dear: you promised Mr. Peake some breakfast?"

"Of course. Right away. Come along!"

Ernest could scarcely believe the transformation in his life. About noon a delegation from the village waited on him—he had to use the archaic term, for they were so determined to make it a formal occasion—led by Hiram Stoddard, who presented his publican brother's apologies, as well as Henry Ames, who practically overnight seemed to have been accepted as a full member of the community, and into the bargain Gaffer Tatton, who declared more than once that it would have taken far worse than rheumatism to keep him at home today. Apparently he was some sort of distant cousin of the Gibsons; probably, Ernest thought wryly, they all were.

They moved a vote of thanks to him in the drawing-room and uttered three solemn cheers, which struck him as rather silly since there were only eight of them, but kindly intended. Trying not to seem unappreciative, he contrived at last to drag the conversation around to something that interested him far more, and sent Tinkler for his sketches.

"Of course, I still haven't seen your brother's photographs, Mr. Stoddard," he said as he diffidently removed them from the portfolio. "But would something on these lines serve? You'll notice"—he recalled and consciously echoed Tinkler's remark—"they are in a sense relevant to certain recent events around here."

For a moment they seemed not to catch the reference. Then, unexpectedly, Gaffer Tatton banged the floor with his stick. "'Tes the very thing!" he exclaimed. "Bain't it to do *her* honour as we dress the wells? She'm bound to be pleased. Don't all on 'em show ladies?"

Ernest was about to comment light-heartedly—light-headedly?—that "lady" was perhaps a misnomer for somebody like Mary Magdalene, when he realised it would have struck a false note. Grave, they were all nodding their agreement.

"Well, sir, we'll get the boards cut by the weekend," Hiram said. "And puddle the clay ready. Can you tell us what colours you have in mind, so we can set the young 'uns to gathering the right bits and pieces?"

"I haven't finished working that out," Ernest admitted. "But I can give you a rough idea. For instance . . ."

And spent a happy quarter of an hour explaining.

It was not until they had left that an odd, disturbing point occurred to him.

The central female figure in each of his three designs bore a remarkable likeness—in his imagination, at least—to Alice Pollock.

What had Gaffer Tatton said? That "she" would certainly be pleased! But he, equally certainly, must have been thinking of a different "she" . . .

Customary doubt assailed him yet again. This time, though, he drove it back, secure in the conviction he had found a worthwhile task at last.

"You may be pleased to hear," the vicar said at lunch a few days later, "that the eviction of the Gibsons from their cottage may not prove as simple as Lady Peake might hope."

Ernest, who had been thinking as little as possible about his aunt and as much as possible about the wells, came to himself with a start.

"How is that?" he inquired.

"The chief fire-officer who attended the conflagration has submitted a report, a copy of which I saw this morning. He says the chimney of the cottage had been long neglected, and its upkeep is not the responsibility of the tenant, but of the landlord. A high proportion of the Gibsons' belongings were inevitably damaged, many beyond recall. One of my nephews is a solicitor and he informs me that the possibility arises of a claim for financial recompense."

"You mean the Gibsons might get some money out of my aunt?" The family were lodging as best they could in one of the vicarage stables, but while this was tolerable in warm weather their stay could not be indefinitely prolonged.

"Blood from a stone," Alice sighed. "But it's worth a try."

"I meant to ask!" Ernest exclaimed. "Sorry to change the subject, but what did the bishop say?"

A twinkle came and went in Mr. Pollock's eyes. "At the risk of sounding vain, I think I may claim that my knowledge of my superiors is as much—ah—*superior* to her ladyship's as is my acquaintance with the principles of doctrine. He went so far as to ask why I had let such an interesting old custom lapse for so long."

"*She* will be pleased," Ernest murmured.

"I beg your pardon?"

"Nothing—nothing. Just quoting someone from the village, one of the people who've been advising me about the well-dressings. By the way, I'm not quite as sure as you about their having completely forgotten the patron spirit of water. But we can discuss that some other time. For now, just remind me of the date of Ascension Day. Since moving here I've lost track of time."

"It's next Thursday," Alice supplied.

"Really! Then I'd better tell them to get a move on!"

"Don't."

"Excuse me . . . ?"

"I said don't!"—with a smile. "They set too much store by this to brook delay. Everything you need will be ready, that I promise."

That evening, strolling in the garden after dinner, he dared to kiss her for the first time. And on Sunday he attended church and sat beside her, and took much pleasure in ignoring his aunt's glares.

The glint was in her eye again, though, and thinking of it made shivers tremble down his spine.

The wells that had drawn the first settlers to the site of this village would, Ernest felt, more properly have been called springs. The first he visited was the closest to his own vision of a well, being surrounded by a stone coping and covered with a makeshift roof, but that was of corrugated iron, and there was neither windlass nor bucket and chain. The second was even more disappointing, for its water had been diverted to first a pump in the main square, then public taps at various points nearby, and eventually individual homes. Now only isolated cottages—like the Gibsons'—lacked at least cold water in the scullery. As to the third, which supplied the part of the village nearest the Hall, there was no sign of it at all below the stone facing that supported the track up to the church. (There were two others, in the grounds of the Hall and the vicarage, but they had of course never been available for general use . . . or dressing at Ascensiontide.)

Leaning on his stick in unconscious imitation of his guide Gaffer Tatton, whom he sometimes found hard to understand, he ventured, "One would scarcely imagine there was a well below here, would one?"

"Ah, but there be!" was the prompt response. "Don't go too close, will 'ee, sir? I recall last time the cover on it were made good—see, 'tes under mould now, and that there grass." He pointed at the base of the wall with his stick. "Deepest on 'em all, it were. Time and past time we dug un out and mended tiles."

"Tiles?"

"Can't see en, but they're there. I recall helping to mend un. I were a boy then. Saw the way on un. Jes' a few tiles. Ah, but good mortar! Best kind! Mr. Howard the builder, 'twere as done it. Still, 'tes in the nature o' things. Don't last for ever, do un? And 'tes time and past time we mended un again. She don't care for being overlooked, she don't."

Greatly daring, Ernest countered, "She . . . ?"

"Ah, 'tes all old stories, sir. We tell un round the chimney-corner come winter, that we do. Fine day like this bain't no time for such chitter-chatter . . . Well, sir, what do you think o' the way they changed your drawings for to fit the boards?"

"I think there's more talent in the village than people admit," Ernest answered honestly. "They could have worked something out by themselves. I don't think you needed me."

"Ah, sir!" Gaffer Tatton leaned firmly on his stick again, staring his companion directly in the eyes. "That's where you be wrong. If you'll excuse me. It's you exactly that we do be needing."

And, before Ernest could inquire what he meant, he was consulting an old pocket-watch.

"Time be a-wasting, sir. Waits for no man, as they say."

"Just a moment!" Ernest exclaimed. "When you said 'she,' were you referring to—?"

"I bain't saying more, sir," the old man grunted. "There be some as believes and some as don't. Though when you've lived in Welstock long as me—"

"I haven't had to," Ernest said.

It was the other's turn to be puzzled. He said, "Do I understand 'ee right, sir?"

"I hope so." Ernest drew back a pace or two and gazed up at the Hall, silhouetted against the bright sky. "*She* can be kind, but she can also be cruel. Isn't that so?"

Gaffer Tatton was totally at a loss. Eventually, however, he found words.

"I knew it!" he burst out. "Couldn't a-drawn them pictures 'less . . ."

"Well? Go on!"—impatiently.

"The rest bain't for me to say, sir, but for you to find out. Same as we all do. Same as we all must. But I'll tell 'ee this: you'm on the right track. Good day!"

"What do you think he meant?" Ernest fretted to Alice after dinner that night.

"Could he have been talking about nature?" she suggested.

"I suppose so, but—"

"Nature personified? You hinted that you don't believe grandfather when he claims they've all forgotten the origin of well-dressing."

"It fits," he admitted. "People always say 'Mother' Nature, don't they? Even though—"

"What?"

He drew a deep breath. "Living here instead of at the Hall, even though I recall what my aunt has said and done, I find it incredibly hard to believe the cruel side of her."

"You aren't talking about your aunt," Alice said perceptively.

"No, I'm not."

"But she's an aspect of the female principle, too."

"I can't think of her that way!"

"Then what about Kali—Kali Durga?"

Taken aback, he demanded, "How do you know about her?"

"From Grandfather's library, of course. You were brought up in India, a place I've never been and very likely never shall, and it's no secret that I want to know more about you, is it? So I've made a start. Grandfather has a lot of old books about missionary work abroad . . . Did you ever witness one of her ceremonies?"

"No, and I'm rather glad!"

"I think I'd be interested—provided, of course, I could just watch from a distance . . . But do you accept my point? There are all those millions of people, much closer to the primitive state than we are, or at any rate believe we are, and they know nature can be cruel as well as kind."

"Yes, of course. But if you're thinking of the well-dressing—"

"Every seventh year there used to be a human sacrifice. Grandfather said so. This year Mr. Ames is offering a pig. Did you ever hear a pig squeal when they slaughter it—? Oh, that was a rotten thing to say. I keep forgetting, because you're such a nice person. You've heard men scream while they were dying, haven't you?"

"Did"—his mouth was suddenly dry as though he had found himself confronting an unexpected rival—"did Gerald tell you about that?"

"He had to tell someone."

"Yes. Yes, of course." Ernest licked his lips.

"Have you ever told anyone? Tinkler?"

"I don't have to tell him. We went through it together."

The glint in my aunt's eyes, the same as that general's—and he recognised it too . . .

"Then a doctor?"

"The doctors I've talked to weren't there. Maybe they can imagine it, but they never saw it."

"Surely, though, doctors too see people die. Horribly, sometimes. In railway accidents, for instance—or burning houses. Worse yet, after operations that went wrong."

"An accident can't be helped. War is deliberate."

"Yes, of course . . . So you haven't ever found anyone to tell?"

He shook his head.

"Then what about me?" She reached for his hand and drew him unresisting to a seat. "I know you think of India as an old unchanging land, but there are more things in England that haven't changed than most people are prepared to admit. Under the veneer of 'tradition' and 'ancient custom' there remain the superstitions that were once a religious faith. Isn't the central mystery of Christianity a human sacrifice? And, come to that, communion involves symbolic cannibalism!"

"What would your grandfather say if—?"

"If he heard me talking like this? He'd accuse me of plagiarism."

"You mean it was he who—?"

"He's a very broad-minded person. Hadn't you noticed? Why do you think I can spend so much time unchaperoned?"

Ernest looked a desperate question that he did not dare to formulate in words.

"I can read your thoughts from your face," Alice murmured. "Did he know about me and Gerald? I don't know. I never asked. I never shall. He very likely guessed, but he never behaved any differently towards me, and when the bad news came"—a quiver in her voice— "he was wonderful . . . Are you jealous of Gerald?"

"No. Sometimes I wonder why not. But I can't be. I find myself wishing that I'd met him. I think we'd have been friends."

"I think so, too." She squeezed his hand. "Now tell me what you couldn't say to anyone before."

"I'll try," he whispered. "I will try . . ."

And out it came, like pus from a boil: the remembered and the imaginary horrors, the images from a borderland between nightmare come alive and reality become nightmare; what it was like to realise you were obeying the orders of a crazy man, and had no escape from them; how it felt to choke one's guts up in a gale of poison gas, to watch one's comrades' very bodies rotting in the putrefaction of the sodden trenches, to shake a man's hand knowing it must be for the last time, for impersonal odds decreed that one or the other of you would be dead by sundown; taking aim at an enemy sniper spotted in a treetop or a belfry, as coolly as at a sitting rabbit, and not remembering until the flailing arms had vanished that the target was a human being like oneself . . .

And endlessly the howling-crashing of the shells, the chatter of machine guns, the racket, the hell-spawned racket that had silenced the very songbirds in the man-made desolation all around.

She sat very still, face pale in the dim light, without expression, never letting go his hand no matter how he cramped her fingers. When he finished he was crying, tears creeping down his cheeks like insects.

But he felt purged. And what she said, as she drew him close and kissed his tears away, was this:

"I met a woman from London who visited the Hall during the war. She called on us and boasted about her 'war work.' It consisted in handing out white feathers to men who weren't in uniform. I remember how I wished I could have kidnapped her and sent her to the Front with the VAD's."

He said, completely unexpectedly, "I love you."

"Yes. I know," was her reply. "I'm glad."

"You—knew?"

"Oh, my dear!" She let go his hand at last and leaned back, laughing aloud. "That's something that you've never learned to hide! The talk in the servants' hall has been of nothing else all week, and all around the village, I imagine. Your aunt, I hear, is absolutely scandalised, but since her setback *vis-à-vis* the bishop—"

"Stop, for pity's sake! You're making my head spin!"

At once she was contrite.

"Yes, of course. It was a dreadful thing to pour your heart out as you did, and I should have left you in peace immediately. But"—she was rising and withdrawing—"if anyone has bad dreams tonight, let it be me who wasn't there and wished she could have been, to help."

And she was gone, as instantly as the embodiment of . . .

Suddenly I know who She is, that Gaffer Tatton spoke of. The thought came unbidden. It seemed to echo from the waters that underlay the hill, and phrases from childhood crowded his mind: *the waters beneath the earth* . . .

Also he remembered Kali, garlanded with human skulls, and could not stop himself from shuddering.

"Well, Mr. Ernest!" Hiram Stoddard said. "What do you think of what we've made out of your sketches? Have we done them justice?"

Ernest stared at the three great boards on which his designs had been interpreted by pressing odds and ends, all natural, into white soft clay. Half his mind wanted to say that this wasn't what he had envisaged, this transformation into bones and leaves and cones and feathers—yet the other, perhaps the older and the wiser half, approved at once. How ingeniously, for example, in every case, they had caught the implication of another, older woman's half-turned back as she spurned the central figure, calling her a sinner justifiably due for punishment! Indeed, they had added something by taking something away. His detestation of his aunt had led him, as he abruptly recognised, to give too much emphasis to her effigy. Now, as he studied the pictures ranked before him, he noticed that the villagers had left her prominent in the first that would be blessed tomorrow, reduced her in the second, left her isolated in a corner of the third which would be set in Old Well Road . . .

Primitive it may be, he thought. *But many of the major French artists, and not a few of our own, have turned to the art not just of primitives but of savages in recent years. Maybe it's because of the savagery we so-called civilised nations have proved capable of . . . Yes, they're right. Their changes are correct.*

He said as much aloud, and those who had been anxiously standing by relaxed and set off to install the boards at their appointed places, ready for tomorrow morning's ceremony. Only at the last moment did it occur to him that he must take one final glance.

Checking in dismay as he called them back, they waited for his ultimate verdict.

But it was all right after all. He already knew that the resemblance between the main female figures and Alice had been efficiently disguised by its interpretation into whatever could be pressed into the clay, with pebbles for eyes and twigs and leaves for hair. For a moment, though, he had been afraid that he might have put too much of himself into the other major figure, who was Jesus . . .

"Don't you fret, sir," muttered Gaffer Tatton at his side, arriving heralded by the stump-stump of his stick. "You do understand. Didn't need me to tell 'ee."

And he was gone again before Ernest could reply, and the board-carriers, escorted by a gang of cheering children and Miss Hicks the teacher, seizing the chance for an open-air history lecture, were on their way to the wells.

He lay long awake that night, as though on the eve of his first one-man show, the kind of thing he had dreamed of when as a boy in India he had marvelled at the images contrived from *ghee* and leaves and petals to celebrate a Hindu festival. Why had he not noticed the connection sooner? Perhaps the iron curtain of the War had shut it out. But tonight he could sense a pulsing in the very landscape, as though an aboriginal power were heaving underground.

The waters beneath the earth . . .

Waking afraid in darkness, feeling as though the old and solid house were rocking back and forth like Noah's Ark, he groped for matches on the bedside table. There was an electric generator at the Hall, but the vicarage was still lit by lamps and candles. When he could see, he forced out faintly, "Alice!"

She was closing the door behind her. In a flimsy nightgown and barefoot, she stole across the floor as if she knew which boards might creak and could avoid them.

"I didn't mean to come," she said in a musing voice, as though puzzled at herself. "Not yet, at any rate. Not until tomorrow when it's over. But I couldn't stop myself. Do you feel something changing, Ernest?"

The match burned his fingers. By touch she prevented him from lighting another, and guided the box back to the table. He heard it rattle as it fell. Something else fell too, with a faint swishing sound, and she was beside him, arms and legs entwined with his.

"Do you feel something changing?" she insisted.

"I feel as though the whole world is changing!"

"Perhaps it is. But not for the worse. Not now, at any rate . . . Oh, my beloved! *Welcome back from hell!*"

Her hands were tugging at his pyjamas, and in a moment there was nothing but the taste and scent of love, and its pressure, and delight.

"If . . ." he said later, into darkness.

Understanding him at once, she interrupted. "So what? You're going to marry me, I hope."

"Of course. Even so—"

She closed his lips with a finger. "Remember this is a part of the world where the old ways endure. Did anyone you met here condemn Mrs. Gibson, for example?"

"Just my aunt."

"Did anybody tell you how soon after the wedding Mrs. Gibson bore her first?"

"Ah—no!"

"It must have been conceived last time the seventh year came round. They didn't marry until he got his call-up papers, though they were long engaged. The second followed one of his leaves, and you know about the third. They take it as natural. Some may think ill of us. I won't. Nor they."

"I won't think ill of you! Ever!" He sealed the promise with a frantic kiss.

"Even if I steal away now?"

"Alice darling—"

"I cannot be found here in the morning, can I? No matter how tolerant Grandfather is! No, you must let me go." She was suiting action to word, sliding out of bed, donning her nightgown again. "We have a lifetime before us. Let's not squander it in advance."

"You're right," he sighed. "I wish I had half your sense."

"And I wish I had half the presence of mind you showed when Mrs. Gibson's fire broke out. Between us"—she bent to bestow a final kiss on his forehead—"we should make quite a team . . . *What was that?*"

The air had been rent by a scream: faint, distant, but unbelievably shrill, like the cry of a damned soul.

Sitting up, Ernest snatched at a possibility.

"It sounded like a stuck pig! Mr. Ames has offered a pig for tomorrow—does the tradition include sacrificing it at midnight?"

"Not that I know of! But it'll have woken half the neighbourhood, whatever it is! I must fly!"

And she was gone.

For a moment Ernest was determined to ignore the noise. He wanted to lie back and recall the delicious proof of love that she had given him. It was no use, though. Within moments he heard noises from below. The rest of the household was awake. After what he had done on the night of the fire, it behooved him to rouse himself. He was already struggling back into his clothes when Tinkler tapped on the door.

"Coming!" he said resignedly.

And, when he descended to the hallway, found Alice there—attired again in jersey and trousers, and looking indescribably beautiful.

Not just looking. Being. Something has entered into that girl . . . Wrong. She was a girl. Now she's a woman.

And an extraordinary corollary followed.

I wonder whether anybody else will notice.

They did.

This time it wasn't he who wore the mantle of authority. She did. She quieted Mrs. Kail, sent her to tell her grandfather he could go back to sleep, and found a lantern and set forth with him down towards Old Well Road and the site of the third of the well-dressings.

Where others had already begun to gather, also bearing lanterns. Among them was Gaffer Tatton, fully dressed. Sensing Ernest's surprise, Alice murmured, "He lives in that cottage opposite. And alone. I don't suppose he takes his clothes off very often."

Ernest couldn't help smiling. That explained a lot!

But why was he so happy? Why was he blatantly holding his companion's hand as they joined the others? He couldn't work it out. He felt as though he were in the grip of a power beyond himself, and kept looking to Alice for guidance.

But she offered none, and none came from anyone else, until they had reached the bottom of the slope and were able to see what the rest of the people were staring at.

The well-dressing was unharmed. But, immediately before it, at the spot where Gaffer Tatton had told him grass was growing on leaf-mould that had accumulated over nothing stronger than tiles and mortar, there was a gaping hole.

And, lying on the ground nearby, there was a mallet.

Realisation slowly dawned. Ernest said faintly, "Is it . . . ?"

"We think so, sir." Hiram Stoddard emerged into the circle of light cast by the lanterns. "It were young Roger as tipped us off. Here, young feller, you're old enough to speak for yourself."

And Roger the coachman was thrust forward from the crowd.

"Well, sir," he began awkwardly, "since you left the Hall her ladyship has been acting stranger and stranger. In the middle of the night we heard her getting up. I was roused by May—that's her maid, sir, as sleeps in the room next to hers. She said the mistress had gone out, muttering to herself like." An enormous gulp. "She said she thought— excuse me, sir—she must have taken leave of her senses!"

"So?"

Ernest would have liked to be the one to say that. In fact it was Alice. Very calm, totally heedless of what the men around might think of her masculine attire.

"Well, sir . . ." Roger shifted uneasily from foot to foot. "As you know, sir, there's a mallet kept next to the dinner gong at the Hall. I saw it were gone. I couldn't think on anyone else as mighta taken it."

Ernest bent to pick up the mallet. He said, turning it over, "Yes, I recognise it. You think she set out to smash the well-dressings?"

Everyone relaxed, most noticeably Gaffer Tatton, who nudged those nearest to him in the ribs.

"It would fit," Alice said in a strained voice. "Only she didn't know how weak the cover was. Being so fat . . ."

"Ah!"—from Gaffer Tatton. "She'll do for two, she will."

The others pretended not to understand, but even Ernest got the point. At length:

"Weren't nothing anybody could do," Hiram declared, and there was a murmur of agreement.

Ernest glanced from face to face. He knew, in that moment, that this was what they'd hoped might happen. It would be no use arguing that if they had turned out sooner in response to the scream they might have saved his aunt's life. Anyway, why should they? He would not have wanted to . . .

Again he sensed the presence of a power beneath the ground. Here, in the lonely small hours of the night, he could clearly hear for the first time the rushing of the water far below.

No longer pure, of course.

"Bring hooks and ropes," he ordered gruffly. "We'll pull her up. And people who use the water from this well had best avoid it for the time being."

"We thought of that, sir," Hiram said. "Those who draw on it will let their taps run the rest of the night."

"Wash her away," said Gaffer Tatton with a gap-toothed smile, and plodded back across the road to home.

"Will you carry on with the well-dressing?" Ernest said, red-eyed at an early breakfast-table.

"Yes, of course."

"You don't think it's inappropriate in the circumstances?"

"My dear Mr. Peake—or may I now address you as Ernest, given the degree of affection that you display towards my granddaughter?"

He is a wise old owl, isn't he? And doesn't he look pleased?

"Of course," he said mechanically.

"Well, then, my dear Ernest: you don't think it inappropriate, do you?"

"Absolutely not!"

"Then we shall go ahead. In fact"—he produced a watch that reminded Ernest of Gaffer Tatton's—"it's time to leave."

Virtually the entire village had turned out for the procession, despite this being officially a working day. The vicar went at its head, attended by Roger the coachman bearing a stoup of holy water and a bundle of herbs bound to make a kind of brush, with which he asperged the decorations at each well before pronouncing a benediction. The church choir came next, singing a traditional hymn, and after there followed the villagers roughly in order of age, while the rear was brought up by the children from the school under Miss Hicks's stern direction, except for one boy and one girl who had been allotted the coveted duty of leading the way with branches of greenery.

Listening to the singing—quiet at first, then lusty—it occurred to Ernest that since his arrival he had never seen so many smiles at once.

During the blessing of the second well, he felt a shy tug at the hand with which he wasn't clasping Alice's. He glanced down to see a woman's face, drawn and lined under prematurely grey hair. It was Mrs. Gibson.

"Me and my littluns got a lot to thank 'ee for already," she whispered. "Now all on us folk got 'ee to thank for bringing back the well-dressing . . . God bless 'ee, Mr. Ernest!"

And she had withdrawn into the throng.

But across the group he caught the eye of Gaffer Tatton, and he was beaming as to say, "What did I tell 'ee?"

Then at last it was time to make for their final destination, the one in Old Well Road. The air was tense with expectation. The ceremony here proceeded exactly as before, with the same prayers and the same quotations about the Water of Life. But more was clearly expected, and of a sudden it came.

Abandoning any prepared text, the vicar surveyed his congregation and said abruptly, "Friends! For I trust after so many years of tribulation I may call you so!"

The smiles came back, in even greater number.

"There are some who have called it wrong, indeed evil, to keep up the tradition we have today renewed. I am not one of them."

Nor are we, was the silent response.

"We all know that our very lives are a miracle—that we are born, that we can think and reason, and that we can learn to praise our Creator: yes, that's a miracle!"

Almost, there was an outburst of applause. The Stoddard brothers frowned it down.

"For the food we eat, and the water we drink: should we not give thanks? And that the land yields bountifully, and our cattle and our other livestock? And, indeed, that we can leave children to follow in our footsteps when we, as must inevitably ensue, are called to join the company of the righteous . . . Met here today, we have acknowledged our indebtedness to the Maker of all things. Today in particular we have celebrated the gift of water. It behooves us all, and always, to remember it is one of many gifts, and the greatest of these is love. God bless you all!"

And he turned back to the well-dressing on which Ernest and all its makers had lavished so much care, and recited the Doxology at the top of his voice. Many of the listeners joined in.

Gaffer Tatton, though, was not among them. He had made for home, bent perhaps on the kind of errand that an old man's weak bladder might make urgent. Just as the vicar finished, however, he burst out once more from his cottage door.

"It's sweet!"

Every head turned.

"The water's sweet! Bain't no more taint to un! I drunk this water all me life, and 'spite o' her as went *she's* made it clean again!"

"He means," Alice began, whispering close to Ernest's ear, and he cut her short.

"I know. What he means is that no matter how awful she was, and how long she lay in the well, she didn't foul the water . . . When we get married, my love, would you mind if we did it twice?"

"How can that be?" She drew back to arm's length, studying him with her wide grey eyes.

"We'll do it once for me, the man, in the name of the Father and the Son. And we'll do it once for you, in the name of—*her*. How about it?"

"But no one knows her name!"

"Does it matter? We know she's there, don't we?"

She thought awhile, and eventually nodded.

"Yes, I've known for years, like Gaffer Tatton. I'm surprised you found out so quickly, but I'm terribly glad . . . Shall we live at the Hall?"

"Most of the time, I suppose. After all, I'm the heir. But I want to take you on honeymoon to India. Even if I can't promise a private view of Kali-worship."

Smiling, she pressed his hand. "I think I've seen enough of the wicked side of the female principle for the time being—" She broke off, aghast. "Ernest, this is terrible! She's scarcely cold, and here we are talking about a honeymoon! We ought to be planning her funeral!"

"Excuse me, Mr. Ernest."

They turned to find the Stoddard brothers at their side.

"Before we go, we'd just like to offer our congratulations and say we hope you'll both be very happy."

How in the world—?

Then he recalled what Alice had said about the talk in the servants' hall, and all around the village. He let his face relax into a grin.

"Thanks awfully! What time's the feast tonight? We'll see you there!"

Afterwards, when Mr. Ames's pig had been distributed in slices, special care being taken to deliver enough to Mrs. Gibson and her children, he said to Alice in the darkness of her room, "I don't think we need the second wedding after all."

"Hmm?"—nuzzling his neck with soft warm lips.

"As far as *she's* concerned we're married, aren't we?"

"Mm-hm. That's what surprised me when you mentioned it . . . Can we again?"

"I think so— Yes! Oh, *yes!*"

Later, though, just before, for the first time, they went to sleep in one another's arms, having agreed to stop worrying about scandal or offending old Mr. Pollock—or even Tinkler—he said musingly, "It's funny, though."

"What is?"

"How close a connection there is between what you see in India and what you find at home."

"But why?" She raised herself on one elbow, her breasts enchantingly visible in the faint light from the window. "Isn't it the same with science?"

"What?"

"You wouldn't expect science to stop working because it's a different country, would you?"

"No, of course not!"

"Well, then!" She lay down again. "Why not the same with religion? After all, we're all human."

"You mean—"

"What I mean," she said firmly, "is that whoever *she* is who guards the wells of Welstock, and brought you and me so splendidly together, she can't be anything else except another aspect of what you are, and I am, and everybody else. That goes for India too, and every countless world we find our way to in our dreams. Which is where, with my lord's permission, I propose to adjourn to. Good night."

He lay awake a while longer, pondering what she had said, and at last inquired, "How do you think the villagers will take to having people here with views like ours?"

"So long as we honour the mistress of the water," came the sleepy answer, "why in the world should they worry?"

Yes indeed. Why should they?

His doubts resolved, the new lord of the manor of Welstock dozed off contentedly beside his lady.

The Fellowship of the Dragon

Patricia A. McKillip

great cry rose throughout the land: Queen Celandine had lost her harper. She summoned north, south, east, west; we rode for days through mud and rain to meet, the five of us, at Trillium; from there we rode to Carnelaine. The world had come to her great court, for though we lived too far from her to hear her fabled harper play, we heard the rumor that at each full moon she gave him gloves of cloth of gold and filled his mouth with jewels. As we stood in the hall among her shining company, listening to her pleas for help, Justin, who is the riddler among us, whispered, "What is invisible but everywhere, swift as wind but has no feet, and has as many tongues that speak but never has a face?"

"Easy," I breathed. "Rumor."

"Rumor, that shy beast, says she valued his hands far more than his harping, and she filled his mouth with more than jewels."

I was hardly surprised. Celandine is as beautiful close as she is at a distance; she has been so for years, with the aid of a streak of sorcery she inherited through a bit of murkiness, an imprecise history on the distaff side, and she is not one to waste her gifts. She had married honorably, loved faithfully, raised her heirs well. When her husband died a decade ago, she mourned him with the good-hearted efficiency she had brought to marriage and throne. Her hair showed which way the wind was blowing, and the way that silver, ash and gold worked among the court was magical. But when we grew close enough to kneel before her, I saw that the harper was no idle indulgence, but had sung his way into her blood.

"You five," she said softly, "I trust more than all my court. I rely on you." Her eyes, green as her name, were grim; I saw the tiny lines of fear and temper beside her mouth. "There are some in this hall who—because I have not been entirely wise or tactful—would sooner see the harper dead than rescue him."

"Do you know where he is?"

She lowered her voice; I could scarcely hear her, though the jealous knights behind me must have stilled their hearts to catch her answer. "I looked in water, in crystal, in mirror: every image is the same. Black Tremptor has him."

"Oh, fine."

She bent to kiss me: we are cousins, though sometimes I have been more a wayward daughter, and more often, she a wayward mother. "Find him, Anne," she said. We five rose as one and left the court.

"What did she say?" Danica asked as we mounted. "Did she say Black Tremptor?"

"Sh!"

"That's a mountain," Fleur said.

"It's a bloody dragon," Danica said sharply, and I bellowed in a whisper, "Can you refrain from announcing our destination to the entire world?"

Danica wheeled her mount crossly; peacocks, with more haste than grace, swept their fine trains out of her way. Justin looked intrigued by the problem. Christabel, who was nursing a cold, said stoically, "Could be worse." What could be worse than being reduced to a cinder by an irritated dragon, she didn't mention. Fleur, who loved good harping, was moved.

"Then we must hurry. Poor man." She pulled herself up, cantered after Danica. Riding more sedately through the crowded yard, we found them outside the gate, gazing east and west across the grey, billowing sky as if it had streamed out of a dragon's nostrils.

"Which way?" Fleur asked. Justin, who knew such things, pointed. Christabel blew her nose. We rode.

Of course we circled back through the city and lost the knights who had been following us. We watched them through a tavern window as they galloped purposefully down the wrong crossroad. Danica, whose moods swung between sun and shadow like an autumn day, was being enchanted by Fleur's description of the object of our quest.

"He is a magnificent harper, and we should spare no pains to rescue him, for there is no one like him in all the world, and Queen Celandine might reward us with gold and honor, but he will reward us forever in a song."

Christabel waved the fumes of hot spiced wine at her nose. "Does anyone know this harper's name?"

"Kestral," I said. "Kestral Hunt. He came to court a year ago, at old Thurlow's death."

"And where," Christabel asked sensibly, "is Black Tremptor?"

We all looked at Justin, who for once looked uncomfortable. "North," she said. She is a slender, dark-haired, quiet-voiced woman with eyes like the storm outside. She could lay out facts like an open road, or mortar them into a brick wall. Which she was building for us now, I wasn't sure.

"Justin?"

"Well, north," she said vaguely, as if that alone explained itself. "It's fey, beyond the border. Odd things happen. We must be watchful."

We were silent. The tavern keeper came with our supper. Danica, pouring wine the same pale honey as her hair, looked thoughtful at the warning instead of cross. "What kinds of things?"

"Evidently harpers are stolen by dragons," I said. "Dragons with some taste in music."

"Black Tremptor is not musical," Justin said simply. "But like that, yes. There are so many tales, who knows which of them might be true? And we barely know the harper any better than the northlands."

"His name," I said, "and that he plays well."

"He plays wonderfully," Fleur breathed. "So they say."

"And he caught the queen's eye," Christabel said, biting into a chicken leg. "So he might look passable. Though with good musicians, that hardly matters."

"And he went north," Justin pointed out. "For what?"

"To find a song," Fleur suggested; it seemed, as gifted as he was, not unlikely.

"Or a harp," I guessed. "A magical harp."

Justin nodded. "Guarded by a powerful dragon. It's possible. Such things happen, north."

Fleur pushed her dish aside, sank tableward onto her fists. She is straw-thin, with a blacksmith's appetite; love, I could tell, for this fantasy, made her ignore the last of her parsnips. She has pale, curly hair like a sheep, and a wonderful, caressing voice; her eyes are small, her nose big, her teeth crooked, but her passionate, musical voice has proved Christabel right more times than was good for Fleur's husband to know. How robust, practical Christabel, who scarcely seemed to notice men or music, understood such things, I wasn't sure.

"So," I said. "North."

And then we strayed into the country called "Remember-when," for we had known one another as children in the court at Carnelaine, and then as members of the queen's company, riding ideals headlong into trouble, and now, as long and trusted friends. We got to bed late, enchanted by our memories, and out of bed far too early, wondering obviously why we had left hearth and home, husband, child, cat and goosedown bed for one another's surly company. Christabel sniffed, Danica snapped, Fleur babbled, I was terse. As always, only Justin was bearable.

We rode north.

The farther we travelled, the wilder the country grew. We moved quickly, slept under trees or in obscure inns, for five armed women riding together are easily remembered, and knights dangerous to the harper as well as solicitous of the queen would have known to track us. Slowly the great, dark crags bordering the queen's marches came closer and closer to meet us, until we reached, one sunny afternoon, their shadow.

"Now what?" Danica asked fretfully. "Do we fly over that?" They were huge, barren thrusts of stone pushing high out of forests like bone out of skin. She looked at Justin; we all did. There was a peculiar expression on her face, as if she recognized something she had only seen before in dreams.

"There will be a road," she said softly. We were in thick forest; old trees marched in front of us, beside us, flanked us. Not even they had found a way to climb the peaks.

"Where, Justin?" I asked.

"We must wait until sunset."

We found a clearing, where the road we followed abruptly turned to amble west along a stream. Christabel and Danica went hunting. Fleur checked our supplies and mended a tear in her cloak. I curried the horses. Justin, who had gone to forage, came back with mushrooms, nuts and a few wild apples. She found another brush and helped me.

"Is it far now?" I asked, worried about finding supplies in the wilderness, about the horses, about Christabel's stubbornly lingering cold, even, a little, about the harper. Justin picked a burr out of her mount's mane. A line ran across her smooth brow.

"Not far beyond those peaks," she answered. "It's just that—"

"Just what?"

"We must be so careful."

"We're always careful. Christabel can put an arrow into anything that moves, Danica can—"

"I don't mean that. I mean: the world shows a different face beyond those peaks." I looked at her puzzledly; she shook her head, gazing at the mountains, somehow wary and entranced at once. "Sometimes real, sometimes unreal—"

"The harper is real, the dragon is real," I said briskly. "And we are real. If I can remember that, we'll be fine."

She touched my shoulder, smiling. "I think you're right, Anne. It's your prosaic turn of mind that will bring us all home again."

But she was wrong.

The sun, setting behind a bank of sullen clouds, left a message: a final shaft of light hit what looked like solid stone ahead of us and parted it. We saw a faint, white road that cut out of the trees and into the base of two great crags: the light seemed to ease one wall of stone aside, like a gate. Then the light faded, and we were left staring at the solid wall, memorizing the landscape.

"It's a woman's profile," Fleur said. "The road runs beneath the bridge of her nose."

"It's a one-eared cat," Christabel suggested.

"The road is west of the higher crag," Danica said impatiently. "We should simply ride toward that."

"The mountains will change and change again before we reach it," I said. "The road comes out of that widow's peak of trees. It's the highest point of the forest. We only need to follow the edge of the trees."

"The widow," Danica murmured, "is upside-down."

I shrugged. "The harper found his way. It can't be that difficult."

"Perhaps," Fleur suggested, "he followed a magical path."

"He parted stone with his harping," Christabel said stuffily. "If he's that clever, he can play his way out of the dragon's mouth, and we can all turn around and go sleep in our beds."

"Oh, Christabel," Fleur mourned, her voice like a sweet flute. "Sit down. I'll make you herb tea with wild honey in it; you'll sleep on clouds tonight."

We all had herb tea, with brandy and the honey Fleur had found, but only Fleur slept through the thunderstorm. We gathered ourselves wetly at dawn, slogged through endless dripping forest, until suddenly there were no more trees, there was no more rain, only the unexpected sun illumining a bone-white road into the great upsweep of stone ahead of us.

We rode beyond the land we knew.

I don't know where we slept that first night: wherever we fell off our horses, I think. In the morning we saw Black Tremptor's mountain, a dragon's palace of cliffs and jagged columns and sheer walls ascending into cloud. As we rode down the slope toward it, the cloud wrapped itself down around the mountain, hid it. The road, wanting nothing to do with dragons, turned at the edge of the forest and ran off the wrong direction. We pushed into trees. The forest on that side was very old, the trees so high, their green boughs so thick, we could barely see the sky, let alone the dragon's lair. But I have a strong sense of direction, of where the sun rises and sets, that kept us from straying. The place was soundless. Fleur and Christabel kept arrows ready for bird or deer, but we saw nothing on four legs or two: only spiders, looking old as the forest, weaving webs as huge and intricate as tapestry in the trees.

"It's so still," Fleur breathed. "As if it is waiting for music."

Christabel turned a bleary eye at her and sniffed. But Fleur was right: the stillness did seem magical, an intention out of someone's head. As we listened, the rain began again. We heard it patter from bough to bough a long time before it reached us.

Night fell the same way: sliding slowly down from the invisible sky, catching us without fresh kill, in the rain without a fire. Silent, we rode until we could barely see. We stopped finally, while we could still imagine one another's faces.

"The harper made it through," Danica said softly; what Celandine's troublesome, faceless lover could do, so could we.

"There's herbs and honey and more brandy," Christabel said. Fleur, who suffered most from hunger, having a hummingbird's energy, said nothing. Justin lifted her head sharply.

"I smell smoke."

I saw the light then: two square eyes and one round among the distant trees. I sighed with relief and felt no pity for whoever in that quiet cottage was about to find us on the doorstep.

But the lady of the cottage did not seem discomfitted to see five armed, dripping, hungry travellers wanting to invade her house.

"Come in," she said. "Come in." As we filed through the door, I saw all the birds and animals we had missed in the forest circle the room around us: stag and boar and owl, red deer, hare and mourning dove. I blinked, and they were motionless: things of thread and paint and wood, embroidered onto curtains, carved into the backs of chairs, painted on the rafters. Before I could speak, smells assaulted us, and I felt Fleur stagger against me.

"You poor children." Old as we were, she was old enough to say that. "Wet and weary and hungry." She was a bird-like soul herself: a bit of magpie in her curious eyes, a bit of hawk's beak in her nose. Her hair looked fine and white as spider web, her knuckles like swollen tree boles. Her voice was kindly, and so was her warm hearth, and the smells coming out of her kitchen. Even her skirt was hemmed with birds. "Sit down. I've been baking bread, and there's a hot meat pie almost done in the oven." She turned, to give something simmering in a pot over the fire a stir. "Where are you from and where are you bound?"

"We are from the court of Queen Celandine," I said. "We have come searching for her harper. Did he pass this way?"

"Ah," she said, her face brightening. "A tall man with golden hair and a voice to match his harping?"

"Sounds like," Christabel said.

"He played for me, such lovely songs. He said he had to find a certain harp. He ate nothing and was gone before sunrise." She gave the pot another stir. "Is he lost?"

"Black Tremptor has him."

"Oh, terrible." She shook her head. "He is fortunate to have such good friends to rescue him."

"He is the queen's good friend," I said, barely listening to myself as the smell from the pot curled into me, "and we are hers. What is that you are cooking?"

"Just a little something for my bird."

"You found a bird?" Fleur said faintly, trying to be sociable. "We saw none . . . Whatever do you feed it? It smells good enough to eat."

"Oh, no, you must not touch it; it is only bird-fare. I have delicacies for you."

"What kind of bird is it?" Justin asked. The woman tapped the spoon on the edge of the pot, laid it across the rim.

"Oh, just a little thing. A little, hungry thing I found. You're right: the forest has few birds. That's why I sew and paint my birds and animals, to give me company. There's wine," she added. "I'll get it for you."

She left. Danica paced; Christabel sat close to the fire, indifferent to the smell of the pot bubbling under her stuffy nose. Justin had picked up a small wooden boar and was examining it idly. Fleur drifted, pale as cloud; I kept an eye on her to see she did not topple into the fire. The old woman had trouble, it seemed, finding cups.

"How strange," Justin breathed. "This looks so real, every tiny bristle."

Fleur had wandered to the hearth to stare down into the pot. I heard it bubble fatly. She gave one pleading glance toward the kitchen, but still there was nothing to eat but promises. She had the spoon in her hand suddenly, I thought to stir.

"It must be a very strange bird to eat mushrooms," she commented. "And what looks like—" Justin put the boar down so sharply I jumped, but Fleur lifted the spoon to her lips. "Lamb," she said happily. And then she vanished: there was only a frantic lark fluttering among the rafters, sending plea after lovely plea for freedom.

The woman reappeared. "My bird," she cried. "My pretty." I was on my feet with my sword drawn before I could even close my mouth. I swung, but the old witch didn't linger to do battle. A hawk caught the lark in its claws; the door swung open, and both birds disappeared into the night.

We ran into the dark, stunned and horrified. The door slammed shut behind us like a mouth. The fire dwindled into two red flames that stared like eyes out of the darkened windows. They gave no light; we could see nothing.

"That bloody web-haired old spider," Danica said furiously. "That horrible, putrid witch." I heard a thump as she hit a tree; she cursed painfully. Someone hammered with solid, methodical blows at the door and windows; I guessed Christabel was laying siege. But nothing gave. She groaned with frustration. I felt a touch and raised my sword; Justin said sharply, "It's me." She put her hand on my shoulder; I felt myself tremble.

"Now what?" I said tersely. I could barely speak; I only wanted action, but we were blind and bumbling in the dark.

"I think she doesn't kill them," Justin said. "She changes them. Listen to me. She'll bring Fleur back into her house eventually. We'll find someone to tell us how to free her from the spell. Someone in this wilderness of magic should know. And not everyone is cruel."

"We'll stay here until the witch returns."

"I doubt she'll return until we're gone. And even if we find some way to kill her, we may be left with an embroidered Fleur."

"We'll stay."

"Anne," she said, and I slumped to the ground, wanting to curse, to weep, wanting at the very least to tear the clinging cobweb dark away from my eyes.

"Poor Fleur," I whispered. "She was only hungry . . . Harper or no, we rescue her when we learn how. She comes first."

"Yes," she agreed at that, and added thoughtfully, "The harper eluded the witch, it seems, though not the dragon."

"How could he have known?" I asked bitterly. "By what magic?"

"Maybe he had met the witch first in a song."

Morning found us littered across tree roots like the remains of some lost battle. At least we could see again. The house had flown itself away; only a couple of fiery feathers remained. We rose wordlessly, feeling the empty place where Fleur had been, listening for her morning chatter. We fed the horses, ate stone-hard bread with honey, and had a swallow of brandy apiece. Then we left Fleur behind and rode.

The great forest finally thinned, turned to golden oak, which parted now and then around broad meadows where we saw the sky again, and the high dark peak. We passed through a village, a mushroom patch of a place, neither friendly nor surly, nor overly curious. We found an inn, and some supplies, and, beyond the village, a road to the dragon's mountain that had been cleared, we were told, before the mountain had become the dragon's lair. Yes, we were also told, a harper had passed through . . . He seemed to have left little impression on the villagers, but they were a hard-headed lot, living under the dragon's shadow. He, too, had asked directions, as well as questions about Black Tremptor, and certain tales of gold and magic harps and other bits of country lore. But no one else had taken that road for decades, leading, as it did, into the dragon's mouth.

We took it. The mountain grew clearer, looming high above the trees. We watched for dragon wings, dragon fire, but if Black Tremptor flew, it was not by day. The rain had cleared; a scent like dying roses and aged sunlit wood seemed to blow across our path. We camped on one of the broad, grassy clearings where we watched the full moon rise, turn the meadow milky, and etch the dragon's lair against the stars.

But for Fleur, the night seemed magical. We talked of her, and then of home; we talked of her, and then of court gossip; we talked of her, and of the harper, and what might have lured him away from Celandine into a dragon's claw. And as we spoke of him, it seemed his music fell around us from the stars, and that the moonlight in the oak wood had turned to gold.

"Sh!" Christabel said sharply, and, drowsy, we quieted to listen. Danica yawned.

"It's just harping." She had an indifferent ear: Fleur was more persuasive about the harper's harping than his harping would have been. "Just a harping from the woods."

"Someone's singing," Christabel said. I raised my brows, feeling that in the untroubled, sweetly scented night, anything might happen.

"Is it our missing Kestral?"

"Singing in a tree?" Danica guessed. Christabel sat straight.

"Be quiet," she said sharply. Justin, lying on her stomach, tossing twigs into the fire, glanced at her surprisedly. Danica and I only laughed, at Christabel in a temper.

"You have no hearts," she said, blowing her nose fiercely. "It's so beautiful and all you can do is gabble."

"All right," Justin said soothingly. "We'll listen." But, moonstruck, Danica and I could not keep still. We told raucous tales of old loves while Christabel strained to hear, and Justin watched her curiously. She seemed oddly moved, did Christabel; feverish, I thought, from all the rain.

A man rode out of the trees into the moonlight at the edge of the meadow. He had milky hair, broad shoulders; a gold mantle fanned across his horse's back. The crown above his shadowed face was odd: a circle of uneven gold spikes, like antlers. He was unarmed; he played the harp.

"Not our harper," Danica commented. "Unless the dragon turned his hair white."

"He's a king," I said. "Not ours." For a moment, just a moment, I heard his playing, and knew it could have parted water, made birds speak. I caught my breath; tears swelled behind my eyes. Then Danica said something and I laughed.

Christabel stood up. Her face was unfamiliar in the moonlight. She took off her boots, unbraided her hair, let it fall loosely down her back; all this while we only watched and laughed and glanced now and then, indifferently, at the waiting woodland harper.

"You're hopeless boors," Christabel said, sniffing. "I'm going to speak to him, ask him to come and sit with us."

"Go on then," Danica said, chewing a grass blade. "Maybe we can take him home to Celandine instead." I rolled over in helpless laughter. When I wiped my eyes, I saw Christabel walking barefoot across the meadow to the harper.

Justin stood up. A little, nagging wind blew through my thoughts. I stood beside her, still laughing a little, yet poised to hold her if she stepped out of the circle of our firelight. She watched Christabel. Danica watched the fire dreamily, smiling. Christabel stood before the harper. He took his hand from his strings and held it out to her.

In the sudden silence, Justin shouted, "Christabel!"

All the golden light in the world frayed away. A dragon's wing of cloud brushed the moon; night washed toward Christabel, as she took his hand and mounted; I saw all her lovely, red-gold hair flowing freely in the last of the light. And then freckled, stolid, courageous, snuffling Christabel caught the harper-king's shoulders and they rode down the fading path of light into a world beyond the night.

We searched for her until dawn.

At sunrise, we stared at one another, haggard, mute. The great oak had swallowed Christabel; she had disappeared into a harper's song.

"We could go to the village for help," Danica said wearily.

"Their eyes are no better than ours," I said.

"The queen's harper passed through here unharmed," Justin mused. "Perhaps he knows something about the country of the woodland king."

"I hope he is worth all this," Danica muttered savagely.

"No man is," Justin said simply. "But all this will be worth nothing if Black Tremptor kills him before we find him. He may be able to lead us safely out of the northlands, if nothing else.

"I will not leave Fleur and Christabel behind," I said sharply. "I will not. You may take the harper back to Celandine. I stay here until I find them."

Justin looked at me; her eyes were reddened with sleeplessness, but they saw as clearly as ever into the mess we had made. "We will not leave you, Anne," she said. "If he cannot help us, he must find his own way back. But if he can help us, we must abandon Christabel now to rescue him."

"Then let's do it," I said shortly and turned my face away from the oak. A little wind shivered like laughter through their golden leaves.

We rode long and hard. The road plunged back into forest, up low foothills, brought us to the flank of the great dark mountain. We pulled up in its shadow. The dragon's eyrie shifted under the eye; stone pillars opened into passages, their granite walls split and hollowed like honeycombs, like some palace of winds, open at every angle yet with every passage leading into shadow, into the hidden dragon's heart.

"In there?" Danica asked. There was no fear in her voice, just her usual impatience to get things done. "Do we knock, or just walk in?" A wind roared through the stones then, bending trees as it blasted at us. I heard stones thrum like harp-strings; I heard the dragon's voice. We turned our mounts, flattened ourselves against them, while the wild wind rode over us. Recovering, Danica asked more quietly, "Do we go in together?"

"Yes," I said, and then, "No. I'll go first."

"Don't be daft, Anne," Danica said crossly. "If we all go together at least we'll know where we all are."

"And fools we will look, too," I said grimly, "caught along with the harper, waiting for Celandine's knights to rescue us as well." I turned to Justin. "Is there some secret, some riddle for surviving dragons?"

She shook her head helplessly. "It depends on the dragon. I know nothing about Black Tremptor, except that he most likely has not kept the harper for his harping."

"Two will go," I said. "And one wait."

They did not argue; there seemed no foolproof way, except for none of us to go. We tossed coins: two peacocks and one Celandine. Justin, who got the queen, did not look happy, but the coins were adamant. Danica and I left her standing with our horses, shielded within green boughs, watching us. We climbed the bald slope quietly, trying not to scatter stones. We had to watch our feet, pick a careful path to keep from sliding. Danica, staring groundward, stopped suddenly ahead of me to pick up something.

"Look," she breathed. I did, expecting a broken harp string, or an ivory button with Celandine's profile on it.

It was an emerald as big as my thumbnail, shaped and faceted. I stared at it a moment. Then I said, "Dragon-treasure. We came to find a harper."

"But Anne—there's another—" She scrabbled across loose stone to retrieve it. "Topaz. And over there a sapphire—"

"Danica," I pleaded. "You can carry home the entire mountain after you've dispatched the dragon."

"I'm coming," she said breathlessly, but she had scuttled crab-wise across the slope toward yet another gleam. "Just one more. They're so beautiful, and just lying here free as rain for anyone to take."

"Danica! They'll be as free when we climb back down."

"I'm coming."

I turned, in resignation to her sudden magpie urge. "I'm going up."

"Just a moment, don't go alone. Oh, Anne, look there, it's a diamond. I've never seen such fire."

I held my breath, gave her that one moment. It had been such a long, hard journey I found it impossible to deny her an unexpected pleasure. She knelt, groped along the side of a boulder for a shining as pure as water in the sunlight. "I'm coming," she assured me, her back to me. "I'm coming."

And then the boulder lifted itself up off the ground. Something forked and nubbled like a tree root, whispering harshly to itself, caught her by her hand and by her honey hair and pulled her down into its hole. The boulder dropped ponderously, earth shifted close around its sides as if it had never moved.

I stared, stunned. I don't remember crossing the slope, only beating on the boulder with my hands and then my sword hilt, crying furiously at it, until all the broken shards underfoot undulated and swept me in a dry, rattling, bruising wave back down the slope into the trees.

Justin ran to help me. I was torn, bleeding, cursing, crying; I took a while to become coherent. "Of all the stupid, feeble tricks to fall for! A trail of jewels! They're probably not even real, and Danica got herself trapped under a mountain for a pocketful of coal or dragon few-mets—"

"She won't be trapped quietly," Justin said. Her face was waxen. "What took her?"

"A little crooked something—an imp, a mountain troll—Justin, she's down there without us in a darkness full of whispering things—I can't believe we were so stupid!"

"Anne, calm down, we'll find her."

"I can't calm down!" I seized her shoulders, shook her. "Don't you disappear and leave me searching for you, too—"

"I won't, I promise. Anne, listen." She smoothed my hair with both her hands back from my face. "Listen to me. We'll find her. We'll find Christabel and Fleur, we will not leave this land until—"

"How?" I shouted. "How? Justin, she's under solid rock!"

"There are ways. There are always ways. This land riddles constantly, but all the riddles have answers. Fleur will turn from a bird into a woman, we will find a path for Christabel out of the wood-king's country, we will rescue Danica from the mountain imps. There are ways to do these things, we only have to find them."

"How?" I cried again, for it seemed the farther we travelled in that land, the more trouble we got into. "Every time we turn around one of us disappears! You'll go next—"

"I will not, I promise—"

"Or I will."

"I know a few riddles," someone said. "Perhaps I can help."

We broke apart, as startled as if a tree had spoken: perhaps one had, in this exasperating land. But it was a woman. She wore a black cloak with a silver edging; her ivory hair and iris eyes and her grave, calm face within the hood were very beautiful. She carried an odd staff of gnarled black wood inset with a jewel the same pale violet as her eyes. She spoke gently, unsurprised by us; perhaps nothing in this place surprised her anymore. She added, at our silence, "My name is Yrecros. You are in great danger from the dragon; you must know that."

"We have come to rescue a harper," I said bitterly. "We were five, when we crossed into this land."

"Ah."

"Do you know this dragon?"

She did not answer immediately; beside me, Justin was oddly still. The staff shifted; the jewel glanced here and there, like an eye. The woman whose name was Yrecros said finally, "You may ask me anything."

"I just did," I said bewilderedly. Justin's hand closed on my arm; I looked at her. Her face was very pale; her eyes held a strange, intense light I recognized: she had scented something intangible and was in pursuit. At such times she was impossible.

"Yrecros," she said softly. "My name is Nitsuj."

The woman smiled.

"What are you doing?" I said between my teeth.

"It's a game," Justin breathed. "Question for answer. She'll tell us all we need to know."

"Why must it be a game?" I protested. She and the woman were gazing at one another, improbable fighters about to engage in a delicate battle of wits. They seemed absorbed in one another, curious, stone-deaf. I raised my voice. "Justin!"

"You'll want the harper, I suppose," the woman said. I worked out her name then and closed my eyes.

Justin nodded. "It's what we came for. And if I lose?"

"I want you," the woman said simply, "for my apprentice." She smiled again, without malice or menace. "For seven years."

My breath caught. "No." I could barely speak. I seized Justin's arm, shook her. "Justin. Justin, please!" For just a moment I had, if not her eyes, her attention.

"It's all right, Anne," she said softly. "We'll get the harper without a battle, and rescue Fleur and Christabel and Danica as well."

"Justin!" I shouted. Above us all the pillars and cornices of stone echoed her name; great, barbed-winged birds wheeled out of the trees. But unlike bird and stone, Justin did not hear.

"You are a guest in this land," the woman said graciously. "You may ask first."

"Where is the road to the country of the woodland king?"

"The white stag in the oak forest follows the road to the land of the harper king," Yrecros answered, "if you follow from morning to night, without weapons and without rest. What is the Song of Ducirc, and on what instrument was it first played?"

"The Song of Ducirc was the last song of a murdered poet to his love, and it was played to his lady in her high tower on an instrument of feathers, as all the birds in the forest who heard it sang her his lament," Justin said promptly. I breathed a little then; she had been telling us such things all her life. "What traps the witch in the border woods in her true shape, and how can her power be taken?"

"The border witch may be trapped by a cage of iron; her staff of power is the spoon with which she stirs her magic. What begins with fire and ends with fire and is black and white between?"

"Night," Justin said. Even I knew that one. The woman's face held, for a moment, the waning moon's smile. "Where is the path to the roots of this mountain, and what do those who dwell there fear most?"

"The path is fire, which will open their stones, and what they fear most is light. What is always coming yet never here, has a name but does not exist, is longer than day but shorter than day?"

Justin paused a blink. "Tomorrow," she said, and added, "in autumn." The woman smiled her lovely smile. I loosed breath noiselessly. "What will protect us from the dragon?"

The woman studied Justin, as if she were answering some private riddle of her own. "Courtesy," she said simply. "Where is Black Tremptor's true name hidden?"

Justin was silent; I felt her thoughts flutter like a bird seeking a perch. The silence lengthened; an icy finger slid along my bones.

"I do not know," Justin said at last, and the woman answered, "The dragon's name is hidden within a riddle."

Justin read my thoughts; her hand clamped on my wrist. "Don't fight," she breathed.

"That's not—"

"The answer's fair."

The woman's brows knit thoughtfully. "Is there anything else you need to know?" She put her staff lightly on Justin's shoulder, turned the jewel toward her pale face. The jewel burned a sudden flare of amethyst, as if in recognition. "My name is Sorcery and that is the path I follow. You will come with me for seven years. After that, you may choose to stay."

"Tell me," I pleaded desperately, "how to rescue her. You have told me everything else."

The woman shook her head, smiling her brief moon-smile. Justin looked at me finally; I saw the answer in her eyes.

I stood mute, watching her walk away from me, tears pushing into my eyes, unable to plead or curse because there had been a game within a game, and only I had lost. Justin glanced back at me once, but she did not really see me, she only saw the path she had walked toward all her life.

I turned finally to face the dragon.

I climbed the slope again alone. No jewels caught my eye, no voice whispered my name. Not even the dragon greeted me. As I wandered through columns and caverns and hallways of stone, I heard only the wind moaning through the great bones of the mountain. I went deeper into stone. The passageways glowed butterfly colors with secretions from the dragon's body. Here and there I saw a scale flaked off by stone; some flickered blue-green-black, others the colors of fire. Once I saw a chip of claw, hard as horn, longer than my hand. Sometimes I smelled sulphur, sometimes smoke, mostly wind smelling of the stone it scoured endlessly.

I heard harping.

I found the harper finally, sitting ankle-deep in jewels and gold, in a shadowy cavern, plucking wearily at his harp with one hand. His other hand was cuffed and chained with gold to a golden rivet in the cavern wall. He stared, speechless, when he saw me. He was, as rumored, tall and golden-haired, also unwashed, unkempt and sour from captivity. Even so, it was plain to see why Celandine wanted him back.

"Who are you?" he breathed, as I trampled treasure to get to him.

"I am Celandine's cousin Anne. She sent her court to rescue you."

"It took you long enough," he grumbled, and added, "You couldn't have come this far alone."

"You did," I said tersely, examining the chain that held him. Even Fleur would have had it out of the wall in a minute. "It's gold, malleable. Why didn't you—"

"I tried," he said, and showed me his torn hands. "It's dragon magic." He jerked the chain fretfully from my hold. "Don't bother trying. The key's over near that wall." He looked behind me, bewilderedly, for my imaginary companions. "Are you alone? She didn't send her knights to fight this monster?"

"She didn't trust them to remember who they were supposed to kill," I said succinctly. He was silent, while I crossed the room to rummage among pins and cups and necklaces for the key. I added, "I didn't ride from Carnelaine alone. I lost four companions in this land as we tracked you."

"Lost?" For a moment, his voice held something besides his own misery. "Dead?"

"I think not."

"How did you lose them?"

"One was lost to the witch in the wood."

"Was she a witch?" he said, astonished. "I played for her, but she never offered me anything to eat, hungry as I was. I could smell food but she only said that it was burned and unfit for company."

"And one," I said, sifting through coins and wondering at the witch's taste, "to the harper-king in the wood."

"You saw him?" he breathed. "I played all night, hoping to hear his fabled harping, but he never answered with a note."

"Maybe you never stopped to listen," I said, in growing despair over the blind way he blundered through the land. "And one to the imps under the mountain."

"What imps?"

"And last," I said tightly, "in a riddle-game to the sorceress with the jewelled staff. You were to be the prize."

He shifted, chain and coins rattling. "She only told me where to find what I was searching for, she didn't warn me of the dangers. She could have helped me! She never said she was a sorceress."

"Did she tell you her name?"

"I don't remember—what difference does it make? Hurry with the key before the dragon smells you here. It would have been so much easier for me if your companion had not lost the riddle-game."

I paused in my searching to gaze at him. "Yes," I said finally, "and it would have been easier than that for all of us if you had never come here. Why did you?"

He pointed. "I came for that."

"That" was a harp of bone. Its strings glistened with the same elusive, shimmering colors that stained the passageways. A golden key lay next to it. I am as musical as the next, no more, but when I saw those strange, glowing strings I was filled with wonder at what music they might make and I paused, before I touched the key, to pluck a note.

It seemed the mountain hummed.

"No!" the harper cried, heaving to his feet in a tide of gold. Wind sucked out of the cave, as at the draw of some gigantic wing. "You stupid, blundering— How do you think I got caught? Throw me the key! Quickly!"

I weighed the key in my hand, prickling at his rudeness. But he was, after all, what I had promised Celandine to find, and I imagined that washed and fed and in the queen's hands, he would assert his charms again. I tossed the key; it fell a little short of his outstretched hand.

"Fool!" he snapped. "You are as clumsy as the queen."

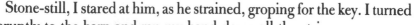

Stone-still, I stared at him, as he strained, groping for the key. I turned abruptly to the harp and ran my hand down all the strings.

What travelled down the passages to find us shed smoke and fire and broken stone behind it. The harper groaned and hid behind his arms. Smoke cleared; great eyes like moons of fire gazed at us near the high ceiling. A single claw as long as my shin dropped within an inch of my foot. Courtesy, I thought frantically. Courtesy, she said. It was like offering idle chatter to the sun. Before I could speak, the harper cried,

"She played it! She came in here searching for it, too, though I tried to stop her—"

Heat whuffed at me; I felt the gold I wore burn my neck. I said, feeling scorched within as well, "I ask your pardon if I have offended you. I came, at my queen's request, to rescue her harper. It seems you do not care for harping. If it pleases you, I will take what must be an annoyance out of your house." I paused. The great eyes sank a little toward me. I added, for such things seemed important in this land, "My name is Anne."

"Anne," the smoke whispered. I heard the harper jerk in his chain. The claw retreated slightly; the immense flat lizard's head lowered, its fiery scales charred dark with smoke, tiny sparks of fire winking between its teeth. "What is his name?"

"Kestral," the harper said quickly. "Kestral Hunt."

"You are right," the hot breath sighed. "He is an annoyance. Are you sure you want him back?"

"No," I said, my eyes blurring in wonder and relief that I had finally found, in this dangerous land, something I did not need to fear. "He is extremely rude, ungrateful and insensitive. I imagine that my queen loves him for his hair or for his harper's hands; she must not listen to him speak. So I had better take him. I am sorry that he snuck into your house and tried to steal from you."

"It is a harp made of dragon bone and sinew," the dragon said. "It is why I dislike harpers, who make such things and then sing songs of their great cleverness. As this one would have." Its jaws yawned; a tongue of fire shot out, melted gold beside the harper's hand. He scuttled against the wall.

"I beg your pardon," he said hastily. A dark curved dragon's smile hung in the fading smoke; it snorted heat.

"Perhaps I will keep you and make a harp of your bones."

"It would be miserably out of tune," I commented. "Is there something I can do for you in exchange for the harper's freedom?"

An eye dropped close, moon-round, shadows of color constantly disappearing through it. "Tell me my name," the dragon whispered. Slowly I realized it was not a challenge but a plea. "A woman took my name from me long ago, in a riddle-game. I have been trying to remember it for years."

"Yrecros?" I breathed. So did the dragon, nearly singeing my hair.

"You know her."

"She took something from me: my dearest friend. Of you she said: the dragon's name is hidden within a riddle."

"Where is she?"

"Walking paths of sorcery in this land."

Claws flexed across the stones, smooth and beetle-black. "I used to know a little sorcery. Enough to walk as man. Will you help me find my name?"

"Will you help me find my friends?" I pleaded in return. "I lost four, searching for this unbearable harper. One or two may not want my help, but I will never know until I see them."

"Let me think . . ." the dragon said. Smoke billowed around me suddenly, acrid, ash-white. I swallowed smoke, coughed it out. When my stinging eyes could see again, a gold-haired harper stood in front of me. He had the dragon's eyes.

I drew in smoke again, astonished. Through my noise, I could hear Kestral behind me, tugging at his chain and shouting.

"What of me?" he cried furiously. "You were sent to rescue me! What will you tell Celandine? That you found her harper and brought the dragon home instead?" His own face gazed back at him, drained the voice out of him a moment. He tugged at the chain frantically, desperately. "You cannot harp! She'd know you false by that, and by your ancient eyes."

"Perhaps," I said, charmed by his suggestion, "she will not care."

"Her knights will find me. You said they seek to kill me! You will murder me."

"Those that want you dead will likely follow me," I said wearily, "for the gold-haired harper who rides with me. It is for the dragon to free you, not me. If he chooses to, you will have to find your own way back to Celandine, or else promise not to speak except to sing."

I turned away from him. The dragon-harper picked up his harp of bone. He said, in his husky, smoky voice,

"I keep my bargains. The key to your freedom lies in a song."

We left the harper chained to his harping, listening puzzledly with his deaf ear and untuned brain, for the one song, of all he had ever played and never heard, that would bring him back to Celandine. Outside, in the light, I led dragon-fire to the stone that had swallowed Danica, and began my backward journey toward Yrecros.

The Decoy Duck

Harry Turtledove

he Videssian dromon centipede-walked its oared way into
Lygra Fjord. Something about it struck Skatval the Brisk as
wrong, wrong. Wondering what, the Haloga chief used the
palm of a horn-hard hand to shield eyes against morning
sun as he stared out to sea.

He reluctantly decided it was not the imperial banner
itself, gold sunburst on blue, that fluttered from the top of
the dromon's mast. He had seen that banner before, had
clashed with those who bore it, too often to suit him.

Nor was it the twin suns the Videssians drew to help the
warship see its proper path, though his own folk would have
painted eyes instead. Coming from the far south, the Videssians naturally had more confidence in the sun than Halogai
could give it. Hereabouts, in the ice and dark and hunger
of winter, the sun seemed sometimes but a distant, fading
memory. Not for the first time, Skatval wondered why the Empire of
Videssos, which had so much, sought to swallow Halogaland and its
unending dearth.

But that thought led him away from the mark he had set for himself.
He peered further, sought once more for strangeness, something small,
something subtle . . .

"By the gods," he said softly, "it's the very shadows." The northern
men, who had to contend with the wild seas and savage storms of the

Bay of Haloga, always built their boats clinker-style, each plank over-lapping the one below and pegs driven through both for surer strength. The planks on the dromon were set edge to edge, so its sides seemed indecently smooth—*rather like the Videssians themselves*, Skatval thought with a thin smile.

The men he led could fill half a dozen war galleys. The arrogant dromon had already sailed past the inlets where four of them rested. Let the fightfire be kindled—and torches lay always to hand—and that brash captain would never hie back to his hot homeland. Skatval had but to say the word.

The word went unsaid. For one thing, in the bow of the dromon stood a white-painted shield hung on a spearshaft, the Videssian sign of truce. For another, the dromon was alone. If he sank it and slew its sailors, a swarm would sally forth for vengeance. Stavrakios, the man who sat on the Empire's throne, was very like a Haloga in that.

The dromon halted perhaps a furlong from the end of the fjord. Skat-val watched the loincloth-clad sailors (his lips twisted in a scornful smile as he imagined how they would fare in such garb here, more than a month either way from high summer) lower a boat into the gray-blue water. Four men scrambled down a rope into that boat. The ragged way they worked the oars told him at once they were no sailors. Now the corners of his mouth turned down. What were they, then?

As they moved out of the dromon's shadow, the sun shone off their shaven pates. For a moment, Skatval simply accepted what he saw. Then he cursed, loud, long, and fierce. So the Videssians were sending another pack of priests to Halogaland, were they? Had they not yet learned the northern folk cared nothing for their god? Or was it that their Phaos sometimes demanded blood sacrifice?

Skatval chewed on the new thought some little while, for it made the Videssian god more like those he venerated. But in the end he spat it out. He had seen imperials at worship. They gave their effete god hymns, not gore.

With the boat gone, the dromon turned almost in its own length (there was oarwork worth respect) and made for the outlet of the fjord. Skatval frowned again. Not even the bloodless Videssians were in the habit of leaving priests behind to perish.

Instead of beaching, the boat paused half a bowshot from shore. The blue-robed priests began to chant. One stood, looked up at the sun, and sketched a circle above his left breast. Skatval knew that was a gesture of respect. The other priests raised their hands to the heavens. The chant went on. The standing blue-robe sketched the sun-circle again, then made a quick pass, and another, and another.

A broad bridge of sunlight suddenly sprang from boat to beach. The priests swung knapsacks over their shoulders and strode across it as confidently as if they walked on dry land. When the last of them had crossed, the bridge vanished. The boat bobbed in the fjord, lonely and forgotten.

So, Skatval thought, *they are sorcerers.* The magic, which likely awed any watching crofters, impressed him as well, but only so far: he would have thought more of it had it brought the boat in, too. Still, the Halogai also boasted wizards, though their craft was earthier, often bloodier, than this play with light itself. Skatval refused to be awed. He had no doubt that was what the blue-robes sought, else they simply would have rowed ashore.

"Like to brag of themselves, do they?" he muttered. "I'll choke their brags in their throats, by the gods."

He set hand on swordhilt and strode shorewards. Should he slay the blue-robes now, he wondered, or was that Stavrakios' purpose, to seek to incite him and give the Empire excuse to turn loose its ships and soldiers? Videssos played a slipperier game of statecraft than most. Perhaps it were wiser to let the priests first commit some outrage, as they surely would, to justify their slaughter.

The unwelcome newcomers saw him tramping down the track from the longhouse. As one, they turned his way. *As one indeed,* he thought. Videssian priests were like as so many peas in a pod. Before he drew near enough to make out faces, he was sure what he would find. Some would be older, some younger, but all small and slight and swarthy by his standards.

Three of the four priests fit the expected pattern. Even their ages were hard to judge, save by the grayness of their untrimmed beards: as much as their matching robes, their naked, gleaming skulls made them seem all the same.

Perhaps because he foresaw uniformity, Skatval needed longer than he should have to note that the fourth man out of the boat broke the mold. Robed he was like his companions, and shaven, but the beard that burgeoned on cheeks and chin was neither black nor gray, but rather a golden tangle that reached halfway down his chest. His face was square; his nose short; his eyes not dark, heavy-lidded, and clever but open, friendly, and the exact color of the waters of Lygra Fjord.

Skatval's firm step faltered. He tugged at his own beard, more neatly kept than that of the fourth priest but of the same shade. Here was something unlooked for. How had Videssos made a Haloga into a priest of Phaos? More to the point, what sort of weapon was he?

All the priests had been praying since they left *Merciless* for the boat that had brought them to this inhospitable shore. But now Antilas, Nephon, and Tzoumas stood silent, watching the barbarian approach. They knew martyrdom might lie only moments away, knew their fate rested in Phaos' hands alone, knew the good god would do with them as he willed.

Kveldulf knew all those things, knew them as well as his brethren. Nevertheless, he recited the creed yet again: "We bless thee, Phaos, lord with the great and good mind, watchful beforehand that the great test of life may be decided in our favor."

"Your piety, as always, does you credit, Kveldulf," Tzoumas said. Like all imperials, the old priest pronounced Kveldulf's name as if it were a proper Videssian appellation: *Kveldoulphios.* He had grown so used to hearing it thus that it was nearly as if he'd borne it that way since birth. Nearly.

Not wishing to contradict his superior, he modestly lowered his eyes. He'd spoken Phaos' creed not so much to beg favor from the good god as to anchor himself, to recall what he'd willed himself to become, in a world where he needed such anchor as much as a shipwrecked sailor needed a spar to support himself in a sea suddenly turned all topsy-turvy.

Though he'd not set foot in Halogaland for twenty years and more, everything here smote him with a familiarity the stronger for being so unexpected: the way the land sloped sharply up from the sea; the grim gray of bare rock; the air's cool salt tang; the dark cloaks of arrow-straight fir and pine that covered the shoulders of the hills; the turf walls of the chief's longhouse and the way those walls turned in toward each other to accommodate the shape of the roof, which was not in fact a roof by original intention, but rather an upside-down boat outworn for any other use. He'd passed his boyhood in just such a longhouse.

But he was boy no more. Taken back to the Empire as prize of war, he'd grown to manhood—grown to priesthood—in its great cities, in golden Skopentzana and in the mighty imperial capital, Videssos the city itself. Now he saw through the eyes of a man who better knew a different world what he had taken for granted as a child.

"They're so poor," he whispered. The green fields were brave with

growing barley and beans, but pitifully narrow. And the crops, by Videssian standards, could not help being small. Under the smiling southern
sun, some favored provinces brought in two harvests a year. Here in the
north, getting one was by no means guaranteed. The kine were small,
the pigs scrawny; only the sheep seemed as fine and woolly as he remembered. They had need for fine wool here, wool to ward against
winter.

Even the longhouse was at the same time a match for his memories
and less than he had looked for it to be. This chief was richer than
Kveldulf's father had dreamed of being; his home was bigger and
stronger than that from which Kveldulf had fled, nose running and
throat raw from smoke, as the imperials set it ablaze. Yet beside a score
of homes, palaces, temples in Skopentzana, beside a score of scores in
Videssos the city, it was but a hovel, and a filthy hovel at that.

The chief himself still stumped toward the priests. He was a big,
broad-shouldered man with the same pale hair, fair skin, and light eyes
as Kveldulf's. The massive gold brooch that closed his cloak also declared his rank. But his baggy wool trousers had dirt-stained knees, perhaps from stooping in the fields but as likely from the earthen floor of
the longhouse. Recalling his father's holding burning over his head
made Kveldulf notice the chief's red-tracked eyes, the soot forever
ground into the lines of his forehead: the Halogai knew of chimneys,
but in winter they often chose not to let heat flee through them.

The chief paused about ten feet in front of the priests, spent a full
minute surveying them. Then he said, "Why came you here, where you
know your kind are not welcome?" His deep, slow voice, the sonorous,
mouth-filling words he spoke, made Kveldulf shiver. Not since boyhood
had he heard anyone save himself speak the pure Haloga tongue; he had
taught it to his comrades here, but they gave it back with a staccato
Videssian intonation.

Just the sound of the chief's voice set Kveldulf's heart crying to reply,
but that was not his proper place. Modestly, he cast his eyes to the
ground as Tzoumas, senior and most holy of the four, answered in the
northern speech: "We come to tell you of the good god Phaos, the lord
with the great and good mind, whom you must worship for the sake of
your souls."

"Here is a new thing," the chief said, raising straw-colored eyebrows.
Suddenly, he shifted into Videssian: "Not a few of us know your language, but few southern men have bothered learning ours."

Behind Kveldulf, Nephon nudged Antilas, whispered, "Few of Videssos would waste their time on this barbarous jargon." Antilas grunted
agreement. The Haloga chief could not have heard him. Kveldulf
frowned anyhow, though Nephon was far from wrong; only a direct order from the patriarch had produced even three to learn the northern
tongue and the ways of the Halogai. Most Videssians assumed anyone
unwilling to take on their own ways was not worth saving.

The chief went on, still in Videssian, "I dare say this decoy duck
taught it to you." His gaze swung to Kveldulf and he returned to his
birthspeech as he asked, "Who are you, and how came you among the
southrons?"

"By your leave, holy sir?" Kveldulf murmured to Tzoumas, who
dipped his head in assent. Only then did Kveldulf speak directly to the
Haloga: "I am Kveldulf, a priest of Phaos like any other."

"Not like any other, by the gods," the chief said. "And Kveldulf *what?*
Are you a slave or a woman, that you have neither ekename nor father's
name to set beside your own?" He thumped his chest with a big fist.
"Me, I am Skatval the Brisk, otherwise Skatval Raud's son."

"Honor to you and yours, Brisk Skatval," Kveldulf said, giving the
chief proper greeting. "I am—Kveldulf. It is enough. If you like, I am
a slave, but a willing slave to the good god, as are all his priests. We
have no other titles, and need none."

"You—own yourself a slave?" Skatval's sword slid from its sheath.
"And you would fain enslave the free folk of Halogaland?"

"To the good god, yes." Kveldulf knew death walked close. Among
themselves, the Halogai kept no slaves. Videssos did. Kveldulf had been
a slave of the most ordinary sort, until his fervent love for the god of
whom he learned within the Empire persuaded his master, a pious man
himself, to free him to serve Phaos. He unflinchingly met Skatval's glare.
"Slay me if you must, sir. I shall not flee, nor fight. But while I live, I
shall preach."

The Haloga chief began to bring up his bright blade. Then, all at
once, he stopped, threw back his head, and roared laughter till it echoed
from the hills. "Preach as you will, where you will, nithing of a priest.
Let us see how many northern men would willingly shackle themselves
forever to anything, even a god."

Kveldulf felt angry heat rise from his throat to the top of his head.
With his pale, almost transparent skin, he knew how visible his rage had
to be. He did not care. Of themselves, his hands curled into clumsy,

unpracticed fists. He took a step toward Skatval. "Hold!" Tzoumas said sharply.

Skatval laughed still, threw aside his sword. "Let him come, Videssian. Perhaps I can pound sense into his shaven head, if it will enter there in no other way."

"Hold, holy sir," Tzoumas told Kveldulf again, and waited for him to obey before turning back to Skatval. To the chief, he said, "Pick up your weapon, sir, for in the battle about to be joined, you will find Kveldulf well armed."

"Well armed? With what?" Skatval jeered.

"With words," Tzoumas answered. Skatval suddenly stopped smiling.

Kveldulf preached in a pasture, a clump of cow dung close by his sandals. From everything Skatval knew of Videssians, that in itself would have been plenty to put them off stride. But Kveldulf noticed no more than any of the chief's smallholders might have. And too many of those smallholders to suit Skatval stood in the field to listen.

Skatval watched from the edge of the woods that lay by the pasture. He had called Kveldulf a woman for bearing an unadorned name. Now, as if in revenge for that taunt, women flocked to hear the Haloga unaccountably turned Videssian priest. When he thought to be so, Skatval was just enough. Much as he despised Kveldulf, he could not deny the blue-robe made a fine figure of a man, save for his naked skull. And even that, repulsive as it still seemed on the Videssian clerics, might be reckoned but an exotic novelty on a man who was in every other way a perfect northerner. By the sighs from the womenfolk, they reckoned it so, which only annoyed Skatval the more.

Among those womenfolk was his own daughter Skjaldvor; he saw her bright gold hair in the second row of the crowd around Kveldulf. He rumbled something discontented, down deep in his throat. If Skjaldvor took this southron nonsense seriously, how could he hope to rid himself of Kveldulf when the time came for that? He rumbled again. His daughter should have been wed two years ago, maybe three or four, but he'd indulged, indeed been flattered by, her wish to stay in his own longhouse. Now he wondered what sort of price he would have to pay for that indulgence.

He could all but hear his own stern, bloodthirsty gods laughing at him. They knew one always paid for being soft. He scowled. Would they willingly let themselves be supplanted, just for the sake of teaching him a lesson he already knew by heart? They might. Halogai who went after vengeance pursued it for its own sake, without counting coins to see if it was worth the cost.

The summer breeze, so mild as to befool a man who did not know better into thinking such fine days would last forever, blew Kveldulf's words to Skatval's ears. The priest had a fine, mellow voice, a man's voice, and was no mean speaker: to northern directness he married a more sophisticated Videssian style, as if he were holding up ideas in his hands and examining them from all sides.

He paused. His listeners, who should have been making the most of the short summer season instead of standing around listening to sweet-tasting nonsense, broke into applause. Skatval saw Skjaldvor's hands meet each other, saw in profile her bright eyes aimed straight at Kveldulf, her mouth wide and smiling.

He began to worry in earnest.

After some days' preaching, Kveldulf began to worry in earnest. The Halogai, once his people—*still* his people if blood counted as well as dwelling, as it surely did—flocked to hear him. They listened to him with greater, more serious attention than a crowd of Videssians would have granted; every imperial fancied himself a theologian, and wanted to argue every shade of meaning in Phaos' holy scriptures. The Halogai listened respectfully; they nodded soberly; they declined to convert.

It was not that they had no questions for him; they had many. But those questions did not spring from the holy scriptures; they did not assume those scriptures were true, and argue from or about their premises. To the Halogai, everything pertaining to Phaos, even his existence, was open to debate. Kveldulf had been warned of that before he sailed for his birthland. Only now, though, was he discovering what it meant.

No Videssian, for instance, would have asked, as did a herder whose rawhide boots were stained with sheepshit, "Well, just how d'you ken this Phaos o'yours is what you say he is?"

"Things act for good in this world, and others for evil," Kveldulf answered. "Phaos is the architect of all that is good, while Skotos works without pause to pull down all he does." He spat between his feet in rejection of the dark god.

The shepherd spat, too. "So you say. Who said so to you?"

"So say the good god's own holy words, written down in ancient days." Kveldulf nodded to Tzoumas, who held up a copy of the scriptures. The words within meant nothing to the watching Halogai; they did not write their own language, let alone Videssian. But the cover, of brass polished till it gleamed like gold and decorated with precious stones and an enamelwork portrait of Phaos' stern, majestic countenance, promised that what lay within was worthy of consideration. As the Videssian proverb put it, *a robe is revealed in advance by its border.*

But the stubborn shepherd said, "Did your god speak these words straight to you?" Kveldulf had to shake his head. The shepherd went on, "Then why put faith in 'em? When I hear the thunder, or see the grain spring green from the ground, or futter my woman, these are things whose truth I know for myself; I feel no shame to worship the gods that shaped them. But a god who spoke long ago, if he spoke at all? Pah!" He spat again.

Behind Kveldulf, one of his Videssian colleagues—he thought it was Nephon—softly said, "Blasphemy!" Kveldulf himself felt brief heat run through his body, heat warmer than that which the watery sunshine of Halogaland could engender. Along with their hair, Videssian priests gave up carnal congress as a mark of their devotion to the good god. Kveldulf had worn his celibacy a long time now; it rarely chafed him. But imperials did not talk about futtering as casually as the shepherd had, either. The naked word made Kveldulf feel for a moment what he had given up.

He said, "If the good god's holy words will not inspire you, think on the deeds of those who follow him. They hold sway from the borders of Makuran far in the southwest, round the lands which touch the Videssian Sea and the Sailors' Sea, and sweep up along the edge of the Northern Sea till their lands march with yours as well. And all this under the rule of one man, the mighty Emperor Stavrakios, Avtokrator of the Videssians, where small Halogaland is split among countless chiefs. Does this not speak for the strength of Phaos?"

Behind him, Nephon said, "This argument is unscriptural. The barbarians must come to Phaos' faith because of the glory of the good god, not that of those who follow him."

"Don't call them barbarians," Antilas said quietly. "He's one of them, remember?"

Nephon grunted. Tzoumas said, "How worshipers find Phaos matters little; that they find him matters much. Let Kveldulf go on, if he will."

The byplay had been in Videssian. The Halogai to whom Kveldulf preached took no notice of it. And now, for the first time since he'd come to Halogaland, he had hearers who listened seriously. He wondered why, for Nephon was right: an argument from results was weaker than one from doctrine. But the men of the north respected strength; perhaps reminding them of the power of Videssos had not hurt.

"Cast forth the evil from your own lives!" he called. "Accept Phaos into your hearts, into your spirits. Turn toward the good which rests in each of you. Who will show me now that he is ready to cleave to the lord with the great and good mind, and reject evil forevermore?"

He'd asked that before at the close of every sermon, and been answered with stony silence or with jeers. The Halogai were happy enough to listen to him; it gave them something unusual and interesting to do with their time. But hearing and hearkening were two different things, and for all his passionate exhortation, he'd not convinced anyone, not until today. Now a woman raised her hand, then another, and then a man.

Kveldulf sketched the sun-sign over his heart. As he looked up to the heavens to thank Phaos for allowing him to be persuasive, his eyes filled with grateful tears. At last the good god had given a sign he would not forsake the folk of the north.

Skatval slashed the horse's throat. As the sacrificial beast staggered, he held the *laut*-bowl under its neck to gather the gushing blood. The horse fell. From the *laut*-bowl he filled *laut*-sprinklers and stained the wooden walls of the temple with shining red. He also daubed his own cheeks and hands, and those of the clansfolk who had gathered with him for the offering.

As he moistened men and women with the holy blood, his priest, Grimke Grankel's son, declared, "May goodness flow down from the god as the gore goes out of the offering."

"So may it be," Skatval echoed. So did his warriors and their women—those that were here. He did his best to hide his unease as he began to butcher the horse, but it was not easy. Sacrifice should have brought together the whole of the clan, to receive the gods' blessing and to feast on horseflesh and ale afterwards. Most of his people had come, but far too many were missing.

Among the missing was Skjaldvor. Skatval's eyebrows came together above his long, thin nose. Of all the people who might listen to this southron twaddle about Phaos, he'd expected his daughter to be one of the last.

He glanced over at Ulvhild, his wife. After they'd lived together in that longhouse the whole of their grown lives, she picked thoughts from his head as if he'd shouted them aloud. Now she shrugged, slowly and deliberately, telling him there was nothing she could do about Skjaldvor: his daughter was a woman now. He snorted. No one could do anything with a girl, once she turned into a woman. Ulvhild heard the snort and glared at him—she'd stolen that thought, too.

Hastily, he turned back to roasting horseflesh. The first pieces were done enough to eat. Someone held out a birchwood platter. He stabbed a gobbet, plopped it onto the plate. Beside him, Grimkel plied a dipper, filled a mug with ale. "The gods bless us with their bounty," he intoned.

Some time later, his belly full of meat and his head spinning slightly from many mugs of ale, Skatval strode out of the temple. He was one of the last folk to leave: not least of his chiefly requirements was being able to outeat and outdrink those he outranked. The rich taste of hot marrow still filled his mouth.

He thumped his middle with the flat of his hand. Life was not so bad. The fields bore as well as they ever did; no murrain had smote the flocks, nor sickness his people. No raiders threatened. Winter would be long, but winter was always long. The gods willing, almost all the clan would see the next spring. He had been through too many years where dearth and death displayed themselves long months in advance.

Then satisfaction leaked from him as if he were a cracked pot. There at the edge of a hayfield walked Skjaldvor and Kveldulf, not arm in arm but side by side, their heads close together. Kveldulf explained something with extravagant gestures he must have learned from the Videssians; no man of Halogaland would have been so unconstrained. Skjaldvor laughed, clapped her hands, nodded eagerly. Whatever point he'd made, she approved of it.

Or more likely, she just approves of Kveldulf, Skatval thought with bleak mirth. The chief wondered if she drew a distinction between the blue-robe's doctrines and himself. He had his doubts. But what could he do? What could anyone do with a girl, once she turned into a woman?

He'd answered that question for himself back inside the temple. He did not like the conclusion he'd reached there, but found none better now.

. . .

"Tell me, Kveldulf," Skjaldvor said, "how came you to reverence the Videssian god?" She stopped walking, cocked her head, and waited for his reply.

The light that filtered through the forest canopy overhead was clear, pale, almost colorless, like the gray-white trunks of the birch trees all around. The air tasted of moss and dew. When he paused too, Kveldulf felt quiet fold round him like a cloak. Somewhere far in the distance, he heard the low, purring trill of a crested tit. Otherwise, all was still. He could hear his own breath move in and out, and after a moment Skjaldvor's as well.

As she looked at him, so he studied her. She was tall for a woman, the crown of her head reaching higher than his chin. Flowing gilt hair framed her face, a strong-chinned, proud-cheekboned visage which, along with the unshrinking gaze of her wide-set eyes, spoke volumes about the legendary stubbornness of the Halogai. She had, in fact, a close copy of her father's features, though in her his harshness somehow grew fresh and lovely. But Kveldulf, unpracticed with either families or women, could not quite catch that.

He did know she made him nervous, and also knew he spent more time with her than he should. All of Skatval's clansfolk had souls that wanted saving. Still, Kveldulf told himself, winning the chief's daughter to the worship of the good god would greatly strengthen Phaos here. And she could have chosen nothing apter to ask him.

The years blew away as he looked back inside himself. "I was a lad yet, my beard not sprouted, sold as a house slave: Videssian spoil of war. I learned the Empire's tongue fast enough to suit my master. He was far from the worst of men; he worked me hard, but he fed me well, and beat me no worse than I deserved." The hairs of his mustache tickled his lips as they quirked into a wry smile. Remembering some of his pranks, he reckoned Zoïlos merciful now, though he hadn't thought so at the time.

"How could you live—a slave?" Skjaldvor shuddered. "You come of free folk. Would you not liefer have lost your life than live in chains?"

"I wore no chains," Kveldulf said.

"That may be worse," she told him, scorn in her voice. "You stayed in slavery when you could have—should have—fled?" She turned her back on him. Her long wool skirt swirled around her, showing him for a moment her slim white ankles.

"How was I to flee?" he asked, doing his best to inform his voice with reason rather than wrath. "Skopentzana is far from Halogaland, and I was but a boy. And before long, I came to see my capture as a blessing, not the sorrow I had held it to be."

Skjaldvor looked at him again, but with hands on her hips. "A blessing? Are you witstruck? To have to walk at the whim of another man's will—I would die before I endured it."

"As may be," Kveldulf said soberly. A slave as lovely as Skjaldvor was all too likely to have to lie down at the whim of another man's will. Zoïlos, fortunately, had not bought Kveldulf for that. He shook his head to dislodge the distracting carnal thought, went on: "But you asked of me how I found Phaos. Had I not been Zoïlos' slave, I doubt I should have. He often went out of morning, and one day I asked where. He told me he prayed at the chief temple in Skopentzana, and asked in turn if I cared to go there with him."

"And you said aye?"

"I said aye." Kveldulf laughed at his younger self. "It seemed easier than my usual morning drudgery. So he let me bathe, and gave me a shirt less shabby than most, and I walked behind him to the temple. We went inside. I had never smelt incense before. Then I looked up into the dome . . ."

His voice trailed away. Across a quarter of a century, he could still call up the awe he'd known, looking up into the golden dome and seeing Phaos stern in judgment, staring down at him—seemingly at him alone, though the temple was crowded—and weighing his worth. Then the priestly choir behind the altar lifted up its many-voiced voice in exaltation and praise of the lord with the great and good mind, and then—

Kveldulf remembered to speak: "I knew not whether I was still on earth or up in the heavens. I saw the holy men in the blue robes who lived with the good god every moment of every day of every year of their lives, and I knew I had to be of their number. Next morning, I asked Zoïlos if I might go with him, not he me, and the morning after that, and the one after that. At first, when I was but shirking, he'd hoped me pious. Now, when I truly touched piety, he reckoned me a shirker. But I kept on; I was drunk with the good god. Once I found Phaos, I wished for nothing else. Well, not nothing; I wished for but one thing more."

"What is that?" Skjaldvor leaned toward him. The silver chains that linked the two large brooches she wore on her breast clinked softly (the shape of those brooches reminded Kveldulf of nothing so much as twin tortoise shells). All at once he was conscious of how close she stood.

Nonetheless, he answered as he had intended: "I wished the good god might grant me the boon of leading my birthfolk out of Skotos' darkness and into the light of Phaos. For those who die without knowing the lord with the great and good mind shall surely spend all eternity in the icepits of Skotos, a fate I wish on no man or woman, Videssian or Haloga, slave or free."

"Oh." Skjaldvor straightened. Where before her voice had been low and breathy, now it went oddly flat. She studied him again, as if wondering whether to go on. At last she did: "I thought perhaps you meant you wished you might enjoy all the pleasures of other men."

Kveldulf felt himself grow hot, and knew his fair skin only made embarrassment more obvious. He looked to see if Skjaldvor also blushed. Though fairer even than he, she did not. She knew herself free to say what she would, act as she would. He stammered a little as he answered, "I may not, not without turning oathbreaker, and that I shall never do."

"The more fool you, and the worse waste, for you are no mean man," she said. "The other blue-robes are less stupid."

"What do you mean?" he demanded.

"Do you not know? *Can* you not know, without being deaf and blind? Your fellows are far from passing all their nights alone and lonely in their tents."

"Is it so?" Kveldulf said, but by her malicious satisfaction he knew it surely was. Sorrow pressed upon him but left him unsurprised. He bent his head, sketched the sun-circle over his heart. "All men may sin. I shall pray for them."

She stared at him. "Is that all?"

"What else would you have me do?" he asked, honestly curious.

"Were it not for your beard, I should guess the southrons made you a eunuch when they set the blue robe upon you." Skjaldvor took a deep breath, let it hiss out through flaring nostrils. "What else would I have you do? This, to start." As she stepped into his arms, her expression might have been that of a warrior measuring a foe over sword and shield.

The gold of her brooches pressed against him through his robe, then the softer, yielding firmness that was herself. His arms still hung by his sides, but that mattered little, for she held him to her. From the sweat that prickled on his forehead and shaven pate, the cool wood might suddenly have become a tropic swamp. Then she kissed him. Not even a man of stone, a statue like one of those in Skopentzana's central square, could have remained unroused.

She stepped back and eyed not his red face but his groin to gauge her effect on him. That effect was all too visible, which only made his face grow redder. But when she reached out to open his robe, he slapped her hand aside. "No, by the good god," he said harshly.

Now she reddened too, with anger. "Why ever not? The Videssians do not stint themselves; why should you, when you are not of their kindred nor born to their faith?"

"That they do wrong is no reason for me to follow them. Were they murdering instead of fornicating, would you bid me do likewise?"

"How can anything so full of joy be wrong?" Skjaldvor tossed her shining hair in scorn at the very idea.

"It is forbidden to Phaos' priests, thus wrong for them," Kveldulf declared. "And though I was not born to faith in Phaos, in it I am a son fostered to a fine father. Whatever I was by birth, Phaos' is the house wherein I would dwell evermore."

All he said was true, yet he knew it was incomplete. As a foster son in Phaos' household, he was held to closer scrutiny than the Videssians who entered it by right of birth: they might be forgiven sins that would condemn him, the outsider who presumed to ape their ways. Another man might have grown resentful, struggling against that double standard. But it spurred Kveldulf. If extra devotion was required of him, extra devotion he would give.

"You will not?" Skjaldvor said.

"I will not," Kveldulf answered firmly. Never since donning the blue robe had he known such temptation; the memory of her body printed against him, he knew, would remain with him till his last breath. He still throbbed from wanting her. But priests were taught to rule their flesh. Over and over he repeated Phaos' creed to himself, focusing on the good god rather than his fleshly lust, and at length that lust began to lessen.

Skjaldvor drew near him again. This time, he thought, he would be proof against her embraces. But she did not embrace him. Serpent-swift, she slapped his left cheek, then, on the backhand, his right. He cherished the sudden pain, which seared the last of his desire from him.

"May the lord with the great and good mind keep you in his heart until you place him in yours," he said. "I shall pray that that time be soon, as you have seemed better disposed than most of your fellows to learning of his faith."

She tossed her head again and laughed, an ugly sound despite the sweetness of her voice. Then she spat full in his face. "This for your Phaos and his faith." She spat again. "And this for you!" She spun on her heel and stormed away.

Kveldulf stood and watched her go while her warm spittle slid down into his beard. Very deliberately, he bent his head and spat himself, down between his feet in the age-old Videssian gesture that rejected Skotos. He recited Phaos' creed once more. When he was through, he walked slowly back toward the tents by the shore.

Skatval watched the small crowd of crofters and herders raise hands to the heavens. The sound of their prayers to Phaos reached him faintly. Save for the name of the Videssian god, the words were in the Haloga tongue. Skatval had heard worse poetry from bards who lived by traveling from chief to chief with their songs. *Kveldulf's work, no doubt,* he thought; the blond-bearded priest was proving a man of more parts than he had looked for.

Absent from the converts' conclave was Skjaldvor. For that Skatval sent up his own prayers of thanks to his gods. He had not asked what passed between her and Kveldulf, but where before she had gone to his services, looked on him with mooncalf eyes, now all at once the sight of him made her face go hard and hateful, hearing his name brought curses from her lips. She was in no danger of coming to follow Phaos, not any more.

But the priests from the Empire had won more folk to their faith than Skatval expected (truth to tell, he'd thought his people would laugh Kveldulf and the rest away in disgrace, else he would have slain them as soon as they set foot on his soil). That worried him. Followers of Videssos' faith would mean Videssian priests on his land henceforward, and that would mean . . . Skatval growled wordlessly. He stalked toward the prayer meeting. He would show his people what that meant.

Kveldulf bowed courteously as he drew nigh. "The good god grant you peace, Skatval the Brisk. May I hope you have come to join us?"

"No," he said, biting off the word. "I would ask a couple of questions of you."

Kveldulf bowed again. "Ask what you will. Knowledge is a road to faith."

"Knowledge is a road around the snare you have set for my people," Skatval retorted. "Suppose some of us take on your faith and then fall out over how to follow it. Who decides which of us is in the right?"

"Priests are brought up from boyhood in Phaos' way," Kveldulf said. "Can newcomers to that way hope to match them in knowledge?"

Skatval grimaced. The Haloga priest—no, the blond Videssian, that was the better way to think of him—was not making matters easy. But the chief bulled ahead regardless: "Suppose the blue-robes disagree, as they may, men being what they are? Who then says which walks the proper path?"

"The prelates set over them," Kveldulf said, cautious now. Skatval had probed at him before, but in private, not in front of the people.

"And the priest against whom judgment falls?" the chief said. "If he will not yield, is he then an outlaw?"

"A heretic, we name one who chooses his own false doctrine over that ordained by his elders." Kveldulf considered the question, then added, "But no, he is not to be outlawed—excommunicated is the word the temples use—yet, for he has right of appeal to the patriarch, the most holy and chiefest priest, the head of all the faith."

"Ah, the patriarch!" Skatval exclaimed, as if hearing of the existence of a supreme prelate for the first time. "And where dwells this prince of piety?"

"In Videssos the city, by the High Temple there," Kveldulf answered.

"In Videssos the city? Under the Avtokrator's thumb, you mean." Skatval showed teeth in something more akin to a lynx's hunting snarl than to a smile. "So you would have us put to Stavrakios' judgment aught upon which we may disagree, is that what you say?" He turned to the converts, lashed them with wounding words: "I reckoned you freemen, not slaves to Videssos through the Empire's god. Your holy Kveldulf here is but the thin edge of the wedge, I warn you."

"The patriarch rules the church, not the Avtokrator," Kveldulf insisted. Behind him, his Videssian colleagues nodded vigorously.

Skatval ignored them; without Kveldulf, they were nothing here. At Kveldulf, he snapped, "And if your precious patriarch dies, what then?"

"Then the prelates come together in conclave to choose his successor," Kveldulf answered.

Skatval quite admired him; without lying, he had twisted truth to his purposes. Against many Halogai, even chiefs, his words would have wrought what he intended. But Skatval, mistrusting the Empire more than most, had learned more of it than most. "By the truth you hold in your god, Kveldulf, who names the three men from whom the prelates pick the patriarch?"

Just for a moment, he saw hatred in those blue eyes so like his own. Just for a moment—and when it cleared, it cleared completely. Skatval also saw the Videssian priests visibly willing Kveldulf to lie. But when he answered at last, his voice was firm, if low: "The Avtokrator names those candidates."

"There, you see?" Skatval turned to the converts who had heard him argue with Kveldulf. "You see? Aye, follow Phaos, if you fancy the Avtokrator telling you how to go about it. Videssos has not the strength to vanquish us by the sword, so she seeks to strangle us with the spider's silk spun by her god. And you—you seek to aid the Empire!"

He had hoped forcing Kveldulf to concede that Phaos' faith was dominated by the Emperor would of itself make his people turn away from the Videssian god. And indeed, a couple of men and women left the gathering, shaking their heads at their own foolishness. To the Halogai, Videssos' autocracy seemed like a whole great land living in chains.

But more folk than he expected stayed where they were, waiting to hear how Kveldulf would answer him. The priest, too canny by half to suit Skatval, saw that as well, and grew stronger for it. He said boldly, "No matter whence the faith comes, friends, its truth remains. You have heard that truth in Phaos' holy scriptures, heard it in my own poor words, and accepted it of your free will. Apart from the cost to your souls in the life to come, turning aside from it now at your chief's urging is surely as slavish as his imagined claim that you somehow serve the Empire by accepting the good god."

Skatval ground his teeth when he saw several men soberly nodding. People stopped leaving the field in which the returned Haloga was holding his service. Kveldulf did not display the triumph he must have felt. A Videssian would have done so, and lost the people whose respect he'd regained. Kveldulf merely continued the service as if nothing had happened: he was a Haloga at heart, and knew the quiet gesture was the quicker killer.

Skatval stormed away. Forcing the fight further now would but cost him face. As he tramped into the woods, he almost ran over Grimke Grankel's son. "Are you coming to cast your lot with Phaos, too?" he snarled.

"A man may watch a foe without wishing to join him," the servant of the Haloga gods replied.

"At least you see he is a foe: more than those cheeseheads back there care to notice," Skatval said. "A deadly dangerous foe." His eyes narrowed as he looked back toward Kveldulf, who was leading his converts in yet another translated hymn. "Why, then, does he not deserve some deadly danger?"

Grimke glanced at the sword he wore on his belt. "You could have given it to him."

"I wanted to, but feared it would set his followers forever in his path. If you, however, were to slay the southrons—and Kveldulf, their stalking horse—by sorcery, all would see our gods are stronger than the one for whom he prates."

Grimke Grankel's son stared, then slowly smiled. "This could be done, my chief."

"Then do it. Too long I tolerated the traitor among us, long enough for his treachery to take root. Now, as I say, simply to slay Kveldulf and his Videssian cronies would stir more strife than it stopped. But you would not *simply* slay him, eh?"

"No, not simply." Grimke's face mirrored anticipation and calculation. "Hmm . . . 'twere best to wait till midnight, when the power of his god is at its lowest ebb."

"As you reckon best. In matters magical, you know—" Skatval broke off, stared at his sorcerer. "Do you say that even you acknowledge Phaos a true god?"

"This for Phaos." Grimke spat between his feet, as a Videssian would in rejecting Skotos. "But any god is true to one who truly believes, and may ward against wizardry. Given a choice between sorceries, I would choose the simpler when I may. Thus, midnight serves me best."

"Let it be as you wish, then," Skatval said. "But let it be tonight."

Even at midnight, the sky was not wholly dark. Sullen red marked the northern sky, tracing the track of the sun not far below the ground. Seeing that glow, Skatval thought of blood. Only a few of the brightest stars pierced the endless summer twilight.

A small fire crackled. Bit by bit, Grimke Grankel's son fed it with chips of wood and other, less readily identifiable, substances. The fickle breeze flicked smoke into Skatval's face. He coughed and nearly choked; it had not the savor of honest flames. Almost, he told Grimke to stamp it out and set sorcery aside.

Grimke set a silver *laut*-bowl in the fire, which licked around it until the gods and savage beasts worked in relief on its outside seemed to writhe with a life of their own. Skatval rubbed his eyes. Heat-shimmers he knew, but none like these. The bowl held a thick jelly. When it began to bubble and seethe, Grimke nodded as if satisfied.

Above the bowl he held two cups of similar work, one filled with blood (some was his own, some Skatval's), the other with bitter ale. Slowly, slowly, he poured the twin thin streams down into the *laut*-bowl. "Drive the intruders from our land, drive them to fear, drive them to death," he intoned. "As our blood is burnt, find for them fates bitter as this beer. May they know sorrow, may they know shame, may they forget their god and gain only graves."

Filled with assonance and alliteration, the chant rolled on. Hair rose on Skatval's forearms and at the back of his neck; though the magic was not aimed at him, he felt its force, felt it and was filled with fear. The gods of the Halogai were grim and cold, like the land they ruled. As Grimke prodded them to put forth their power, Skatval wondered for a moment if Phaos would not make a better, safer master for his folk. He fought the thought down, hoping his gods had not seen it.

Too late for second thoughts anyhow. Grimke's voice rose, almost to a scream. And other screams, more distant, rose in answer from the tents in which the priests dwelt. Hearing the horror in them, Skatval wondered again if he should have chosen Phaos. He shook his head. Phaos might make his folk a fine master, but the Avtokrator Stavrakios would not, and he could not have the one without the other.

Grimke Grankel's son set down the silver cups. The flickering flames showed sweat slithering down his face, harsh lines carved from nose to mouth corners. Voice slow and rough with weariness, he said, "What magic may wreak, magic has wrought."

Kveldulf woke from dreams filled with dread. The sun shining through the side of his tent made him sigh with relief, as if he had no right to see it. He shook his head, feeling foolish. Dreams were but dreams, no matter how frightening: when the sun rose, they were gone. But these refused to go.

He had slept in his robe. Now he belted it on again, went outside to offer morning prayers to the sun, the symbol of his god. Tzoumas, Nephon, and Antilas remained in their tents. *Slugabeds,* he thought, and lifted hands to the heavens. "We bless thee, Phaos, lord with the great and good mind—" Out of the corner of his eye, he saw Skatval bearing down on him, but took no true notice of the chief until he had finished the creed.

"You live!" Skatval shouted, as if it were crime past forgiving.

"Well, aye," Kveldulf said, smiling. "The good god brought me safe through another night. Am I such an ancient, though, that the thought fills you with surprise?"

"Look to your fellows," Skatval said, staring at him still.

"I would not disturb them at their rest," Kveldulf said. Tzoumas in particular could be a bear with a sore paw unless he got in a full night.

"Look to them!" Skatval said, so fiercely Kveldulf had to obey. He went over to Nephon's tent, pulled back the flaps that closed it, stuck his head inside. A moment later, he drew back, face pale, stomach heaving. Of themselves, his fingers shaped Phaos' sun-circle. He went to Antilas' tent, and Tzoumas', hoping for something better, but in each he found only twisted death, with terror carved irremovably onto all the priests' features.

He turned back to Skatval. "Why did you spare me? I would sooner have died with my fellows." He knew the chief did not favor his faith, but had not imagined he held such hatred as to do . . . what he had done to the Videssians. By his own standards, Skatval seemed a reasonable man. But where was the reason in this?

Skatval supplied it: "The gods know I hoped Grimke's wizardry would overfall you too, you more than any of the others. They without you were nothing; you without them remain deadly foe to all I hold dear: deadlier now, for having survived. Your god I could perhaps live with, or suffer my folk to do so. But with Phaos you bring Stavrakios, and that I will not have. Flee now, Kveldulf, while life remains in you, if you would save yourself."

Slowly, Kveldulf shook his head. He knew Skatval spoke some truth; half-overheard whispers from Videssian hierarchs said as much. In one of its aspects, the faith of Phaos was the glove within which moved the hand of imperial statecraft. If the Halogai served Phaos, they might one day come to serve Stavrakios or his successors as well.

But that was not the portion of the faith to which Kveldulf had been drawn. He believed with all his soul in the lord with the great and good mind, believed others needed to believe for the sake of their souls, believed most of all his native people had been blind in spirit far too long,

that too many of them suffered forever in Skotos' ice because they knew
not Phaos. That the good god might have singled him out to lead the
Halogai to the light filled him with holy joy he had not known since the
day when he first set eyes on Phaos stern in judgment in the temple in
Skopentzana.

And so he shook his head once more, and said, "I shall not flee,
Skatval. I told you as much when first I came here. You may slay me,
but while I draw breath I shall go on glorifying Phaos to your folk. The
good god demands no less of me. He is my shield, my protector, against
all evil; if I die here, he shall receive my soul."

To his amazement, Skatval bellowed laughter. "You may follow the
southrons' god, but you have a Haloga's soul. We are stubborn, not
slippery or subtle like the Videssians. Those three priests dead in their
tents, they would have given me all manner of lies, then tried to squirm
around them. That way has served Videssos for centuries."

"It is not mine," Kveldulf said simply.

"So I have seen." Skatval's eyes narrowed, sharpened, until they
pierced Kveldulf like blued blades. "And so, likely, you still live. Oh,
I'll not deny those Videssians served their god—"

"My god," Kveldulf broke in.

"However you would have it. They served him, in their fashion, but
they served Stavrakios as well. You, though, you're so cursed full of
Phaos, you have no room in you for anything else. Thus your faith
warded you, where theirs, thinner, went for naught."

"It may well be so." Kveldulf remembered how Skjaldvor had jeered,
saying the three Videssian priests ignored their vows of celibacy. Remembering Skjaldvor, he remembered also her body pressed against his,
remembered his manhood rising in desire. He said, "Yet I am no great
holy man, to be revered by the generations yet to come. I am as full of
sin as anyone, fight it though I may."

"To what man is it given to know in his lifetime how the generations
yet to come will look on him?" Skatval said. "We do what we will and
what we may with the time we have. Among men, that must be enough;
the gods alone see how our purposes intertwine."

"There, for once, but for your choice of words, we agree." To his
surprise, Kveldulf found himself bowing to Skatval, as he might have
before an ecclesiastical superior. More clearly than ever before, he saw
the Haloga chief was also fighting for a way of life he reckoned right.
That saddened Kveldulf, for he had always believed those who failed to

follow Phaos were without any sort of honor. Yet he remained convinced his own way was best, was true. He said, "But for our choice of creeds, we might have been friends, you and I."

"So we might, though your unbending honesty makes you a dangerous man to keep by one's side: you are a sharp sword without sheath." Skatval stroked his chin, considering. "It might still come to pass. How's this? Instead of bidding us throw down our gods, give over your Phaos, grow out your hair, and live the rest of your days as a Haloga—as you were born to live."

Kveldulf shook his head, though startled at the sadness that surged in him. "Tell my heart to give over beating before you bid me abandon the lord with the great and good mind."

"If you do not, your heart will give over beating." Skatval touched his swordhilt.

Kveldulf bowed again. "If it be so, it shall be so. I will not flee, I will not cease. Do what you will with me on that account. My fate lies in Phaos' hands."

"I would not slay a man I admire, but if I must, I will." Skatval sighed. "As I say, by blood you belong to us. Many are the bold warriors sung of in our lays who chose death over yielding."

"I remember the songs from my boyhood," Kveldulf said, nodding. "But Phaos' faith has its martyrs, too, Videssians who gave all for the good god, and gladly would I be reckoned among their number. Will you give me a shovel, Skatval, that I may bury my friends?"

"I will," Skatval said. "And Kveldulf—"

"Aye?"

"Dig a fourth grave, as well."

Wearing helm and hauberk, ash-hafted spear at the ready, Skatval stalked toward the meeting in the field. Half a dozen chosen men, likewise armed and armored, tramped behind him. One also carried a length of rope. Kveldulf must have seen them, but preached on. By his demeanor, he might have thought they were coming to join his converts.

Before long, perhaps warned by clanking byrnies, some of the converts turned away from Kveldulf. None of them wore mail, nor were they armed for war. Nonetheless, they moved to ring the priest with their bodies; those who bore belt knives drew them. Skatval's jaw tightened. Slaughtering the priest was one thing, fighting his own folk quite another.

"Stand aside," he said. Neither men nor women moved. "Are you so many sparrows, serving to save the cuckoo's spawn Stavrakios has set among you?"

"He is a holy man, a good man," said Kalmar Sverre's son, a fine crofter and not the worst of men himself.

"I do not deny it," Skatval said, which caused more than one of Kveldulf's guards to stare at him in surprise. He went on, "That makes him the greater danger to all that is ours. Ask him yourself, if you believe it not of me." His voice roughened. "Go on, ask him."

Though none of the converts gave way, they did look back to Kveldulf. The blue-robe stared past them to Skatval. Unafraid, he sketched the sun-sign, then set right fist over heart in formal Videssian military salute. He said, "Skatval speaks the truth. Having taken the lord with the great and good mind into your hearts, you cannot remain what you once were. His truth will melt the falsehoods in your spirit as the summer sun slays the snows of Halogaland."

"By his own words he brands himself our foe," Skatval said. "Would you let him make you into milksop southrons?"

"Kveldulf is no milksop," Kalmar said stoutly. He held his knife low, ready to stab up in the way of those who knew how to fight with short blades. But a few people left the converts' circle and stood apart from it, watching to see what would happen next.

Kveldulf said, "I would not see brother spill brother's blood. Stand aside; I told Skatval I would not flee him. Phaos will receive me into his palace; the world to come is finer than the one in which we live now. If your chief would send me to it, I will go."

"But, holy sir—" Kalmar protested. Kveldulf shook his head. The son of Sverre muttered a word that ran round the ring of converts. Skatval heard it, too: "Fey. He is fey." Kalmar looked back to Kveldulf once more. Again Kveldulf shook his head. Tears brightening his eyes, Kalmar lowered the knife to his side and stepped away. One by one, the other converts moved to right or left, until no one stood between Kveldulf and Skatval.

The chief spoke to the men behind him. "We'll take him to the trees over there and tie him."

"No need for that," Kveldulf said. He had gone pale, but his voice stayed steady. "I said I would not flee, and meant it. Do as you deem you must, and have done."

" 'Twere easier the other way, priest," Skatval said doubtfully.

"No. I need not be bound to show I would gladly lay down my life for the lord with the great and good mind; I act by my own will." Kveldulf paused for one long breath. "A favor once I am dead, though, if you would."

"If I may, without hurt to my own," Skatval said.

"Pack my head in salt, as if it were a mackerel set by for the winter, and give it into the hands of the next Videssian shipmaster who enters Lygra Fjord. Tell him the tale and bid him take it—and me—back to the temples, that the prelates there might learn of my labors for the good god's sake."

Skatval stroked his beard as he pondered. Stavrakios might shape the return of such a relic into a pretext for war, but then Stavrakios was a man who seldom needed pretext if he aimed to fight. The chief nodded. "It shall be as you say—my word on it."

"Strike, then." Kveldulf raised hands and eyes to the sky. "We bless thee, Phaos, lord with the great and good mind, watchful beforehand that—"

Skatval struck with all the strength that was in him, to give Kveldulf as quick an end as he might. The spearhead tore out through the back of the blue robe. The priest prayed on as he crumpled. Skatval's followers shoved spears into him as he lay on the green grass. Blood dribbled from the corner of his mouth. He writhed, jerked, was still.

Wearily, Skatval turned to the converts who had watched the killing. "It is over," he said. "Go to your homes; go to your work. You see whose gods are stronger. Would you worship one who lets those who love him die like a slaughtered sow? This Phaos is all very well for Videssians, who serve nobles and Avtokrator like slaves. Give me a god who girds his own to go down fighting, as a Haloga should." He locked eyes with Kalmar Sverre's son. "Or say you otherwise?"

Kalmar met his gaze without flinching, as Kveldulf had before him. In his own good time, he looked away to Kveldulf's corpse. He sighed. "No, Skatval; it is so."

Skatval sighed too, somber still but satisfied. A low murmur rose from the rest of the converts when they heard Kalmar acknowledge the might of the old Haloga gods. They too took a long look at Kveldulf, lying in a pool of his own blood. A couple of women hesitantly signed themselves with the sun-circle. Most, though, began to drift out of the field where they had worshiped. Skatval did not smile, not outside where it showed. By this time next year, his folk's brief fling with Phaos would be as forgotten as a new song sung for a summer but afterwards set aside.

Pleased with the way the event had turned, he said to a couple of his followers, "Vasa, Hoel, take him by the heels and haul him to the hole he dug. But hack off his head before you throw him in; a promise is a promise."

"Aye, Skatval," they said together, as respectfully as they had ever spoken to him: almost as respectfully as if he were Stavrakios of Videssos, sole Avtokrator of a mighty empire, not Skatval the Brisk of Halogaland, one among threescore squabbling chiefs. The feeling of power, strong and sweet as wine from the south, puffed out his chest and put pride in his step as he strode up the path to his longhouse.

But when Skjaldvor spied the bright blood that reddened his spear-shaft, she ran weeping through the garden and into the woods. He stared after her, scratching his head. Then he plunged the iron point of the spear into the ground several times to clean it, wiped it dry with a scrap of cloth so it would not rust.

"Try and understand women," he grumbled. He leaned the spear against the turf wall of his longhouse, opened the door, nodded to Ulvhild his wife. "Well, I'm back," he said.

Nine Threads of Gold

Andre Norton

he way along the upper sea cliff had always been the secondary road into the Hold. Erosion had left only a narrow thread of a trail, laced with ice from the touch of storm-driven waves.

It was midafternoon but there was no sun, the sullen greyness of the sky all of a piece with the cracked rock underfoot. The wayfarer leaned under the leash of a frost wind, digging the point of a staff into such crevices as would give her strength to hold when the full blasts struck.

The traveler paused, to face inland and stare at a tall pillar of rock ending in a jagged fragment pointing skyward like a broken talon. Then the staff swung up and, for a second, there was a play of bluish glimmer about that spear of rock, which vanished in a breath as if the next gust of wind had blown out a taper.

Now the path turned abruptly away from the sea. Here the footing was smoother, the way wider, as if the land had preserved more than the wave-beaten cliffs allowed. It followed for a space the edge of a valley, narrow as an arrow-point at the sea tip, widening inland. The stream that bisected the valley ran toward the sea, but where it narrowed abruptly stood a building, towered, narrow of window, twined with a second structure, a bridge connecting them, allowing the stream full passage between.

In contrast to the grey stone of the cliffs the blocks that formed the walls of those two structures were a dull green, as if painted by moss growth undisturbed by a long flow of years.

The traveler paused at the head of a steep-set stairway descending from the cliff trail, for a searching survey of what lay below. There were no signs of life. Those slits of windows were lightless, blind black eyes. The fields beyond lay fallow and now thick with tough grass.

"Sooo—" The wayfarer considered the scene. In her mind one picture fitted over another. The land she surveyed was spread with an overcoating of another season, another time. And life in many forms was there.

She gathered her cloak closer at her throat and started to pick a careful way down the stair. The clouds at last broke, as they had threatened to do all that day. Rain began as a sullen drizzle, coating those narrow steps dangerously.

However, she did not halt again until she reached what had once been a wider and better-traveled way leading inward from the sea. In spite of the rain she stopped again, peering very intently at the building. Holding her staff a little free from the pavement, she swung it back and forth. No, she had not mistaken that tug. But a warning was as good as a coat of armor might be—sometimes.

Such a long time— Seasons sped into each other in her thoughts, and she did not draw on any one memory.

The road had been well set long ago but now its pavement was akilter from the push of thick-stemmed shrubs, grey and leafless at this season. It still led straight to an arch giving on the nearer end of the bridge that united the two buildings. Down below, the stream gurgled sullenly, but the birds who had haunted the cliffs had been left behind, and there was no other sound—save now and then a roll of distant thunder. She stepped out on the bridge, her staff still held free of the pavement, the lower end pointed a little forward. If only a small portion of what she suspected was the truth, there was that which must be warded against.

Now the archway leading to the courtyard of the larger building was an open gape. Suddenly her staff swung forward at knee level.

There was a flash of blue flame, a speeding of sparks both to right and left as she took a single step on into the courtyard.

"Here entered no darkness—" She spoke that sentence aloud as if it were a charm—or password—at the same time pushing back the hood that had concealed her face, so displaying a countenance like a statue

meant to honor a Queen or Goddess long forgot. While the hair wound
tightly about her head was silver, there were no marks of age on her,
only that calm which comes to one who has seen much, weighed much,
known the pull of duty.

"Come—" Her staff moved in a small beckoning.

The two who first advanced into the open moved warily and plainly
showed that they were coming against their will. There was a boy, his
bony frame loosely covered with a patchwork of badly cured skins cobbled together. Both his hands were so tight about the smaller end of a
club that the knuckles showed, nearly piercing the skin. But the girl was
not far behind him, and she weighed in her two hands a lump of stone,
jagged and large enough to be a good threat.

There was also movement from the wall behind, wherein that gate
was, though the traveler made no attempt to turn or even look over her
shoulder. Another boy, near as thin as the taut bowstring arming the
weapon he carried, and a girl, with a dagger in hand, sprang from some
perch above. A second boy, also with bow in hand, joined them. The
three sidled around the stranger, their weapons at ready, their faces
showing that they were not ignorant of the lash of fear nor the use of the
arms they carried.

Five—

"The others of you?" The traveler made a question of that.

Those arose out of hiding as if the fact that she asked drew them into
sight. Two boys, twins, so alike that one might be the shadow of the
other, each armed with a spear of wood, the points of which had been
hardened by careful fire charring and rubbing. Another girl, who had
no weapon, but carried a younger child balanced on her hip.

Nine. In so much— Yet this was not what she had expected. The
traveler looked intently from one gaunt face to the next. No, not what
she had expected. But in a time of need a weaver must make do with
the best there is to hand.

It was the eldest of the boys, he who had leaped first from the wall,
who gave challenge. He was of an age to have been a squire, and he
wore a much too large and rusty coat of mail, a belt with an empty sword
scabbard bound about it to hold it to his body.

"Who are you?" His demand was sharp and there were traces of the
old high tongue in the inflection of his speech. "How came you here?"

"She came the sea path—" It was the girl who had lain in hiding
with him on the upper wall who spoke then, and her dagger remained

unsheathed. However, it was the younger one who carried the baby who spoke, her gaze holding full upon the traveler:

"Do you not see, Hurten, she is one of *Them*."

They stood in a semicircle about the woman. She could taste fear, yes, but also with that something else, the grim determination that had brought them to this ancient refuge, kept them alive when others had died. They would be stout for the weaving, these nine threads distilled from a broken and ravaged land.

"I am a seeker," the woman answered. "If I must answer to a name let it be Lethe."

"One of *Them*," repeated she who played nursemaid, stubbornly.

The boy Hurten laughed. "Alana, *They* are long gone. You see tales in all about you. Lethe—" He hesitated, and then with now more than a touch of the courtly tongue, "Lady, there is nothing here—" Still holding bow, he spread his hands wide apart, as if to encompass all that lay about him. "We mean no harm. We can spare you a place by a fire, a measure of food, a roof against the storm—little more. We have long been but wayfarers also."

Lethe raised her head so that the folds of her hood slid even farther back.

"For your courtesy of roof and hearth, I give thanks. For the goodwill that prompted such offers, may that be returned to you a hundredfold."

Alana had allowed the small boy in her arms to wriggle to the ground. Now, before she could seize him back in a protective hold, he trotted forward, one hand outstretched to catch full hold on Lethe's cloak, supporting himself as he looked up into her face.

"Maman?" But even as he asked that his small face twisted and he let out a cry. "No—maman—no, maman!"

Alana swooped to catch him up again and Lethe spoke to her softly: "This one is of your blood kin?"

The girl nodded. "Robar, my brother. He . . . doesn't understand, Lady. We were with a pilgrim party. The demons caught us by a bridge. Maman, she told me to jump and she threw Robar down to me. We hid in the reeds— He—he didn't see her again."

"But you did?"

For a moment there was stark horror in Alana's eyes. Her lips formed a word she did not appear to have the strength to voice. Lethe's staff raised; the point of it touched ever so lightly on the little girl's tangle of hair.

"Fade," the woman said, "let memory fade, child. There will come a balancing in good time. Now," she spoke to Hurten, "young sir, I am right ready to make acquaintance of this promised fire and roof of yours."

It would seem that any suspicion they had held was already eased. The weapons were no longer tightly in hand, though the children still surrounded her in a body as she walked ahead, well knowing where she was bound, through the doorway that led into the great presence chamber.

Outside the day was fast darkening into twilight; herein there was light of a sort. Globes set in the walls gave off a faint glimmer as if that which energized them was close to the end of its power. What this dim radiance showed was shadow-cloaked decay.

Once there had been strips of weaving along the walls. Now there were webs of dwindling threads from which all but the faintest of patterns had been lost. There was a dais on which had stood an impressive line of chairs, tall-backed, carven. Most of those had been hacked apart and, as they passed, the children each went forward and picked up an armload of the broken wood, even small Robar taking up one chunk, as if this were a duty to which all of them were sworn.

They passed beyond a carven screen through another door and down a hall until they came into another chamber, which gave evidence of being a camping place. Here was a mighty cavern of a fireplace wherein was hung a pot nearly large enough to engulf Robar himself, and about it other tools of cookery.

A long table, some stools, had survived. Near the hearth to one side was a line of pallets fashioned from the remains of cloaks, patched with small skins, and apparently lumpily stuffed with what might be leaves or grass.

There was a fire on the hearth, and to that one of the twins added wood from the pile where they had dumped their loads, while the other stirred the sullen glow within to greater life.

Hurten, having rid himself of his load, turned, hesitated, and then said gruffly:

"We keep sentinel. It is my duty hour." And was gone.

"There have been others—those you must watch for?" Lethe asked.

"None since the coming of Truas and Tristy." The oldest girl nodded toward the twins. "They came over mountain three tens ago. But the demons had wrought evil down by the sea—earlier. There was a village there once.

"Yes," Lethe agreed, "there was once a village."

"It had been taken long ago," the boy who had borne the club volunteered. "We—we are all from over mountain, Lusta and I—I'm Tyffan, Hilder's son, of Fourth Bend. We were in the fields with Uncle Stansals. He bid us into th' wood when there was smoke from th' village over hill. But"—the boy's fists clenched and there was a grim set to his young jaw—"he did not come back. We had heard of th' demons an' what they did to villages, still we waited in hiding. No one came."

The girl Lusta looked into the heart of the now bravely burning fire. "We wanted to go back—but we saw th' demons riding an' we knew we could never make it."

Truas, tending the fire, looked over his shoulder. "We're shepherds and were out after a stray. They saw us but we knew th' rock trails better. At least those devils cannot fly!"

"Hurten was shield-bearer for Lord Vergan," the oldest girl spoke up. "He was hit on the head and left for dead in the pass battle. I am Marsila and he"—she pointed to the younger boy who had been on the wall— "is my brother, Orffa. Our father was marshal of the Outermost Tower. We were hunting when they came and so were cut off—"

"How came you together?" Lethe asked.

Marsila glanced about as if for the first time she herself had faced that question.

"Lady, we met by chance. Alana and Robar, they fled to Bors Wood and there met with Lusta and Tyffan. And Orffa and I, we found Hurten and stayed with him until his head was healed, then we, too, took the wood road. There was, we hoped, a chance that Skylan or Varon might have held—only, when we met the others, Alana said the demons had swept between to cut us off."

"You decided then to come over mountain? Why?" Lethe must know—already she sought the beginning of the pattern she had sensed. There was one or she, the weaver, would not have been summoned.

It was Lusta who answered, in a low voice, her head down as if she must confess some fault. "The dreams, Lady. Always the same dream an' each time I saw clearer."

"Lusta's gran was *Wise*," Tyffan broke in. "All of Fourth Bend thought she had part of the gift, too. Lusta dreamed us here."

Marsila smiled and put her arm around the younger girl's shoulders. "Not many have the *Wise* gifts now, but we had records of such at the Tower and—well—we had no other place to go, so why not trust a dream?"

Her face became bleak again. "At least the demons did not try the mountains then. When we found this place we knew that fortune favored us a little. There is farm stock running wild in the valley, even some patches of grain we are harvesting, and fruit. Also—this place, it seemed somehow as if we were meant to shelter here."

"Dreams led!" Lethe moved to Lusta and, as she had with Alana, touched the girl's head with her staff. There was a spark of blue. Lethe smiled.

"Dreamer, you have wrought well. Good will follow in a way now past your understanding."

Then she drew back to survey them all, her gaze resting for a long moment on each face. So this was indeed the beginning.

"Truly," she spoke, "this is the place for such as you."

These were from very different beddings, these seedlings, yet their roots were the same. That had been clear to her from their first sighting. Their hair, tangled, unkempt, was of the same pale silver blond, their eyes shared the same clear sword-blade grey. Yes, the old stock had survived after all, though the seed might have been wide flung.

Lethe shifted the bag she had carried from her shoulder to the top of the table. She loosed the string and reached within, drawing forth a packet of dried meat, another of herbs.

There was already something steaming in the great pot; she was certain that they had not lost the chance for a day's hunting. Now she shook forth her own offerings and added them to that. They watched her closely.

"Traveler's fare, but it may add to your store as is the custom," she told them.

Marsila had watched her very closely. Now, in spite of the fact that she wore breeches patched with small skins, she made the curtsy of a daughter of a House in formal acknowledgment.

"If this be your kin, hold our thanks for shelter." Still there was a measure of questioning in her eyes.

However, it was Alana who spoke, and she did so almost with accusation. "You are one of *Them* so this *is* your place."

"What do you know of *Them*, child?" Lethe had shrugged off her cloak. Her breeches and jerkin were of a dull green not unlike the walls about her.

"They had strange powers," Alana answered. She reached out and drew Robar to her. "Powers which gave them rule. None could stand against them—like the demons!"

Lethe had taken a ladle from a hook in the hearth wall. Now she looked directly at the small girl. "Powers to take rule like the demons—that is what they say of us now?"

For a long moment Alana was silent and then she flushed. "*They*—*They* did not hunt people—*They* did not . . . kill—"

"*They* were guardians!" Marsila broke in. "When *They* were in the land there could be no death there."

"Why did *They* go?" One of the twins sat back on his heels.

"When *They* had strong keeps like this, if *They* ruled th' land, what did *They* do?"

Lethe stirred the pot. She did not look around.

"The land is old, many have been rooted here. When years pass another blood comes to masterage."

For the first time Orffa spoke: "So this is the time for demons to rule, is that what you tell us?" There was a fierce challenge in his voice and he was scowling.

"Demons?" Lethe looked to the fire and the steaming pot. "Yes, to this land at this hour, they are demons."

Marsila moved closer. "How else can we see them? Tell me that, once guardian!"

Lethe sighed. "No way else." She turned to face the children. Children? Save for Robar, there was little childlike in those faces ringing her in. They had seen much, and none of it good. But that was the working of the Way, the spinning of the weaver's threads. Standing in shadow behind each was the faint promise of what might be.

"Why have you come? Will others follow you?" demanded Orffa.

"I have come because I was summoned. I alone." She gave them the truth. "The kinblood have passed to another place, only it would seem that I am tied to this day."

"That is magic." Tyffan pointed to her staff where she had laid it across the table. "But you're one against many. Those raiders hold th' land from Far River to th' Sea, from Smore Mount Mouth to Deep Yen."

Lethe looked directly at him. His mop of hair reached barely above her shoulder, but his sturdy legs were planted a little apart, and he stood with his fist-curled hands on his hips as if in defiance.

"You speak as one who knows," she commented.

To her mild surprise he grinned. "Not claimin' magic, mistress, that. You find us here now, that's not sayin' as how we is always here. We has our ways o' learnin'. What chances over mountain—and it ain't by dreams."

Lethe pursed her lips. Looking at him she could believe in what he

hinted. This one had stated that he was land-born, land-trained; and
the young learned swiftly when there was need.

"So you have used your eyes and ears to good purpose." He nodded
briskly. "Well enough. And what have you learned with your non-
magic?"

Orffa pushed past the younger boy. "Enough," he snapped.

"And the demons have not disturbed you here?" she asked.

"There was a scouting company," Marsila answered. "They followed
the sea road inward but there came a sudden rockfall which closed that.
At night they camped near that . . ."

Tyffan grinned widely and the twins echoed his expression.

"They didn't like what they heard nor saw. We didn't either, but then
we guessed as how it weren't meant for th' likes of us. They ran—an'
some o' them went into th' river. Hurten, he brought down one with an
arrow—he's a champion shot—an' we bashed a couple with rocks.
Wanted to get their weapons but river took 'em an' we didn't dare go
after 'em. They ain't been this way since."

"It wasn't us, not all of it," Marsila said slowly. "There was something
there—we felt it but it did not try to get us—only them."

Lusta held to the other girl's arm. "The rocks made shadow things,"
she said.

"So the old guards hold somewhat," Lethe commented. "But those
were never meant to stand against any who meant no harm. This"—she
gestured with her hand—"was once a place of peace under the sign of
Earth and Air, Flame and Water.

"Now," she pointed to the pot, "shall we eat? Bodies need food, even
as minds need knowledge."

But her thoughts were caught in another pattern. Here was a mixture
which only danger could have, and had, cemented—delvers, shepherds,
soldier and lordly blood all come by chance together and seemingly already united. Chance? No, she thought she dared already believe not.

They brought bowls and marshalled in line. Some had battered metal,
time-darkened, which they must have found here; there were cups
shaped of bark pinned together with pegs. Lethe tendered the ladle to
Marsila and watched the girl dip careful portions to each. One over she
set aside and Lethe took it up.

"For your sentinel? Let this be my service."

Before any protested she headed out of the great kitchen. The dark
had deepened despite the globe light, but she walked with the sure step

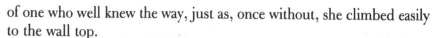

of one who well knew the way, just as, once without, she climbed easily to the wall top.

"No need for that." She had heard rather than seen the draw of a belt knife, could picture well the spare young body half acrouch. "Your supper, sentinel, also your relief."

Shadow moved out of shadows. In her left hand the staff diffused a pale radiance. Though Hurten reached for the bowl, the dagger was still drawn. However, Lethe took no notice of his wariness. Instead she had swept the staff along the outer edge of the parapet that sheltered them a little from the incoming sea wind.

"So are guards set, Hurten. I promise you that there need be no watch on duty this night. And there is much we all have to talk of . . ."

She could sense the edge of the resentment that was rightfully his. What leadership this group had known in the arts of war must have come from him.

"Shield Chief," deliberately Lethe used the old tongue, "there is a time for the blooding of blades and a time for planning, that those blades may be better sharpened for the blooding."

"By Oak, by Stream, by Storm, by Fire—" The words came in the old tongue—

Lethe nodded, though he might not be able to see that gesture of approval in the gloom.

"By Sword and Staff, by Horn, by Crown." The old words came so easily in this place, though it was another time when they were common here. "So warrior, you have at least trod a stride or two down that path?"

"My lord was of the House of Uye. When we were given our swords as men he held by the old oaths."

Swords as men! she thought. These must be dire days when boys were counted men. But only dire days could have drawn her here.

"Then you know that this is a place of peace."

She heard the faint snick of the dagger being sent once more into sheath.

"Lady, in this land there is no longer any place of peace." His words were stark and harsh.

"To that we shall take council. Come—"

Hurten hesitated, still unwilling to admit that the watch he had taken on himself might no longer be necessary, but she had already started back as if she thought there could be no questioning, and he followed.

They found the rest about the fire. Orffa and Marsila both looked up in question as Hurten came in, but Lethe was quick to explain:

"There is a guard, and one which will keep the watch well. For now there is that which we must discuss among ourselves." Deliberately she chose her words to ally herself at once with these chosen for a purpose she could not question.

"Time may change but not the seasons." Lethe had waited until they had cleaned their bowls. "The sea winds herald ill coming. There was once some command over wind and weather in this place, but that was long ago. We shall need that for day and night"—she pointed to the fire—"and food—"

"We have been gathering," Marsila answered sharply as if some action of hers had been called into question. "We have a storeroom."

Lethe nodded. "That I do not question. Save that if the dire storms hit, as well they may, there shall be needed every scrap of food, every stick of wood. Herb-craft also, for there are the illnesses which come with weather changes, and some of those are severe."

There was movement at the other side of the table. Alana carried a nearly asleep Robar to one of the fireside pallets.

Hurten leaned forward.

"What are we to you?" His voice was a little hoarse. "We are not of your breed. No." He glanced briefly at the others. "Nor are we even of one House or blood ties ourselves. We make no claim of vassalage rights—"

"Why did you come here?" Marsila planted one elbow on the table and rested her chin upon her hand. "There has been no tale of your kind among us since the High Queen Fothuna died, leaving no daughter for the rule, and all the land fell apart, with quarrels between lordlings and War Ladies. And that was a legend length of years ago. We have none of the old power—

"Lusta, yes. Twice she dreamed us out of fell dangers—but our race was and is wise in our own way only. Thus we ask, why do you come to speak as a chatelaine here?"

"And I ask again, what do you want with us?" Hurten repeated.

He was frowning, and that frown was echoed by a stronger scowl drawing together Orffa's straight brows. The impish humor that had looked ever ready to curve Tyffan's lips was gone, and the twins were blank-faced.

Lusta's tongue showed a pink tip between her lips but she did not speak, and Alana's hands clasped together tightly on the table top before her.

"You, in a manner, called me. No"—Lethe shook her head, aware of the denial already on Hurten's lips—"I do not say that you knew of me. But in those days of far legend Marsila has mentioned there were gaes laid, and this was mine: that I was tied to Kar-of-the-River—this keep in which we shelter. And so I fulfill now that set upon me. I did not know until I came hither what I would find.

"As to what you mean to me—that we both must learn. For I must in right tell you this, that you are bound even as I—"

Hurten's hand balled into a fist. He moved as if to stand. He was of no temper to play with words, as Lethe saw, yet what more could she tell him yet?

It was Orffa who got to his feet and moved behind the older boy, as a liege man would back-cover his lord. But of him Hurten took no notice as he said:

"Lady, we are not those for your binding."

Lethe sighed. Patience, ever patience. A weaver must be sure that no knotting despoiled her threads. It was Marsila who put an end to it.

"The hour grows late." She had pulled Alana closer beside her, and the child leaned heavily against her shoulder. "With the morrow there will be time enough for questions."

It seemed that even Hurten was willing to surrender to that. So the fire was set for long burning and they took their places on the pallets within its warmth, Lethe lying down upon a cushion of her cloak—though she did not sleep. For her kind needed little of such rest. Instead, behind closed eyelids, she rebuilt what now closed her in as she had seen it last in other days. Out of the past she summoned others who moved as shades where they had once been true life.

A sound broke through her half-dream. She opened her eyes. One of those on the pallets had sat up, shrugged aside a covering of skins. The fire flickered to show a face—

Lusta, the dreamer!

Lethe's keen sight was not deadened by the gloom. The girl's eyes were closed. Nor did she open them as her head swung around as if in answer to some summons. On hands and knees, eyes still shut, she crawled away from the hearth into inner darkness, and then got to her feet. Lethe allowed her a small start and followed after.

Down the hall into the great presence chamber. The globe light was gone, it was totally dark here, yet Lusta went with the confidence of one who saw perfectly. Lethe followed. To break the girl's trance—no—that was a dangerous folly. She must know what drove Lusta into the night.

They came forth from the hall into the open of the courtyard. Up the stairs Lusta went without a stumble. A moon shone warily between moving clouds, and to Lethe this was light enough. Lusta had sought out the very perch where Hurten had earlier made his sentry post.

She turned slowly, facing outward, and then her hand went out to the parapet and her fingers tapped along it. Sparks flew as if she used a wand of iron instead of her own flesh.

Lethe's head went back. Her nostrils flared as if to catch some faint scent. She was already up the stairs; now she moved forward, and, standing behind Lusta, put out her own two hands, touching fingers lightly to both the girl's temples.

The woman's lips flattened into something closer than a snarl. This—but she had not thought that the new invaders were so knowledgeable. Or were they only symptoms of an older and fouler plague?

She applied pressure, flesh to flesh, and forced will upon dream. Lusta's own hands paused in their tapping. Then she cried out sharply and crumpled as if all life had been withdrawn in a matter of a breath or two.

Lethe did not kneel at once beside her; rather she now turned all attention to the danger at hand. Where Lusta had wrought a breaking spell, she relaid the guard, this time reinforcing it with will enough to leave her feeling nearly as drained as the unconscious girl at her feet.

It was not well—what she had done would alert that other power that had already made this first move. Yet Lusta taken over, with a gift she had not been trained to protect, was a key which must not be used.

Lethe crouched down to gather the girl into her arms, pulling her cloak about the both of them. Lusta's face was as chill as if she had been brought out of a snowbank, but both of her hands, which Lethe took into one of hers, were warm, near fire-hot. That which the girl had not finished projecting into the break spell was turned back upon her, eating in. She moaned and twisted in the woman's hold.

"Lusta!" There came a call from below, then the scrape of boots on stone.

Tyffan came in a scrambling run. "Lusta!" He went down on his knees beside the two of them. "What—"

"She is safe—for now." Under Lethe's touch the fire had cooled from the girl's hands. "Tyffan, you say she dreamed you here?"

"What is wrong with her?" He paid no attention to that question.

"She has been possessed." Lethe gave him the truth. "Perhaps even her dreaming you here was by another's purpose. This night that which held her in bond used her to attack the guards."

Tyffan stared at the woman. "But Lusta would not—"

"No!" Lethe assured him quickly. "She would not have brought harm to you willingly. But she was not taught to guard her gift, and that laid her open to—"

"The demons!" But how—"

"We do not know by whom or why she was sent to do this," Lethe said quickly. "But she has overused her strength, and we must get her into warmth now."

Hurten and Orffa met them at the door of the presence chamber, and Tyffan gave them a confused answer as to what had happened as Lethe hurried the girl, who was on her feet but barely so, into the warmth of the kitchen place.

She oversaw the brewing up of an herbal potion and stood over Lusta until the girl drank it to the dregs. Lusta seemed but half awake, dazed, mumbling, and unaware of where she was or what had happened. Lethe saw her back to the pallet and then faced the others.

"You asked me earlier what I wanted of you," she said directly. "That I do not yet fully know. But it may also be that another power brought you here and is prepared to make use of you." And she explained what Lusta had been led to do.

"Lusta is not a demon!" Tyffan near shouted.

It was Marsila who answered him. "She is *Wise*. That is a power. Lusta would never use it for any but good. In truth"—now she spoke to Lethe—"she never used it by her will; the dreams came to her without her seeking or bidding."

"We speak of power as a gift," Lethe said. "It may also be a burden, even a curse, if it is not used with control. I do not think that Lusta was given any aid in learning what she could do—"

Tyffan stirred. "She—she didn't know as how it meant anything." He looked toward where the girl lay. "Her mam, she died when Lusta was just a mite. M' mam, she was closest kin an' took her. But we had no *Wise* for a long time. T'wasn't 'til after th' demons came that she dreamed—or at least told her dreams. But she's no demon—ask Hurten—ask Truas and Tristy. She dreamed us together!"

"The demons," Lethe returned. "Have you heard that they have some form of the Wisdom among them?"

The children looked to one another and then Marsila shook her head.

"They came like—like storm clouds—and there was no standing against them. There were so many and they seemed to appear without any warning. But my father said we fared so badly in the field against them because the lords and War Ladies had been cut adrift from any one leader. Each fought for their own holds, and one by one those Holds fell. There was no High Queen. It was almost as if we were all blinded—"

Hurten nodded. "My lord—he tried to send for help to the Hold of Iskar, and the lord there told him no because he feared those of Eldan more than the demons. He told the messenger that the rumors of demons were put about to frighten timid Hold-keepers. That was before Iskar was taken in two days and left but bloodied stone. There, it is true"—he spoke thoughtfully now, almost as if he were examining memory and seeing a new pattern in it—"that the Holders did not come together. And what they gave as reasons were mainly wariness of their own neighbors. Was that—could that have been some power of the demons?"

His hand had gone once more to the hilt of his dagger and he stared at Lethe as if he would have the truth even at a point of steel.

"It could be so."

It was Alana who came a step or so closer and looked up into Lethe's face.

"Lady, why would the demons want us who are here in this place—unless to kill us as"—she hesitated a second and the old fear came flooding back into her firelit eyes—"they did all the others? Lusta dreamed us here—but there were no demons waiting."

"This was waiting, and perhaps your entrance here would open doors for them or something else." Lethe was searching—her senses weighing first the children and then the very walls about them. No, there had been no tampering save that she had caught this night. There was no taint of dark in this company.

"What lies here then?" flared Hurten. "The demons came upon us from the north; they are not of our kind. Perhaps"—his eyes narrowed—"they are of yours—Lady." And there was little goodwill in the title he gave her.

"Before your demons," she answered him, "there were other powers abroad. Some were always of the Dark. Open your mind, youth: is this such a place as welcomes the Dire Shadows?"

For a moment there was a silence. Hurten's frown did not fade. Then tentatively his right hand arose between them and the fingers moved in a gesture that brought a sigh of relief from Lethe.

"Bite of iron, warrior." She held out her own hand. He hesitated, then drew his dagger. She deliberately touched the end of the blade, withstanding a stab of flame pain that was true fire. When she took her hand away and turned it over, she held it well into the light.

There was an angry red blotch on her pale skin. She endured the pain for a space, that they might see, and then willed healing into the skin.

"Cold iron." Hurten looked down at his own weapon as if it possessed a potential unknown to him.

"The demons," Orffa broke in, "can die but from edge and point. Only the First Ones—" He drew a deep breath.

"Only those of the Right-Hand Path," Marsila interrupted her brother, "cannot hold iron."

"And our wards still held here," Lethe pointed out. "Still there must be that which would put an end to weaving by destroying loom and weaver."

"You speak of weaving," Marsila said then. "You are the weaver?"

"So it has been set upon me."

"It remains." Hurten turned to the earlier problem. "Lusta led us here, by whose will?"

"Who can tell that?" Lethe spoke wearily, for again the truth burdened her down.

"Will—will she be possessed again?" Marsila approached Lusta with caution. The younger girl appeared deep in sleep, unaware of all about her now.

"I have set guards," Lethe answered. "For now those will hold."

None of them questioned that—as if they avoided voicing doubts. Hurten settled by the fire, but not to sleep. Instead he brought from a belt pouch a whetstone, and with this he set about giving edge to his dagger, working as one who must occupy himself with even so small a preparation against trouble to come. Marsila dragged her pallet up beside Lusta's, just as Tyffan barricaded the girl on the other side.

Hurten's belt with its empty scabbard—without a sword—

Without a sword, that symbol of manhood for his race. Lethe once more closed her eyes, but her thoughts were awake. A sword—she resisted, having the feeling that she was being pushed too swiftly into decisions. It was not for her to deal with weapons as this land now knew them, but neither could she deny to others the safety a blade could offer. However, this could wait until tomorrow. Hurten had stopped the push of the whetstone, returned it to his pouch, was stretching out to sleep.

Lethe lengthened the narrowest edge of thought as a field commander would dispatch a trained scout. The guards were firm, nothing tried them. Lusta? The girl was so deep in slumber that no invader could reach her. Safe? Were any of them safe?

Lusta had offered a gate to some old power—what of the other children? Lethe shrank from what she must do—this was something that could only be justified by dire danger. Did they face that?

She made her decision and began the search. Alana, one arm thrown about her little brother in constant protection—nothing there.

The shepherd twins? A hazy dream picture, partly shared, of a fair morning in home heights. Tyffan—dark shadows acreep—the beginning of a nightmare in which he struggled to reach a farmhouse where Lusta awaited him. That she could banish, and she did.

Marsila—fall woodlands in brilliant color, a sun-warmed morning—rightness and loving memory. Her brother—deep sleep as untroubled as Lusta's. Hurten—the sentry on the wall, a pressing need to hold off some threat that had not yet shown itself—a need the greater because he had no weapon. She had been right—this one needed the talisman of a blade.

Lethe searched memory. She had read them and there was no taint here. So assured, she could await the coming day.

They broke their morning fast with a rough mush of wild grain only made palatable by a handful of dried berries. Lethe waited until they were done before she spoke.

"You have two bows, two daggers among you—that is not enough."

Hurten laughed angrily. "The truth, Lady. But here there is no forge, nor are any of us smiths. Is there an enemy we can hope to plunder?"

"Come—"

Lethe led them back to the presence chamber, all, even Robar, trailing her. She came to face the wall behind the dais. There hung one of the time-ravished lengths of weaving. This was no tapestry like the others, rather the remains of what might once have been a banner.

So hard had time treated what lay here! However, she was not saddened, rather stirred by the need to be about her task. The chairs that
had once stood against the wall were debris. But the long table there
was intact, save it was covered with dust and splinters of wood.

She swept out with her staff, and the litter was lifted and blown away
by a strong puff of breeze. Lethe pointed now to the frail banner.

With the staff she drew a careful outline around what hung there while
she hummed—a faint drone of sound, like the sigh of wind in a wood.
On the wall the banner moved. Dust motes shifted down, but none of
the frail fabric parted. As a single piece it was loosed while her staff
moved back and forth as might that of a shepherd guiding a flock around
some danger. Down came the length of ancient weaving, to lie full-length
on the table.

"Do not touch it!" she ordered. "That time is not yet. We have other
needs."

Once more her staff moved, now pointing directly to the wall the
banner had curtained. She spoke aloud in command, words that had
not been uttered since the days of deep legend.

Cracks appeared between stones, lines formed a doorway. That
opened.

"Come!" Lethe waved them on.

The staff itself gave forth the light here, bringing answering gleams
from racks, from shelves for storage. Here were weapons. She heard a
cry from Hurten as he pushed forward, his hand out to the hilt of a
sword. He stood looking down at it in joyful wonder. The others ventured farther in, eyeing what was there as if they did not quite dare touch.
Then Orffa took up a sword, and Tyffan, after glancing to Lethe as if
she might forbid it even now, closed hand upon the haft of a double-
bladed axe.

A moment later Hurten turned accusingly to the woman. "What folly
is this? No true steel—" He had been running his hand along the blade
of his choice.

She laughed. "Cold iron is not to be found here, young warrior. These
are forged of battle silver, but none the less sharp and strong."

For a moment it seemed as if he might dispute that, then he nodded.
"To each people their own secrets. This balances well at least." He
swung it in a practice thrust.

"No—no—Robar!"

Alana was engaged in a tug of war with her brother. Face red with rising anger, he was struggling to get full hold on a dagger near long enough to be deemed a short sword.

"Want—want—now! Robar wants—!"

Alana seemed unable to break his grip. Truas caught the little boy by the shoulders from behind.

"Here now, young'un, that's naught to play with. Give it to Alana an'—" He had turned his head to view the racks of weapons but was plainly baffled as to what might be offered as a counter to Robar's first choice.

"Want!" Robar howled and then aimed a kick at his sister that struck home before Truas could pull him out of reach.

"Robar—no—!" There was an expression of fear on Alana's face. "Give it to Alana, please!"

As the boy fought and wriggled to free himself, Alana pried his fingers loose one by one. His screaming was enough to bring all the others to the battle. Once his sister had forced one hand open, Robar swung that up and drew his nails down her cheek. She cried out and jerked back, her eyes wide, staring at her brother as if she had never seen him before.

Marsila pushed her aside, but it was Hurten who took command:

"Give him to me!" And when Truas had surrendered the still wildly fighting boy into his hold he added, "Get that thing away from him!"

In spite of having to ward off kicks, which, to Lethe, appeared too well aimed to be allied with blind rage, Truas was able to capture the dagger. Then Hurten carried the still struggling child out of the room.

Alana's whole body was shaking. Tears diluted the blood from the scratches on her cheeks.

"He—he never did that before. Oh, Robar!" She pushed aside Marsila and ran after Hurten and her brother.

There was a subdued quiet. Lethe stooped to pick up the disputed weapon. To both her eyes and her inner touch it was no more than it appeared to be. For a moment a wisp of thought had troubled her. But the scene could have risen simply from the fact that an over-guarded and indulged child—for Alana's care was easy to see—had wanted a choice like the other boys. He was passing out of babyhood and perhaps had been unconsciously resentful of Alana's protectiveness for some time.

The others made their choices quickly. Marsila chose four bows and matching quivers of silver-tipped arrows, gathering them into an unwieldy bundle. Lusta and the others selected daggers, testing the points on fingertips. But for major weapons the twins wanted short-shafted javelins, taking a trio of these apiece. Tyffan held to the axe, Orffa the sword with a belt and sheath to go with it.

Lethe was interested in their choices. Each must have chosen those arms with which they felt the most comfortable. She replaced the dagger Robar had clung to in the rack, and followed the company out. Behind her the door closed and once more disappeared.

Marsila laid the bows down on the table, taking care not to disturb the banner. She motioned to Lusta and Orffa, and they each chose one. Then she selected hers, leaving the other.

"Hurten's"—she nodded to that—"a far better one than he has, and one to serve him well."

Alana sat by the pallet when they reentered the kitchen. Robar lay there curled in upon himself sniffling. As the others drew near his sister pulled at his shoulder.

"Robar?" Her voice both admonished and encouraged.

He sat up. The anger had gone out of his eyes. Instead tears marked his cheeks.

"Sorry—Robar's sorry." His voice was hardly above a whisper.

Alana smiled. "It's true, he is sorry."

Marsila went closer. "Very well, Robar. But being sorry does not take away the scratches on your sister's cheek, now does it?"

He smeared both hands across his face. "Robar's sorry," he repeated woefully. Alana caught him in a tight hug.

"Of course, Alana knows. Robar's really sorry."

Tyffan, fingering the new axe, had seemed to pay little attention. Now he said:

"'Tis a fair day out. Maybe there will be a beast in the grasslands— easy to be downed with new bows."

"Of course!" Hurten appeared with the bow Marsila had left for him. "Get us perhaps that yearling bull calf we saw two days ago."

Lethe watched them scatter to what must have been the occupations they had settled to since they had come to the keep. In the day there was no fear of the outlands.

Even Robar shared in the gathering of supplies, disputing with a number of angry squirrels for the harvest of fallen nuts, while his sister and Tristy beat the tree branches to bring more down.

Lusta was using her new dagger to cut ragged stands of wild grain still slippery from yesterday's storm. Her harvesting sent grain-eating birds flying, and she turned to her bow. Though it was apparent she was no well-trained archer, she did not always miss.

Lethe left the scene of labor and followed the river, pausing now and then to stand, staff in hand, spying out toward the hills in her own fashion. But if Lusta had nearly opened a door to something of the Dark last night, it was not to be sensed now.

Though her warning sense kept guard, her main thoughts turned to what had drawn her here and why. These children seedlings, threads—hers would be the planting, the weaving. She tightened hold on her staff. After all the years to have once more a purpose!

Lethe returned to the keep at midday to stand again in the presence chamber, looking down at the ghostly banner. Her fingers moved as they might, without direction but from long habit. Slowly she turned to survey the huge chamber. Where there was desolation—yes, there would be life again.

In the kitchen was truly the bustle of life. Hurten had indeed brought down the bull calf and roughly butchered it. And now it lay bundled in its own spotted hide; containers of bark, even large leaves pinned together with thorns, were full of the last of the berries, nuts, edible roots, all of which Lusta was sorting with the help of Alana; while Marsila had brought in a string of ducks.

Hurten appeared again with the twins, and this time they had not plundered the moldering furniture in the other rooms, but had good loads of wood, storm gleanings—though these must be set to dry.

They shared the work as if they had done this many times before, and Lethe nodded. Already these were bonded after their own fashion; her task would be the lighter.

Through her self-congratulation broke a cry of fear. Alana had pulled away from the table.

"Robar—where is Robar? Tyffan, did he follow you again? Where is he?"

"Never saw him." There was an odd note in the older boy's voice. "What do you mean, followed me?" He was so quickly angry, as if he had been accused of some wrongdoing.

Lethe tensed. Now there was something awakening here, hostile to the accord that had lulled her.

Orffa was also showing signs of anger. "Little pest, always creeping around where he shouldn't be," he muttered.

Alana was confronting Tyffan. There was fear but anger also in the words she flung at him.

"When you passed us you said you were going to the pond. You know how he loves to go there."

Tyffan shook his head. "He wasn't with me, I tell you."

She turned then on Orffa. "You were hunting up on the hill, you must have seen him."

"I never saw the brat. He's always in some trouble or other. Best tie him to you and be done with it, trader trash!"

"Mind your mouth!" Marsila snapped at her brother. "If Robar did go to the pool—"

Alana let out a keening cry and darted for the doorway, Marsila but a step or so behind her. A crash sounded from the table: Lusta had dropped one of the metal bowls. Hurten caught Orffa by the shoulder and jerked him around to face him.

"That pool is deep, Orffa. Also, there are no 'trader trash' here. Keep that tongue of yours clean!"

Orffa's face was scarlet as he jerked free from the other's grip.

"I never saw the brat!"

Lethe shivered. She had been a sentry—surely she would have sensed evil in the valley this morning if it had lain in waiting there. The contentment that had been here only moments earlier was shattered as if she had willed it away herself.

Lusta? Her gift; that was understandable. Robar? Lethe had sensed no power in him, but he was so young a child that at his age he would have very few natural defenses. Robar—!

Not the pool, no. What was wanted for Robar was not danger for him, but through him. And what was wanted must lie within these walls.

"Fool!" Hurten snarled at Orffa. The younger boy's hand flew to his sword hilt. Now the twins moved in and Tyffan was rounding the table to join them. Lusta stood with her hands pressed to her whitened cheeks.

"Keep your tongue to yourself!" Orffa cried. "Do not try to play the high lord with me! I do not know where the brat went—"

"He came here," Truas said. "Saw him on the bridge."

Orffa showed teeth. "Why didn't you speak up before, thickhead—or were you so gagged with the dirty wool you couldn't?"

"Here now," Tristy answered before his brother. He still held the bloody knife he had been using on Hurten's kill. "What's gotten into you, Orffa?"

"Orffa?" He made a near threat of his own name. "Who are you to name me so familiarly, beast-keeper? I am of the blood of Ruran who was lord—"

"Stop!" Lethe's staff was between the boys. Her eyes had narrowed as she looked from one furious scowl to another. "You saw Robar come here? Then let us find him." Either the tone of her voice or some effect of the staff brought them together again—temporarily.

"We'll search—" Hurten agreed.

"Perhaps there is no need to go far." Lethe beckoned to Lusta and asked, "Which of those boxes of nuts there did Robar fill?"

Lusta shivered, and her hands whipped behind her back. "No! No!" She turned her head from side to side, like a small trapped animal gnawed by fear.

"Yes!" There was no escaping that order.

Lusta's right arm moved outward, her fingers hooked like claws. She was staring down at the array of the morning's harvest with fear-rounded eyes. Her hand swung, steadied over one of those containers.

Instantly Lethe raised the staff and touched the crude basket.

She had their full attention now, their quarreling forgotten. Her grip on the staff was loose enough to allow it play, swing of its own accord. She followed that direction, the others close behind her.

Back into the presence chamber—to the wall of the hidden room. She had been a fool to underestimate this other power. That early scene with Robar in there—why had she been so blind?

She strove within her to trace, to know—

"There must be all of you here. Find Marsila—Alana—"

Lethe did not look to see if she had been obeyed, but she heard the shuffle of badly worn boots across the hall.

"Lady." Lusta had crept to her side. "Lady I am afraid—I cannot—I do not know what you would have me do."

"Nor do I know yet what has to be done, child. As for can and cannot, Lusta, that will wait upon what we learn."

She fought within her to set aside all the lives about her, to think only in terms of her weapon—no blade nor axe, spear nor bow, only what was her own. As she wove life, so now she must weave another sort of web, one to be both defense and trap.

"Robar! Please." There was a tug at her arm. "Is Robar truly here?" Lethe looked around quickly—not only Alana was here, but all the rest.

She began a chant, the words issuing stiffly from her lips as if it were
so long since they had been used that they had grown as rusty as un-
tended armor. Once more the concealed door opened.

Around them the globe lights dimmed as if their radiance was being
sucked out of them.

Lethe threw out her arm to catch Alana, who would have darted before
her.

"Robar!" his sister screamed, and then her voice was muffled, for
which Lethe was briefly grateful.

The light of the staff flared. In the armory a shadow sprang forth from
shadows—and the light caught on a bared blade.

Lethe's weapon swung down between her body and that intended
blow. Robar crouched. His face was not that of a child. That which had
entered him had molded his features, was blazing from his eyes.

The staff swung, pointed. Sparks formed into a tongue of light, but
that was fended, curled back, before it touched the child.

"Join!" Lethe's other hand moved as her voice rose above the insane
shrieks from the small figure before her. Spittle flecked from his lips.
Dread intelligence stared grimly and grotesquely from his eyes.

"Join!" Her free hand was gripped, she felt the surge of energy, then
came a second and a third—that which had first brought them together
was still in force.

The staff warmed. The thread of solid light from it was still held away
from Robar, but the space was less and less.

"You are Robar!" Lethe called upon the power that lay in names.
"You are one with this company. You are Robar!"

Small lips twisted into a sneer.

"Fratch!"

Lethe was prepared. That challenger name did not surprise her. As
there were the weavers among the kin, so there had been destroyers. But
time was long, and that which destroyed never grew without feeding.
Had it been the invaders who had fed this one awake again?

"You are Robar!"

She sought the Touch, to seek out, to shift one personality from another. The light spear was now less than a finger-width from the grimacing child.

"Robar!" That was meant as a call, a summoning. At the same time
she drew deeper on the energy fed her by the others.

The light touched the child's forehead. His features writhed and he howled, a cry no human could have uttered. Then—it was as if something that had been confined in too small a prisoning burst forth.

Robar fell like a crumpled twist of harvest grain. Above his body wavered a mist into which bored the spear of light. Then the mist spiraled downward upon itself until it was but a grey blot which the blue bolt licked into nothingness.

"Robar!" Alana threw herself at her brother, pulling him close, twisting her own body about him as if to wall him from all harm.

"What—what happened, Lady?" Tyffan asked hoarsely.

"That was a shadow, of something which should have died long ago." Lethe tried to take a step and tottered.

Strong young arms closed about her as Hurten and Marsila moved in. "A shadow of a will. First it tried to fasten onto Lusta, for her gift offered it power. Then it turned to Robar because he was too young to have those safeguards which come through living. Fratch—Styreon who was"—she addressed the empty air—"you were ever greedy for that which was not yours—nor shall it ever be!"

They went out of the armory, Orffa carrying Robar, who lay limp in his arms, Alana seemingly content to have it so. Marsila and Hurten kept their hold on Lethe, the end of her staff dragging on the floor, though she still kept it within her grasp.

Here was the table on which lay the banner. What was to be done was clear now, and the sooner done the better. Lethe spoke to Lusta:

"This is a beginning. Sister, take your dagger, that which is of the great forging, and not made of fatal iron, and cut from the head of each of these comrade-kin of yours a lock."

They asked no questions, and submitted to Lusta's knife. For the first time Lethe set aside her staff. From her belt purse she brought forth a large needle, which glistened gold in the light. This she threaded with a strand of hair and set about weaving it into the webbing as one would darn a very old and precious thing. So she did again and again as they watched. And with each new strand she repeated aloud the name of him or her to which it had belonged, forming so a chant.

Thus Lethe wrought in moments lifted out of time, for none spoke nor moved, only watched. When she was done they looked upon a length of silver-gold on which faint patterns formed, changed, reformed, growing ever the stronger.

Lethe withdrew her needle. "One is combined of many, even as you united in your flight out of death, as you gave me of your strength to free Robar—you are indeed one.

"But from that one weaving there will come much which is to be welcomed—and time will welcome it and you."

It is told that in the fell days when the Ka-sati had laid totally waste the land and those of the barbarian blood would raise a temple to the Eternal Darkness, there came a company out of the northern hills, riding under a banner bearing nine stripes of gold. Those who bore it were of the blood of legends and what they wrought was to the glory of earth and sky, flood and flame—the darkness being utterly blinded by their light.

The Conjure Man

Charles de Lint

I do not think it had any friends, or mourners, except myself and a
pair of owls.
—J. R. R. Tolkien, from the introductory note to *Tree and Leaf*

You only see the tree by the light of the lamp. I wonder when
you would ever see the lamp by the light of the tree.
—G. K. Chesterton, from *The Man Who Was Thursday*

The conjure man rode a red, old-fashioned bicycle with fat
tires and only one, fixed gear. A wicker basket in front contained a small mongrel dog that seemed mostly terrier. Behind the seat, tied to the carrier, was a battered brown
satchel that hid from prying eyes the sum total of all his
worldly possessions.

What he had was not much, but he needed little. He was,
after all, the conjure man, and what he didn't have, he could
conjure for himself.

He was more stout than slim, with a long grizzled beard
and a halo of frizzy grey hair that protruded from under his
tall black hat like ivy tangled under an eave. Nesting in the
hatband were a posy of dried wildflowers and three feathers:
one white, from a swan; one black, from a crow; one brown,
from an owl. His jacket was an exhilarating shade of blue,
the colour of the sky on a perfect summer's morning. Under it he wore
a shirt that was as green as a fresh-cut lawn. His trousers were brown
corduroy, patched with leather and plaid squares; his boots were a deep
golden yellow, the colour of buttercups past their prime.

His age was a puzzle, somewhere between fifty and seventy. Most
people assumed he was one of the homeless—more colourful than most,
and certainly more cheerful, but a derelict all the same—so the scent of
apples that seemed to follow him was always a surprise, as was the good

humour that walked hand in hand with a keen intelligence in his bright
blue eyes. When he raised his head, hat brim lifting, and he met one's
gaze, the impact of those eyes was a sudden shock, a diamond in the
rough.

His name was John Windle, which could mean, if you were one to
ascribe meaning to names, "favoured of god" for his given name, while
his surname was variously defined as "basket," "the red-winged thrush,"
or "to lose vigor and strength, to dwindle." They could all be true, for
he led a charmed life; his mind was a treasure trove storing equal
amounts of experience, rumour and history; he had a high clear singing
voice; and though he wasn't tall—he stood five-ten in his boots—he had
once been a much larger man.

"I was a giant once," he liked to explain, "when the world was young.
But conjuring takes its toll. Now John's just an old man, pretty well all
used up. Just like the world," he'd add with a sigh and a nod, bright
eyes holding a tired sorrow. "Just like the world."

There were some things even the conjure man couldn't fix.

Living in the city, one grew used to its more outlandish characters, eventually noting them in passing with an almost familial affection: The pigeon lady in her faded Laura Ashley dresses with her shopping cart filled
with sacks of birdseed and bread crumbs. Paperjack, the old black man
with his Chinese fortune-teller and deft origami sculptures. The German
cowboy who dressed like an extra from a spaghetti western and made
long declamatory speeches in his native language to which no one listened.

And, of course, the conjure man.

Wendy St. James had seen him dozens of times—she lived and
worked downtown, which was the conjure man's principal haunt—but
she'd never actually spoken to him until one day in the fall when the
trees were just beginning to change into their cheerful autumnal party
dresses.

She was sitting on a bench on the Ferryside bank of the Kickaha River,
a small, almost waif-like woman in jeans and a white T-shirt, with an
unzipped brown leather bomber's jacket and hightops. In lieu of a purse,
she had a small, worn knapsack sitting on the bench beside her, and she
was bent over a hardcover journal which she spent more time staring at
than actually writing in. Her hair was thick and blonde, hanging down

past her collar in a grown-out pageboy with a half-inch of dark roots showing. She was chewing on the end of her pen, worrying the plastic for inspiration.

It was a poem that had stopped her in mid-stroll and plunked her down on the bench. It had glimmered and shone in her head until she got out her journal and pen. Then it fled, as impossible to catch as a fading dream. The more she tried to recapture the impulse that had set her wanting to put pen to paper, the less it seemed to have ever existed in the first place. The annoying presence of three teenage boys clowning around on the lawn a half-dozen yards from where she sat didn't help at all.

She was giving them a dirty stare when she saw one of the boys pick up a stick and throw it into the wheel of the conjure man's bike as he came riding up on the park path that followed the river. The small dog in the bike's wicker basket jumped free, but the conjure man himself fell in a tangle of limbs and spinning wheels. The boys took off, laughing, the dog chasing them for a few feet, yapping shrilly, before it hurried back to where its master had fallen.

Wendy had already put down her journal and pen and reached the fallen man by the time the dog got back to its master's side.

"Are you okay?" Wendy asked the conjure man as she helped him untangle himself from the bike.

She'd taken a fall herself in the summer. The front wheel of her ten-speed struck a pebble, the bike wobbled dangerously and she grabbed at the brakes, but her fingers closed over the front ones first, and too hard. The back of the bike went up, flipping her right over the handlebars, and she'd had the worst headache for at least a week afterwards.

The conjure man didn't answer her immediately. His gaze followed the escaping boys.

"As you sow," he muttered.

Following his gaze, Wendy saw the boy who'd thrown the stick trip and go sprawling in the grass. An odd chill danced up her spine. The boy's tumble came so quickly on the heels of the conjure man's words, for a moment it felt to her as though he'd actually caused the boy's fall.

As you sow, so shall you reap.

She looked back at the conjure man, but he was sitting up now, fingering a tear in his corduroys which already had a quiltwork of patches on them. He gave her a quick smile that traveled all the way up to his eyes, and she found herself thinking of Santa Claus. The little dog pressed its nose up against the conjure man's hand, pushing it away from the tear. But the tear was gone.

It had just been a fold in the cloth, Wendy realized. That was all.

She helped the conjure man limp to her bench, then went back and got his bike. She righted it and wheeled it over to lean against the back of the bench before sitting down herself. The little dog leaped up onto the conjure man's lap.

"What a cute dog," Wendy said, giving it a pat. "What's her name?"

"Ginger," the conjure man replied as though it was so obvious that he couldn't understand her having to ask.

Wendy looked at the dog. Ginger's fur was as grey and grizzled as her master's beard without a hint of the spice's strong brown hue.

"But she's not at all brown," Wendy found herself saying.

The conjure man shook his head. "It's what she's made of—she's a gingerbread dog. Here." He plucked a hair from Ginger's back, which made the dog start and give him a sour look. He offered the hair to Wendy. "Taste it."

Wendy grimaced. "I don't think so."

"Suit yourself," the conjure man said. He shrugged and popped the hair into his own mouth, chewing it with relish.

Oh boy, Wendy thought. She had a live one on her hands.

"Where do you think ginger comes from?" the conjure man asked her.

"What, do you mean your dog?"

"No, the spice."

Wendy shrugged. "I don't know. Some kind of plant, I suppose."

"And that's where you're wrong. They shave gingerbread dogs like our Ginger here and grind up the hair until all that's left is a powder that's ever so fine. Then they leave it out in the hot sun for a day and half—which is where it gets its brownish colour."

Wendy only just stopped herself from rolling her eyes. It was time to extract herself from this encounter, she realized. Well past the time. She'd done her bit to make sure he was all right and since the conjure man didn't seem any worse for the wear from his fall—

"Hey!" she said as he picked up her journal and started to leaf through it. "That's personal."

He fended off her reaching hand with his own and continued to look through it.

"Poetry," he said. "And lovely verses they are, too."

"Please. . . ."

"Ever had any published?"

Wendy let her hand drop and leaned back against the bench with a sigh.

"Two collections," she said, adding, "and a few sales to some of the literary magazines."

Although, she corrected herself, "sales" was perhaps a misnomer since most of the magazines only paid in copies. And while she did have two collections in print, they were published by the East Street Press, a small local publisher, which meant the bookstores of Newford were probably the only places in the world where either of her books could be found.

"Romantic, but with a very optimistic flavour," the conjure man remarked as he continued to look through her journal where all her false starts and incomplete drafts were laid out for him to see. "None of that *Sturm und Drang* of the earlier romantic era and more like Yeats's twilight or, what did Chesterton call it? *Mooreeffoc*—that queerness that comes when familiar things are seen from a new angle."

Wendy couldn't believe she was having this conversation. What was he? A renegade English professor living on the street like some hedgerow philosopher of old? It seemed absurd to be sitting here, listening to his discourse.

The conjure man turned to give her a charming smile. "Because that's our hope for the future, isn't it? That the imagination reaches beyond the present to glimpse not so much a sense of meaning in what lies all around us, but to let us simply see it in the first place?"

"I . . . I don't know what to say," Wendy replied.

Ginger had fallen asleep on his lap. He closed her journal and regarded her for a long moment, eyes impossibly blue and bright under the brim of his odd hat.

"John has something he wants to show you," he said.

Wendy blinked. "John?" she asked, looking around.

The conjure man tapped his chest. "John Windle is what those who know my name call me."

"Oh."

She found it odd how his speech shifted from that of a learned man to a much simpler idiom, even referring to himself in the third person. But then, if she stopped to consider it, everything about him was odd.

"What kind of something?" Wendy asked cautiously.

"It's not far."

Wendy looked at her watch. Her shift started at four, which was still a couple of hours away, so there was plenty of time. But she was fairly certain that interesting though her companion was, he wasn't at all the sort of person with whom she wanted to involve herself any more than she already had. The dichotomy between the nonsense and substance that peppered his conversation made her uncomfortable.

It wasn't so much that she thought him dangerous. She just felt as though she was walking on boggy ground that might at any minute dissolve into quicksand with a wrong turn. Despite hardly knowing him at all, she was already sure that listening to him would be full of the potentiality for wrong turns.

"I'm sorry," she said, "but I don't have the time."

"It's something that I think only you can, if not understand, then at least appreciate."

"I'm sure it's fascinating, whatever it is, but—"

"Come along, then," he said.

He handed her back her journal and stood up, dislodging Ginger, who leapt to the ground with a sharp yap of protest. Scooping the dog up, he returned her to the wicker basket that hung from his handlebars, then wheeled the bike in front of the bench, where he stood waiting for Wendy.

Wendy opened her mouth to continue her protest, but then simply shrugged. Well, why not? He really didn't look at all dangerous and she'd just make sure that she stayed in public places.

She stuffed her journal back into her knapsack and then followed as he led the way south along the park path up to where the City Commission's lawns gave way to Butler University's common. She started to ask him how his leg felt, since he'd been limping before, but he walked at a quick, easy pace—that of someone half his apparent age—so she just assumed he hadn't been hurt that badly by his fall after all.

They crossed the common, eschewing the path now to walk straight across the lawn towards the G. Smithers Memorial Library, weaving their way in between islands of students involved in any number of activities, none of which included studying. When they reached the library, they followed its ivy-hung walls to the rear of the building, where the conjure man stopped.

"There," he said, waving his arm in a gesture that took in the entire area behind the library. "What do you see?"

The view they had was of an open space of land backed by a number of other buildings. Having attended the university herself, Wendy recognized all three: the Student Center, the Science Building and one of the dorms, though she couldn't remember which one. The landscape enclosed by their various bulking presences had the look of recently having undergone a complete overhaul. All the lilacs and hawthorns had been cut back, brush and weeds were now just an uneven stubble of ground covering, there were clumps of raw dirt, scattered here and there, where trees had obviously been removed, and right in the middle was an enormous stump.

It had been at least fifteen years since Wendy had had any reason to come here in behind the library. But it was so different now. She found herself looking around with a "what's wrong with this picture?" caption floating in her mind. This had been a little cranny of wild wood when she'd attended Butler, hidden away from all the trimmed lawns and shrubbery that made the rest of the university so picturesque. But she could remember slipping back here, journal in hand, and sitting under that huge . . .

"It's all changed," she said slowly. "They cleaned out all the brush and cut down the oak tree. . . ."

Someone had once told her that this particular tree was—had been— a rarity. It had belonged to a species not native to North America—the *Quercus robur,* or common oak of Europe—and was supposed to be over four hundred years old, which made it older than the university, older than Newford itself.

"How could they just . . . cut it down . . . ?" she asked.

The conjure man jerked a thumb over his shoulder towards the library.

"Your man with the books had the work done—didn't like the shade it was throwing on his office. Didn't like to look out and see an untamed bit of the wild hidden in here disturbing his sense of order."

"The head librarian?" Wendy asked.

The conjure man just shrugged.

"But—didn't anyone complain? Surely the students . . ."

In her day there would have been protests. Students would have formed a human chain around the tree, refusing to let anyone near it. They would have camped out, day and night. They . . .

She looked at the stump and felt a tightness in her chest as though someone had wrapped her in wet leather that was now starting to dry out and shrink.

"That tree was John's friend," the conjure man said. "The last friend I ever had. She was ten thousand years old and they just cut her down."

Wendy gave him an odd look. Ten thousand years old? Were we exaggerating now or what?

"Her death is a symbol," the conjure man went on. "The world has no more time for stories."

"I'm not sure I follow you," Wendy said.

He turned to look at her, eyes glittering with a strange light under the dark brim of his hat.

"She was a Tree of Tales," he said. "There are very few of them left, just as there are very few of me. She held stories, all the stories the wind brought to her that were of any worth, and with each such story she heard, she grew."

"But there's always going to be stories," Wendy said, falling into the spirit of the conversation even if she didn't quite understand its relevance to the situation at hand. "There are more books being published today than there ever have been in the history of the world."

The conjure man gave her a sour frown and hooked his thumb towards the library again. "Now you sound like him."

"But—"

"There's stories and then there's stories," he said, interrupting her "The ones with any worth change your life forever, perhaps only in a small way, but once you've heard them, they are forever a part of you. You nurture them and pass them on and the giving only makes you feel better.

"The others are just words on a page."

"I know that," Wendy said.

And on some level she did, though it wasn't something she'd ever really stopped to think about. It was more an instinctive sort of knowledge that had always been present inside her, rising up into her awareness now as though called forth by the conjure man's words.

"It's all machines now," the conjure man went on. "It's a—what do they call it?—high tech world. Fascinating, to be sure, but John thinks that it estranges many people, cheapens the human experience. There's no more room for the stories that matter, and that's wrong, for stories are a part of the language of dream—they grow not from one writer, but from a people. They become the voice of a country, or a race. Without them, people lose touch with themselves."

"You're talking about myths," Wendy said.

The conjure man shook his head. "Not specifically—not in the classical sense of the word. Such myths are only a part of the collective story that is harvested in a Tree of Tales. In a world as pessimistic as this has become, that collective story is all that's left to guide people through the encroaching dark. It serves to create a sense of options, the possibility of permanence out of nothing."

Wendy was really beginning to lose the thread of his argument now.

"What exactly is it that you're saying?" she asked.

"A Tree of Tales is an act of magic, of faith. Its existence becomes an affirmation of the power that the human spirit can have over its own destiny. The stories are just stories—they entertain, they make one laugh or cry—but if they have any worth, they carry within them a deeper resonance that remains long after the final page is turned, or the storyteller has come to the end of her tale. Both aspects of the story are necessary for it to have any worth."

He was silent for a long moment, then added, "Otherwise the story goes on without you."

Wendy gave him a questioning look.

"Do you know what 'ever after' means?" he asked.

"I suppose."

"It's one bookend of a tale—the kind that begins with 'once upon a time.' It's the end of the story when everybody goes home. That's what they said at the end of the story John was in, but John wasn't paying attention, so he got left behind."

"I'm not sure I know what you're talking about," Wendy said.

Not sure? she thought. She was positive. It was all so much . . . well, not exactly nonsense, as queer. And unrelated to any working of the world with which she was familiar. But the oddest thing was that everything he said continued to pull a kind of tickle out from deep in her mind so that while she didn't completely understand him, some part of her did. Some part, hidden behind the person who took care of all the day-to-day business of her life, perhaps the same part of her that pulled a poem onto the empty page where no words had ever existed before. The part of her that was a conjurer.

"John took care of the Tree of Tales," the conjure man went on.

"Because John got left behind in his own story, he wanted to make sure that the stories themselves would at least live on. But one day he went wandering too far—just like he did when his story was ending—and when he got back she was gone. When he got back, they'd done *this* to her."

Wendy said nothing. For all that he was a comical figure in his bright clothes and with his Santa Claus air, there was nothing even faintly humourous about the sudden anguish in his voice.

"I'm sorry," she said.

And she was. Not just in sympathy with him, but because in her own way she'd loved that old oak tree as well. And—just like the conjure man, she supposed—she'd wandered away as well.

"Well then," the conjure man said. He rubbed a sleeve up against his nose and looked away from her. "John just wanted you to see."

He got on his bike and reached forward to tousle the fur around Ginger's ears. When he looked back to Wendy, his eyes glittered like tiny blue fires.

"I knew you'd understand," he said.

Before Wendy could respond, he pushed off and pedaled away, bumping across the uneven lawn to leave her standing alone in that once wild place that was now so dispiriting. But then she saw something stir in the middle of the broad stump.

At first it was no more than a small flicker in the air like a heat ripple. Wendy took a step forward, stopping when the flicker resolved into a tiny sapling. As she watched, it took on the slow stately dance of time-lapse photography: budded, unfurled leaves, grew taller, its growth like a rondo, a basic theme that brackets two completely separate tunes. Growth was the theme, while the tunes on either end began with the tiny sapling and ended with a full-grown oak tree as majestic as the behemoth that had originally stood there. When it reached its full height, light seemed to emanate from its trunk, from the roots underground, from each stalkless, broad saw-toothed leaf.

Wendy stared, wide-eyed, then stepped forward with an outstretched hand. As soon as her fingers touched the glowing tree, it came apart, drifting like mist until every trace of it was gone. Once more, all that remained was the stump of the original tree.

The vision, combined with the tightness in her chest and the sadness the conjure man had left her, transformed itself into words that rolled across her mind, but she didn't write them down. All she could do was stand and look at the tree stump for a very long time, before she finally turned and walked away.

Kathryn's Café was on Battersfield Road in Lower Crowsea, not far from the university but across the river and far enough that Wendy had to hurry to make it to work on time. But it was as though a black hole had swallowed the two hours from when she'd met the conjure man to when her shift began. She was late getting to work—not by much, but she could see that Jilly had already taken orders from two tables that were supposed to be her responsibility.

She dashed into the restaurant's washroom and changed from her jeans into a short black skirt. She tucked her T-shirt in, pulled her hair back into a loose bun, then bustled out to stash her knapsack and pick up her order pad from the storage shelf behind the employees' coat rack.

"You're looking peaked," Jilly said as Wendy finally got out into the dining area.

Jilly Coppercorn and Wendy were almost a matched pair. Both women were small, with slender frames and attractive delicate features, though Jilly's hair was a dark curly brown—the same as Wendy's natural hair colour. They both moonlighted as waitresses, saving their true energy for creative pursuits: Jilly for her art, Wendy her poetry.

Neither had known the other until they began to work at the restaurant together, but they'd become fast friends from the very first shift they shared.

"I'm feeling confused," Wendy said in response to Jilly's comment.

"You're confused? Check out table five—he's changed his mind three times since he first ordered. I'm going to stand here and wait five minutes before I give Frank his latest order, just in case he decides he wants to change it again."

Wendy smiled. "And then he'll complain about slow service and won't leave you much of a tip."

"If he leaves one at all."

Wendy laid a hand on Jilly's arm. "Are you busy tonight?"

Jilly shook her head. "What's up?"

"I need to talk to someone."

"I'm yours to command," Jilly said. She made a little curtsy that had

Wendy quickly stifle a giggle, then shifted her gaze to table five. "Oh bother, he's signaling me again."

"Give me his order," Wendy said. "I'll take care of him."

It was such a nice night that they just went around back of the restaurant when their shift was over. Walking the length of a short alley, they came out on a small strip of lawn and made their way down to the river. There they sat on a stone wall, dangling their feet above the sluggish water. The night felt still. Through some trick of the air, the traffic on nearby Battersfield Road was no more than a distant murmur, as though there was more of a sound baffle between where they sat and the busy street than just the building that housed their workplace.

"Remember that time we went camping?" Wendy said after they'd been sitting for a while in a companionable silence. "It was just me, you and LaDonna. We sat around the campfire telling ghost stories that first night."

"Sure," Jilly said with a smile in her voice. "You kept telling us ones by Robert Aickman and the like—they were all taken from books."

"While you and LaDonna claimed that the ones you told were real and no matter how much I tried to get either of you to admit they weren't, you wouldn't."

"But they were true," Jilly said.

Wendy thought of LaDonna telling them that she'd seen Bigfoot in the Tombs and Jilly's stories about a kind of earth spirit called a gemmin that she'd met in the same part of the city and of a race of goblin-like creatures living in the subterranean remains of the old city that lay beneath Newford's subway system.

She turned from the river to regard her friend. "Do you really believe those things you told me?"

Jilly nodded. "Of course I do. They're true." She paused a moment, leaning closer to Wendy as though trying to read her features in the gloom. "Why? What's happened, Wendy?"

"I think I just had my own close encounter of the weird kind this afternoon."

When Jilly said nothing, Wendy went on to tell her of her meeting with the conjure man earlier in the day.

"I mean, I know why he's called the conjure man," she finished up.

"I've seen him pulling flowers out of people's ears and all those other stage tricks he does, but this was different. The whole time I was with him I kept feeling like there really was a kind of magic in the air, a *real* magic just sort of humming around him, and then when I saw the . . . I guess it was a vision of the tree. . . .

"Well, I don't know what to think."

She'd been looking across the river while she spoke, gaze fixed on the darkness of the far bank. Now she turned to Jilly.

"Who is he?" she asked. "Or maybe should I be asking *what* is he?"

"I've always thought of him as a kind of anima," Jilly said. "A loose bit of myth that got left behind when all the others went on to wherever it is that myths go when we don't believe in them anymore."

"That's sort of what he said. But what does it mean? What is he really?"

Jilly shrugged. "Maybe what he is isn't so important as *that* he is." At Wendy's puzzled look, she added, "I can't explain it any better. I . . . Look, it's like it's not so important that he is or isn't what he says he is, but *that* he says it. That he believes it."

"Why?"

"Because it's just like he told you," Jilly said. "People are losing touch with themselves and with each other. They need stories because they really are the only thing that brings us together. Gossip, anecdotes, jokes, stories—these are the things that we used to exchange with each other. It kept the lines of communication open, let us touch each other on a regular basis.

"That's what art's all about, too. My paintings and your poems, the books Christy writes, the music Geordie plays—they're all lines of communication. But they're harder to keep open now because it's so much easier for most people to relate to a TV set than it is to another person. They get all this data fed into them, but they don't know what to do with it anymore. When they talk to other people, it's all surface. How ya doing, what about the weather. The only opinions they have are those that they've gotten from people on the TV. They think they're informed, but all they're doing is repeating the views of talk show hosts and news commentators.

"They don't know how to listen to real people anymore."

"I know all that," Wendy said. "But what does any of it have to do with what the conjure man was showing me this afternoon?"

"I guess what I'm trying to say is that he validates an older kind of value, that's all."

"Okay, but what did he want from me?"

Jilly didn't say anything for a long time. She looked out across the river, her gaze caught by the same darkness as Wendy's had been earlier when she was relating her afternoon encounter. Twice Wendy started to ask Jilly what she was thinking, but both times she forbore. Then finally Jilly turned to her.

"Maybe he wants you to plant a new tree," she said.

"But that's silly. I wouldn't know how to begin to go about something like that." Wendy sighed. "I don't even know if I believe in a Tree of Tales."

But then she remembered the feeling that had risen in her when the conjure man spoke to her, that sense of familiarity, as though she was being reminded of something she already knew, rather than being told what she didn't. And then there was the vision of the tree. . . .

She sighed again.

"Why me?" she asked.

Her words were directed almost to the night at large, rather than just her companion, but it was Jilly who replied. The night held its own counsel.

"I'm going to ask you something," Jilly said, "and I don't want you to think about the answer. Just tell me the first thing that comes to mind—okay?"

Wendy nodded uncertainly. "I guess."

"If you could be granted one wish—anything at all, no limits—what would you ask for?"

With the state the world was in at the moment, Wendy had no hesitation in answering: "World peace."

"Well, there you go," Jilly told her.

"I don't get it."

"You were asking why the conjure man picked you and there's your reason. Most people would have started out thinking of what they wanted for themselves. You know, tons of money, or to live forever—that kind of thing."

Wendy shook her head. "But he doesn't even know me."

Jilly got up and pulled Wendy to her feet.

"Come on," she said. "Let's go look at the tree."

"It's just a stump."

"Let's go anyway."

Wendy wasn't sure why she felt reluctant, but just as she had this afternoon, she allowed herself to be led back to the campus.

Nothing had changed, except that this time it was dark, which gave the scene, at least to Wendy's way of thinking, an even more desolate feeling.

Jilly was very quiet beside her. She stepped ahead of Wendy and crouched down beside the stump, running her hand along the top of it.

"I'd forgotten all about this place," she said softly.

That's right, Wendy thought. Jilly'd gone to Butler U. just as she had—around the same time, too, though they hadn't known each other then.

She crouched down beside Jilly, starting slightly when Jilly took her hand and laid it on the stump.

"Listen," Jilly said. "You can almost feel the whisper of a story . . . a last echo. . . ."

Wendy shivered, though the night was mild. Jilly turned to her. At that moment, the starlight flickering in her companion's blue eyes reminded Wendy very much of the conjure man.

"You've got to do it," Jilly said. "You've got to plant a new tree. It wasn't just the conjure man choosing you—the tree chose you, too."

Wendy wasn't sure what was what anymore. It all seemed more than a little mad, yet as she listened to Jilly, she could almost believe in it all. But then that was one of Jilly's gifts: she could make the oddest thing seem normal. Wendy wasn't sure if you could call a thing like that a gift, but whatever it was, Jilly had it.

"Maybe we should get Christy to do it," she said. "After all, he's the story writer."

"Christy is a lovely man," Jilly said, "but sometimes he's far more concerned with how he says a thing, rather than with the story itself."

"Well, I'm not much better. I've been known to worry for hours over a stanza—or even just a line."

"For the sake of being clever?" Jilly asked.

"No. So that it's right."

Jilly raked her fingers through the short stubble of the weeds that passed for a lawn around the base of the oak stump. She found something and pressed it into Wendy's hand. Wendy didn't have to look at it to know that it was an acorn.

"You have to do it," Jilly said. "Plant a new Tree of Tales and feed it with stories. It's really up to you."

Wendy looked from the glow of her friend's eyes to the stump. She remembered her conversation with the conjure man and her vision of the tree. She closed her fingers around the acorn, feeling the press of the cap's bristles indent her skin.

Maybe it *was* up to her, she found herself thinking.

The poem that came to her that night after she left Jilly and got back to her little apartment in Ferryside, came all at once, fully-formed and complete. The act of putting it to paper was a mere formality.

She sat by her window for a long time afterward, her journal on her lap, the acorn in her hand. She rolled it slowly back and forth on her palm. Finally, she laid both journal and acorn on the windowsill and went into her tiny kitchen. She rummaged around in the cupboard under the sink until she came up with an old flowerpot, which she took into the backyard and filled with dirt—rich loam, as dark and mysterious as that indefinable place inside herself that was the source of the words that filled her poetry and that had risen in recognition to the conjure man's words.

When she returned to the window, she put the pot between her knees. Tearing the new poem out of her journal, she wrapped the acorn up in it and buried it in the pot. She watered it until the surface of the dirt was slick with mud, then placed the flowerpot on her windowsill and went to bed.

That night she dreamed of Jilly's gemmin—slender earth spirits that appeared outside the old three-story building that housed her apartment and peered in at the flowerpot on the windowsill. In the morning, she got up and told the buried acorn her dream.

Autumn turned to winter and Wendy's life went pretty much the way it always had. She took turns working at the restaurant and on her poems; she saw her friends; she started a relationship with a fellow she met at a party in Jilly's loft, but it floundered after a month.

Life went on.

The only change was centered around the contents of the pot on her windowsill. As though the tiny green sprig that pushed up through the dark soil was her lover, every day she told it all the things that had happened to her and around her. Sometimes she read it her favorite stories from anthologies and collections, or interesting bits from magazines and newspapers. She badgered her friends for stories, sometimes passing them on, speaking to the tiny plant in a low but animated voice, other times convincing her friends to come over and tell the stories themselves.

Except for Jilly, LaDonna and the two Riddell brothers, Geordie and Christy, most people thought she'd gone just a little daft. Nothing serious, mind you, but strange all the same.

Wendy didn't care.

Somewhere out in the world, there were other Trees of Tales, but they were few—if the conjure man was to be believed. And she believed him now. She had no proof, only faith, but oddly enough, faith seemed enough. But since she believed, she knew it was more important than ever that her charge should flourish.

With the coming of winter, there were less and less of the street people to be found. They were indoors, if they had such an option, or perhaps they migrated to warmer climes like the swallows. But Wendy still spied the more regular ones in their usual haunts. Paperjack had gone, but the pigeon lady still fed her charges every day, the German cowboy continued his bombastic monologues—though mostly on the subway platforms now. She saw the conjure man, too, but he was never near enough for her to get a chance to talk to him.

By the springtime, the sprig of green in the flowerpot had grown into a sapling that stood almost a foot high. On warmer days, Wendy put the pot out on the backporch steps where it could taste the air and catch the growing warmth of the afternoon sun. She still wasn't sure what she was going to do with it once it outgrew its pot.

But she had some ideas. There was a part of Fitzhenry Park called the Silenus Gardens that was dedicated to the poet Joshua Stanhold. She thought it might be appropriate to plant the sapling there.

One day in late April, she was leaning on the handlebars of her tenspeed in front of the public library in Lower Crowsea, admiring the yellow splash the daffodils made against the building's grey stone walls, when she sensed, more than saw, a red bicycle pull up onto the sidewalk behind her. She turned around to find herself looking into the conjure man's merry features.

"It's spring, isn't it just," the conjure man said. "A time to finally forget the cold and bluster and think of summer. John can feel the leaf buds stir, the flowers blossoming. There's a grand smile in the air for all the growing."

Wendy gave Ginger a pat, before letting her gaze meet the blue shock of his eyes.

"What about a Tree of Tales?" she asked. "Can you feel her growing?"

The conjure man gave her a wide smile. "Especially her." He paused to adjust the brim of his hat, then gave her a sly look. "Your man Stanhold," he added. "Now there was a fine poet—and a fine storyteller."

Wendy didn't bother to ask how he knew of her plan. She just returned the conjure man's smile and then asked, "Do you have a story to tell me?"

The conjure man polished one of the buttons of his bright blue jacket.

"I believe I do," he said. He patted the brown satchel that rode on his back carrier. "John has a thermos filled with the very best tea, right here in his bag. Why don't we find ourselves a comfortable place to sit and he'll tell you how he got this bicycle of his over a hot cuppa."

He started to pedal off down the street, without waiting for her response. Wendy stared after him, her gaze catching the little terrier, sitting erect in her basket and looking back at her.

There seemed to be a humming in the air that woke a kind of singing feeling in her chest. The wind rose up and caught her hair, pushing it playfully into her eyes. As she swept it back from her face with her hand, she thought of the sapling sitting in its pot on her back steps, thought of the wind, and knew that stories were already being harvested without the necessity of her having to pass them on.

But she wanted to hear them all the same.

Getting on her ten-speed, she hurried to catch up with the conjure man.

[For J. R. R. Tolkien; may his own branch of the tree live on forever.]

The Halfling House

Dennis L. McKiernan

e sent Tynvyr on ahead, riding her fox, while the rest of us slithered through the slip and squish of the alley.

"Ow, Fiz!" someone hissed, Marley I think. "Keep your filthy wings to yourself! You nearly poked my eye out."

"Listen, Gnome," shot back Fiz, her silvery voice gone all iron, "you keep your scuzzy eye out of my wings."

Great, just great. Here we were in the middle of the night on a secret rescue mission, and already the Gnome and Pixie were at each other's throats.

And our tempers weren't improved by the reek of sewage and rot that hung upon the air, putrid to the nose and causing our gorges to rise until we were near to gagging. Too, a trickle of foul water seemed always underfoot, and we slithered and slipped in the mud and the slime, jerking this way and that to keep from falling.

"Bork," came Fiz's voice back to me, "tell me again the stupid reason I've got to muck along in this muck instead of flying."

Before I could answer, Rafferty spoke up. "Faith, lass, isn't't told that this divil hisself has wingedy creatures, anow? Blood-suckin' bats and sich, they say. Flyin' about up there in th' dark. Sure and wouldn't they jist love t'get a bit o' y'r delicate, delicious self?"

If Rafferty's source had been right, Khassan *did* have creatures of the

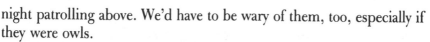

night patrolling above. We'd have to be wary of them, too, especially if they were owls.

Big owls.

Big enough to carry any one of us off in its talons.

And if owls or bats didn't get us, then surely the alley rats would snatch us away down some dark hole.

"Oof!" grunted Marley, stepping in a rut *slsh!* full of malodorous water. "I can't see a blasted thing."

Well, he *was* after all just a Gnome, and their Fairy Vision is worse than that of nearly all the Wee Folk. Of course, mine isn't much to be proud of either, not like Tynvyr's or Fiz's.

Oh, if only the overcast fouling the night sky would blow away, so that just a little starlight shone down, or better yet if the Moon was up and full and the clouds gone, well then, none of us would have even the tiniest bit of trouble.

But as it was, the night was dark and overcast, and here we were in a pitch black alley—a Pixie, a Gnome, a Leprechaun, and a Brownie . . . while somewhere ahead was a Pysk riding a fox—all of us sneaking among the ramshackle buildings looming up in the ebon darkness all about, trying to avoid the owls and bats and rats, any one of which could probably rip us to shreds.

I mean, when you stand only a foot or two high, these things are terrible foes.

And the stinking alley and the stinking night seemed to be filled with their stinking menace. And we couldn't see and we didn't know exactly where we were going or what we were going to do once we got there, or even whether or not we were on the right trail.

Hèl, I didn't even know who it was we were out to rescue!

Talk about your bright plans—I mean, what else could go wrong?

And then we heard the *Mmrrawing* yowl of an alley cat hunting for something to eat.

Damn!

It all started a day or so ago, when, after finishing up a solid month of cobbling shoes, I decided to go on holiday while I had a chance. You see, the Halfling House had appeared in the glen a week earlier, and I knew that it wouldn't be about too long. And since I'd heard it was the very best way to travel, to see new and wonderful places, I thought I would take a room before it and the entire inn vanished.

So in the daytime, when there are no owls about, I betook myself down to the glen and there it stood, where nothing had been just a week earlier: the Halfling House.

How the inn arrives, none that I had spoken to knew. Rudd and Meech, a couple of barn Bwca—cousins of mine, you might say—tell that it materializes out of thin air . . . but then, they had been drinking when they claimed they had witnessed its appearance, and who can believe anything seen through the eyes of drunken Bwca?

Others say that it seeps up from the ground . . . after all, the roof *is* made of sod.

In any case, it seems to come overnight from nowhere, and if that's true then the other tales about it are probably true, too, and some dark-tide soon or late it will vanish just as well!

At least that was what I was counting on.

If the tales were true.

Yet whether it did or did not materialize in the wee witching hours, the fact is, here it was where nought had been before, in the glen, at least for the time present.

I took a long hard look. Some would say that the building was quaint and pastoral, and it did fit right in with the surroundings. I could see by the placement of oddly shaped windows that it was nearly three storeys tall, and I gauged the peak of the low-canted sod roof to be some fifteen feet above the ground. That would make the ceilings inside some four to five feet high. More than tall enough for me at my eighteen inches. Truly, this had to be an inn large enough for Halflings, though I'd been told that all Wee Folk were welcome.

As I approached the small, roofed-over front porch, I noted that although the windows adorning the white stuccoed walls seemed normal, there appeared to be something strange and slightly sparkly about the light reflecting from the glass. When I stepped up to the windows by the door and tried to peer through, the view to the inside was oddly distorted, as if the panes were utterly muddled, yet each seemed clear and smooth to the touch.

The way in was through a stout oaken door some four feet tall, iron banded, with latches and handles placed at varying heights, as if for the convenience of different-sized Wee Folk. In the center of the door was mounted a plaque proclaiming:

```
┌─────────────────────────────────┐
│                                 │
│      The Halfling House         │
│         Any and All             │
│    Halflings and Wee Folk       │
│         WELCOME                 │
│   Dando Thistledown, Prop.      │
│                                 │
└─────────────────────────────────┘
```

This was the place, alright.

Grasping one of the handles and raising its latch, I pushed, expecting a struggle; but the door swung smoothly open, and I stepped into the inn.

Like all places of its kind, it was larger on the inside than out.

Before I could get much more than a glimpse, though, this pointy-eared fellow, a tall Halfling with Elfy-welfy slanty but jewellike eyes came over. Hey, he had to be more than twice my height, three foot five if he was an inch—a regular high pockets.

He peered down from his lofty height at me. "Welcome to the Halfling House. My name is Dando Thistledown, and I'm the proprietor. Will you be needing a room?"

"Uh"—I looked around at the place, noting that there were several other of these tall ones about. But here and there, I could also see folk of my size, as well as some even smaller—"yes, your loftiness, a room please. That is unless you keep owls on the premises, in which case, I'm leaving."

"No, no." He blinked his sparkly eyes at me. "No owls. Also no cats, rats, dogs, bats, hawks, weasels, cobras, mongooses or mongeese, or any other thing of the sort.

"The last time there was anything *dangerous* in here was when we went to the Emerald Isle, and this *fool* drove a massive herd of snakes right over the top of us. Filled the place right up, he did, and for that you can blame Rafferty, who ran in just ahead of them and forgot to shut the door. We had to go to Iceland to chill 'em into a torpor, then to a desert far to the west, where we shoveled them out the door and into the fields of tall cacti as fast as we could, before they had a chance to recover in the desert heat and start that wriggling and rattling again."

Cor blimey! Here I had been afraid only of owls, and Stretch, here, was telling me about cats, rats, dogs, bats, hawks, weasels, cobras, mongooses or mongeese (whatever they are, but I can imagine), and snakes that go slither and rattle. Now I could worry about a whole new pantheon of things what could grab me in the dark. I peered closely at the floor and under the furniture. "There's none of those blighters about now, is there?"

Again he blinked his sparklies at me, and I thought I saw him cross his fingers behind his back. "Oh no. All gone. I swear."

You could say that there was just the tee tiniest bit of doubt lingering in my mind, but, I *did* need holiday rest. "Well, then, your tallness, just give me a room and some food, and ale . . . yes, a good jug of ale."

"If you'll have a seat," he said, waving his hand in the direction of the other patrons gathered 'round one of the common-room hearths, "I'll see to it straightaway." He turned to go and as he walked away, I heard a faint buzzing, as of dried seeds shaken in a small gourd. Proprietor Dando leapt sideways away from the nearby cabinet he was passing, hurriedly walking on.

As I approached the other patrons, I looked about. The curtains were drawn back from the muddled windows to let sunlight brighten the interior, yet I could see that at night the warm amber glow of lamp and candle would illume the room, along with the ruddy cast of a crackling fire should the weather warrant. The ceilings were what I judged to be about four feet or so high. The furniture, large by my standards, was most suitable for Halflings.

To my back was what I'll call the east fireplace, and before it stood a commodious longtable, and to the center of the room was another smaller one; when occupied by a happy crowd, they would no doubt give the place the genial atmosphere of a joyously rowdy pub.

Before the west fireplace, where I was headed, was a soft couch flanked by what looked to be several cozy chairs. Throughout the rest of the common room, other tables and chairs were placed about, and toward the "north" wall stood a cheery bar with what I hoped would be excellent ale. In the southeast corner, a spiral staircase twined upward to the second floor, where I assumed the guest rooms were.

I came in among the other patrons: a Pixie, a Pysk, a Gnome, and a Leprechaun: these I recognized. But then there was another one of these Halflings, a different kind from Proprietor Dando, but a Halfling still. Rotund of girth, as best as I could judge with him sitting down, he was maybe three foot eight or nine. Unlike Dando, this one had no Elven ears and jewellike eyes, but instead he had these enormously large hairy feet! Bare! Propped on a footstool before him. And, oh my, what clod-hoppers they were. Cor! These had to be the biggest pair of dogs I ever clapped eyes on. And I know feet! I'm a cobbler, after all. Lor! If I had to make a pair of shoes for him, blimey! it'd take a whole cow just to get the job done.

"I'm Fiz," said a voice next to me.

Wrenching my amazed eyes away from those enormous feet, I saw that the Pixie was speaking to me. She was a little bit of a thing, twelve inches or so, the top of her head with its straw-colored hair just reaching my ribcage, though the upper tips of her gauzy wings o'ertopped my head slightly.

"H'llo, Fiz; glad to make your acquaintance," I responded. "My name is Bork, and I'm a cobbler by trade."

"Oh, I'm a house sprite, spreading cheer among the children of the family I watch over." Her smile lit up the whole room. "At the nonce, I am between children: they've grown up, but will soon have babes of their own. Then will I return to the family."

Oh, how lovely was this Pixie. I could feel myself staring, and so could she, turning pink under my gaze.

Wresting my attention away from her beatific smile, I turned to the Gnome. "Bork's the name. Shoes are my game."

He was a couple inches shorter than me, say one foot four or so, and he had a pointy hat and a pale skin and his dark beard reached down to his belt. With disgust, he looked at my extended hand as if it were an obscene thing. "This is one hand of a pair of hands that handle dirty shoes? Dirty shoes that fit smelly feet? Feet of all folk, no matter what disease might rack their bodies? And you want me, *me* to come into contact with it, to grip it, to squeeze it? Yuck!"

"Oi," I protested, "I'll have you know—"

"Say," he interrupted, "you're not one of those foot fetishists, now, are you?"

As my mouth dropped open, Fiz looked startled and backed away from me, kneeling down on a large cushion, hiding her feet underneath her.

"Ah, now m'lad," said the Leprechaun, "pay him no heed. He's f'r needin' holiday, too. Gone spotty in th' head, what with all that ham-merin' day and night. Sure and his name is Marley, and me, wellanow,

I am called Rafferty by some what know me, and I'm jist along f'r th' roide, keepin' auld Marley here company."

Black-haired, Rafferty was perhaps an inch taller than me, and dressed in several shades of green, just as I dress in varying shades of brown. He had large silver buckles on his shiny black shoes, and a silver belt buckle, too. His grip was firm when I shook his hand, and I thought I detected a merry twinkle in his black, black eyes, though it was hard to tell, given the darkness of his gaze and all.

I could see Proprietor Dando approaching, bearing my tray of food and my flagon of ale.

In that moment, though, the Pysk stepped forward, and except for the fact that she had no wings, she could have been Fiz's twin. "I am Tynvyr, from the land far to the west, and this is Rufous."

She turned and called, *"Rufous,"* and from behind the couch that Bigfoot sat on, there came a—

"Yaaa . . . !" I shrieked, leaping backward, crashing into Proprietor Dando, the tray flying wide, dishes and flatware and stew and bread and ale sailing through the air to clatter and smash and slosh and phoomp and splash and shatter and tinkle and run and dribble hither and thither and yon.

"Save me," I screamed, rolling over on top of Dando, staring him in the eye.

Somewhere in the distance, it seemed, I could hear the Gnome shrieking, too, something about being covered with filthy, disease-laden food.

Dando grabbed me by my tunic front, pulling me down into his snarling face, gritting, "Save you from *what*?"

"The dog, you fool!" I shouted. "You said that there were no dogs here, but one is attacking me right now! Ripping out my throat, my jugular vein!"

Still gripping my tunic, Dando got to his feet, hauling me up with him. "Look!"

I looked.

So, alright already, maybe it wasn't a dog. Maybe instead it was a red fox. So what if it wasn't snarling and attacking. So what if it was merely sitting and waiting, its tongue lolling from grinning mouth. Still, it *could* have torn me to shreds, it *could* have ripped out my throat, it *could* have slashed my jugular veins. And it *did* seem to be licking its chops as it eyed me.

I looked at Tynvyr, too, her with a tentative smile on her face, standing beside the sitting fox, reaching up and holding tightly to its collar.

"Tame?" I asked.

She nodded, still grinning hesitantly, though she kept a firm grip.

"Not dangerous?"

Solemnly, she shook her head, pulling back on the collar as the fox seemed to strain forward.

"Rufous?"

Her timorous smile returned, and she nodded, Rufous salivating, licking his chops. She reached up and tapped the fox on the nose, and he looked sideways at her, a bit disgruntled, but seemed to settle down. At least he stopped the licking.

Somewhat reassured, I looked up at three-foot-five Dando. "So turn me loose, oh tall one."

"Look, Mister . . ." Dando paused, staring down at me.

"Bork," I supplied.

". . . Mister Bork," he continued smoothly, "I judge you are going to have to pay for"—he waved his hand vaguely in the general direction of everywhere—"the meal and broken dishes and spilled ale. After all it was *you* who crashed into *me*."

"You should have warned me about the dog," I said, supremely.

"It's a fox," he replied.

"Fox shmox, still you should have warned me."

"Mister Bork, I told you that we have nothing dangerous here in the inn"—he cast a surreptitious glance at the cabinet in the hall, the one whence came the rattle—"I specifically said that we have no owls, cats, rats, dogs, bats, hawks, weasels, cobras, and no mongooses or mongeese."

"Well, what about rattly snakes?" I didn't know what a rattly snake was but—

"No. They're all gone. Indeed. Yessir. No mice either."

He paused a moment and then said, "Tell you what: you pay half, I'll pay half, and we'll call it even."

I thought it over, eyeing the fox. The fox licked its chops and smiled. I flinched.

"See?" crowed Dando, having witnessed my reaction to Rufous.

"Alright, alright, your tallness," I said. "You've proved your point."

Dando smiled and bustled off for a broom and a mop and bucket, and to fetch me another meal.

"What *is* he?" I asked Rafferty as I watched Dando walk away. "Pointy ears, slanty jewellike eyes, Halfling sized. I'd call him an Elf, but for his eyes and his size."

"Wellanow, laddie," said Rafferty as he stared at Marley frantically scrubbing the back of his hand where a single tiny droplet of flung stew had landed on the Gnome, "Dando, he's what y' moight call a Warrow, or some sich. Nobody t' fool about with, them Warrows, from what I hear. Especially whin riled."

From behind came a comment. "They are much more prone to violence than my folk."

I turned about. The speaker was Bigfoot. "We live in small hamlets," he added, "much the same as they do, but we'd rather eat and sleep and work in our gardens, whereas they hunt and herd and farm and shoot bows and arrows and at times are rather warlike. Fierce, you might say, and *active*. They are, indeed, Elflike, but they live only a hundred and twenty years or so, in contrast with Elves, who live forever if you believe the tales. I'm not certain that I do, what with all the travel I've done, the many and varied quests and great adventures that I've undertaken, throughout all the lands and across all the oceans, cities and hamlets and woodlands and intricate underground caverns and halls and . . ."

He droned on and on, never shutting up. My meal came and went, and still he rambled on, endlessly, circuitously, tortuously . . . torturously, too, all the while jotting notes in a journal, recording, I believe, what he was saying at that very moment. Drone, drone, drone. Scribble, scribble, scribble. Drone, scribble, drone. I never did find out his name. Bigfoot would have to do.

He didn't even notice when we all got up and left, he just kept right on talking and writing and writing and talking, simultaneously, never missing a beat.

Maybe instead of shoes for Bigfoot, I'd take that cowhide and make a full-body gag for him.

I'd consider it on the morrow if he was still talking, and I was sure he would be.

As I was escorted up the spiral stairs to my room by another tall Warrow, this one a female (a damman, I believe they're called), I saw Dando down on the floor with a forked stick and a gunny sack cautiously peering and poking a broom handle under the foot of the cabinet where the rattling sound had come from.

The next morning, when I came downstairs, the inn was—how shall I put this?—the inn was *elsewhere*.

Where? . . . *I* don't know, though someone said we were near a Shire.

But Bigfoot was gone, waddled off across the countryside a couple of hours ago, going home, said Tynvyr, and now this dreadful black rider was coming down the road, and Dando was severely alarmed, and so we got the Hèl out of there.

Dando slammed the door in the guy's face, and twisted at his own left hand, and the windows got all sparkly and glittery, and everything inside got dark, even though when last I looked it was daylight outside.

The dammen (several female Warrows) lighted lanterns and candles. But I went to the windows and cupped my hands to shade out the light and tried to peer through.

I almost went cross-eyed.

Beyond the glass there were strange cyclopean shapes twisting obscenely in what I knew had to be a cruel, etheric, icy void, and the cold phosphorescent luminance beyond was cosmic and singular, a hideous unknown blend of colour, a colour out of—

I wrenched my cross-eyed gaze from the glass and whirled about dizzily, stumbling and staggering to a nearby table, plopping down beside two Marleys the Gnome, who at that moment was complaining about the filthy clean white towels in his and Rafferty's room, eyeing the Leprechaun as if he were dungeon slime.

Too, Marley seemed obsessed with where the toilets flushed, and where the water came from, claiming that it was one and the same place.

Hey, good questions, I thought, as I eyed Rufous and he eyed me, the fox licking his chops and checking to see if Tynvyr was looking (she was). *Where* did *the water come from and where* did *the toilets flush to? This inn can't have a well or a septic system, the whole building flying around as it does from perdition to who knows where.*

Rafferty supplied the answer. "Marley, m' bucko, don't y' know? Th' handpumps are magic, drawing their water from cool mountain streams in th' land far to th' west. Wan o' these days, somewan will most loikely settle nearby and brew th' most wanderful beer from th' very same waters, Cor, if I do say so meself.

"And as to th' privies, wellanow, they flush magically, too, droppin' their loads in th' marshy meadowlands o' th' east coast o' th' very same western land far away.

"Why, laddie, the Halfling House itself is a powerful magic artifact, able to travel here and there and in between th' very 'dimensions' themselves, or so I hear, whatever 'tis that a 'dimension' might be, for I don't

even know what't is they might be talkin' about whin they use that word
'dimension.' But regardless o' the meaning o' that word, we do know
f'r a fact that th' Halfling House *does* go thither and yon, and from place
to place. How it's controlled, this Halfling House, what device or object
is used to cause it to go from wan place to anither . . . wellanow, I have
me suspicions, but I'll keep them to meself."

*Oh well, magic—magic pumps, magic privies, in the wonderful magic
travelling inn—I should have known.* At last my eyes uncrossed and I
glanced over at Fiz, who glared back at me and pulled a blanket tighter
about her feet.

Suddenly with a thump, the sparkly glow from the windows subsided,
and once again daylight, wan and thin, streamed in through the muddled
glass.

"Where are we?" asked one of the dammen, the elder one, Dando's
mate, I think. A regular Amazon, towering some three feet high.

"I don't know, Molly," answered Dando. "I didn't have time to select
a destination."

Molly burst into tears. "This is just like the time you lost Tip and
Perry. And who knows where they might be?"

Dando hung his head. "Wull, I didn't have much choice. That black
rider—"

"Black rider *this* time," wailed Molly, "Black Dragon last time. And
the time before it was—"

"Now, now," interrupted Dando, his eyes darting this way and that,
glancing about at all of us, "there's no call to upset our guests."

"A pox on our guests," spat Molly, and Marley reeled back in horror,
examining his hands, feeling his face, as she continued. "Dando Thistledown, all I know is that the last time we fled, the Dragon, it was, and
landed somewhere, and put out the fire on the roof, and repainted the
scorched porch, Tip and Perry stepped out that door off on some lark
of their own and were never seen again." Once more she burst into tears.

"There, there, Molly, someday we'll find them. Someday when I can
remember how I twisted the—" He glanced down at the ring he wore.

Beside me, Tynvyr slapped Rufous on the nose. *"No!"* she hissed
sharply, and the fox stopped looking at me with his pointy-toothed grin
and, disgruntled, lay down.

"Tynvyr," I whispered, *"who are Tip and Perry, and are they really
small enough to ride larks?"*

Tynvyr smiled and shook her head, *No,* and whispered back, *"Tip is their son, and Perry is his cousin."*

Tall Molly pulled herself up to her thirty-six inches, stifling her tears at last. "Well, Dando, you don't know exactly where we are, you say, but you can send someone out to look about."

"Now, Molly, I shouldn't leave the inn." Dando glanced significantly at his ring, and Molly nodded. "And none of you dammen should go. I mean, look at what just happened, the black rider and all. And that only leaves . . ." Dando looked around and down at Fiz, Marley, Tynvyr and Rufous, Rafferty, and me.

Rafferty sighed. "Alright, Dando, m'lad, I'll go. But remember what happened back in auld Eire, what with th' rattly snakes and all. If I come arunnin' back in, somewan needs to shut th' door after me quick as a cat, else there moight be th' divil t' pay."

As best as I can tell, Rafferty was gone for two days, and when he got back he was drunk.

And dressed in a paper sack.

And covered with filth.

Marley took one look at the filthy wretch and ran shrieking up the stairs and leapt into a bathtub and began frantically scrubbing himself.

I'm not certain that he even took his clothes off.

The rest of us rushed to Rafferty's side, where he had fallen inward through the door and to the floor.

He was singing some ditty under his wine-laden breath, and only now and again could I catch a word or two—something about mushroom rings and the ones who dance there.

We couldn't make any sense of what he was saying, and so Dando got Molly to brew this almost-black drink made from little dark brown beans, ground up, and they poured gallons of it down the inside of Rafferty's neck, and soon we had this very alert drunk on our hands, singing at the top of his lungs:

> *"Whin th' Fairies dance,*
> *Oh they sometimes ware no pants . . ."*

Fiz shrieked, "You peeked!" She turned to Tynvyr. "He peeked!"

Outraged, Tynvyr turned up her nose and spun away from the drunken Leprechaun, snatching away the cold cloth she had been holding to his head. "Come, Fiz, Peeping Raffertys don't deserve our help." And they marched off in high dudgeon.

Gee, when he sobered up, I would have to find out from Peeping Rafferty precisely where this mushroom ring was.

Marley came back downstairs just in time to see Rafferty throw up all over, and the Gnome ran shrieking back up to the bathing room and we could hear him moaning and sobbing amid more sounds of frantical scrubbing.

Rafferty, on the other hand, groaned and passed out.

"Garn!" exclaimed Dando. "Well, let's clean him up and lay him on the couch and wait for him to come to."

And so we did, covering Rafferty with a blanket.

It was late in the day when Rafferty came 'round, and then it was that we found out where he'd been and what he had been up to.

I wish I'd been elsewhere.

But, there we were, near Rafferty: me, Fiz, Tynvyr and Rufous, and Marley, the Gnome now as clean as a pin, though his skin was nigh rubbed raw—you've heard of dishpan hands, well Marley had an entire dishpan body. Dando and Molly were there, too.

Anyway, as Rufous—just tasting—took a tiny lick of me and Tynvyr slapped him away, Rafferty sat up with a start, and grabbed his head, groaning, and looked wildly about. Seeing Dando—"I've found them!" exclaimed the Leprechaun, wincing at the loudness of whoever it was that was talking, discovering that it was himself. "I've found them," he repeated, softly this time. "Tip and Perry. I know whare they be."

Dando leapt forward and grabbed the Leprechaun by the shoulders, jerking him back and forth and back and forth. "Where, Rafferty? Where?"

Rafferty just screamed and clutched his thrashing head.

Molly shoved Dando aside. "Where?" she shrieked in the Leprechaun's ear, grabbing him by the shoulders, taking up where Dando had left off. But suddenly, as if the news were too much for her, she swooned, falling on top of Dando.

Finding himself free, in spite of his throbbing head, Rafferty leapt over the back of the couch, aiming to keep it between him and Dando and Molly.

"Faith, now, boyo," he called out to Dando, the Warrow rising to his feet, "ye've got t' stop bashin' me brain about in me head. I'll tell ye. I'll tell ye. Jist leave me alone."

Dando helped Molly to the couch, where she lay down, and he took up a cold cloth, one that they'd been using on Rafferty, and applied it to her forehead. Then he turned to the Leprechaun. "Tell me."

Rafferty came around the end of the couch and that was when he discovered— "I'm naked as a woodpecker!" he shrieked, snatching at the blanket, covering himself, turning red, refusing to look at Tynvyr and Fiz, who were struggling to stifle laughter, hands over their mouths. Then Rafferty put a finger to his own lips, mumbling, "Oh, now I remember."

His modesty reclaimed by the blanket, Rafferty took a seat. "Wellanow, Dando, m'lad, in y'r rush t' get away from that black roider, it seems that y've managed to twist that ring o' y'rs and bring us back to th' very same place whare y' went whin y' escaped the Dragon, back t' th' very same location whare y' lost Tip and Perry in th' first place."

The ring! So *that's* how Dando controls the flight of the inn. By twisting his ring! The same ring that at this very moment he was trying to hide by shoving his hands in his pockets. So *that's* what he had in his pockets—the controlling ring.

"Anyway," continued Rafferty, "by accident or instinct, in y'r panic, wance again y' managed t' come t' here. Here whare they are. On this w'rld. In this wicked city. Trapped. Captured. Locked up."

Molly gasped, and Dando gritted his teeth but remained silent, neither saying ought as Rafferty went on.

"They are being held somewhare in an opium den, in a dope den, th' Yellow Poppy. Th' owner's name is Khassan, and he's a slaver on th' side, and as mean a one as ever there was, if I am t' believe me ears, and I do. They say he's got mean guards, too, patrollin' th' grounds. And if I'm t' believe me ears, them what told me say that there's them what's patrollin' under th' soil below and up in th' skies above, as well.

"As to Tip and Perry, Khassan's got 'em up f'r sale, at an exorbitant price. 'Special,' he calls 'em, 'cause o' their sparkly eyes. And there's hundreds o' bounty hunters in this town, beatin' th' bushes and searchin' th' alleyways and storm drains and anywhare else they figure Wee Folk with eyes what sparkle could be hidin'.

"Y'see, Khassan has put up a big reward f'r more sparkly-eyed folk, no questions asked.

"I learned all this from a couple o' droonks who were layin' in an alley and who thought me t' be a bottle-born figment o' their sodden minds. T' keep 'em talking, o' course, I had t' take a wee nip from their bottle ev'ry now and again—kept it in a paper bag, they did.

"And then, before y' could say thimbletythumb, there I was, droonk on cheap wine.

"We sold m' silver buckles f'r more wine, then m' clothes. And whin it all ran out—th' buckles, m' clothes, th' money, th' wine—I took th' empty out o' th' paper sack and came home in the bag."

A flinty glint came into Dando's eye. "Where is this Yellow Poppy?"

Rafferty held out his hand, palm out, as if to press the Warrow back into his seat. "Oi, now, and sure y' wouldn't be f'r thinkin' t' be goin' after Tip and Perry y'rself, now, would y'? Y' f'rget, there be a high bounty on all heads loike y'rs, what with y'r sparkly eyes and all.

"Oh, no, me auld friend, y'r not goin' on no rescue mission, sure, and that's final."

Dando ground his teeth in rage, and now I could see just why these folk were considered to be dangerous when riled. "If not me and mine, Rafferty," he gritted, "then who? Who will rescue them?"

That's when Rafferty looked at Fiz and Marley and Tynvyr and Rufous . . . and me.

And now here we were, stumbling along in a dark alley on a dark night, slipping in filth and slime, trapped between high buildings, with bats and rats and perhaps owls prowling the night, and somewhere in the blackness a cat was stalking.

Stalking us.

Great.

Just great.

An animal the size and ferocity of a cat, of a hungry cat, of an alley cat, could rip any and all and each of our tiny little bodies to shreds with but one swipe of its claws.

Mrrawww!

Fiz shrieked. Marley jerked. Rafferty ducked. I jumped.

It sounded as if the cat were practically on top of us.

Then I looked up.

It *was* practically on top of us. Black on black, dark against dark, I could barely see this vague blot atop the wall, silhouetted 'gainst the ebon sky.

It moved.

It was the cat.

"Look out above!" I shouted, just as it leaped, landing in the alley before us.

Somewhere.

We couldn't see it now. But I could hear it creeping closer.

Then I heard other paws padding. *Oh, Hèl, there's more than one. MMMRRAWW!*

"I can see it!" cried Fiz, her Fairy Vision better than any of ours. "It's going to spring."

"Save yourself, honey," I shouted. "Use your wings! Fly!"

Padding paws broke into a run. The other one was coming apace to join the first.

Turning about in confusion and fear, I didn't know which way to flee.

Suddenly the alley was full of snarling and *mrawwing* and the sounds of animals fighting, fighting like cats and do—

Rufous! It had to be Rufous! Then I heard Tynvyr shouting.

Lor! It *was* Rufous! We'd been saved by the fox!

With a yowl, the cat left the alleyway, leaping back up to the fence and bounding away in the darkness.

Rafferty lit a match and there they were, Tynvyr and Rufous, the fox dancing on his hind legs with his front paws against the fence, there where the cat had fled.

Without thinking, I ran to Rufous and hugged him. He turned and looked at me and began grinning and salivating.

I leapt back, bumping into someone soft, and turned to discover Fiz gazing up at me, adoration in her eyes.

Uh oh.

"You called me 'honey,'" she said, some kind of smarmy look descending over her. "You told me to save myself and called me 'honey.'"

Next I knew, she was pressing herself against me, her arms locked about my waist.

Between the upright tips of her wings I saw Rafferty smiling at me, and beyond him was Marley the Gnome, looking by matchlight around at the filth in the alley, shock and dismay on his face, seemingly about to faint but refusing to, for if he did he would fall into the filth itself:

foetid garbage and discarded refuse and squishy black mud and other things of slime and excrement better left unmentioned.

Then the match went out and we were plunged back into the blackness of the alleyway, and I could feel Rufous's hot breath panting down the back of my neck, and saliva dripping onto me.

"Another hundred feet or so"—it was Tynvyr speaking in the darkness—"and you'll round a corner, and there's light to see by. It's coming from the outside lanterns of the Yellow Poppy.

"There is a rusted wrought-iron fence surrounding it, and the inside grounds are patrolled by a guard, accompanied by a big dog of some kind. Another guard stands at the front door, letting people enter. Humans all.

"All of us can easily slip through the bars of the fence, even Rufous, though he'd have to squeeze a bit. But there are additional dogs in a kennel at the rear, and I'm certain that they'd warn the sentry should strangers attempt to enter the back way.

"Fiz could fly, were it not for the bloodsuckers in the sky above—and, no, Bork, before you ask, I didn't see any owls aloft.

"The Poppy itself is large, two-and-a-half or three Human storeys high, perhaps thirty feet from the ground to the peak of the roof. I judge it to be sixty or seventy feet wide, and maybe as much as a hundred feet long. How it ever got plunked down here in the middle of back alleyways, I'll never know. Regardless, there's a door in front and another in back, but the handles are set at Human height.

"There's barred windows about, but they look to be boarded up. We could get down the chimneys, except that there's smoke coming out.

"In my judgement, with the guards, the dogs, the boarded up windows, and the fires in the fireplaces, this will be a tough, if not impossible place to break into. Probably made so to keep anyone from stealing drugs.

"So, Rafferty, it looks as if we'll have to try one of the fallback plans after all."

Rafferty lit another match, and Tynvyr pulled Rufous back from my saliva-dripped-on neck, the fox looking guilty, though not necessarily repentant.

Fiz still had an arm about my waist, and once again she smarmed up at me, but I was all business. "Which plan, mine or Marley's?" I asked. "Mine, where we act as a travelling troupe of entertainers, or Marley's,

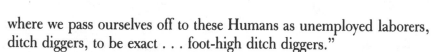

where we pass ourselves off to these Humans as unemployed laborers, ditch diggers, to be exact . . . foot-high ditch diggers."

"Well, if we only had some calluses," said Marley, peering at his hands by wavering matchlight, "then the choice would be obvious. But as it is, I think it's a toss-up as to which plan we choose."

We all looked at Rafferty, our unofficial leader, waiting for his decision.

He watched the match burn a bit more, then glanced up at us, his head cocked sideways, and he flung his arms open wide, and a great open-mouthed smile lit up his face. He gave his head a little shake and said, "Coo coo-ca choo, folks! It's showtime!"

And so, singing lustily at the tops of our voices, we marched down the alley and into the lantern light and up to the goggling guard gaping at us beside the front door of the Yellow Poppy.

We were escorted through the door and into a foyer, a foyer filled with a blue haze, and a cloying, sickeningly sweet odor pervaded the air. Fortunately, down at floor level, where we were, the haze thinned out a bit.

There was a black-haired receptionist, a Human, I think, though her eyes did have an Elven slant to them. Her skin was sallow, or yellow—it was difficult to tell through the blue smoke.

Her tilted eyes flew wide at the sight of us, and when Rafferty explained to her that we were Professor Marvel's Travelling Wonder Show (where he got that name, I'll never know) and that he himself was Professor Marvel and that we'd come to entertain, harrumph, for a small fee, of course, harrumph, well then she escorted us up a spiral stairway and onto the second floor.

We passed by two or three rooms, a door or two open, and inside were—Fiz gasped—naked Humans, lolling about on small satin sheets and silken pillows, lying atop a deep-pile carpet, woven with a geometric pattern, covering the floor of the room. The Humans seemed to be enthralled in some sort of trance, lost in an inner vision.

Past these rooms and through another door we went, coming before a final door, this one closed.

The receptionist knocked softly.

"What is it?" called a voice, strangely accented.

"Master, there are those here you should see."

We waited a moment, and suddenly the door was jerked open. "Who?"

The speaker was a Man. Black hair, black eyes, swarthy skin. A scar ran down his left cheek. He was slender, for a Human, with long-fingered hands. I judged that he was nearly six feet tall. A behemoth, towering some four times over my own considerable height. I mean, for a Brownie, at eighteen inches I'm fairly large, but this guy was a monster.

"Who?" he repeated.

The attendant pointed down, and there we were.

He started back, clearly surprised. A wide smile came over his face as Rafferty, er, Professor Marvel explained who we were.

He invited us into his quarters to audition our acts and to talk over our wages, telling the attendant to have Drak and his Men come and act as an audience. Hèl, this was going to be even easier than I had imagined. We had him fooled completely.

Fifteen minutes later, they hauled us down the stairs and into the basement and through the secret door and threw us in our cell, Drak bitching because "the damn fox bit me."

As soon as the door slammed shut behind, Marley whirled on me and snarled, "See! I *told* you that my plan was better! But in the face of overwhelming logic, would Mister High-and-Mighty Showbusiness listen? Oooohhh noooo, says he. They'll never believe that we are ditch diggers, says he. But a travelling show, now, says he, will pull the wool right over their eyes. Well, let me tell you, Bork, we put on the best damn show this town has ever seen, and where did it get us? In a cell! That's where! In a crummy cell, laden with"—for the first time he looked around and blanched—"rotten"—he sniffed—"sour-smelling (urp) filthy straw."

Trying to not touch the floor, Marley stepped over to peer into one of two buckets that were placed on opposite sides of the cell, one probably a drinking bucket and the other a privy pot. He looked into the one and shrieked, reeling back, his hand out in a warding gesture. He then looked into the other, and shrieked again.

"Which one has the dipper?" I asked. "Then we'll know."

Marley gagged and would have thrown up except he knew he couldn't stand the sight of it.

Rufous sat down and began scratching vigorously behind one ear. "We've got to get out of here," said Tynvyr, desperation in her voice.

Rufous now began frantically scratching at his neck.

Fiz looked adoringly up at me. "Don't worry," she responded to Tynvyr, "Bork will think of something."

All of this adoration just for one slip of the tongue.

Rufous began biting at the base of his tail, chasing after something in his fur. Thank the stars for Rufous, otherwise we'd all be crawling with vermin.

"Hoosh up, anow," shushed Rafferty, placing his ear against the cell wall, "I hear voices."

We all rushed over and listened.

"Hiyo! Lookit this bug, Perry, its legs work backwards . . . Hey! This part of the straw smells rottener than that part! . . . Lor! You can see patterns in the wood grain of the door! Here's one that looks like your nose, and here's another that looks like your—"

"Shut up, Tip! Just shut the Hèl up! I'm working on another escape plan, and I can't think! Your chatter is driving me crazy! So shut up!"

"Gee, Perry, sure I'll shut up. I'm probably better at shutting up than anyone else I know. Tippy is my name and shutting up is my game. I won't make a peep. Not a one. No sound. No sir. Perry is working on escape plan number four thousand five hundred and fifty three and he needs absolute quiet, and by golly I'm gonna give it to him. After all—"

"SHUT UP!"

I took my ear away and looked around at our cell, at the impenetrable stone walls, the thick, solid, locked wooden door, the vermin-ridden sour rotten straw, and the pair of who-knows-which-is-which privy and water buckets. We'd been trapped by a slaver and locked away in a heavily guarded secret room beneath a dope den. And locked in another cell adjacent to ours, we found the ones we'd come to set free.

Success at last!

Rafferty paced back and forth. "We need an escape plan," he said, "or there'll be th' divil t' pay."

I looked up at Rafferty. "I'd deal with a Demon if it'd get us out of here."

Fiz beamed at me. "Oh, Bork, I just *knew* you'd come up with a good plan."

"Huh?" I said brilliantly, and in that same moment we heard a rattling at the door. It was flung open.

It was Drak. He towered there, all six feet or so, glaring down at us, sucking the side of his hand where Rufous had bitten him.

Drak didn't look fully Human, but rather like he had some Goblin or Troll blood mixed in. But that's clearly impossible, for no one but another Goblin or Troll could stand a Goblin or Troll.

I could be mistaken, though, for behind Drak hulked the other guards, like him, Goblinoid as well.

"Keep yer dog under control," Drak growled at Tynvyr, all the while eyeing Rufous. But the fox was too busy scratching and nipping at his own fur to even notice Drak.

"Mister Drak," Marley started to say—

"Shaddup, you!" snarled Drak, glaring at him and then at each of us. "It's time you began earning yer keep. We're not just gonna feed ya fer free. So the boss wants ta know and *I* want ta know what yer names are and what ya do for a livin."

"My name is Marley and I am a ditch digger," said Marley, glaring triumphantly at me. I just sadly shook my head, knowing that he'd come to regret his words.

"Ditch digger, eh?" snorted Drak. "We got just the job fer you."

He glowered at me. "Next!"

"Bork. Cobbler," said I.

One by one he took our names and professions. "Fiz, house sprite"; "Rafferty, bartender"; "Tynvyr and Rufous, ratters."

I spent all day repairing shoes and racking my brains for a way to escape. But every time I came up with a plan, either it called for skills we didn't have, or it wouldn't work, or it would take years to accomplish, or it would get one or more of us killed. Hey, what can I say? Not all of us are escape artists.

Late, when I got back to the cell, Tynvyr and scratching Rufous were already there. There's one good thing to say about the vermin: at least they kept Rufous's mind off me. Even so, still I felt sorry for the fox, who, to my eye, was beginning to look a bit mangy.

Before Tynvyr and I had said more than a word or two, a guard rattled the door open and Fiz flew in, winging directly to me and giving me a peck on the cheek even before landing.

As soon as the door closed, Fiz said, "I've been upstairs, talking to the rugs, getting ready to carry out your plan."

My plan? Talking to the rugs? Clearly this Pixie has cracked under the strain. I glanced over to Tynvyr and she merely shrugged and gave one of those looks which says, *How should I know?*

"How was your day, dear?" Fiz asked domestically, looking up at me.

I sighed. "In the escape department, not very productive, though I *did* manage to steal this." I took a leather-working awl out from under my apron.

Fiz squealed, snatching it from me. "Oh, you are so very clever"— she gave me another peck on the cheek—"this is just perfect for unravelling the bindings on the rugs."

Again the door rattled open, and as Fiz hid the awl, the Goblinoid guards threw Rafferty into the cell. Damn! He was falling down drunk and singing about the Fairies Who Dance, again.

The Goblinoids started to shut the door, but someone yelled, and in came Marley, whimpering, covered from head to toe in Human feces. They'd put him to work shovelling out privies.

"What a Hèl hole," I growled, dragging Rafferty into the corner and onto some softer straw.

"Worse than you think," said Tynvyr. "Rufous and I did our ratting upstairs, on the first floor, and it's filled with row upon row of bunks, double-decker and triple. Humans lie in them, smoking dope, snorting powder up their noses, sticking needles in their veins, swallowing pills.

"They collapse on their beds and smile their meaningless smiles, their unfocused eyes staring inward, their abandoned souls lost within unremembered dreams of paradise, while stoic attendants wander silently among the wretches, bringing them even more opiates to feed their unslaked desires.

"And all the while, other lost souls shuffle in, seeking only an empty bunk for themselves. It's as if they don't see or don't want to see the others who shake and tremble and beg for more, the ones who offer to do *anything* for it, the ones who are wasting away, choosing narcotics instead of food, as if they'd rather have drug-driven dreams than a healthy body and mind.

"What fools they are to have ever begun, and what a hideous place is this Yellow Poppy."

Upon hearing Tynvyr's tale, Fiz shuddered. "Oh, how awful. But where I was, was awful, too:

"I worked on the second floor, as an attendant in the Rooms of Forbidden Illusions.

"There's five rooms up there, each with its lush carpet strewn with silken pillows. One by one, Humans come in and strip off all their clothes, be they male or female. My job was to give them small satin sheets, and they lie on these.

"As each new Human comes in and lies down, slowly he begins to lose consciousness as he falls under the web of the spell; his eyes lose focus, and then close, the lids flutter as his eyes shudder and whip side to side beneath; spittle begins to drool from his mouth, and his breathing becomes heavy and gasping; perspiration begins to bead until his whole body becomes wet and slick; then a look of intense rapture crosses his face, and his entire being tenses and spasms, only to fall completely slack, unconscious. Oh Bork, some of them totally lost control of their bodily functions, and I and the other attendants had to clean up the messes.

"The long-time attendants say that all those who seek the forbidden illusions are affected the same: slowly they lose interest in real life, and they become listless and completely unmotivated; the only reality and joy for them is found among silken pillows on satin sheets on a lush carpet within those rooms on the second floor of the Yellow Poppy.

"And you know what? They don't even know what's truly happening up there. I suppose it's because they don't have Fairy Sight. But you see, their very souls are slowly being eaten away, a bit at a time with each visit, traded for illusion. Bit by bit, each loses fragments of his soul, until he doesn't have any left. You see, the Demon trapped in whichever rug the victim is addicted to ultimately will have eaten it all. And—"

Rafferty began throwing up. And whimpering, Marley crawled over, dragging one of the buckets after, intending to clean up the vomit with his bare hands. Tynvyr and I stopped him, and led him back to his corner, and he looked at us with unfocused eyes, weeping all the while. What the masters of the Yellow Poppy had done to this poor Gnome was beyond forgiveness.

Too, I could not but help reflect upon what Tynvyr and Fiz had seen in the den above, and I knew that Khassan and his henchmen must somehow be made to pay for their crimes.

And I raged at the sheer stupidity of *anyone* who would get addicted to *anything*, whether it be narcotics or illusion or drink or pipeweed or *anything*. And that not only included Humans being addicted, but *anyone*—Halflings, Hobbits, Warrows, and Wee Folk included . . . even Leprechauns.

I glanced at Marley, the Gnome shivering and shuddering and weeping in his corner. Damn! We just had to get out of this Hèlhole!

We made our big break the next day, Fiz executing my plan to perfection, even though it nearly got all of us killed forever. What's that, you say? You didn't know I had a plan? Well, join the club, friend, 'cause neither did I.

It happened this way.

The door rattled open again and there was Drak, as usual. "Out, slime!" he snarled. "Time to sew leather, catch rats, tend the rugheads, and shovel shit. And you, Rafferty, no more bartending; you're gonna shovel shit, too."

We all groaned to our feet—Marley somewhat recovered, Rafferty holding his head—and began to file out, Fiz flying.

"Oi, Cap'n," shouted one of the Goblinoid guards, pointing up at Fiz, "she's got some kinda weapon!"

I looked. Fiz was carrying the awl.

All Hèl broke loose.

Fiz, darting and dodging swatting hands, flew toward the open secret door. Snarling, Rufous attacked Drak, the fox's slashing teeth hamstringing the shrieking Goblinoid Human to come crashing down, clutching his leg, blood flying wide. Tynvyr darted out and leapt astride the raging fox, and Marley smashed a bucket down on Drak's head, cracking his skull open like a rotten egg.

Rafferty and I ran to the adjacent cell, and I scrambled up onto his shoulders, heaving the bar out from the hooks to come crashing down. And together, we flung open the wooden door.

Gaping at us were two Warrows, Tip and Perry, though which was which, I knew not.

"Rafferty!" they shouted together in unison.

"Don't jist stand there loike a couple o' harebrained ninnies," shrieked Rafferty, "don't y' recognize a prison break whin y' see wan?"

They bolted outward, Perry scooping up the door bar in passing, to bring it smashing into a Goblinoid Human's knee, shattering the cap, the guard falling screeching to the floor, where his days were ended by Marley and his lethal bucket.

"Bork!" I heard a shriek, and looked up in time to see Tynvyr and Rufous bearing down on me. *"Up behind! We've got to help Fiz!"*

I leapt astraddle Rufous behind Tynvyr, and through milling legs and stomping feet we darted for the exit. While behind, Tip with Drak's sword, Perry with a bar, Rafferty with a nightstick scooped up from a fallen foe, and Marley with his killer bucket battled the remaining guards.

But two of the Goblinoids, shouting at the tops of their lungs, raced after Tynvyr and Rufous and me.

Up the spiral stairs we ran, Rufous leaping up three steps at a time, the Goblinoids right behind. Up from the basement and to the first floor, we fled, Rufous darting down a long hall, toward the stairs at the far end, Tynvyr crying *"Yah! Yah!"*

Behind us thundered the guards, yelling for aid, but we did not slow to see if they were answered.

Up the second set of spiral stairs twisted Rufous, the fox beginning to labor, for he was carrying double, not used to bearing someone of my massive size.

Even so, ahead of the guards we bounded onto the second floor, and with claws scrabbling and Tynvyr shouting and guards thudding up after, Rufous charged down the long hall to come unto the Rooms of Forbidden Illusions.

Past doors we flashed, glancing into the rooms as Rufous ran by. And at the third door, I caught a fleeting glimpse of Fiz—*"Stop!"* shrieked Tynvyr, the fox planting his front feet stiff-leggedly while hunkering down his rear, skidding on the slippery floor, sliding and spinning, whirling me off to fly through the air, arms flailing and legs thrashing. I crashed to a stop against a wall ten feet beyond.

Dizzily, I scrambled up. Even now, the Goblinoid Humans were charging toward us. Rufous with Tynvyr still aboard scrabbled back toward the door where we had seen Fiz, and I darted after. We made it into the room just ahead of the pursuers.

And there was Fiz.

There, too, was Khassan, across the room, on his knees, crying "No! Please no!" *He was begging!*

And Fiz was at the border of the carpet, my awl in her hand, poised over the rug's edge binding.

What the . . . ?

"No!" shrieked Khassan. "I'll let you all go! I'll set you all free! Just please don't do it. *He* will get out!"

Footsteps thudded behind us. *The guards!*

"No, no!" Khassan screamed.

I looked at the carpet, and hidden down deeply within the pattern, I could barely make something out. And with my poor Fairy Sight, so very weak when compared with Fiz's, I could just discern a huge face peering up through the geometrical design, a deep red face with yellow, viperous eyes and a leering mouth filled with glistening fangs, the face of a—

plink

The barely audible *plink* of a breaking thread sounded as Fiz broke the binding on the carpet.

RRRRAAAWWWW!

Explosively expanding out from the carpet, swelling upward and crashing through the ceiling, shattering open the Yellow Poppy like a rotten melon, exposing the grublike patrons to the Sun, suddenly, the gigantic form of a massive Demon towered high above, laughing ghoulishly and shouting "Free! Free!"

Wreckage crashed down all around us, and flames blasted upward as something below caught fire. *"Fiz, get out of there! Use your wings! Fly! Flee!"* I shouted, darting toward the ruin of the stairs, the front stairs, they were closer.

"Bork!" Once again Tynvyr and Rufous came to my aid, and I leapt upon the back of the fox, and he ran like Hèl.

Khassan fled, too, as did his guards, running before us.

But then a great hand came down and scooped up shrieking Khassan, lifting him high into the air. Suddenly there was a squashing sound, as of a bug being smashed, chopping off Khassan's screams in mid-shriek.

Downward we fled, Rufous bounding in great leaps from stair fragment to stair fragment, from shattered rubble to tumbled ruin, flying across gaps that took my breath away. And I knew then that neither Tynvyr nor I would have made it without the fox.

The front of the building was burst open, and we bolted outward into the alleyway street. Behind us, flames raged.

"Hiyo!" came a call, and out from the wreckage stumbled Tip and Perry and Rafferty and Marley, the Gnome still carrying his killer bucket. And flying down from above came Fiz.

And towering upward into the sky loomed a gigantic Demon, red pulp dripping from his closed right fist, and he laughed horribly, madly, his yellow viperous eyes wide and glaring insanely.

Reaching down into the flames, the Demon lifted something up from the burning wreck. It was another of the rugs. He pulled loose one thread, and a second gigantic Demon appeared, towering up into the sky.

Swiftly, three more Demons were loosed, making five in all. And they looked at one another and laughed their mad laughs. Then, as if of one mind, they sped away from one another, to come to five points equidistant on the perimeter of the city.

Rafferty looked and with trepidation in his voice said, "Saints presarve us, they are at th' points o' a pentagram."

At that moment, violent ocherous energy crackled along a five-pointed web between the Demons, and suddenly, there we were, us and the whole wicked city, under a dark maroon Sun, while overhead a black Moon sailed through a sulfurous yellow sky.

"Neddra, Neddra," howled the Demons, and then I knew that somehow the entire city had been transported to the Lower Realms. And across the endless dust-laden plains and past the bubbling pools of lava came marching great ravening hordes: the Legions of the Undead.

We had gone to Hèl.

We were in Hèl.

We were surrounded by Hèl.

We ran like Hèl.

Just ahead of gibbering corpses, slavering black-fanged baying things, flaming devils, tall stalking creatures made of bones, yellow-eyed leathery-webbed howlers, ebon wraiths, and other things too hideous to describe. And racing past us and through the city streets veered thundering chariots, drawn by Hèlsteeds and bearing howling ghouls waving jagged lances, great spinning blades upon the wheels, each ghoul swerving to try to impale us on that whirling death. Yet we dodged and darted, and fled before them, running for our very lives, trying to reach the Halfling House.

And as we ran, great shudders racked the city, thunderous explosions booming, buildings blasting apart, ruby fire flaring upward into the sulfurous sky. Crowds of people raced this way and that, screaming dopers and slavers and sadistic guards, panderers, thieves, ruffians, brigands, muggers, burglars, the entire population of this wicked city, all of them of one vile sort or another, the entire population and us, too, fleeing before the ravenous Hordes of Hèl.

Just ahead of death, we ran, and at last, there was our goal: the Halfling House.

Darting and dashing, Fiz flying, across the final rubble-strewn field we fled and onto the porch, slamming inward through the door, Rafferty coming last, bolting inward and under a table, crying "Dando! Away! Fly! Foe! Flee!"

Dando twisted his ring.

Nothing happened.

"The door, Rafferty!" he shrieked. "Shut the door!"

But I was closest and scrambled for the door just as this huge, claw-handed, skull-faced Giant came ripping up out of the soil—*RRRRAAAWWWW!*—lunging forward, reaching for the opening, just as I slammed it shut.

This time, as the damman lighted the candles and lanterns, I didn't even attempt to peer out the sparkly windows, knowing what it would do to my eyes. Instead, I relaxed on the couch and rubbed Fiz's feet, her exquisite tiny feet, lust stealing into my loins.

Most of us were there in the great room, worn out, exhausted, catching our breath, except for Marley, who'd gone upstairs lugging his killer bucket, and I could hear sounds of frantic scrubbing drifting down from the bathing room above.

Molly and Dando were having a tearful reunion with Tip and Perry, and Rafferty was smacking his lips over a flagon of ale. Fiz was explaining to everyone how with our Fairy Sight she and I had seen the rug-trapped Demons the very first time we had passed the Rooms of Forbidden Illusions on our way to meet Khassan, and how in the cell I had hatched my very clever plan to deal with a Demon. And all the while she told the tale she beamed adoringly at me.

I don't think I'll ever tell her the truth.

When Marley came back down, skin scrubbed raw, bucket in hand, Tynvyr borrowed some flea soap and led Rufous toward the stairs, the fox stopping every now and again to nip at his fur or to scratch. I figured that with a bath it wouldn't be long ere he would once more begin eyeing me and salivating. Oh well, I would deal with that in its own due time.

I sat reflecting, slowly relaxing. If I'd learned one thing, it was this: anytime anyone ever says, "Well, I'll be go to Hèl," I can say, "I've been there, and believe me, you don't want to go."

My musing was interrupted by a faint buzzing. "What's that rattling?"

Dando jumped up and whirled to face me. "Nothing! No one! No owls, cats, rats, dogs, bats, hawks, weasels, cobras, mongooses or mongeese, or any other thing of the sort. And no rattly snake. No sir. No way. No how. And certainly no mice; they've all disappeared."

Suddenly, with a soft thump, we landed. The windows stopped sparkling. And a harsh dark lavender glare shone in.

Rafferty looked up at the violet blare. "Wellanow, Dando, me bucko. Jist whare d'we be this toime?"

Dando coughed and shrugged. "Well, as to that . . . um . . . you see, I'm not exactly sure, what with that skull-faced Giant who was coming at us, and all . . . anyway, I just didn't have time to select a destination."

Just then, from outside came a bellowing roar.

The Halfling House began to shake.

The front door crashed open.

Purple light blasted inward.

Someone screamed. . . .

Silver or Gold

Emma Bull

oon Very Thin sat on the raised hearth—the only place in
the center room out of the way—with her chin on her
knuckles. She would have liked to be doing something more,
but the things she thought of were futile, and most were
undignified. She watched Alder Owl crisscross the slate floor
and pop in and out of the stillroom and the pantry and the
laundry. Alder Owl's hands were full of things on every
crossing: clean clothes, a cheese, dried yellow dock and
feverfew, a tinderbox, a wool mantle. She was frowning
faintly all over her round pink face, and Moon knew that
she was reviewing lists in her head.

"You can't pack all that," said Moon.

"You couldn't," said Alder Owl. "But I've had fifty years
more practice. Now remember to cure the squash before you
bring them in, or there'll be nothing to eat all winter but
onions. And if the squirrels nest in the thatch again, there's a
charm—"

"You told me," Moon sighed. She shifted a little to let the fire roast
a slightly different part of her back. "If I forget it, I can look it up. It's
awfully silly for you to set out now. We could have snow next week."

"If we did, then I'd walk through it. But we won't. Not for another
month." Alder Owl wrapped three little stoneware jars in flannel and
tucked them in her wicker pack.

Moon opened her mouth, and the thing she'd been busy not saying for three days hopped out. "He's been missing since before Midsummer. Why do you have to go now? Why do you have to go at all?"

At that, Alder Owl straightened up and regarded her sternly. "I have responsibilities. You ought to know that."

"But why should they have anything to do with *him*?"

"He is the prince of the Kingdom of Hark End."

Moon stood up. She was taller than Alder Owl, but under that fierce gaze she felt rather stubby. She scowled to hide it. "And we live in Hark End. Hundreds—*thousands* of people do. A lot of them are even witches. They haven't all gone tramping off like a pack of questing youngest sons."

Alder Owl had a great many wrinkles, which deepened all over her face when she was about to smile. They deepened now. "First, youngest sons have never been known to quest in packs. Second, all the witches worth their salt and stone have tried to find him, in whatever way suits them best. All of them but me. I held back because I wanted to be sure you could manage without me."

Moon Very Thin stood still for a moment, taking that in. Then she sat back down with a thump and laced her fingers around her knees. "Oh," she said, halfway between a gasp and a laugh. "Unfair, unfair. To get at me through my pride!"

"Yes, my weed, and there's such a lot of it. I have to go, you know. Don't make it harder for me."

"I wish I could do something to help," said Moon after a moment.

"I expect you to do all your work around here, and all of mine besides. Isn't that enough?" Alder Owl smoothed the flap down over the pack and snugged the drawstring tight.

"You know it's not. Couldn't I go with you?"

Alder Owl pulled a stool from under the table with her foot and sat on it, her hands over her knees. "When I travel in my spirit," she said, "to ask a favor of Grandmother, you can't go with me."

"Of course not. Then who'd play the drum, to guide you back?"

Alder Owl beamed. "Clever weed. Open that cupboard over the mantel-shelf and bring me what you find there."

What Moon found was a drum. It was nothing like the broad, flat, cowhide journey-drum, whose speech echoed in her bones and was like a breathing heartbeat under her fingers, whose voice could be heard in the land where there was no voice. This drum was an upright cylinder no bigger than a quart jar. Its body was made of some white wood, and the skins of its two heads were fine-grained and tufted with soft white hair around the lashings. There was a loop of hide to hold it with, and a drumstick with a leather beater tucked through that.

Moon shook her head. "This wouldn't be loud enough to bring you home from the pump, let alone from—where *are* you going?"

"Wherever I have to. Bring it to me."

Moon brought her the drum, and Alder Owl held it up by the loop of hide and struck it, once. The sound it made was a sharp, ringing *tok*, like a woodpecker's blow.

Alder Owl said, "The wood is from an ash tree planted at the hour of my birth. The skins are from a ewe born on the same day. I raised the ewe and watered the tree, and on my sixteenth birthday, I asked them for their lives, and they gave them gladly. No matter how far I go, the drum will reach me. When I cannot hear it, it will cease to sound.

"Tomorrow at dawn, I'll leave," Alder Owl continued. "Tomorrow at sunset, as the last rind of the sun burns out behind the line of the Wantnot Hills, and at every sunset after, beat the drum once, as I just did."

Moon was a little shaken by the solemnity of it all. But she gathered her wits at last and repeated, "At sunset each day. Once. I'll remember."

"Hmph. Well." Alder Owl lifted her shoulders, as if solemnity was a shawl she could shrug away. "Tomorrow always comes early. Time to put the fire to bed."

"I'll get the garden things," Moon said. She tossed her cloak on and went out the stillroom door into the night.

Her namesake was up, and waxing. Alder Owl would have good light, if she needed to travel by night. But it would be cold traveling; frost dusted the leaves and vines and flagstone paths like talcum. Moon shivered and sighed. "What's the point of having an able-bodied young apprentice, if you're not going to put all that ableness to use?" she muttered to the shifting air. The cold carried all her S's off into the dark.

She pinched a bloom from the yellow chrysanthemum, and a stalk of merry-man's wort from its sheltered bed. When she came back into the house she found that Alder Owl had already fed the fire and settled the logs with the poker, and fetched a bowl of water. Moon dropped the flowers into it.

"Comforter, guard against the winter dark," Alder Owl said to the fire, as always, as if she were addressing an old friend. She stirred the water with her fingers as she spoke. "Helpmeet, nourisher of flesh and heart, bide and watch, and let no errant spark leap up until the sun should take thy part."

Firelight brushed across the seamed landscape of Alder Owl's face, flashed yellow in her sharp, dark eyes, turned the white in her hair to ivory. *Tomorrow night*, Moon thought, *she won't be here. Just me.* She could believe it only with the front of her mind, where all untested things were kept. The rest of her, mind and lungs and soles of feet, denied it.

Alder Owl flicked the water from her hand onto the hearth, and the line of drops steamed. Then she handed the bowl to Moon, and Moon fed the flowers to the fire.

After a respectful silence, Moon said, "It's water." It was the continuation of an old argument. "And the logs were trees that grew out of the earth and fed on water, and the fire itself feeds on those and air. That's all four elements. You can't separate them."

"It's the hour for fire, and it's fire that we honor. At the appropriate hours we honor the other three, and if you say things like that in public, no educated person in the village will speak to you." Alder Owl took the bowl out of Moon's hands and gathered her fingers in a strong, wet clasp. "My weed, my stalk of yarrow. You're not a child anymore. When I leave, you'll be a grown woman, in others' eyes if not your own. What people hear from a child's mouth as foolishness becomes something else on the lips of a woman grown: sacrilege, or spite, or madness. Work the work as you see fit, but keep your mouth closed around your notions, and keep fire out of water and earth out of air."

"But—"

"Empty the bowl now, and get on to bed."

Moon went into the garden again and flung the water out of the bowl—southward, because it was consecrated to fire. Then she stood a little while in the cold, with a terrible hard feeling in her chest that was beyond sadness, beyond tears. She drew in great breaths to freeze it, and exhaled hard to force the fragments out. But it was immune to cold or wind.

"I'd like to be a woman," she whispered. "But I'd rather be a child with you here, than a woman with you gone." The sound of the words, the knowledge that they were true, did what the cold couldn't. The terrible feeling cracked, melted, and poured out of her in painful tears. Slowly the comforting order around her, the beds and borders Alder

Owl had made, stopped the flow of them, and the kind cold air wiped them off her face.

At dawn, when the light of sunrise lay tangled in the treetops, Alder Owl settled her pack on her back and went out by the front door. Moon went with her as far as the gate at the bottom of the yard. In the uncertain misty land of dawn, Alder Owl was a solid, certain figure, cloaked in shabby purple wool, her silver and black hair tucked under a drunken-brimmed green hat.

"I don't think you should wear the hat," Moon said, past the tightness in her throat. "You look like an eggplant."

"I *like* it. I'm an old woman. I can wear what I please."

She was going. What did one say, except "Goodbye," which wasn't at all what Moon wanted? "When will you come back?"

"When I've found him. Or when I know he can't be found."

"You always tell me not to try to prove negatives."

"There are ways," Alder Owl replied, with a sideways look, "to prove this one."

Moon Very Thin shivered in the weak sun. Alder Owl squinted up at her, pinched her chin lightly. Then she closed the gate behind her and walked down the hill. Moon watched her—green and purple, silly and strong—until the trees hid her from sight.

She cured the squash before she put them in the cellar. She honored the elements, each at its own hour. She made cheese and wine, and put up the last of the herbs, and beat the rugs, and waxed all the floors against the coming winter muck. She mended the thatch and the fence, pruned the apple trees and turned the garden beds, taking comfort from maintaining the order that Alder Owl had established.

Moon took over other established things, too. By the time the first snow fell, her neighbors had begun to bring their aches and pains to her, to fetch her when a child was feverish, to call her in to set a dog's broken leg or stitch up a horse's gashed flank. They asked about the best day to sign a contract, and whether there was a charm to keep nightshade out of the hay field. In return, they brought her mistletoe and willow bark, a sack of rye flour, a tub of butter.

She didn't mind the work. She'd been brought up for it; it seemed as natural as getting out of bed in the morning. But she found she minded the payment. When the nearest neighbor's boy, Fell, trotted up to the gate on his donkey with the flour sack riding pillion, and thanked

her, and gave it to her, she almost thrust it back at him. Alder Owl had
given her the skill, and had left her there to serve them. The payment
should be Alder Owl's. But there was no saying which would appear
first, Alder Owl or the bottom of the sack.

"You look funny," Fell said.

"You look worse," Moon replied, because she'd taught him to climb
trees and to fish, and had thus earned the privilege. "Do you know those
things made out of wood or bone, with a row of little spines set close
together? They call them 'combs.'"

"Hah, hah." He pointed to the flour. "I hope you make it all into
cakes and get fat." He grinned and loped back down the path to the
donkey. They kicked up snow as they climbed the hill, and he waved at
the crest.

She felt better. Alder Owl would never have had that conversation.

Every evening at sunset, Moon took the little drum out of the cupboard over the mantel. She looked at it, and touched it, and thought of
her teacher. She tried to imagine her well and warm and safe, with a
hot meal before her and pleasant company near. At last, when the rim
of the sun blinked out behind the far line of hills, she swung the beater
against the fine skin head, and the drum sounded its woodpecker knock.

Each time Moon wondered: Could Alder Owl really hear it? And if
she could, what if Moon were to beat it again? If she beat it three times,
would Alder Owl think something was wrong, and return home?

Nothing was wrong. Moon put the drum away until the next sunset.

The Long Night came, and she visited all her neighbors, as they visited her. She brought them fir boughs tied with bittersweet, and honey
candy, and said the blessing-charm on their doorsteps. She watched the
landscape thaw and freeze, thaw and freeze. Candle-day came, and she
went to the village, which was sopping and giddy with a spell of warmer
weather, to watch the lighting of the new year's lamps from the flame
of the old. It could be, said the villagers, that no one would ever find
the prince. It could be that the King of Stones had taken him beneath
the earth, and that he would lie there without breath, in silence, forever.
And had she had any word of Alder Owl, and hadn't it been a long time
that she'd been gone?

Yes, said Moon, it had been a long time.

The garden began to stir, almost invisibly, like a cat thinking of breakfast in its sleep. The sound of water running was everywhere, though

the snow seemed undisturbed and the ice as thick as ever. Suddenly, as if nature had thrown wide a gate, it was spring, and Moon was run off her legs with work. Lambing set her to wearing muddy paths in the hills between the cottage and the farmsteads all around. The mares began to foal, too. She thanked wisdom that women and men, at least, had no season.

She had been with Tansy Broadwater's bay thoroughbred since late morning. The foal had been turned in the womb and tied in his cord, and Moon was nearly paralyzed thinking of the worth of the two of them, and their lives in her hands. She was bloody to the elbows and hoarse with chanting, but at last she and Tansy regarded each other triumphantly across the withers of a nursing colt.

"Come up to the house for a pot of hot tea," Tansy said as Moon rinsed soap off her hands and arms. "You won't want to start out through the woods now until moonrise, anyway."

Moon lifted her eyes, shocked, to the open barn door. The sun wore the Wantnot Hills like a girdle.

"I have to go," she said. "I'm sorry. I'll be all right." She headed for the trail at a run.

Stones rolled under her boots, and half-thawed ice lay slick as butter in the shadows. It was nearly night already, under the trees. She plunged down the hill and up the next one, and down again, slithering, on all fours sometimes. She could feel her bones inside her brittle as fire-blasted wood, her ankles fragile and waiting for a wrench. She was afraid to look at the sun again.

The gate—the gate at the bottom of the path was under her hands. She sobbed in relief. So close . . . She raced up through the garden, the cold air like fire in her lungs. She struggled frantically with the front door, until she remembered it was barred inside, that she'd left through the stillroom. She banged through the stillroom door and made the contents of the shelves ring and rattle. To the hearth, and wrench the cupboard door open . . .

The drum was in her hands, and through the window the sun's rind showed, thin as thread, on the hills. She was in time. As the horizon closed like a snake's eyelid over the disk of the sun, Moon struck the drum.

There was no sound at all.

Moon stared at the drum, the beater, her two hands. She had missed, she must have. She brought the beater to the head again. She might as well have hit wool against wool. There was no woodpecker knock, no sharp clear call. She had felt skin and beater meet, she had seen them. What had she done wrong?

Slowly Alder Owl's words came back to her. *When I cannot hear it, it will cease to sound.* Moon had always thought the drum would be hard to hear. But never silent. *Tell me if you can't hear this,* she thought wildly. Something else they'd said as she left, about proving negatives—that there were ways to prove the prince couldn't be found.

If he were dead, for example. If he were only bones under the earth.

And Alder Owl, beyond the drum's reach, might have followed him even to that, under the dominion of the King of Stones.

She thought about pounding the drum; she could see herself doing it in her mind, hammering at it until it sounded or broke. She imagined weeping, too; she could cry and scream and break things, and collapse at last exhausted and miserable.

What she did was to sit where she was at the table, the drum on her knees, watching the dark seep in and fill the room around her. Sorrow and despair rose and fell inside her in a slow rhythm, like the shortening and lengthening of days. When her misery peaked, she would almost weep, almost shriek, almost throw the drum from her. Then it would begin to wane, and she would think, *No, I can bear it,* until it turned to waxing once again.

She would do nothing, she resolved, until she could think of something useful to do. She would wait until the spiders spun her white with cobwebs, if she had to. But she would do something better than crying, better than breaking things.

The hide lashing of Alder Owl's drum bit into her clenched fingers. In the weak light of the sinking fire, the wood and leather were only a pale mass in her lap. How could Alder Owl's magic have dwindled away to this—a drum with no voice? What voice could reach her now?

And Moon answered herself, wonderingly: *Grandmother.*

She couldn't. She had never gone to speak with Grandmother herself. And how could she travel there, with no one to beat the drum for her when she was gone? She might be lost forever, wandering through the tangled roots of Grandmother's trees.

Yet she stood and walked, stiff-jointed, to the stillroom. She gathered up charcoal and dried myrtle and cedar. She poured apple wine into a wooden cup, and dropped in a seed from a sky's-trumpet vine. It was a familiar set of motions. She had done them for Alder Owl. She took down the black-fleeced sheepskin from the wall by the front door, laid it out on the floor, and set the wine and incense by it, wine to the east, charcoal to the south. Another trip, to fetch salt and the little bone-handled knife—earth to the north, the little conical pile of salt, and the knife west, for air. (Salt came from the sea, too, said her rebellious mind, and the knife's metal was mined from earth and tempered with fire and water. But she was afraid of heresy now, afraid to doubt the knowledge she must trust with the weight of lives. She did as she'd been taught.)

At last she took the big drum, the journey-drum, out of its wicker case and set it on the sheepskin. The drum would help her partway on her travels. But when she crossed the border, she would have to leave body, fingers, drum all at the crossing, and the drum would fall silent. She needed so little: just a tap, tap, tap. Well, her heart would have to do.

Moon dropped cross-legged on the sheepskin. Right-handed she took up the knife and drew lightly on the floor around herself as if she were a compass. She passed the knife to her left hand behind her back, smoothly, and the knife point never left the slate. That had been hard once, learning to take the knife as Alder Owl passed it to her. She drew the circle again with a pinch of salt dropped from each hand, and with cedar and myrtle smoking and snapping on their charcoal bed. Finally she drew the circle with wine shaken from her fingers, and drank off the rest. Then she took up the drum.

She tried to hear the rhythm of her breathing, of her heart, the rhythm that was always inside her. Only when she felt sure of it did she begin to let her fingers move with it, to tap the drum. It shuddered under her fingers, lowing out notes. When her hands were certain on the drum head, she closed her eyes.

A tree. That was the beginning of the journey, Moon knew; she was to begin at the end of a branch of the great tree. But what kind of tree? Was it night, or day? Should she imagine herself as a bird or a bug, or as herself? And how could she think of all that and play the drum, too?

Her neck was stiff, and one of her feet was going to sleep. *You think too much,* she scolded herself. Alder Owl had never had such trouble. Alder Owl had also never suggested that there was such a thing as too much thinking. More of it, she'd said, would fix most of the world's problems.

Well, she'd feel free to think, then. She settled into the drumbeat, imagined it wrapped around her like a featherbed.

—A tree too big to ever see all at once, one of a forest of trees like it. A tree with a crown of leaves as wide as a clear night sky on a hilltop. Night time, then. It was an oak, she decided, but green out of season. She envisioned the silver-green leathery leaves around her, and the rough black bark, starry with dew in the moonlight. The light came from the end of the branch. Cradled in leaves there was a pared white-silver crescent, a new moon cut free from the shadow of the old. It gave her light to travel by.

The rough highroad of bark grew broader as she neared the trunk. She imagined birds stirring in their sleep and the quick, querulous *chirk* of a squirrel woken in its nest. The wind breathed in and out across the vault of leaves and made them twinkle. Moon heard her steps on the wood, even and measured: the voice of the drum.

Down the trunk, down toward the tangle of roots, the knotted mirror-image of the branches above. The trunks of other trees were all around her, and the twining branches shuttered the moonlight. It was harder going, shouldering against the life of the tree that always moved upward. Her heartbeat was a thin, regular bumping in her ears.

It was too dark to tell which way was down, too dark to tell anything. Moon didn't know if she'd reached the roots or not. She wanted to cry out, to call for Grandmother, but she'd left her body behind, and her tongue in it.

A little light appeared before her, and grew slowly. There were patterns in it, colors, shapes—she could make out the gate at the bottom of the garden, and the path that led into the woods. On the path—was it the familiar one? It was bordered now with sage—she saw a figure made of the flutter of old black cloth and untidy streamers of white hair, walking away from her. A stranger, Moon thought; she tried to catch up, but didn't seem to move at all. At the first fringes of the trees the figure turned, lifted one hand, and beckoned. Then it disappeared under the roof of the woods.

Moon's spirit, like a startled bird, burst into motion, upward. Her eyes opened on the center room of the cottage. She was standing unsteadily on the sheepskin, the journey-drum at her feet. Her heart clattered under her ribs like a stick dragged across the pickets of a fence, and she felt sore and prickly and feverish. She took a step backward, overbalanced, and sat down.

"Well," she said, and the sound of her voice made her jump. She licked her dry lips and added, "That's not at all how it's supposed to be done."

Trembling, she picked up the tools and put them away, washed out the wooden bowl. She'd gathered up the sheepskin and had turned to hang it on the wall when her voice surprised her again. "But it worked," she said. She stood very still, hugging the fleece against her. "It worked, didn't it?" She'd traveled and asked, and been answered, and if neither had been in form as she understood them, still they were question and answer, and all that she needed. Moon hurried to put the sheepskin away. There were suddenly a lot of things to do.

The next morning she filled her pack with food and clothing, tinderbox and medicines, and put the little ash drum, Alder Owl's drum, on top of it all. She put on her stoutest boots and her felted wool cloak. She smothered the fire on the hearth, fastened all the shutters, and left a note for Tansy Broadwater, asking her to look after the house.

At last she shouldered her pack and tramped down the path, through the gate, down the hill, and into the woods.

Moon had traveled before, with Alder Owl. She knew how to find her way, and how to build a good fire and cook over it; she'd slept in the open and stayed at inns and farmhouses. Those things were the same alone. She had no reason to feel strange, but she did. She felt like an impostor, and expected every chance-met traveler to ask if she was old enough to be on the road by herself.

She thought she'd been lonely at the cottage; she thought she'd learned the size and shape of loneliness. Now she knew she'd only explored a corner of it. Walking gave her room to think, and sights to see: fern shoots rolling up out of the mushy soil, yellow cups of wild crocuses caught by the sun, the courting of ravens. But it was no use pointing and crying, "Look!," because the only eyes there had already seen. Her isolation made everything seem not quite real. It was harder each night to light a fire, and she had steadily less interest in food. But each night at sunset, she beat Alder Owl's drum. Each night it was silent, and she sat in the aftermath of that silence, bereft all over again.

She walked for six days through villages and forest and farmland. The weather had stayed dry and clear and unspringlike for five of them, but on the sixth she tramped through a rising chill wind under a lowering sky. The road was wider now, and smooth, and she had more company on it: Carts and wagons, riders, other walkers went to and fro past her. At noon she stopped at an inn, larger and busier than any she'd yet seen.

The boy who set tea down in front of her had a mop of blond hair over a cheerful, harried face. "The cold pie's good," he said before she could ask. "It's rabbit and mushroom. Otherwise, there's squash soup.

But don't ask for ham—I think it's off a boar that wasn't cut right. It's awful."

Moon didn't know whether to laugh or gape. "The pie, then, please. I don't mean to sound like a fool, but where am I?"

"Little Hark," he replied. "But don't let that raise your hopes. Great Hark is a week away to the west, on foot. You bound for it?"

"I don't know. I suppose I am. I'm looking for someone."

"In Great Hark? Huh. Well, you can find an ant in an anthill, too, if you're not particular which one."

"It's that big?" Moon asked.

He nodded sympathetically. "Unless you're looking for the king or the queen."

"No. A woman—oldish, with hair a little more white than black, and a round pink face. Shorter than I am. Plump." It was hard to describe Alder Owl; she was too familiar. "She would have had an eggplant-colored cloak. She's a witch."

The boy's face changed slowly. "Is she the bossy-for-your-own-good sort? With a wicker pack? Treats spots on your face with witch hazel and horseradish?"

"That sounds like her . . . What else do you use for spots?"

"I don't know, but the horseradish works pretty well. She stopped here, if that's her. It was months ago, though."

"Yes," said Moon. "It was."

"She was headed for Great Hark, so you're on the right road. Good luck on it."

When he came back with the rabbit pie, he said, "You'll come to Burnton High Plain next—that's a two-day walk. After that you'll be done with the grasslands pretty quick. Then you'll be lucky if you see the sun 'til you're within holler of Great Hark."

Moon swallowed a little too much pie at once. "I will? Why?"

"Well, you'll be in the Seawood, won't you?"

"Will I?"

"You don't know much geography," he said sadly.

"I know I've never heard that the Seawood was so thick the sun wouldn't shine in it. Have you ever been there?"

"No. But everyone who has says it's true. And being here, I get to hear what travelers tell."

Moon opened her mouth to say that she'd heard more nonsense told in the common rooms of inns than the wide world had space for, when a woman's voice trumpeted from the kitchen. "Starling! Do you work here, or are you taking a room tonight?"

The blond boy grinned. "Good luck, anyway," he said to Moon and loped back to the kitchen.

Moon ate her lunch and paid for it with a coin stamped with the prince's face. She scowled at it when she set it on the table. *It's all your fault,* she told it. Then she hoisted her pack and headed for the door.

"It's started to drip," the blond boy called after her. "It'll be pouring rain on you in an hour."

"I'll get wet, then," she said. "But thanks anyway."

The trail was cold, but at least she was on it. The news drove her forward.

The boy was right about the weather. The rain was carried on gusts from every direction, which found their way under her cloak and inside her hood and in every seam of her boots. By the time she'd doggedly climbed the ridge above Little Hark, she was wet and cold all through, and dreaming of tight roofs, large fires, and clean, dry nightgowns. The view from the top of the trail scattered her visions.

She'd expected another valley. This was not a bowl, but a plate, full of long, sand-colored undulating grass, and she stood at the rim of it. Moon squinted through the rain ahead and to either side, looking for a far edge, but the grass went on out of sight, unbroken by anything but the small rises and falls of the land. She suspected that clear weather wouldn't have shown her the end of it, either.

That evening she made camp in the midst of the ocean of grass, since there wasn't anyplace else. There was no firewood. She'd thought of that before she walked down into the plain, but all the wood she could have gathered to take with her was soaked. So she propped up a lean-to of oiled canvas against the worst of the rain, gathered a pile of the shining-wet grass, and set to work. She kept an eye on the sun, as well; at the right moment she took up Alder Owl's drum and played it, huddling under the canvas to keep it from the wet. It had nothing to say.

In half an hour she had a fat braided wreath of straw. She laid it in a circle of bare ground she'd cleared, and got from her pack her tinderbox and three apples, wrinkled and sweet with winter storage. They were the last food she had from home.

"All is taken from thee," Moon said, setting the apples inside the straw wreath and laying more wet grass over them in a little cone. "I have taken, food and footing, breath and warming, balm for thirsting. This

I will exchange thee, with my love and every honor, if thou'lt give again thy succor." With that, she struck a spark in the cone of grass.

For a moment, she thought the exchange was not accepted. She'd asked all the elements, instead of only fire, and fire had taken offense. Then a little blue flame licked along a stalk, and a second. In a few minutes she was nursing a tiny, comforting blaze, contained by the wreath of straw and fueled all night with Alder Owl's apples.

She sat for a long time, hunched under the oiled canvas lean-to, wrapped in her cloak with the little fire between her feet. She was going to Great Hark, because she thought that Alder Owl would have done so. But she might not have. Alder Owl might have gone south from here, into Cystegond. Or north, into the cold upthrust fangs of the Bones of Earth. She could have gone anywhere, and Moon wouldn't know. She'd asked—but she hadn't insisted she be told or taken along, hadn't tried to follow. She'd only said goodbye. Now she would never find the way.

"What am I doing here?" Moon whispered. There was no answer except the constant rushing sound of the grass in the wind, saying *hush, hush, hush*. Eventually she was warm enough to sleep.

The next morning the sun came back, watery and tentative. By its light she got her first real look at the great ocean of golden-brown she was shouldering through. Behind her she saw the ridge beyond which Little Hark lay. Ahead of her there was nothing but grass.

It was a long day, with only that to look at. So she made herself look for more. She saw the new green shoots of grass at the feet of the old stalks, their leaves still rolled tight around one another like the embrace of lovers. A thistle spread its rosette of fierce leaves to claim the soil, but hadn't yet grown tall. And she saw the prints of horses' hooves, and dung, and once a wide, beaten-down swath across her path like the bed of a creek cut in grass, the earth muddy and chopped with hoofprints. As she walked, the sun climbed the sky and steamed the rain out of her cloak.

By evening she reached the town of Burnton High Plain. Yes, the landlord at the hostelry told her, another day's walk would bring her under the branches of the Seawood. Then she should go carefully, because it was full of robbers and ghosts and wild animals.

"Well," Moon said, "robbers wouldn't take the trouble to stop me, and I don't think I've any quarrel with the dead. So I'll concentrate on the wild animals. But thank you very much for the warning."

"Not a good place, the Seawood," the landlord added.

Moon thought that people who lived in the middle of an eternity of grass probably *would* be afraid of a forest. But she only said, "I'm searching for someone who might have passed this way months ago. Her name is Alder Owl, and she was going to look for the prince."

After Moon described her, the landlord pursed his lips. "That's familiar. I think she might have come through, heading west. But as you say, it was months, and I don't think I've seen her since."

I've never heard so much discouraging encouragement, Moon thought drearily, and turned to her dinner.

The next afternoon she reached the Seawood. Everything changed: the smells, the color of the light, the temperature of the air. In spite of the landlord's warning, Moon couldn't quite deny the lift of her heart, the feeling of glad relief. The secretive scent of pine loam rose around her as she walked, and the dark boughs were full of the commotion of birds. She heard water nearby; she followed the sound to a running beck and the spring that fed it. The water was cold and crisply acidic from the pines; she filled her bottle at it and washed her face.

She stood a moment longer by the water. Then she hunched the pack off her back and dug inside it until she found the little linen bag that held her valuables. She shook out a silver shawl pin in the shape of a leaping frog. She'd worn it on festival days, with her green scarf. It was a present from Alder Owl—but then, everything was. She dropped it into the spring.

Was that right? Yes, the frog was water's beast, never mind that it breathed air half the time. And silver was water's metal, even though it was mined from the earth and shaped with fire, and turned black as quickly in water as in air. How *could* magic be based on understanding the true nature of things if it ignored so much?

A bubble rose to the surface and broke loudly, and Moon laughed. "You're welcome, and same to you," she said, and set off again.

The Seawood gave her a century's worth of fallen needles, flat and dry, to bed down on, and plenty of dry wood for her fire. It was cold under its roof of boughs, but there were remedies for cold. She kept her fire well built up, for that, and against any meat-eaters too weak from winter to seek out the horses of Burnton High Plain.

Another day's travel, and another. If she were to climb one of the tallest pines to its top, would the Seawood look like the plain of grass: undulating, almost endless? On the third day, when the few blades of sun that reached the forest floor were slanting and long, a wind rose.

Moon listened to the old trunks above her creaking, the boughs swishing like brooms in angry hands, and decided to make camp.

In the Seawood the last edge of sunset was never visible. By then, beneath the trees, it was dark. So Moon built her fire and set water to boil before she took Alder Owl's drum from her pack.

The trees roared above, but at their feet Moon felt only a furious breeze. She hunched her cloak around her and struck the drum.

It made no noise; but from above she heard a clap and thunder of sound, and felt a rush of air across her face. She leaped backward. The drum slid from her hands.

A pale shape sat on a low branch beyond her fire. The light fell irregularly on its huge yellow eyes, the high tufts that crowned its head, its pale breast. An owl.

"Oo," it said, louder than the hammering wind. "Oo-whoot."

Watching it all the while, Moon leaned forward, reaching for the drum.

The owl bated thunderously and stretched its beak wide. "Oo-wheed," it cried at her. "Yarrooh. Yarrooh."

Moon's blood fell cold from under her face. The owl swooped off its branch quick and straight as a dropped stone. Its talons closed on the lashings of the drum. The great wings beat once, twice, and the bird was gone into the rushing dark.

Moon fell to her knees, gasping for breath. The voice of the owl was still caught in her ears, echoing, echoing another voice. *Weed. Yarrow. Yarrow.*

Tears poured burning down her face. "Oh, my weed, my stalk of yarrow," she repeated, whispering. "Come back!" she screamed into the night. She got no answer but the wind. She pressed her empty hands to her face and cried herself to sleep.

With morning, the Seawood crowded around her as it had before, full of singing birds and softness, traitorous and unashamed. In one thing, at least, its spirit marched with hers. The light under the trees was gray, and she heard the patter of rain in the branches above. Moon stirred the cold ashes of her fire and waited for her heart to thaw. She would go on to Great Hark, and beyond if she had to. There might yet be some hope. And if there wasn't, there might at least be a reckoning.

All day the path led downward, and she walked until her thighs burned and her stomach gnawed itself from hunger. The rain came down harder, showering her ignominiously when the wind shook the branches. She meant to leave the Seawood before she slept again, if it meant walking all night. But the trees began to thin around her late in the day, and shortly after she saw a bare rise ahead of her. She mounted it and looked down.

The valley was full of low mist, eddying slowly in the rain. Rising out of it was the largest town Moon had ever seen. It was walled in stone and gated with oak and iron, and roofed in prosperous slate and tile. Pennons flew from every wall tower, their colors darkened with rain and stolen away by the gray light. At the heart of the town was a tall, white, red-roofed building, cornered with round towers like the wall.

The boy was right about this, too. She could never find news of one person in such a place, unless that person was the king or the queen. Moon drooped under a fresh lashing of rain.

But why not? Alder Owl had set off to find the prince. Why wouldn't she have gone to the palace and stated her business, and searched on from there? And why shouldn't Moon do the same?

She flapped a sheet of water off her cloak and plunged down the trail. She had another hour's walk before she would reach the gates, and she wanted to be inside by sundown.

The wall loomed over her at last, oppressively high, dark and shining with rain. She found the huge double gates open, and the press of wagons and horses and pedestrians in and out of them daunting. No one seemed to take any notice when she joined the stream and passed through, and though she looked and looked, she couldn't see anyone who appeared to be any more official than anyone else. Everyone, in fact, looked busy and important. *So this is city life,* Moon thought, and stepped out of the flow of traffic for a better look around.

Without her bird's-eye view, she knew she wouldn't find the palace except by chance. So she asked directions of a woman and a man unloading a cart full of baled hay.

They looked at her and blinked, as if they were too weary to think; they were at least as wet as Moon was, and seemed to have less hope of finding what they were looking for. Their expressions of surprise were so similar that Moon wondered if they were blood relations, and indeed, their eyes were much alike, green-gray as sage. The man wore a dusty brown jacket worn through at one elbow; the woman had a long, tattered black shawl pulled up over her white hair.

"Round the wall that way," said the man at last, "until you come to a broad street all laid with brick. Follow that uphill until you see it."

"Thank you." Moon eyed the hay cart, which was nearly full. Work was ointment for the heart. Alder Owl had said so. "Would you like some help? I could get in the cart and throw bales down."

"Oh, no," said the woman. "It's all right."

Moon shook her head. "You sound like my neighbors. With them, it would be fifteen minutes before we argued each other to a standstill. I'm going to start throwing hay instead." At that, she scrambled into the cart and hoisted a bale. When she turned to pass it to the man and woman, she found them looking at each other, before the man came to take the hay from her.

It was hot, wet, prickly work, but it didn't take long. When the cart was empty, they exchanged thanks and Moon set off again for the palace. On the way, she watched the sun's eye close behind the line of the hills.

The brick-paved street ran in long curves like an old riverbed. She couldn't see the palace until she'd tramped up the last turning and found the high white walls before her, and another gate. This one was carved and painted with a flock of rising birds, and closed.

Two men stood at the gate, one on each side. They were young and tall and broad-shouldered, and Moon recognized them as being of a type that made village girls stammer. They stood very straight, and wore green capes and coats with what Moon thought was an excessive quantity of gold trim. She stepped up to the nearest.

"Pardon me," she said, "I'd like to speak to the king and queen."

The guard blinked even more thoroughly than the couple with the hay cart had. With good reason, Moon realized; now she was not only travel-stained and sodden, but dusted with hay as well. She sighed, which seemed to increase the young man's confusion.

"I'll start nearer the beginning," she told him. "I came looking for my teacher, who set off at the end of last autumn to look for the prince. Do you remember a witch, named Alder Owl, from a village two weeks east of here? I think she might have come to the palace to see the king and queen about it."

The guard smiled. Moon thought she wouldn't feel too scornful of a girl who stammered in his presence. "I suppose I could have a message taken to Their Majesties," he said at last. "Someone in the palace may have met your teacher. Hi, Rush!" he called to the guard on the other side of the gate. "This woman is looking for her teacher, a witch who set out to find the prince. Who would she ask, then?"

Rush sauntered over, his cape swinging. He raised his eyebrows at

Moon. "Every witch in Hark End has gone hunting the prince at one time or another. How would anyone remember one out of the lot?"

Moon drew herself up very straight, and found she was nearly as tall as he was. She raised only one eyebrow, which she'd always found effective with Fell. "I'm sorry your memory isn't all you might like it to be. Would it help if I pointed out that this witch remains unaccounted for?"

"There aren't any of those. They all came back, cap in hand and dung on their shoes, saying, 'Beg pardon, Lord,' and 'Perishing sorry, Lady.' You could buy and sell the gaggle of them with the brass on my scabbard."

"You," Moon told him sternly, "are of very little use."

"More use than anyone who's sought him so far. If they'd only set my unit to it . . ."

She looked into his hard young face. "You loved him, didn't you?"

His mouth pinched closed, and the hurt in his eyes made him seem for a moment as young as Fell. It held a glass up to her own pain. "Everyone did. He was—is the land's own heart."

"My teacher is like that to me. Please, may I speak with someone?"

The polite guard was looking from one to the other of them, alarmed. Rush turned to him and frowned. "Take her to—merry heavens, I don't know. Try the steward. He fancies he knows everything."

And so the Gate of Birds opened to Moon Very Thin. She followed the polite guard across a paved courtyard held in the wide, high arms of the palace, colonnaded all around and carved with the likenesses of animals and flowers. On every column a torch burned in its iron bracket, hissing in the rain, and lit the courtyard like a stage. It was very beautiful, if a little grim.

The guard waved her through a small iron-clad door into a neat parlor. A fire was lit in the brick hearth and showed her the rugs and hangings, the paneled walls blackened with age. The guard tugged an embroidered pull near the door and turned to her.

"I should get back to the gate. Just tell the steward, Lord Leyan, what you know about your teacher. If there's help for you here, he'll see that you get it."

When he'd gone, she gathered her damp cloak about her and wondered if she ought to sit. Then she heard footsteps, and a door she hadn't noticed opened in the paneling.

A very tall, straight-backed man came through it. His hair was white and thick and brushed his shoulders, where it met a velvet coat faced in creweled satin. He didn't seem to find the sight of her startling, which Moon took as a good sign.

"How may I help you?" he asked.

"Lord Leyan?"

He nodded.

"My name is Moon Very Thin. I've come from the east in search of my teacher, the witch Alder Owl, who set out last autumn to find the prince. I think now . . . I won't find her. But I have to try." To her horror, she felt tears rising in her eyes.

Lord Leyan crossed the room in a long stride and grasped her hands. "My dear, don't cry. I remember your teacher. She was an alarming woman, but that gave us all hope. She has not returned to you, either, then?"

Moon swallowed and shook her head.

"You've traveled a long way. You shall have a bath and a meal and a change of clothes, and I will see if anyone can tell you more about your teacher."

Before Moon was quite certain how it had been managed, she was standing in a handsome dark room with a velvet-hung bed and a fire bigger than the one in the parlor, and a woman with a red face and fly-away hair was pouring cans of water into a bathtub shaped and painted like a swan.

"That's the silliest thing I've ever seen," said Moon in wonder.

The red-faced woman grinned suddenly. "You know, it is. And it may be the lords and ladies think so, too, and are afraid to say."

"One of them must have paid for it once."

"That's so. Well, no one's born with taste. Have your bath, and I'll bring you a change of clothes in a little."

"You needn't do that. I have clean ones in my pack."

"Yes, but have they got lace on them, and a 'broidery flower for every seam? If not, you'd best let me bring these, for word is you eat with the King and Queen."

"I do?" Moon blurted, horrified. "Why?"

"Lord Leyan went to them, and they said send you in. Don't pop your eyes at me, there's no help for it."

Moon scrubbed until she was pink all over, and smelling of violet soap. She washed her hair three times, and trimmed her short nails, and looked in despair at her reflection in the mirror. She didn't think she'd put anyone off dinner, but there was no question that the only thing that stood there was Moon Very Thin, tall and brown and forthright.

"Here, now," said the red-faced woman at the door. "I thought this would look nice, and you wouldn't even quite feel a fool in it. What do you say?"

Draped over her arms she had a plain, high-necked dress of amber linen, and an overgown of russet velvet. The hem and deep collar were embroidered in gold with the platter-heads of yarrow flowers. Moon stared at that, and looked quickly up at the red-faced woman. There was nothing out of the way in her expression.

"It's—it's fine. It's rather much, but . . ."

"But it's the least much that's still enough for dining in the hall. Let's get you dressed."

The woman helped her into it, pulling swaths of lavender-scented fabric over her head. Then she combed out Moon's hair, braided it, and fastened it with a gold pin.

"Good," the red-faced woman said. "You look like you, but dressed up, which is as it should be. I'll show you to the hall."

Moon took a last look at her reflection. She didn't think she looked at all like herself. Dazed, she followed her guide out of the room.

She knew when they'd almost reached their destination. A fragrance rolled out of the hall that reminded Moon she'd missed three meals. At the door, the red-faced woman stopped her.

"You'll do, I think. Still—tell no lies, though you may be told them. Look anyone in the eye, though they might want it otherwise. And take everything offered you with your right hand. It can't hurt." With that the red-faced woman turned and disappeared down the maze of the corridor.

Moon straightened her shoulders and, her stomach pinched with hunger and nerves, stepped into the hall.

She gaped. She couldn't help it, though she'd promised herself she wouldn't. The hall was as high as two rooms, and long and broad as a field of wheat. It had two yawning fireplaces big enough to tether an ox in. Banners hung from every beam, sewn over with beasts and birds and things she couldn't name. There weren't enough candles in all Hark End to light it top to bottom, nor enough wood in the Seawood to heat it, so like the great courtyard it was beautiful and grim.

The tables were set in a U, the high table between the two arms. To her dazzled eye, it seemed every place was taken. It was bad enough to dine with the king and queen. Why hadn't she realized that it would be the court, as well?

At the high table, the king rose smiling. "Our guest!" he called. "Come, there's a place for you beside my lady and me."

Moon felt her face burning as she walked to the high table. The court watched her go; but there were no whispers, no hands raised to shield moving lips. She was grateful, but it was odd.

Her chair was indeed set beside those of the king and queen. The king was white-haired and broad-shouldered, with an open, smiling face and big hands. The queen's hair was white and gold, and her eyes were wide and gray as storms. She smiled, too, but as if the gesture were a sorrow she was loath to share.

"Lord Leyan told us your story," said the queen. "I remember your teacher. Had you been with her long?"

"All my life," Moon replied. Dishes came to roost before her, so she could serve herself: roast meat, salads, breads, compotes, vegetables, sauces, wedges of cheese. She could limit herself to a bite of everything, and still leave the hall achingly full. She kept her left hand clamped between her knees for fear of forgetting and taking something with it. Every dish was good, but not quite as good as she'd thought it looked.

"Then you are a witch as well?" the king asked.

"I don't know. I've been taught by a witch, and learned witches' knowledge. But she taught me gardening and carpentry, too."

"You hope to find her?"

Moon looked at him, and weighed the question seriously for the first time since the Seawood. "I hope I may learn she's been transformed, and that I can change her back. But I think I met her, last night in the wood, and I find it's hard to hope."

"But you want to go on?" the queen pressed her. "What will you do?"

"The only thing I can think of to do is what she set out for: I mean to find your son."

Moon couldn't think why the queen would pale at that.

"Oh, my dear, don't," the king said. "Our son is lost, your teacher is lost—what profit can there be in throwing yourself after them? Rest here, then go home and live. Our son is gone."

It was a fine, rich hall, and he was a fair, kingly man. But it was all dimmed, as if a layer of soot lay over the palace and its occupants.

"What did he look like, the prince?"

The king frowned. It was the queen who drew a locket out of the bodice of her gown, lifted its chain over her head and passed it to Moon. It held, not the costly miniature she'd expected, but a sketch in soft pencil, swiftly done. It was the first informal thing she could recall seeing in the palace.

"He wouldn't sit still to be painted," the queen said wistfully. "One of his friends likes to draw. He gave me that after . . . after my son was gone."

He had been reading, perhaps, when his friend snatched that quiet moment to catch his likeness. The high forehead was propped on a long-fingered hand; the eyes were directed downward, and the eyelids hid them. The nose was straight, and the mouth was long and grave. The hair was barely suggested; light or dark, it fell unruly around the sup-porting hand. Even setting aside the kindly eye of friendship that had informed the pencil, Moon gave the village girls leave to be silly over this one. She closed the locket and gave it back.

"You can't know what's happened to him. How can you let him go, without knowing?"

"There are many things in the world I will never know," the king said sharply.

"I met a man at the gate who still mourns the prince. He called him the heart of the land. Nothing can live without its heart."

The queen drew a breath and turned her face to her plate, but said nothing.

"Enough," said the king. "If you must search, then you must. But I'll have peace at my table. Here, child, will you pledge it with me?"

Over Moon's right hand, lying on the white cloth, he laid his own, and held his wine cup out to her.

She sat frozen, staring at the chased silver and her own reflection in it. Then she raised her eyes to his and said, "No."

There was a shattering quiet in the hall.

"You will not drink?"

"I will not . . . pledge you peace. There isn't any here, however much anyone may try to hide it. I'm sorry." That, she knew when she'd said it, was true. "Excuse me," she added, and drew her hand out from under the king's, which was large, but soft. "I'm going to bed. I mean to leave early tomorrow."

She rose and walked back down the length of the room, lapped in a different kind of silence.

A servant found her in the corridor and led her to her chamber. There she found her old clothes clean and dry and folded, the fire tended, the bed turned down. The red-faced woman wasn't there. She took off her finery, laid it out smooth on a chair, and put her old nightgown on. Then she went to the glass to unpin and brush her hair.

The pin was in her hand, and she was reaching to set it down, when she saw what it was. A little leaping frog. But now it was gold.

It *was* hers. The kicking legs and goggle eyes, every irregularity—it was her pin. She dashed to the door and flung it open. "Hello?" she called. "Oh, bother!" She stepped back into the room and searched, and finally found the bell pull disguised as a bit of tapestry.

After a few minutes, a girl with black hair and bright eyes came to the door. "Yes, ma'am?"

"The woman who helped me, who drew my bath and brought me clothes. Is she still here?"

The girl looked distressed. "I'm sorry, ma'am. I don't know who waited on you. What did she look like?"

"About my height. With a red face and wild, wispy hair."

The girl stared, and said, "Ma'am—are you sure? That doesn't sound like anyone here."

Moon dropped heavily into the nearest chair. "Why am I not surprised? Thank you very much. I didn't mean to disturb you."

The girl nodded and closed the door behind her. Moon put out the candles, climbed into bed, and lay awake for an uncommonly long time.

In a gray, wet dawn, she dressed and shouldered her pack and by the simple expedient of going down every time she came to a staircase, found a door that led outside. It was a little postern, opening on a kitchen garden and a wash yard fenced in stone. At the side of the path, a man squatted by a wooden hand cart, mending a wheel.

"Here, missy!" he called out, his voice like a spade thrust into gravel. "Hold this axle up, won't you?"

Moon sighed. She wanted to go. She wanted to be moving, because moving would be almost like getting something done. And she wanted to be out of this beautiful place that had lost its heart. She stepped over a spreading clump of rhubarb, knelt, and hoisted the axle.

Whatever had damaged the wheel had made the axle split; the long splinter of wood bit into Moon's right hand. She cried out and snatched that hand away. Blood ran out of the cut on her palm and fell among the rhubarb stems, a few drops. Then it ceased to flow.

Moon looked up, frightened, to the man with the wheel.

It was the man from the hay wagon, white-haired, his eyes as green and gray as sage. He had a ruddy, somber face. Red-faced, like the woman who'd—

The woman who'd helped her last night had been the one from the hay cart. Why hadn't she seen it? But she remembered it now, and the woman's green eyes, and even a fragment of hay caught in the wild hair. Moon sprang up.

The old man caught her hand. "Rhubarb purges, and rhubarb means advice. Turn you back around. Your business is in there." He pointed a red, rough finger at the palace, at the top of the near corner tower. Then he stood, dusted off his trousers, strolled down the path and was gone.

Moon opened her mouth, which she hadn't been able to do until then. She could still feel his hand, warm and callused. She looked down. In the palm he'd held was a sprig of hyssop and a wisp of broom, and a spiraling stem of convolvulus.

Moon bolted back through the postern door and up the first twisting flight of stairs she found, until she ran out of steps. Then she cast furiously about. Which way was that wretched tower? She got her bearings by looking out the corridor windows. It would be that door, she thought. She tried it; it resisted.

He could have kept his posy and given me a key, she thought furiously. Then: *But he did.*

She plucked up the convolvulus, poked it into the keyhole, and said, "Turn away, turn astray, backwards from the turn of day. What iron turned to lock away, herb will turn the other way." Metal grated against metal, and the latch yielded under her hand.

A young man's room, frozen in time. A jerkin of quilted, painted leather dropped on a chair; a case of books, their bindings standing in bright ranks; a wooden flute and a pair of leather gloves lying on an inlaid cedar chest; an unmade bed, the coverlet slid sideways and half pooled on the floor.

More, a room frozen in a tableau of atrocity and accusation. For Moon could feel it, the thing that had been done here, that was still being done because the room had sat undisturbed. Nightshade and thornapple, skullcap, henbane, and fern grown bleached and stunted under stone. Moon recognized their scents and their twisted strength around her, the power of the work they'd made and the shame that kept them secret.

There was a dust of crushed leaf and flower over the door lintel, on

the sill of every window, lined like seams in the folds of the bed hangings.
Her fingers clenched on the herbs in her hand as rage sprouted up in
her and spread.

With broom and hyssop she dashed the dust from the lintel, the windows, the hangings. "Merry or doleful, the last or the first," she chanted
as she swung her weapons, spitting each word in fury, "fly and be
hunted, or stay and be cursed!"

"What are you doing?" said a voice from the door, and Moon spun
and raised her posy like a dagger.

The king stood there, his coat awry, his hair uncombed. His face was
white as a corpse's, and his eyes were wide as a man's who sees the
gallows, and knows the noose is his.

"You did this," Moon breathed; and louder, "You gave him to the
King of Stones with your own hand."

"I had to," he whispered. "He made a beggar of me. My son was the
forfeit."

"You locked him under the earth. And let my teacher go to her . . .
to her *death* to pay your forfeit."

"It was his life or mine!"

"Does your lady wife know what you did?"

"His lady wife helped him to do it," said the queen, stepping forward
from the shadows of the hall. She stood tall and her face was quiet, as
if she welcomed the noose. "Because he was her love and the other, only
her son. Because she feared to lose a queen's power. Because she was a
fool, and weak. Then she kept the secret, because her heart was black
and broken, and she thought no worse could be done than had been
done already."

Moon turned to the king. "Tell me," she commanded.

"I was hunting alone," said the king in a trembling voice. "I roused
a boar. I . . . had a young man's pride and an old man's arm, and the
boar was too much for me. I lay bleeding and in pain, and the sight
nearly gone from my eyes, when I heard footsteps. I called out for help.

" 'You are dying,' he told me, and I denied it, weeping. 'I don't want
to die,' I said, over and over. I promised him anything, if he would save
my life." The king's voice failed, and stopped.

"Where?" said Moon. "Where did this happen?"

"In the wood under Elder Scarp. Near the waterfall that feeds the
stream called the Laughing Girl."

"Point me the way," she ordered.

The sky was hazed white, and the air was hot and still. Moon dashed sweat from her forehead as she walked. She could have demanded a horse, but she had walked the rest of the journey, and this seemed such a little way compared to that. She hoped it would be cooler under the trees.

It wasn't; and the gnats were worse around her face, and the biting flies. Moon swung at them steadily as she clambered over the stones. It seemed a long time before she heard the waterfall, then saw it. She cast about for the clearing, and wondered, were there many? Or only one, and it so small that she could walk past it and never know? The falling water thrummed steadily, like a drum, like a heartbeat.

In a shaft of sun, she saw a bit of creamy white—a flower head, round and flat as a platter, dwarfed with early blooming. She looked up and found that she stood on the edge of a clearing, and was not alone.

He wore armor, dull gray plates worked with fantastic embossing, trimmed in glossy black. He had a gray cloak fastened over that, thrown back off his shoulders, but with the hood up and pulled well forward. Moon could see nothing of his face.

"In the common way of things," he said, in a quiet, carrying voice, "I seek out those I wish to see. I am not used to uninvited guests."

The armor was made of slate and obsidian, because he was the King of Stones.

She couldn't speak. She could command the king of Hark End, but this was a king whose rule did not light on him by an accident of blood or by the acclaim of any mortal thing. This was an embodied power, a still force of awe and terror.

"I've come for a man and his soul," she whispered. "They were wrongly taken."

"I take nothing wrongly. Are you sure?"

She felt heat in her face, then cold at the thought of what she'd said: that she'd accused him. "No," she admitted, the word cracking with her fear. "But that they were wrongly given, I know. He was not theirs to give."

"You speak of the prince of Hark End. They were his parents. Would you let anyone say you could not give away what you had made?"

Moon's lips parted on a word; then she stared in horror. Her mind churned over the logic, followed his question back to its root.

He spoke her thoughts aloud. "You have attended at the death of a child, stilled in the womb to save the mother's life. How is this different?"

"It *is* different!" she cried. "He was a grown man, and what he was was shaped by what he did, what he chose."

"He had his mother's laugh, his grandfather's nose. His father taught him to ride. What part of him was not made by someone else? Tell me, and we will see if I should give that part back."

Moon clutched her fingers over her lips, as if by that she could force herself to think it all through before she spoke. "His father taught him to ride," she repeated. "If the horse refuses to cross a ford, what makes the father use his spurs, and the son dismount and lead it? He has his mother's laugh—but what makes her laugh at one thing, and him at another?"

"What, indeed?" asked the King of Stones. "Well, for argument's sake I'll say his mind is in doubt, and his heart. What of his body?"

"Bodies grow with eating and exercise," Moon replied. This was ground she felt sure of. "Do you think the king and the queen did those for him?"

The King of Stones threw back his cowled head and laughed, a cold ringing sound. It restored Moon to sensible terror. She stepped back, and found herself against a tree trunk.

"And his soul?" said the King of Stones at last.

"That didn't belong to his mother and father," Moon said, barely audible even to her own ears. "If it belonged to anyone but himself, I think you did not win it from Her."

Silence lay for long moments in the clearing. Then he said, "I am well tutored. Yet there was a bargain made, and a work done, and both sides knew what they pledged and what it meant. Under law, the contract was kept."

"That's not true. Out of fear the king promised you anything, but he never meant the life of his son!"

"Then he could have refused me that, and died. He said 'Anything,' and meant it, unto the life of his son, his wife, and all his kingdom."

He had fought her to a standstill with words. But, words used up and useless, she still felt a core of anger in her for what had been done, outrage against a thing she knew, beyond words, was wrong.

So she said aloud, "It's *wrong*. It was a contract that was wrong to make, let alone to keep. I know it."

"What is it," said the King of Stones, "that says so?"

"My judgment says so. My head." Moon swallowed. "My heart."

"Ah. What do I know of your judgment? Is it good?"

She scrubbed her fingers over her face. He had spoken lightly, but Moon knew the question wasn't light at all. She had to speak the truth; she had to decide what the truth was. "It's not perfect," she answered reluctantly. "But yes, I think it's as good as most people's."

"Do you trust it enough to allow it to be tested?"

Moon lifted her head and stared at him in alarm. "What?"

"I will test your judgment. If I find it good, I will let you free the prince of Hark End. If not, I will keep him, and you will take your anger, your outrage, and the knowledge of your failure home to nurture like children all the rest of your life."

"Is that prophecy?" Moon asked hoarsely.

"You may prove it so, if you like. Will you take my test?"

She drew a great, trembling breath. "Yes."

"Come closer, then." With that, he pushed back his hood.

There was no stone helm beneath, or monster head. There was a white-skinned man's face, all bone and sinew and no softness, and long black hair rucked from the hood. The sockets of his eyes were shadowed black, though the light that fell in the clearing should have lit all of his face. Moon looked at him and was more frightened than she would have been by any deformity, for she knew then that none of this—armor, face, eyes—had anything to do with his true shape.

"Before we begin," he said in that soft, cool voice. "There is yet a life you have not asked me for, one I thought you'd beg of me first of all."

Moon's heart plunged, and she closed her eyes. "Alder Owl."

"You cannot win her back. There was no treachery there. She, at least, I took fairly, for she greeted me by name and said I was well met."

"No!" Moon cried.

"She was sick beyond curing, even when she left you. But she asked me to give her wings for one night, so that you would know. I granted it gladly."

She thought she had cried all she could for Alder Owl. But this was the last death, the death of her little foolish hope, and she mourned that and Alder Owl at once with falling, silent tears.

"My test for you, then." He stretched out his hands, his mailed fingers curled over whatever lay in each palm. "You have only to choose," he said. He opened his fingers to reveal two rings, one silver, one gold.

She looked from the rings to his face again, and her expression must have told him something.

"You are a witch," said the King of Stones, gently mocking. "You read symbols and make them, and craft them into nets to catch truth in. This is the meat of your training, to read the true nature of a thing. Here are symbols—choose between them. Pick the truer. Pick the better."

He pressed forward first one hand, then the other. "Silver, or gold? Left or right? Night or day, moon"—she heard him mock her again—"or sun, water or fire, waning or waxing, female or male. Have I forgotten any?"

Moon wiped the tears from her cheeks and frowned down at the rings. They were plain, polished circles of metal, not really meant for finger rings at all. Circles, complete in themselves, unmarred by scratch or tarnish.

Silver, or gold. Mined from the earth, forged in fire, cooled in water, pierced with air. Gold was rarer, silver was harder, but both were pure metals. Should she choose rareness? Hardness? The lighter color? But the flash of either was bright. The color of the moon? But she'd seen the moon, low in the sky, yellow as a peach. And the light from the moon was reflected light from the sun, whose color was yellow although in the sky it was burning white, and whose metal was gold. There was nothing to choose between them.

The blood rushed into her face, and the gauntleted hands and their two rings swam in her vision. It was true. She'd always thought so.

Her eyes sprang up to the face of the King of Stones. "It's a false choice. They're equal."

As she said the words, her heart gave a single terrified leap. She was wrong. She was defeated, and a fool. The King of Stones' fingers closed again over the rings.

"Down that trail to a granite stone, and then between two hazel trees," he said. "You'll find him there."

She was alone in the clearing.

Moon stumbled down the trail, dazed with relief and the release of tension. She found the stone, and the two young hazel trees, slender and leafed out in fragile green, and passed between them.

She plunged immediately into full sunlight and strangeness. Another clearing, carpeted with deep grass and the stars of spring flowers, surrounded by blossoming trees—but trees in blossom didn't also stand heavy with fruit, like a vain child wearing all its trinkets at once. She saw apples, cherries, and pears under their drifts of pale blossom, ripe and without blemish. At the other side of the clearing there was a shelf of stone thrust up out of the grass. On it, as if sleeping, lay a young man, exquisitely dressed.

Golden hair, she thought. *That's why it was drawn in so lightly. Like amber, or honey.* The fair face was very like the sketch she remembered, as was the scholar's hand palm up on the stone beside it. She stepped forward.

Beside the stone, the black branches of a tree lifted, moved away from their neighbors, and the trunk— Not a tree. A stag stepped into the clearing, scattering the apple blossoms with the great span of his antlers. He was black as charcoal, and his antler points were shining black, twelve of them or more. His eyes were large and red.

He snorted and lowered his head, so that she saw him through a forest of polished black dagger points. He tore at the turf with one cloven foot.

I passed his test! she cried to herself. Hadn't she won? Why this? *You'll find him there*, the King of Stones had said. Then her anger sprang up as she remembered what else he'd said: *I will let you free the prince of Hark End.*

What under the wide sky was she supposed to do? Strike the stag dead with her bare hands? Frighten it away with a frown? Turn it into—

She gave a little cry at the thought, and the stag was startled into charging. She leaped behind the slender trunk of a cherry tree. Cloth tore as the stag yanked free of her cloak.

The figure on the shelf of stone hadn't moved. She watched it, knowing her eyes ought to be on the stag, watching for the rise and fall of breath. "Oh, what a *stupid* trick!" she said to the air, and shouted at the stag, "Flower and leaf and stalk to thee, I conjure back what ought to be. Human frame and human mind banish those of hart or hind." Which, when she thought about it, was a silly thing to say, since it certainly wasn't a hind.

He lay prone in the grass, naked, honey hair every which way. His eyes were closed, but his brows pinched together, as if he was fighting his way back from sleep. One sunbrowned long hand curled and straightened. His eyes snapped open, focused on nothing; the fingers curled again; and finally he looked at them, as if he had to force himself to do it, afraid of what he might see. Moon heard the sharp drawing of his breath. On the shelf of stone there was nothing at all.

A movement across the clearing caught Moon's eye and she looked up. Among the trees stood the King of Stones in his gray armor. Sunshine glinted off it and into his unsmiling face, and pierced the shadows of his eye sockets. His eyes, she saw, were green as sage.

The prince had levered himself up onto his elbows. Moon saw the tremors in his arms and across his back. She swept her torn cloak from her shoulders and draped it over him. "Can you speak?" she asked him. She glanced up again. There was no one in the clearing but the two of them.

"I don't—yes," he said, like a whispering crow, and laughed thinly. He held out one spread and shaking hand. "Tell me. You don't see a hoof, do you?"

"No, but you used to have four of them. You're not nearly so impressive in this shape."

He laughed again, from closer to his chest this time. "You haven't seen me hung all over with satin and beads like a dancing elephant.'

"Well, thank goodness for that. Can you stand up? Lean on me if you want to, but we should be gone from here."

He clutched her shoulder—the long scholar's fingers were very strong—and struggled to his feet, then drew her cloak more tightly around himself. "Which way?"

Passage through the woods was hard for her, because she knew how hard it was for him, barefoot, disoriented, yanked out of place and time. After one especially hard stumble, he sagged against a tree. "I hope this passes. I can see flashes of this wood in my memory, but as if my eyes were off on either side of my head."

"Memory fades," she said. "Don't worry."

He looked up at her quickly, pain in his face. "Does it?" He shook his head. "I'm sorry—did you tell me your name?"

"No. It's Moon Very Thin."

He asked gravely, "Are you waxing or waning?"

"It depends from moment to moment."

"That makes sense. Will you call me Robin?"

"If you want me to."

"I do, please. I find I'm awfully taken with having a name again."

At last the trees opened out, and in a fold of the green hillside they found a farmstead. A man stood in the farmhouse door watching them come. When they were close enough to make out his balding head and wool coat, he stirred from the door; took three faltering steps into his garden; and shouted and ran toward them. A tall, round woman appeared at the door, twisting her apron. Then she, too, began to run.

The man stopped just short of them, open-mouthed, his face a study in hope, and fear that hope will be yanked away. "Your Highness?"

Robin nodded.

The round woman had come up beside the man. Tears coursed down her face. She said calmly, "Teazle, don't keep 'em standing in the yard. Look like they've been dragged backwards through the blackthorn, both of them, and probably hungry as cats." But she stepped forward and touched one tentative hand to the prince's cheek. "You're back," she whispered.

"I'm back."

They were fed hugely, and Robin was decently clothed in linen and leather belonging to Teazle's eldest son. "We should be going," the prince said at last, regretfully.

"Of course," Teazle agreed. "Oh, they'll be that glad to see you at the palace."

Moon saw the shadow of pain pass quickly over Robin's face again.

They tramped through the new ferns, the setting sun at their backs. "I'd as soon . . ." Robin faltered and began again. "I'd as soon not reach the palace tonight. Do you mind?"

Moon searched his face. "Would you rather be alone?"

"No! I've been alone for—how long? A year? That's enough. Unless you don't want to stay out overnight."

"It would be silly to stop now, just when I'm getting good at it," Moon said cheerfully.

They made camp under the lee of a hill near a creek, as the sky darkened and the stars came out like frost. They didn't need to cook, but Moon built a fire anyway. She was aware of his gaze; she knew when he was watching, and wondered that she felt it so. When it was full dark and Robin lay staring into the flames, Moon said, "You know, then?"

"How I was . . . ? Yes. Just before . . . there was a moment when I knew what had been done, and who'd done it." He laced his brown fingers over his mouth and was silent for a while; then he said, "Would it be better if I didn't go back?"

"You'd do that?"

"If it would be better."

"What would you do instead?"

He sighed. "Go off somewhere and grow apples."

"Well, it wouldn't be better," Moon said desperately. "You have to go back. I don't know what you'll find when you get there, though. I called down curse and banishment on your mother and father, and I don't really know what they'll do about it."

He looked up, the fire bright in his eyes. "You did that? To the king and queen of Hark End?"

"Do you think they didn't deserve it?"

"I wish they didn't deserve it." He closed his eyes and dropped his chin onto his folded hands.

"I think you *are* the heart of the land," Moon said in surprise.

His eyes flew open again. "Who said that?"

"A guard at the front palace gate. He'll probably fall on his knees when he sees you."

"Great grief and ashes," said the prince. "Maybe I can sneak in the back way."

They parted the next day in sight of the walls of Great Hark. "You can't leave me to do this alone," Robin protested.

"How would I help? I know less about it than you do, even if you are a year out of date."

"A lot happens in a year," he said softly.

"And a lot doesn't. You'll be all right. Remember that everyone loves you and needs you. Think about them and you won't worry about you."

"Are you speaking from experience?"

"A little." Moon swallowed the lump in her throat. "But I'm a country witch and my place is in the country. Two weeks to the east by foot, just across the Blacksmith River. If you ever make a King's Progress, stop by for tea."

She turned and strode away before he could say or do anything silly, or she could.

Moon wondered, in the next weeks, how the journey could have seemed so strange. If the Seawood was full of ghosts, none of them belonged to her. The plain of grass was impressive, but just grass, and hot work to cross. In Little Hark she stopped for the night, and the blond boy remembered her.

"Did you find your teacher?" he asked.

"No. She died. But I needed to know that. It wasn't for nothing."

He already knew the prince had come back; everyone knew it, as if the knowledge had blown across the kingdom like milkweed fluff. She didn't mention it.

She came home and began to set things to rights. It didn't take long. The garden wouldn't be much this year, but it would be sufficient; it was full of volunteers from last year's fallen seed. She threw herself into work; it was balm for the heart. She kept her mind on her neighbors' needs, to keep it off her own. And now she knew that her theory was right, that earth and air and fire and water were all a part of each other, all connected, like silver and gold. Like joy and pain.

"You're grown," Tansy Broadwater said to her, but speculatively, as if she meant something other than height, that might not be an unalloyed joy.

The year climbed to Midsummer and sumptuous life. Moon went to the village for the Midsummer's Eve dance and watched the horseplay for an hour before she found herself tramping back up the hill. She felt remarkably old. On Midsummer's Day she put on her apron and went out to dig the weeds from between the flagstones.

She felt the rhythm in the earth before she heard it. Hoofbeats, coming up the hill. She got to her feet.

The horse was chestnut and the rider was honey-haired. He drew rein at the gate and slipped down from the saddle, and looked at her with a question in his eyes. She wasn't quite sure what it was, but she knew it was a question.

She found her voice. "King's Progress?"

"Not a bit." He sounded just as she'd remembered, whenever she hadn't had the sense to make enough noise to drown the memory out. "May I have some tea anyway?"

Her hands were cold, and knotted in her apron. "Mint?"

"That would be nice." He tethered his horse to the fence and came in through the gate.

"How have things turned out?" She breathed deeply and cursed her mouth for being so dry.

"Badly, in the part that couldn't help but be. My parents chose exile. I miss them—or I miss them as they were once. Everything else is doing pretty well. It's always been a nice, sensible kingdom." Now that he was closer, Moon could see his throat move when he swallowed, see his thumb turn and turn at a ring on his middle finger.

"Moon," he said suddenly, softly, as if it were the first word he'd spoken. He plucked something out of the inside of his doublet and held it out to her. "This is for you." He added quickly, in a lighter tone, "You'd be amazed how hard it is to find when you want it. I thought I'd better pick it while I could and give it to you pressed and dried, or I'd be here empty-handed after all."

She stared at the straight green stem, the cluster of inky-blue flowers still full of color, the sweet ghost of vanilla scent. Her fingers closed hard on her apron. "It's heliotrope," she managed to say.

"Yes, I know."

"Do . . . do you know what it means?"

"Yes."

"It means 'devotion.'"

"I know," Robin said. He looked into her eyes, as he had since he'd said her name, but something faltered slightly in his face. "A little pressed and dried, but yours, if you'll have it."

"I'm a country witch," Moon said with more force than she'd planned. "I don't mean to *stop* being one."

Robin smiled a little, an odd sad smile. "I didn't say you ought to. But the flower is yours whether you want it or not. And I wish you'd take it, because my arm's getting tired."

"Oh!" Moon flung her hands out of her apron. "*Oh!* Isn't there a plant in this whole wretched garden that means 'I love you, too'? *Bother!*"

She hurtled into his arms, and he closed them tight around her.

Once upon a time there ruled in the Kingdom of Hark End a king who was young and fair, good and wise, and responsible for the breeding of no fewer than six new varieties of apple. Once upon the same time there was a queen in Hark End who understood the riddle of the rings of silver and gold: that all things are joined together without beginning or end, and that there can be no understanding until all things divided are joined. They didn't live happily ever after, for nothing lives forever; but they lived as long as was right, then passed together into the land where trees bear blossom and fruit both at once, and where the flowers of spring never fade.

Up the Side of the Air

Karen Haber

It was cold in the high-vaulted main room of the mage Nestor's house. The fire had died back to sullen embers and an icy wind whistled through a hole in the window and played among the rafters.

The wizard had been studying his spell book, poring over the faded, ancient runes, until the heat of the fire had lulled him to sleep. The gold-edged book of spells lay open in his lap. Now, suddenly awakened by a frigid gust, he sat up sharply, a half-finished snore caught in his throat, and looked around the room.

Shivering in the cold air, he drew his robe of white fur tightly about him, closed the book in his lap with a snap, and got to his feet. His worn black boots creaked: they were old and in need of a good oiling.

The mage Nestor was a sinewy, grizzled man with an airy cloud of white hair, a long, tapering white beard, and clear grey eyes that bore a trace of blue in their depths. His skin was seamed and wrinkled like the fine brown bark of a Yarrow tree. He was in fact a great deal older than the oldest Yarrow tree on Fennet's Mountain. But Nestor moved now with the energy of one less than half his age.

"Fire," he muttered. "The spell for fire. Come now, you know it like you know your own true name." He turned toward the dark hearth, arms upraised, and called out with the voice of a great hunting bird, three

short harsh syllables and then a soft whistling sound. Flames sprang up
at once, bathing the mage's face in orange light. He nodded in satisfaction, white beard bobbing on his chest, and held his long, gnarled fingers
up to the crackling warmth. "A pox on Jotey!" he said. "Trust that boy
to misspell and get himself thinned. Gone and left everything for me to
do." Nestor reached for the black iron kettle, filled it from the bucket
at hearthside, and set it to heat on its brazier.

The water was not quite bubbling in the kettle when the door to the
house creaked on its ancient hinges and slowly swung open. Renno, the
mage's servant of many years' standing, stood there in his winter wrap
of grey fur. He was a small, wiry man whose coal-black hair was drawn
back and woven in a fat braid that trailed halfway down his spine. His
eyes were dark as coal, his cheeks ruddy, and his nose bulbous, glossy,
conspicuous to a fault. He looked much like the dolls sold by the charm-
vendors during festival in the Rondish market. At his side was a small
diffident-looking figure whose features were almost completely obscured
by a coarse black cloak better suited for one of much more imposing
stature. The new apprentice, Nestor realized.

"Good," he said. "You've brought him."

Renno held up his hands. "Uh, wise one—"

"Don't stand in the doorway, Renno. It's cold enough in here. Come
in and close the door. The sooner you're warm the sooner we can set
the boy to his tasks."

"Great and powerful wizard—"

"Enough jabber, man! And stop stumbling around like that. Come.
Come, both of you, and warm yourselves by the fire." The mage set out
two more bowls next to his own and poured the fragrant brew, steaming
with golden mist, from the iron kettle.

The manservant opened his mouth once more as though to offer ar-
gument. Then he shrugged, closed it again, and moved closer to the fire.
The small figure in the cloak paused to shut the door before following
Renno toward the warmth.

"Flame tea," the mage said. "Here. Drink up. Night like this it warms
you right down to your soul."

A small hand reached out from under the cloak to take the tea bowl.

"Drink it down while it's hot," the mage said, not unkindly. It was
best to begin with kindness when one was breaking in a new apprentice.

The bowl was lifted to the hood, tilted, drained without pause. The
newcomer set it down empty.

"A good appetite," the mage said to Renno. "He'll grow like a glass-reed."

Small hands threw back the hood now. A thick tangle of curling red hair came into view, glistening in the dancing firelight. Bright blue eyes blinked up at the mage, and pink lips curved in a hesitant smile. "My name is Dora," the apprentice said softly. "Will I live here now?"

Nestor put down his tea bowl so hard that the iron rang against the green hearthstones. He turned toward Renno and found the servant suddenly quite busy with the wood bin. "What is this?" the mage demanded.

"What is what, master?" Renno asked, taking care to keep his face averted.

"This."

The mage indicated the child.

"I'm not certain I—"

The mage sighed, expelling a great gust of breath. "Don't play foolish with me, Renno. You may be a fool, but I don't think you're a dullard. You've brought me a girl. I specified a boy, did I not?"

Renno's look was meek. "Yes, master."

"Then why do I see a girl here?"

Renno's voice was meeker. "Master, there were no boys to be had."

"None at all?"

"The Duke's contests draw all the young men away to Brobant," said Renno. "At market, there was naught I could find but weary old men and babes barely weaned. And even those came so dearly it was beyond easy belief."

Nestor glared at him. "Better an old man than a foolish girl! What am I to do with her, Renno? Tell me: what mage has a girl for an apprentice? What will they say at the convocation at halfmonth?" The wizard shook his head in fury. "You'll have to take her back."

"Back?" Renno's dark eyes clouded. "You can't mean that, master! The market's closed now. And there's no place for her to go. She's an orphan. She has no one. We can't turn her out into the cold!"

"Pah, you are soft-hearted and soft-headed," Nestor grumbled. "So I've always said. And so you are."

Renno's look was profoundly contrite. "That is true. I would never deign to deny it."

"Don't make matters even worse with your numskull agreeability," the mage thundered. "How can we keep her? What use does she have? I ask you, what good is she?"

"Well, you could try to teach her a few things—"

The wizard's eyes were grey ice. "Teach her what?"

"Things." The manservant gazed down at the broad-planked floor. "She might learn. A little, at least."

Nestor could not be certain that the man's expression was truly rueful or merely crafty.

"You could keep her here until the next market, anyway," Renno went on. "It'll be held at month's end. I'll take her and sell her there, then."

"But that's after the convocation!" Nestor said. "What am I to do about the grand meeting? Greet my brethren without an apprentice to aid me?"

"You could train her."

"In sorcery?"

"That was what I had in mind, master. It won't do to attend the convocation without an apprentice." Renno paused. "Especially if Dalbaeth is there waiting for you."

Nestor scowled. "Pah! Let me worry about Dalbaeth. That pipsqueak has never forgiven me for besting his father long ago. But have no worry. I can handle him, with or without an apprentice." Nestor turned to gaze down at Dora. He shook his head. "Besides, just look at how small she is. And those tiny hands. Useless for spells. Probably not even good for housework."

"That's not so," Dora piped up. "I can clean. And cook. Just watch."

The mage gazed at her thoughtfully and his grey eyes glinted with blue. The wind's wild howling seemed to double and redouble. The child waited, staring up at him fearlessly.

"Oh, very well," he said. "I suppose I can't send you out into the night, can I? You can sleep on that pallet close by the hearth, girl. And not a peep out of you, hear? There's important work to be done and I don't want to be disturbed by some little flibbertigibbet."

"I ain't no flibber—gibber—whatever," she said. And smartly, with a toss of her bright head, she gathered up the tea bowls and popped them into the white stone washtub on its sturdy wooden stand. She busied herself with scouring and drying them. When she was done, the bowls shone in the candlelight, cleaner than they'd been all winter. Without another word the girl climbed onto her rush bed, curled up in her cloak, and was asleep before the mage could unleash even a simple spell of somnolence upon her.

"For the night," Nestor muttered, shaking his head emphatically.

"But only for the night." He leaned back in his big chair by the fire, opened his book of spells, and slipped off into sleep before he had finished reading through the first charm to summon easy dreams.

In the morning, Nestor awakened to the scent of oatcakes baking and milk warming. The spell book was in his lap, and his knees ached with old and familiar complaints.

"Tea's ready," said a strange voice. It was high and lilting, with just a hint of a lisp.

A small hand held out a tea bowl filled with steaming brew.

"Eh?" Nestor stared down in puzzlement at blue eyes and upturned nose. "Girl, what are you doing here?"

A look of impatience crossed her face. "You told me to stay. Remember?"

The last shadows of sleep fled and the mage began to recall the events of the night before. The new apprentice, yes. Very small. Scrawny. A girl, of all things!

"Renno! Renno, where are you?"

"Here, master." The small man hurried into the room carrying a load of firewood in his arms.

"You must take this girl back at once."

"I can't, sir."

"Why not?"

"Because I can't. Where can I take her? The market is closed until month's end. I told you so last night."

The wizard closed his lips over his irritation. "Hmmm. Yes, that's right, I suppose. Of course." He toyed with his beard. "Well then, girl, you'll have to make yourself useful here. I don't suppose you know any spells for cleaning, do you?"

"Spells?" The girl's blue eyes were wide and guileless. "I never magicked, sir. And don't want to, neither." Her fair brows lowered in a frown and she shuddered. In a low voice she said, "S'evil."

From Renno came a sound that could have been a smothered chuckle. Nestor scowled at him. But before he could say anything, his manservant hurried through the front door and disappeared into the yard.

"Well, it can be evil, I suppose," Nestor conceded. The mage scratched his beard thoughtfully. "In the wrong hands. Just as well you don't want to magick. Girls make poor wizards. And I've no patience for training a witch. Not at my age."

She gave him a shrewd look. "How old are you?"

"Just never you mind, missy." Nestor waggled a finger at her. "That hearth needs sweeping. And the bookshelves could use a dusting."

"The entire house is filthy," she said, nodding cheerfully. "I've never seen a mess like this. A good thing you bought me to look after you."

Nestor was tempted to discuss the possibility of using a spell for silence when Renno erupted into the room, looking frantic.

"Fougasse!" he cried. "He's aloft!"

Nestor blinked. "The dragon? Surely not." The mage moved toward the door and peered uncertainly into the pale blue sky, shading his eyes. "It's not swarming season. It can't be. Dragons never fly in cold weather."

On the horizon, what appeared to be a bird flapped lazy wings that reflected the morning sunlight. Nestor squinted. The bird appeared to have a long sinuous body. As it drew nearer, the mage could make out a reptilian head and baleful red eyes.

No, not a bird. Not a bird at all.

The wizard sighed. "It is Fougasse indeed. I should think he would have better sense than to bother me before I've had a proper breakfast."

"Is it really a dragon?" Dora asked. Her eyes were huge with wonder. "I've never seen one before."

"Well, don't stand there gawking, child. Get yourself back. He just might eat a tempting morsel like you."

With a squeak of fear Dora hurried behind the wizard, clinging to the back of his white robe.

The dragon circled above them, eyes glinting, scaly neck gleaming in the sunlight.

"Greetings, Nestor," it called. The dragon spoke in the old tongue.

"Fougasse," the mage said. "What sends you aloft in this cold?"

"Red light in the eastern hills. And now I see what it is. The trees are ablaze."

"What? How?"

"Elven mischief. The woods will be consumed."

"Not if I have anything to say about it."

The dragon let out a draught of steam in what would have been approval. The red eyes blinked once, and the scaled wings beat furiously in the cold air as the creature wheeled and shot upward across the sky. A moment later it was a golden speck on the smoky horizon.

"Foolish elves up to midwinter nonsense," Nestor said. "Probably playing with spells. I've warned them before. Renno, saddle the mule—a proper winter saddle, hear? With two—no, three—blankets."

"You're going alone?" The manservant fixed his dark button eyes upon the wizard.

"Would you come with me, then?"

Renno looked abashed. "I have my family's welfare to consider, your wisdom."

The mage smiled. "As I thought. Stay, then." He glanced toward the girl. "If I'd a proper apprentice, I would bring him along. But not this child."

Dora's lower lip jutted forward. "You should take me," she said sulkily. "You need someone to look after you."

Nestor reared back as though wounded. "I do, do I?"

"Yes. What if the mule fell and broke a leg? What if you got lost in the woods? Who will cook for you? Who'll hold your staff at night? Who'll lead the mule when you tire? Who will—"

"Certainly not you!"

"Well, remember then: if you become lost and tired and hungry it won't be my fault," Dora said. She turned and hurried into the house.

Nestor spat an oath into the chill wind. "Renno, forget the mule! I'll go by air." The mage held his arms up until they arched like wings. He uttered a strange, liquid cry. And where Nestor had stood a moment before was now a great, grey-feathered bird with sharp golden eyes. Soundlessly, it beat its wings until it was high above the house, moving toward the East at a steady pace.

Together, the manservant and child stood in the doorway and watched the great bird dwindle until it was a speck without shape or color, far away. Renno turned to Dora and nodded.

"A good trick for an old wizard," he said thoughtfully. He patted Dora on the shoulder "Best to be about the cleaning, child. I've got to cut a load of firewood or the mage will suffer chilblains upon his return." Whistling a somber tune, Renno shouldered his black metal axe and vanished into a stand of grey-trunked trees at the far edge of the clearing.

Dora stood at the door a moment longer, took a deep breath of the cool air, and walked into the house. She had seen wonders this day. A dragon! A wizard transformed into a huge bird! She paused and looked around the room.

The morning sun had hidden behind a cloud, and the resulting pale light cast a sickly illumination through the front window.

Cobwebs hung from the rafters. The windowsills had a thick layer of grime, and the windows themselves were coated with the residue of many rainstorms and morning dew.

"A bit of magic might not be such a bad idea," she said. "This house hasn't been cleaned since the wizard was young."

She seized the broom from its corner and set about sweeping, clucking her tongue from time to time at the awful mess. Thick clouds of dust rose up as she worked, and she sneezed once, twice, three times.

"The blessings of the archmage upon you," said a deep, pleasant voice.

Dora spun around. "Who's there?"

The room was empty.

"I said, bless you."

"Renno, are you joking with me?"

"I'd forgotten," said the voice cheerfully. "You can't see me, can you?"

The sound of ripping fabric filled the room.

A sleek blue-furred felak appeared, curled up on the fat woven cushion of the three-runged bench. It blinked bright orange eyes at her. "My," it said. "You are rather small for a human, aren't you?"

"Who taught you to talk?" Dora said. Her voice was high and shrill.

"The wizard, who do you think?" The felak stretched its long neck and began scratching its chin with its middle left paw. Midway through a particularly vigorous stroke, it paused and cocked its head at her. "Why are you using the broom? That's doing it the hard way, wouldn't you say? Don't you know the proper spells for cleaning?"

Dora glared at it, hands on hips. "Of course I don't."

"Why not? What kind of apprentice are you?"

"I'm not any kind of apprentice."

"Nestor is getting old," the felak said. "He's starting to forget the kind of basic training an apprentice has to have. Well, no matter. I can help. Here. See that large white and gold sapskin book on the top shelf? Get it."

Dora craned her neck. "That's too high. I can't reach."

"Well, stand on something, then!" said the felak, with a sharp note of impatience in its tone.

Cautiously, Dora balanced herself upon the arm of a chair, grasped the book, and scrambled down. The cover was soft to the touch and shiny in spots, as though many hands had touched the nappy hide, wearing it down.

"Turn to the third page and read the spell aloud."

"I can't read. Most especially I can't read runish."

The felak stopped preening and stared at her with a look of unmistakable distaste. "Can't read? I think I'm beginning not to understand Nestor. Why would he buy an illiterate apprentice? For that matter, why bother to purchase a girl to begin with?"

"He didn't. Renno bought me."

"Ah. Well, then." The felak yawned, showing twin rows of sharp, triangular teeth lining the inside of its green beak. It rose up on its hind legs, leaped onto the arm of Dora's chair, and perched there, peering over her shoulder at the book in her lap. The faded runes of the spellbook danced across the page in gold ink. "Now, listen closely and watch what happens."

It said something in a sibilant whisper. Dora couldn't quite understand the words, try as she might. But as she watched, the red clay baking dish on the hearth floated up into the air, flew across the room, and began to dunk itself in the washtub, splashing water merrily.

The girl stared, goggle-eyed. "How wonderful!"

"All right. Now you try it," the felak said. "With those tea bowls. Repeat these syllables together: Re. Osum. Emosum. Tem."

Dora formed the unfamiliar words haltingly, stumbling over the last one. She waited. But the tea bowls on the hearth sat there, immobile. Her feet tingled as though they were falling asleep. She stamped them, looked down, and gasped. A fine coating of purple fur was sprouting like new grass upon her toes and feet.

"What did I do wrong?" she cried.

The felak uttered a sound much like a human cackle. "The last word is Tem. One syllable. Just one. You gave it an extra one. Which happens to be the hirsute spell." The felak laughed again. "What a lovely shade of purple fur that is," it crowed. "I like the way it complements your hair."

"Make it go away," Dora wailed.

"Don't you like it?" The felak shook its head. "I think it looks just fine." The creature nodded in evident satisfaction, prowled around its cushion several times, sat down, and closed its eyes.

Dora stared in horror at her feet.

"Wait. You can't go to sleep!" she cried. "Help me. Please! I don't want furry feet!"

The felak snored gently.

Renno opened the front door and walked in carrying a bucket filled with water. He nearly dropped it when he saw the purple fur on Dora's feet. "Child," he gasped. "What have you done?"

Tears streamed down Dora's cheeks. "Not me. It was the felak who did it."

"What felak?"

"The wizard's."

The manservant frowned and scratched his head. "But he has no such beast."

"It's asleep on the chair." Dora pointed at the triple-runged bench. But the cushion was empty, the felak gone.

Renno's eyes narrowed with suspicion. "Child, I thought you couldn't read runish."

"It's true. I don't know anything about this magicking." Dora stared woefully at her furry toes. "And what I've seen I don't care for. But what will I do now?"

Renno shrugged. "Wait for the wizard to return. Clean the house and wait."

Dora stared at the bench. There was no help coming from an empty cushion. Nor from Renno.

She was a practical child at heart. She sighed, picked up the broom, and set to work, reminding herself that an empty belly was even worse than a little purple fur.

As the first stars began their icy twinking in the twilight sky, Nestor returned. He was limping, his beard was singed, his eyebrows gone.

"Master!" Renno tucked his shoulder under the mage's arm and half-carried Nestor to his fireside chair. He gestured at Dora. "Child, bring tea. Quickly."

Nestor allowed himself to be helped out of his coat, out of his boots, and onto the well-padded chair. "Fool elves," he said. His voice was hoarse. "First they set the woods ablaze. Then they dry up the riverbed. And while I'm busy quelling the flames, do they give me any help? Not a bit of it. They stand there giggling and pointing, like a flock of silly birds. Even when their own benighted nests were in danger of burning. The fools were too busy setting fires behind me to protect their own homes." Nestor paused and took a long draught from the steaming tea bowl. "Ah, good. And that's done. Now we'll—" He stopped in mid-sentence and stared at Dora's feet. His forehead creased in a frown. "Girl, what is the meaning of this?"

Dora tucked one leg behind the other in embarrassment. "T'weren't me, sir. The felak did it."

"Felak? Don't be absurd. I haven't had a felak here since before Renno was born."

Her eyes locked with his. "If it's invisible most of the time, how would you know when it's here and when it isn't?"

"Eh?" Nestor shook his head and chuckled. "You have a good point, there. Well, perhaps it was a felak. But what were you attempting to do?"

"Use a spell to clean the house."

Nestor glanced quickly around the room. The cobwebs were gone. The windows sparkled as never before. "It appears you found your own spells. Perhaps one or two too many. I don't suppose you want to keep that fur, do you?"

"Nossir."

"I thought not." The mage pointed toward the girl's feet and uttered three harsh words which sounded something like: Ak-Sum-Re.

A tingling sensation swept through Dora's feet. The fur was gone without a trace. The girl beamed at the wizard.

"In the future, be more careful around spells," Nestor told her solemnly. He yawned, closed his eyes, and before Dora could thank him, he was asleep.

When the morning came, the mage's legs and back were as stiff as the old floorboards. Nestor grunted, groaned, struggled to rise, and finally motioned for Dora to help him from his bed. "Gods, it's no fun to get old," he muttered. "Don't do it, girl, if you can avoid it."

He warmed himself by the fire while Dora fixed his breakfast. Gingerly, he partook of the fresh oatcakes and steaming milk. Nestor felt considerably better after his meal. He had work to do. Spells to read. The mage set both feet against the floor and rose slowly, straightening as he went. Pain shot up both his legs and crawled across his back. Gasping, Nestor sank into his seat.

"What's wrong?" Dora said.

"Rheumatism," Nestor said.

"Let me make you a salve. It'll warm up your legs."

The wizard fixed a skeptical eye on her. "A salve? And I suppose a dragon taught you medicine, yes?"

The girl gave him a defiant look. "As a matter of fact, no. I was scullery help to the apothecary in Physte. Learned a bit here and there."

"Hmmph. Well, I'm willing to try anything to unknot these muscles and banish these aches. Mix your potions, child."

Her expression turned anxious. "I'll need blackroot, mannis weed, and tincture of lemonwort."

"You'll find some in the jars by the kitchen window. Just mind that you read the labels. If you know how to read."

"I know what the herbs look like, well enough," Dora said. "I don't need to read. But how am I going to reach them? They're on such a high shelf."

"I'll get them for you," Nestor said. He chanted two words quickly. Three speckled stone canisters floated through the air and came to rest at Dora's feet.

She crushed the herbs carefully in the wizard's mortar and pestle, then mixed them with honey and paraffin to form a soothing balm.

"A-a-h," Nestor sighed. His legs were warming, the pains and aches easing. "Better than magick."

"You could use a hot bath," Dora said.

"Later, girl. Later. I've got work to do. Weather to change. Rats to drive out of the baker's storehouse . . ." The wizard's words trailed off as he watched Dora struggle with the heavy stone canisters as she tried to replace them by the window. "That won't do," he said. "Not at all. Girl, you might as well learn a few useful household spells so I don't end up having to do all the heavy lifting around here."

"I don't know—"

"Well, I do." Nestor's grey eyes glowed. "Sit down here and pay attention."

Dora clambered onto the stool by his side.

"Now repeat this carefully: Cana Ferem Asturem."

Dora spoke the words slowly, in a near-whisper. Nothing happened.

"Louder. And enunciate more clearly, girl. And elongate the first syllable."

"Caa-na. Fe-er-em. A-a-s-turem."

To Dora's amazement, the canisters jumped back to their slots on the window ledge.

"Wonderful!" She clapped her hands. "It's like singing them into place."

Nestor nodded until his beard danced upon his chest. "In a way, I suppose it is." He smiled as Dora instructed the milk bowl to place itself in the cabinet. He almost chuckled when she did the same with the mortar and pestle. But when the thatch-seat chair nearly knocked the mage down in its spell-induced haste to resume its position next to the fire, Nestor held up his hand. "Enough, child! This is serious work, not play. Now come along and I'll teach you properly how to clean the house without draining all your energy. Or endangering me."

Wizard and girl spent the remainder of the day side by side, practicing the odd words and ancient phrases. As Dora could not read, she was forced to learn the spells by sound, Nestor calling them out and Dora repeating carefully until she had committed them to memory. And in this manner she learned the spell for washing, for mixing, for drying, and even for baking.

"Don't much care for that one," she said. "I'll burn the oatcakes with it."

"Practice," Nestor said. "Much practice makes all things easier."

In the days that followed, Dora found that there was much truth in the mage's words. Soon she had mastered the magic of the house and felt quite at ease instructing a cake to mix and bake itself, the flame tea to begin steeping, and the beds to air themselves on the front porch.

Renno, watching her work one morning, broke into a smile so deep that his face became a mass of wrinkles. "I'd say you're a quick learner, girl," he said. "Not such a bad apprentice after all."

Nestor loomed up behind him, a scowl on his face. "Apprentice? What apprentice?" the wizard said. "She's a housekeeper, Renno. I still need an apprentice."

"But she's done so well."

"Oh, I'll grant you that the house is clean. The laundry is dry. The oatcakes are fine. But any first-year kitchen witch could master those tricks. No, what I need is a proper apprentice. A tall boy to fetch my spell book, represent me at the town meeting, carry my staff. And before the convocation. We only have a few days. Renno, you'll have to try the Sporvan market."

The manservant shook his head. "There isn't time, master. The Sporvan market doesn't open until the day past Mass Day. And by then it'll be too late. The convocation begins that same morning."

Nestor made a sour face. "You're right. By the stars, girl, I suppose you'll have to do until after the convocation. Do you think you can learn a few more spells by Mass Day?"

"I don't know," Dora said. She gazed at the mage in despair. "I don't think my poor head can hold much more."

"Try," Nestor said. "Try very hard. Or perhaps I'll decide to give you a new head with a little more room in it—and green hair."

Dora clutched at her red curls. "You wouldn't."

"Don't tempt a wizard when he's cranky, girl. Now come over here, be silent, and learn!"

For six mornings running, after Dora had finished her chores, she dutifully sat beside the mage and practiced the runes for basic magic. At first her spells misfired. More than once, Nestor was forced to cancel a spell in mid-strike to avoid burning the house down or turning every piece of wood in the house to iron. But finally, Dora could float the wizard's ivory staff across the room, douse fire by summoning water from the ground, change spoons and knives into small silvery rodents, and cause empty boots to walk across the floor.

"She's as ready as she'll ever be," Renno said.

"Yes, and I suppose she's better than empty air. But she needs a proper cloak, Renno."

"Aye, master. That she does." Renno nodded. "My good wife can sew her a proper enough cloak from sapskin."

"I think that should do," Nestor said. "And make it blue, Renno."

The manservant turned to stare at the wizard. "Blue?" he said. "Why blue? All your other apprentices wore black."

"None of them were girls, were they? With blue eyes?" Nestor chuckled. "Blue it shall be, Renno. And no more backtalk."

Master and servant exchanged silent smiles.

"Then I'll be off," Renno said. "Good day to you." Whistling a cheerful melody, he hurried toward home.

The morning of the convocation dawned cold and crisp, with low, dark clouds that promised snow by midday.

Nestor squinted up at the sky. "Snow, eh?" he muttered. "We'll see about that." He threw off his white fur cloak and raised both arms high. In his right hand he grasped his burnished ivory staff. It glowed with an amber gleam as does honey in sunlight. Carefully, the mage inscribed circles with the staff. Then he brought its tip to rest sharply against the ground. With his free hand, Nestor gestured broadly, as if to encompass the entire grey bowl of the sky in his embrace.

"Qua-Sachem-Moree!" he cried and his voice was like summer thunder. "Sheft-Kazem-Bansin!"

A dazzling sunbeam split the gloom like a golden knife. Then another. The clouds were rent to tatters by sunlight. Swiftly they dispersed and the sun shone merrily in a bright blue sky. A winter bird filled the air with fluting notes. It would be a clear, beautiful day.

"That's better," Nestor said. He scratched his stomach thoughtfully. The scent of fresh-baked oatcakes came to him, drawing him back into the house.

"Breakfast first," he said. "Then we'll see about the wizards' convocation."

"Will every great wizard in the four quarters be there?" Dora wanted to know.

"From the four quarters and beyond," Nestor said. "So look sharp, girl. And mind that tongue of yours. Apprentices should be seen, not heard." He munched contentedly. When he was finished, his plate and cup whisked themselves away. Dora and Renno had eaten hours before.

Dora appeared in a sky-colored cloak. She grinned eagerly and pirouetted before the mage.

"Very pretty," Renno said.

"Don't go swelling her head," Nestor said.

Dora laughed. "But then I would have more room for spells, wouldn't I?"

Nestor cleared his throat although it sounded much like smothered laughter. "Let's be off," he said. "Renno, watch the house until we return. Child, take my hand."

Silent winds seemed to converge upon them from all corners, sending their clothes billowing and hair flying. The walls of the house faded, faded, and for a moment they were in a strange white space. Then dark walls sprang up around them, heavy with old wood, stained by smoke. Nestor and Dora found themselves in the midst of a fine banquet hall. And all around them were wizards in a rainbow of cloaks.

"Nestor," called one with a thick red beard. "Well met."

"Annesh," Nestor said. "And Rovard."

A short wizard whose hairless head shone in the firelight winked at him. "A fine day, thanks to you."

All were carrying staffs and talking boisterously. Two young mages floated in mid-air, juggling spheres of blue light high above the heads of those assembled. In the corner, a tall wizard in a green cloak began shape-changing: he became a golden dragon whose eyes glittered with red fire, then a white, winged horse with a silver mane, and next a strange beast with clawed feet and green fur.

Dora watched, wide-eyed. She could scarcely hear herself think for the noise. Shyly, she peered at the other apprentices. They were dark-robed boys who towered over her—young giants they seemed, and so much older, so much wiser. With lordly confidence they walked behind their masters, nodding at one another and sharing occasional jests. With great reluctance, Dora threw back her hood. Her red-gold hair glowed in the firelight.

All talk ceased. The assembled wizards and apprentices, the mages and servants, all stared at Dora as though they'd never seen such a sight before.

"Ho, Nestor!" called the hairless wizard named Rovard. A broad smile lit his face. "What's this? A girl for an apprentice? You must be joking."

Nestor drew himself up with enormous dignity. "It's no joke. Why not a girl? She's quick and nimble."

"But such tiny hands," Rovard said.

Annesh nodded until his red beard danced from side to side. "Next we'll be seeing felaks and sphinxes."

All laughed. But above the merry din, one voice rang out, sour and loud.

"So, greybeard! I see you are just as foolish as ever. I can't believe you felt worthy enough to come to this meeting. You should be at home, by the hearth."

Again, the room grew silent.

Nestor turned, grey eyes flaring blue with anger.

The speaker was a man of medium build with dark black hair, a mustache, goatee, and eyes the color of ice. He wore a grey cloak with a full hood lined by dark fur.

"Dalbaeth," Nestor said. "I had hoped we would not meet."

"And so you have been saying since the day you tricked my father and claimed victory," Dalbaeth said. His voice was icy with disdain. "You are afraid that I'll best you."

"I don't fear what isn't possible," Nestor said. He turned to move away.

Dalbeath stepped in front of him and set his black staff down firmly against the brick floor. "I challenge."

Nestor froze. His eyes glinted with blue fire.

"Don't be foolish," Annesh said heatedly. "The contest between Nes-

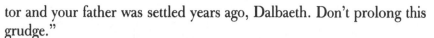

tor and your father was settled years ago, Dalbaeth. Don't prolong this grudge."

"And for long years I have wanted an opportunity to regain the family's honor," Dalbaeth said. His cold gaze never once left Nestor's face.

Nestor nodded sharply. "As you will," he said. "It's best that we settle this matter now."

Everyone began speaking at once. The room filled with voices shouting both protest and approval.

Above the din, Rovard alone could be heard. "Not here," he bellowed. "You must resolve your differences away from this gathering in a secluded place. None may be endangered, none may observe, and none may aid."

"Of course," Nestor said. "I propose the Ganz Valley beyond the river knoll."

"Acceptable," Dalbaeth said. "When?"

Nestor met his gaze squarely. "Now."

His eyes still on Dalbaeth, Nestor spoke five words very quickly.

The room spun around them, walls blurring to white. Then the walls fell away and the two wizards were standing in the midst of a broad meadow lined by tall, leafless trees. A cool wind whispered above, bearing the chill breath of winter.

"What is that child doing here?" Dalbaeth demanded.

Nestor spun around to find Dora sitting on the ground behind him.

"Girl! You weren't to accompany me. Why didn't you remain in the hall?"

"I'm sorry," she said. "But you moved so quickly there wasn't time for me to get free. I couldn't help but cling to your robe and be carried along."

"I'll send you back," he said.

"No, please," Dora said. "I want to stay."

Nestor's brows knotted in a frown. "This isn't any place for children."

"I'm your apprentice." She folded her arms across her chest. "You said so yourself."

Dalbaeth roared with laughter. "A girl for an apprentice, Nestor. How appropriate. And next I suppose you'll train a mule to do spells?"

Nestor's eyes flashed. "Have it your way, girl. Stay, then. But keep back and guard yourself." He pointed to a jumble of green rocks to one side of the meadow. "Get out of the way."

. . .

Dora peered around the side of a slippery smooth boulder. It felt like green ice under her fingers.

The two wizards squared off. For a moment, all time seemed suspended. Both men were motionless, each watching the other. Only the voice of the wind could be heard, sighing in the dry yellow grass.

As though a signal had been given, each man leaned toward the other.

Dalbaeth held his hands above his head and lightning sprang from his fingers.

Nestor roared an oath which rendered the lightning into fireflies that flashed and sparkled a moment before dispersing on the wind.

Without pause, Dalbaeth shouted another spell, and before his voice had died away an answering thunder rocked the meadow. With a terrible ripping sound, the ground beneath Nestor's feet wrenched open.

Nestor fell, desperately grasping at the ragged edge of the chasm to slow his descent. And as he did so, he whistled a charm. His robes rippled wildly. Two broad, white wings appeared upon his back. With much effort, the mage beat his way into the sky, up and away from the threat. A guttural chant gave him an enormous gryphon's head. Nestor inhaled once and began to spit fireballs at his rival.

Dalbaeth held up his hands to shield himself. But his beard was singed by the first shot. Cursing, he summoned a giant mirror from a blade of grass, and held it directly before him. The mirror was angled in such a way that Nestor's winged reflection appeared in its silvery-green depths. And now, each deadly fireball Nestor launched hit the mirror and was repulsed—right back at its source.

A wild ricochet caught Nestor's left wing. In a moment the feathers were ash. Feebly flapping his remaining wing, the mage plummeted to the ground. He struck hard and lay still upon the cold stiff grass. The remaining wing and gryphon's head disappeared.

Dora, watching everything, cried out in horror.

With a nod of satisfaction, Dalbaeth tossed the mirror into thin air where it vanished. He hurried toward the fallen mage and stood over him, his arms held wide.

"Come, spirit of earth," he cried. "Cover this wretch with stone. Imprison him forever."

"No," Dora cried. "No!"

She had to stop him. But how? He was an all-powerful wizard who could control the very elements. All she knew were some household spells. And a felak's trick. Her heart beat quickly at the thought. The felak's spell, yes.

Gasping, she whispered the syllables in quick succession.

Nothing happened.

Dora repeated the spell once more. And then again.

Dalbaeth coughed. He sneezed. Purple fur sprouted on his chin, his hands, even his boot tops. He was covered from head to foot with a coat of purple fur. It was in his eyes, in his nose, even in his mouth. He couldn't see, couldn't breathe. Choking, the wizard fell to the dry ground, uttering muffled curses.

Nestor rose up on one arm, saw what was happening, and gestured with his staff.

A huge iron cage, glowing with unearthly fires, formed around Dalbaeth. The fur-covered wizard scarcely noticed.

For a moment, Nestor sagged to the ground.

"Master," Dora called. "You've won. We must leave."

Nodding weakly, Nestor gestured and drew Dora to him. With another odd motion, he brought them both surging back out of the cold wind and into the noisy, smoke-filled wizards' convocation in Little Harbor.

"Nestor," cried Annesh. "You have returned! So quickly. Where is Dalbaeth?"

Nestor opened his mouth to speak. But no voice came forth.

The old mage gasped for air and fell backwards. If not for Annesh's strong arms and quick reflexes, Nestor would have fallen, senseless, to the polished brick floor of the hall.

"Air! The man has fainted!" Annesh roared. "Give him air! And bring the herbalist."

A tall, thin man with two grey braids approached at a run. He knelt quickly over Nestor and examined the fallen mage carefully. He rose, shaking his head.

"Nestor is old. Very old," the herbalist said. "He has overextended his powers and is rendered impotent. Mute."

Dora bit her lip in despair. "Forever?" she said.

"I do not know," the herbalist said sadly. "Perhaps with time he will recover."

Annesh patted Dora on the head. "Child, it's not fair to you to be apprenticed to an incapacitated wizard. I shall arrange for a more appropriate master. Or would you prefer a witch as mistress?"

A witch as mistress! Dora hesitated in confusion. "I don't know. Haven't thought much about it. A witch, you say? That might be nice. But what will happen to Nestor?"

"You leave him to us. Now run along and have something to eat," Annesh said. "We'll arrange for your transfer afterwards." He shooed her out the door and into a crowded dining hall filled with dark-robed apprentices.

Dora filled a plate with roasted meat and orange sugar bread, and took a place at the far end of the farthest long table. No one looked at her. No one spoke to her. She stared at the food. Chewed a mouthful of bread without tasting it.

She put down her knife. Stood up, left her plate on the table, and hurried from the room.

The great hall was empty. She ran through it, her footsteps echoing, until she found a smaller room off to the side, near the main entrance.

Nestor lay within by the fire. He was stiff and silent, staring glumly into the flames. At the sound of her footsteps he gazed up. His eyes were the color of blue ice.

She could not leave him. Would not. Annesh would understand.

Nestor sat up, scowling.

"Want to go home?" Dora said.

He nodded wanly.

"Well, let's go then." She gestured impatiently.

Nestor shook his head. His lips moved but no sound came from them.

"Oh, that's right. I forgot. You can't talk, can you?" She gave the old wizard a smile that was half exasperated, half affectionate. "And you didn't teach me any spells for transport, did you?"

Her only reply was a look of disgust.

With a sigh, Dora fixed her blue hood into place over her bright hair and sealed her cloak against the cold. "Come along, then. I'll see about hiring a horse. And so much for the grand power of magicks."

Nestor rose slowly and sealed his cloak tightly about him.

Dora reached for his arm. For a moment, the old mage pulled back, eyes blazing. Then he shrugged.

And together, hand in hand, the old wizard and his apprentice set off for home.

The Naga

Peter S. Beagle

AUTHOR'S NOTE: The following tale is a fragment of a recently discovered first-century Roman manuscript, tentatively ascribed to Caius Plinius Secundus, known as Pliny the Elder. It appears to be an addendum to his great Encyclopedia of Natural History, *and to have been written shortly before his death in 79 A.D., in the eruption of Mount Vesuvius. How it fell into the present writer's hands is another story entirely, and is no one's business but his own.—P.S.B.*

. . . et us begin with a creature of which report has reached us only from those half-mythical lands beyond the Indus, where dwell many dragons and unicorns as well. The naga is described by such traders as travel between India and the Roman provinces of Mesopotamia as being a great serpent with seven heads, like the beast known to us as the hydra. Leaving aside the history of Hercules' conquest of the Lernaean Hydra, authorities have related numerous encounters with these animals off the coasts of Greece and Britain. The hydra has between seven and ten heads, like dogs' heads; these are generally depicted as growing at the ends of prodigiously muscular necks or arms, and they do not devour the prey they seize but drag it to a central head, much larger, which then tears it apart with a beak like that of a monstrous African parrot. Further, it is said that these heads and necks, cut in two, do grow again: on the instant, according to the Greek writers, but their capacity both for lying and credulity surpasses all bounds that one might reasonably impose on other peoples. Nevertheless, of the hydra's actual existence there can be little doubt—I have myself spoken with sailors who had lost comrades to the voracity of these beasts, and who, in vengeance, would boil one alive and devour it themselves whenever they should capture one. I am advised that the taste of the hydra is quite similar to that of the boots of which soldiers often make soup in desert extremities. The flavor is not easily forgotten.

But the naga is plainly another nature of being from the hydra, whatever their superficial resemblances. Such accounts as I have received indicate that the folk of India and the lands beyond generally revere this creature, indeed consider it almost as a god, yet at the same time somehow lower than the human. The contradictions do not end here, for though the bite of the naga is reputedly poisonous to all that lives, only certain individuals are regarded as physically dangerous to man. (Indeed, there appears to be no agreement among my sources as to the usual prey of the naga: several authorities even suggest that the beast does not eat at all, but lives on the milk of the wild elephant, which it herds and protects as we do cattle.) Water is the nagas' element: they are believed to have the power to bring rain, or to withhold it, and consequently must be propitiated with sacrifices and other offerings, and treated with constant respect. As do dragons here, they guard great hoards of treasure in deep lairs; but much unlike the dragons we know, the nagas reportedly construct underground palaces of immense richness and beauty, dwelling there in the manner of kings and queens in this world. Yet it is said that they are often restless, pining for something they cannot have, and then they leave their mansions and stir forth into the rivers and brooks of India. The philosophers of that region say that they are seeking enlightenment—there are sects in Rome who would assure us that they hunger for a human soul. I have no opinion in this matter.

It may be of some interest to those who have served the Emperor in Britain to know that a creature similar to the naga is rumored to exist in the far northern marches of that island, where it is worshipped as a bringer of fertility, perhaps because it sleeps out the winter months underground, emerging on the first day of spring. But whether or not these serpents amass treasure in the same manner as the nagas, and as to how many heads they have, I know not.

All nagas are said to possess a priceless jewel, located either in the forehead or the throat, which is the source of their great power. They are, like the elephant, of a religious and even reverential nature, frequently keeping up shrines to the gods of India and making rich offerings of the same sort as they themselves receive. In addition, there are accounts of naga kings presenting their bodies as couches for the gods, spreading their hoods to keep off the rain and sun. Whether or not these tales are true, that they should be credited at all certainly indicates the regard in which the nagas are held in these lands.

A further puzzling contradiction concerning the naga is the general understanding that the female serpent—referred to as a nagini—is capable of assuming the human shape, while this is not so for the male of the species. In this counterfeit form, the nagini is frequently of remarkable beauty, and it is said that there are royal families who trace their descent from the marriage of a mortal prince with a nagini. Regarding this matter, the following tale was related directly to me by a trader in silks and dyestuffs who has traveled widely both in India and in the neighboring realm to the east called by its folk Kambuja. I will repeat it in the manner of his telling, as well as I am able.

In Kambuja, a little way from the palace of the kings, there stands to this day a tower sheathed completely in gold, as is often the style of royalty in those parts. This tower was built very long ago by a young king, as soon as he rose to power, to serve as apartments for himself and his queen when he should marry. But in the arrogance of his youth, he was impatient and impossible to please: this maiden was too plain, that one too dull; this one pretty enough but too quick-tongued, and this other was an unsuitable match for family reasons, and smelled of dried fish to boot. Consequently, his first youth passed in the solitude of majesty, which—as I am often advised—can surely be no substitute for the companionship and loving wisdom of a true wife, whether queen or bondservant. And the king was ever more lonely, though he would not say so, and ill-tempered because of this; and while he was not cruel or capricious in his ways, still he ruled in a listless fashion, doing little of evil and no good, having no heart for either. And the golden tower went untenanted, year on year, save for spiders and small owls raising their own families in the topmost spire.

Now (said the trader), this king was much in the habit of walking disguised among his people in the warm twilight of the streets and the marketplace. He fancied that he gained some knowledge of their true daily lives thereby, which was not at all so: first, because there was no least urchin but recognized him on sight, however wearily cunning his incognito; and secondly, because he had no real desire for such understanding. Nevertheless, he kept his custom faithfully enough, and one evening a beggar-woman with a dirty and ignorant face approached him on his meanderings and inquired in a vulgar dialect, "Your pardon, master potter"—for so he was dressed—"but what is the nature of that shiny thing there?" And she pointed toward the golden tower that the king had designed for his happiness so long ago.

Now the king was apparently not without humor, albeit of a bleak and comfortless sort. He replied courteously to the beggar-woman, saying, "That is a museum consecrated to the memory of one who never lived, and I am no potter but its very guardian. Would you care to satisfy your curiosity? for we welcome visitors, the tower and I." The beggar-woman assented readily, and the king took her by the hand and led her, first through the gardens that he had planted with his own hands, and then through the great shining door to which he always carried the key, though it had never turned in the lock until that day.

From room to room and spire to spire the king led the beggar-woman, conversing with her all the time in grave mockery of his own past dreams. "Here is where he would have dined, this man who never was, and in this room he would have sat with his wife and his friends to hear musicians play. And this place was to have been for his wife's women, and this for children to sleep—as though the unborn could father children." But when they came to the royal bedchamber, the king drew back from the door and would not go in, but said harshly, "There are serpents here, and plague, come away."

But the beggar-woman stepped boldly past him and into the bedchamber with the air of one who has been long away from a place, yet remembers it well. The king called to her in anger, and when she turned he saw (said the trader) that she was no creeping beggar, but a great queen, clad in robes and jewels far richer than any he possessed himself. And she said to him, "I am a nagini, come from my palace and my estates far under the earth, for love and pity of you. From this evening forward, neither you nor I shall sleep elsewhere but in this tower ever again." And the king embraced her, for she was of such royal loveliness that he could do no other; and besides, he had been much alone.

Presently, some degree of order having returned to their joy, the king began to speak of their wedding, of festivals to last for months, and of how they would rule and keep their court together. But the nagini said, "Beloved, we are twice wed already: once when I first saw your face, and again when we first held one another in our arms. As for counselors and armies and decrees, that is all your daytime world and none of mine. My own realm, my own folk, need my care and governance as much as yours need you. But in our night world we will care for each other here, and how can our dutiful days but be happy, with night always to come?"

The king was not content with this, for he wished to present his people with their long-awaited queen, and to have her by his side at every moment of every day. He said to her, "I can see that we shall come to no good end. You will tire of journeying constantly between two worlds and forget me for some naga lord, compared to whom I will seem as a sweeper, a date-seller. And I, in my sorrow, will turn to a street-singer, a common courtesan, or—worse—a woman of the court, and be more lonely and more strange than ever for having loved you. Is this the gift that you have come all this long way to bring me?"

At that, the nagini's long, beautiful eyes flashed, and she caught the king by his wrists, saying, "Never speak to me of jealousy and betrayal, even in jest. My folk are faithful through all their lives—can you say the same of yours? And I will tell you this, my own lord, my *one*— should night ever come to this tower and not bring you with it, it will not be morning before a terrible catastrophe befalls your kingdom. If even once you fail to meet me here, nothing will save Kambuja from my wrath. That is how we are, we nagas."

"And if you do not come to me each night," said the king simply, "I shall die." Then the nagini's eyes filled with tears, and she put her arms about him, saying, "Why do we vex each other with talk of what will never happen? We are home together at last, my friend, my husband." And of their happiness in the golden tower there is no further need to speak, save to add that the spiders and serpents and owls were all gone from there by morning.

Thus it was that the king of Kambuja took a nagini as his queen, even though she came to him only in darkness, and only in the golden tower. He told no one of this, as she bade him; but since he abandoned all matters of state, all show and ceremony, as soon as the sun set, to hurry alone to the tower, rumors that he met a woman there every night spread swiftly through all the country. The curious followed him as closely and as far as they dared; and there were even those who waited all night outside the tower in hopes of spying out the king's secret mistress as she came and went. But none ever saw even the shadow of the nagini—only the king, walking slowly back into the day, calm and pensive, his face shining with the last light of the moon.

In time, however, such gossip and fascination gave way to wonder at the change in the king. For he ruled more and more with a passionate awareness of his people's real existence, as though he had awakened to see them for the first time, in all their human innocence and wickedness and suffering. From caring about nothing but his own bitter loneliness, he now began to work at bettering their lot as intensely as they themselves worked merely to survive. There was no one in the realm who could not see and speak freely to him; no condemned criminal, overtaxed merchant, beaten servant or daughter sold into marriage who could not appeal and be heard. Such zealous concern bewildered many who were accustomed to other sorts of rulers, and a half-mocking saying grew up in the land: "By night we have a queen, but by day we have at least five kings." Yet slowly his people came to return their king's love, if not to comprehend it, and it came also to be said that if justice existed nowhere else in the entire universe, still it had been invented in Kambuja.

The reason for this change, as the king himself well knew, was two-fold: first, that he was happy for the first time in his life and wished to see others happy; second, that it seemed to him that the harder he worked, the faster the day sped its course, carrying him to nightfall and his nagini queen. In its turn, as she had told him, the joy that he took in their love made even their hours apart joyous by reflection, as the sun, long since set, yet brightens our nights through the good offices of the moon. So it is that one learns to treasure, without confusing them, day and night and twilight alike, with all that they contain.

The years passed swiftly, being made up of days and nights as they are. The king never spent a night away from the golden tower—which meant, among many other things, that during his reign Kambuja never went to war—and the nagini was always there when he arrived to greet him by the secret name that the priests had given him as a child, the name that no one else knew. In return she had told him her naga name (and laughed fondly at his attempts to speak it correctly), but she refused ever to let him see her in her true shape, as she went among her own folk. "What I am with you is what I am most truly," she said to him (according to the sworn word of my trader). "We nagas are forever passing between water and earth, earth and air, between one form and another, one world and another, this desire and that, this dream and that. Here in our tower I am as you know me, neither more nor less; and what shape you put on when you sit and give judgment on life and death, I do not ask to see. Here we are both as free as though you were not a king and I were not a naga. Let it remain so, my dear one."

The king answered, "It shall be as you say, but you should know that there are many who whisper that their night queen is indeed a naga. The land has grown too bounteous, the rainfall is too perfect, too reliable—who but a naga could command such precise good fortune? Most of my people have believed for years that you are the true ruler of Kambuja, whatever else you may be. In truth, I find it hard to disagree with them."

"I have never told you how to govern your country," the nagini answered him. "You needed no instruction from me to be a king."

"You think not?" he asked her then. "But I was no king at all until you came to me, and my people know that as well as I. Perhaps you never taught me to build a road or a granary, to devise a just tax or keep my land's borders free of enemies, but without you I would never have cared that I could do such things. Once Kambuja was only to be endured because it contained our golden tower; now, by little and little, the tower has grown to take in all Kambuja, and all my people have come inside with us, precious as ourselves. This is your doing, and this is why you rule here, by day as well as night."

At times he would say to her, "Long ago, when I told you that I would die if you ever failed to meet me here, your face changed and I knew that I had spoken more truth than I meant. I know now—so wise has loving made me—that one night you will not come, and I will die indeed, and for that I care nothing. I have known you. I have lived." But the nagini would never let him speak further, weeping and promising him that such a night would never be, and then the king would comfort her until morning. So they were together, and the years passed.

The king grew old with the nagini as he had been young with her, joyously and without fear. But those most near to him grew old too, and died or retired from the court, and there emerged a rabble of young soldiers and courtiers who grumbled increasingly loudly that the king had provided no heir to the throne, and that the realm would be torn to pieces by his squabbling cousins at his death. They complained further that he was in such thrall to his nagini, or his sorceress, or his leopard-woman (for the belief in such shape-changers is a common one in Kambuja) that he took little care for the glory and renown of the kingdom, so that Kambuja had become a byword for well-fed timidity among other nations. And if none of this was true, still it is well-known that long tranquility makes many restless, ready to follow anyone who promises tumultuous change for its own sake. It has happened so even in Rome.

Several attempted to warn the king that such was the case at his court, but he paid no heed, preferring to believe that all around him were as serene as he. Thus, when a drowsy noon hour abruptly shattered into blood and shouting and the clanging of swords, and even when he found himself with his back to his own throne-room door, fighting for his life, the king was not prepared. If the best third of his army, made up of his strongest veterans, had not remained loyal, the battle would have been over in those first few minutes, and there would be no more than this to my trader's story. But the king's forces held on doggedly, and then rallied, and by mid-afternoon were on the attack; so that as the sun began to set the insurrection had dwindled to a few pockets of a few desperate rebels who fought like madmen, knowing that no surrender would be accepted. It was in combat with one such that the king of Kambuja received his mortal wound.

He did not know that it was mortal. He knew only that night was falling, and that there were yet men standing between him and the golden tower, men who had screamed all afternoon that they would kill him first and then his leopard-woman, his serpent-woman, the monster who had for so long rotted the fiber of the realm. So he struck them down with all his remaining strength, and then he turned, half-naked, covered with blood, and limped away from battle toward the tower. If men barred his way, he killed them; but he fell often, and each time he was slower to rise, which made him angry. The tower seemed to grow no closer, and he knew that he should be with his nagini by now.

He would never have reached the tower, but for the valor of a very young officer, far younger than boys in Rome have ever been permitted to enter the Emperor's service. This boy's commander, whose personal charge was the safety of the king, had been slain early in the rebellion, and the boy had appointed himself the king's shield in his stead, following the king through all the dusty turmoil of battle and ever fighting at his side or his back. Now he ran forward to raise the king and support him, all but carrying him toward that distant door through which he had jestingly led a beggar-woman so long ago. None of either side came near them as they struggled through the twilight; none dared.

By the time they at last attained the tower door, the boy knew that the king was dying. He had no strength to turn the key in the lock, nor could he even speak, save with his eyes, to order the boy to do it; yet once they were within, he pulled himself to his feet and climbed the stairs like any eager young man hastening to his beloved. The boy trailed behind, frightened of this place of his parents' nursery stories, this high darkness rustling with demon queens. Yet care for his king overcame all such terrors, and he was once again at the old man's side when they stood on the bedchamber threshold with the door swinging open before them.

The nagini was not there. The boy hurried to light the torches on the walls, and saw that the chamber was barren of everything but shadows; shadows and the least, least smell of jasmine and sandalwood. Behind him, the king said clearly, "She has not come." The boy was not quick enough to catch him when he fell. His eyes were open when the boy lifted him in his arms, and he pointed toward the bed without speaking. When the boy had set him there, and bound his many wounds as best he could, the king beckoned him close and whispered, "Watch the night. Watch with me." It was no plea, but a command.

So the boy sat all through the night on the great bed where the king and queen of Kambuja had slept in happiness for so long, and he never knew when the king died. He fought to stay awake as hard as he had fought the king's enemies that day, but he was weary and wounded himself, and he dozed and woke and dozed again. The last time he roused, it was because all the torches had gone out at once, with a sound like a ship's sails cracking in the breeze, and because he heard another sound, heavy and slow, some cold, rough burden being dragged over cold stone. In the last moonlight he saw her: the immense body filling the room like greenish-black smoke, the seven cobra heads swaying as one, and a flickering about her, as though she were shimmering between two worlds at a speed his eyes could not understand. She was close enough to the bed for him to see that she too bore fresh, bleeding wounds (he said later that her blood was as bright as the sun, and hurt his eyes). When he hurled himself away, rolling and scrambling into a corner, the nagini never looked at him. She bowed her seven heads over the king as he lay, and her burning blood fell and mingled with his blood.

"My people tried to keep me from you," she said. The boy could not tell whether all the heads spoke, or only one; he said that her voice was full of other voices, like a chord of music. The nagini said, "They told me that today was the day appointed for your death, fixed in the atoms of the universe since the beginning of time, and so it was, and I have always known this, as you knew. But I could not turn away and let it be so, fated or not, and I fought them and came here. He who hides in the shadows will sing that you and I never once failed each other, neither in life nor in death."

Then she called the king by a name that the boy did not recognize, and she took him up onto the coils of her body, as the folk of these parts believe that a naga named Muchalinda supports this world and those to come. Nor did she leave the bedchamber by the door, but passed slowly into darkness, vanishing with no more trace than the scent of jasmine and sandalwood, and the fading music of all her voices. And what became of her, and of the remains of the king of Kambuja, is not known.

Now I find this story open to some question—there is more evidence to be offered for the existence of nagas than proof positive that they do *not* exist; but of their commerce with men, much may safely be doubted. But I set it down even so, in honor of that boy who waited until sunrise in that silent golden tower before he dared walk out among the clamor of kites and the moans of the grieving to tell the people of Kambuja that their king was dead and gone. One of his descendants it was—or so he swore—who told me the tale.

And if there is any sort of message or metaphor in it, perhaps it is that sorrow and hunger, pity and love, run far deeper in the world than we imagine. They are the underground rivers that the nagas forever traverse; they are the rain that renews us when the right respect has been paid, whether to the nagas or to one another. And if there are no gods, nor any other worlds than this, if there is no such thing as enlightenment or a soul, still there remain those four rivers—*sorrow and hunger, pity and love*. We humans can survive for terribly long and long without food, without shelter or clothing or medicine, but it is a fact that we will die very soon if the rain does not come.

Revolt of the Sugar Plum Fairies

Mike Resnick

Arthur Crumm didn't believe in leprechauns.

He didn't believe in centaurs, either.

He also didn't believe in ghosts or goblins or gorgons or anything else beginning with a G. Oh, and you can add H to the list; he didn't believe in harpies or hobbits, either.

In fact, you could write an awfully thick book about the things he didn't believe in. You'd have to leave out only one item: the one about the Sugar Plum Fairies.

Them, he believed in.

Of course, he had no choice. He had a basement full of them. They were various shades of blue, none of them more than eighteen inches tall, and possessed of high, squeaky voices that would have driven his cats berserk if he had owned any cats. Their eyes were large and round, rather as if they had been drawn by someone who specialized in painting children on black velvet, and their noses were small and pug, and each of them had a little potbelly, and they were dressed as if they were about to be presented to Queen Elizabeth. They looked cloyingly cute, and they made Mickey Mouse sound like a baritone—but they had murder on their minds.

They had been in Arthur's basement for less than an hour, but already he had managed to differentiate them, which was harder than you might think with a bunch of tiny blue fairies. There was Bluebell, who struck

Arthur as the campus radical of the bunch. There was Indigo, with his Spanish accent, and old Silverthorne, the arch-conservative, and Purpletone, the politician, and Inkspot, who spoke jive like he had been born to it. Royal Blue seemed to be their leader, and there was also St. Looie Blues, standing off by himself playing a mournful if tiny saxophone.

"Well, I still don't understand how you guys got here," Arthur was saying.

Now, most men are not really inclined to sit on their basement stairs and converse with a bunch of Sugar Plum Fairies, but Arthur was a pragmatist. Their presence meant one of two things: either he was quite mad, or his house was infested with fairies. And since he didn't feel quite mad, he decided to assume that the latter was the case.

"I keep telling you: we came here by inter-dimensional quadrature," snapped Bluebell. "Open your ears, fathead!"

"That's no way to speak to our host," said Purpletone placatingly.

"Host, *schmost*!" snapped Bluebell. "If he was our host, he'd set us free. He's our captor."

"*I* didn't capture you," noted Arthur mildly. "I came down here and found you all stuck to the floor."

"That's because some of the Pepsi you stored leaked all over the floor," said Bluebell. "What kind of fiend stores defective pop bottles in his basement, anyway?"

"You could at least have carpeted the place," added Silverthorne. "It's not only sticky, it's *cold*."

"Now set us free so we can take our grim and terrible vengeance," continued Bluebell.

"On *me*?" asked Arthur.

"You are an insignificant spear carrier in the pageant of our lives," said Royal Blue. "We have a higher calling."

"Right, man," chimed in Inkspot. "You let us free, maybe we don't mess you up, you dig?"

"It seems to me that if I *don't* let you free you won't mess me up, either," said Arthur.

"You see?" said Indigo furiously. "I tole you and I tole you: you can't trust Gringos!"

"If you don't like Gringos, why did you choose *my* basement?" asked Arthur.

"Well, uh, we didn't exactly *choose* it," said Royal Blue uneasily.

"Then how did you get here?"

"By inter-dimensional quadrature, dummy!" said Bluebell, who finally succeeded in removing his feet from his shoes, only to have them stick onto the floor right next to the empty shoes.

"So you keep saying," answered Arthur. "But it doesn't mean anything to me."

"So it's *my* fault that you're a scientific illiterate?" demanded Bluebell, grabbing his left foot and giving it a mighty tug to no avail.

"Try explaining it another way," suggested Arthur, as Bluebell made another unsuccessful attempt to move his feet.

"Let *me* try," said Silverthorne. He turned his head so that he was facing Arthur. "We activated the McLennon/Whittaker Space-Time Displacement Theorem, but we didn't take the Helmhiser Variables or the Kobernykov Uncertainty Principle into account." He paused. "There. Does that help?"

"Not very much," admitted Arthur.

"What difference does it make?" said Royal Blue. "We're here, and that's all that matters."

"I'm still not clear why you're here at all," persisted Arthur.

"It's a matter of racial pride," answered Royal Blue with some dignity.

Arthur scratched his head. "You're proud of being stuck to the floor of my basement?"

"No, of course not," said old Silverthorne irritably. "We're here to defend our honor."

"How?"

"We've mapped out a campaign of pillage and destruction and vengeance," explained Royal Blue. "The entire world will tremble before us. Strong men will swoon, women and children will hide behind locked doors, even animals will scurry to get out of our path."

"A bunch of Sugar Plum Fairies who can't even get their feet unstuck from the floor?" said Arthur with a chuckle.

"Don't underestimate us," said Bluebell in his falsetto voice. "We Sugar Plum Fairies are tough dudes. We are capable of terrorizing entire communities." He grimaced. "Or we would be, if we could just get our feet free."

"And the seven of you are the advance guard?"

"What advance guard? We're the entire invasion force."

"An invasion force of just seven Sugar Plum Fairies?" repeated Arthur.

"Didn't you ever see *The Magnificent Seven*?" asked Royal Blue. "Yul

Brynner didn't need more than seven gunslingers to tame that Mexican town."

"And Toshiro Mifune only needed seven swordsmen in *The Seven Samurai*," chimed in Bluebell.

"Seven is obviously a mystical number of great spiritual power," said Purpletone.

"Besides, no one else would come," added Silverthorne.

"Has anyone thought to point out that you're neither seven swordsmen nor seven gunfighters?" asked Arthur. "You happen to be seven undersized, potbellied, and totally helpless fairies."

"Hey, baby," said Inkspot. "We may be small, but we're wiry."

"Yeah," added Indigo. "We sleet some throats, watch some feelthy videos, and then we go home."

"If we can figure out how to get there," added Silverthorne.

"We tried invading the world *your* way and look where it got us," said Bluebell irritably. "On the way home, we'll take the second star to the right."

"That's an old wives' tale," protested Purpletone.

"Yeah?" shot back Bluebell. "How would *you* do it?"

"Simple. You close your eyes, click your heels together three times, and say 'There's no place like home,'" answered Purpletone. "Any fool knows that."

"Who are you calling a fool?" demanded Bluebell.

"Uh . . . I don't want to intrude on your argument," put in Arthur, "but I have a feeling that both of you are the victims of false doctrine."

"Okay, wise guy!" squeaked Bluebell. "How would *you* do it?"

Arthur shrugged. "I haven't the foggiest notion where you came from."

"From Sugar Plum Fairyland, of course! How dumb can you be?"

"Oh, I can be pretty dumb at times," conceded Arthur. "But I've never been dumb enough to get stuck to the floor of a basement in a strange world with no knowledge of how to get home."

"All right," admitted Bluebell grudgingly. "So we got a little problem here. Don't make a federal case out of it."

"Be sure and tell me when you have a *big* problem," said Arthur. "The mind boggles."

"You stop making fun of us, Gringo," said Indigo, "or we're gonna add you to the list."

"The list of people you plan to kill?"

"You got it, hombre."

"Just out of curiosity, how long *is* this list?" asked Arthur.

"Well," said Royal Blue, "so far, at a rough count, an estimate, so to speak, it comes to three."

"Who are they?" asked Arthur curiously.

"Number One on our hit list is Walt Disney," said Royal Blue firmly.

"And the other two?"

"That choreographer—what was his name—oh, yeah: Balanchine. And the Russian composer, Tchaikovsky."

"What did they ever do to you?" asked Arthur.

"They made us laughing stocks," said Bluebell. "Disney made us cute and cuddly in *Fantasia,* and Balanchine had us dancing on our tippy-toes in *The Nutcracker.* How are we expected to discipline our kids with an image like that? Our women giggle at us when they should be swooning. Our children talk back to us. Our enemies pay absolutely no attention when we lay siege to their cities." The little fairy paused for breath. "We *warned* that Russkie what would happen if he didn't change it to the '*March* of the Sugar Plum Fairy.' Now we're going to make him pay!"

"I don't know how to lay this on you," said Arthur, "but all three of them are dead."

St. Looie Blues immediately began playing a jazz version of "Happy Days Are Here Again" on his saxophone.

"Stop that!" squeaked Bluebell furiously.

"Whassa matter, man?" asked St. Looie Blues.

"This is nothing to celebrate! We've been robbed of our just and terrible vengeance!"

"If they were all the size of this here dude," said St. Looie Blues, indicating Arthur, "you wasn't gonna be able to do much more than bite each of 'em on the great toe, anyway." He went back to playing his instrument.

"Well, what are we going to do?" asked Bluebell in a plaintive whine. "We can't have come all this way for nothing!"

"Maybe we could kill each of their firstborn sons," suggested Purpletone. "It's got a nice religious flavor to it."

"Maybe we should just go home," said Royal Blue.

"Never!" said Bluebell. "They still perform the ballet, they still listen to the symphony, they still show the movie!"

"In seventy millimeters, these days," added Arthur helpfully.

"But how can we stop them?" asked Royal Blue.

"I suppose we'll have to kill every musician and dancer on this world, and destroy all the prints of the movie," said Silverthorne.

"Right!" said Bluebell. "Let's go!"

Nobody moved.

"Arthur, old friend," said Purpletone. "I wonder if we could appeal to you, as one of the potential survivors of our forthcoming bloody war of conquest, to get us unstuck."

Arthur sighed. "I don't think so."

"Why not?" asked Royal Blue. "We've told you everything you want to know, and *you're* not on our hit list."

"It would be murder."

"Definitions change when you're in a state of war," responded Purpletone. "We don't consider ourselves to be murderers."

Arthur shook his head. "You don't understand. *They* would murder *you*."

"Preposterous!" squeaked Bluebell.

"Ridiculous," added Silverthorne.

"Do you have any weapons?" asked Arthur.

"No," admitted Bluebell. "But we've got a lot of gumption. We fear absolutely nothing."

"Well, that's not entirely true," said Purpletone after a moment's consideration. "Personally, I'm scared to death of banshees, moat monsters, and high cholesterol levels."

"*I'm* terrified of heights," added Royal Blue. "And I don't like the dark very much, either."

Soon all of the Sugar Plum Fairies were making long lists of things that frightened them.

"Well, some of us are hardly afraid of anything, with certain exceptions," amended Bluebell weakly. "And the rest can be bold and daring under rigidly defined conditions."

"If I were you, I'd pack it in and go home," said Arthur.

"We can't!" said Bluebell. "Even if we knew how to get there, we can't face our people and tell them that our mission was a failure, that we never even got out of your basement."

"I know you've got our best interests at heart, Arthur," added Silverthorne. "But we've got our pride."

"So now," concluded Royal Blue, "if you'll just help free us, we'll be on our way, leaving a modest trail of death and destruction in our wake."

Arthur shook his head. "You're going about it all wrong."

"What do *you* know about cataclysmic wars of revenge?" demanded Bluebell.

"Nothing," admitted Arthur.

"Well, then."

"But I *do* know that killing a bunch of people, even if you had the power to do it, wouldn't keep *Fantasia* from getting re-released every couple of years."

"That's what *you* say," replied Bluebell with more conviction than he felt.

"That's what I *know,*" said Arthur. He paused. "Look, I don't know why I should want to help you, except that you're cute as buttons"—all seven of them growled high falsetto growls at this—"and I don't think I really believe in you anyway. But if it was *me* planning this operation," he continued, "I'd break into the Disney distribution computer and re-call all the copies of *Fantasia*. I mean, it beats the hell out of going to every theater in the world looking for a handful of prints."

"That's a *great* idea!" said Royal Blue enthusiastically. "Men, isn't that a great idea? Simply marvelous!" He paused for a moment. "By the way, Arthur, what's a computer?"

Arthur explained it to them.

"That's all very well and good," said Silverthorne when Arthur had finished, "but how does it prevent the ballet from ever being performed?"

"I would imagine that Balanchine's notes—the play-by-play, so to speak—have been computerized by now," answered Arthur. "Just find the proper computer and wipe them out."

"And Tchaikovsky's music?"

Arthur shrugged. "That's a little more difficult."

"Well, two out of three ain't bad," said Inkspot. "You're an okay guy, Arthur, for someone what ain't even blue."

"Yeah, Gringo," added Indigo. "My sombrero's off to you. Or it would be, if I could find a sombrero in my size."

"Okay, Arthur," said Royal Blue. "We're primed to go. Just set us free and point us in the right direction."

"We're a long way from California," said Arthur as he began freeing each fairy in turn. "How do you plan to get there?"

"The same way we got here," answered Silverthorne.

"In which case you'll probably end up in Buenos Aires," said Arthur.

"A telling point," agreed Purpletone.

"We could fly," suggested Silverthorne.

"Great idea!" said Purpletone enthusiastically. Then he paused and frowned. "*Can* we fly?"

"I dunno, man," said Inkspot, flapping his arms. "If we can, I sure don't remember how."

"I'm afraid of heights anyway," said Royal Blue. "We'll have to find another way."

"Maybe we could reduce our bodies to their composite protons and electrons and speed there through the telephone lines," suggested Bluebell.

"You first," said Purpletone.

"Me?" said Bluebell.

"Why not? It's your idea, isn't it?"

"Well, I thought of it, so it's only fair that someone else should test it out," said Bluebell petulantly.

"Maybe we could hitchhike," suggested Indigo.

"What do you think, Arthur?" said Royal Blue. He looked around the basement. "Hey, where did Arthur go?"

"If he's reporting us to the authorities, I'm gonna give him such a kick on the shin . . ." said Bluebell.

Suddenly Arthur appeared at the head of the stairs with a large box in his hands.

"I got tired of listening to you squabble," he said, carrying the box down to the basement.

"What's that for?" asked Royal Blue, nervously pointing to the box.

"Get in," said Arthur, starting to pry them loose from the floor.

"All of us?"

Arthur nodded.

"Why?"

"I'm shipping you to the Disney corporate offices," answered Arthur. "Once you're there, you're on your own."

"Great!" cried Royal Blue. "Now we can wreak havoc amongst our enemies and redeem the honor of our race."

"Or at least get a couple of gigs at Disneyland," added St. Looie Blues.

. . .

It was two weeks later that Arthur Crumm returned home from work, a bag of groceries in his arms, and found the seven Sugar Plum Fairies perched on various pieces of furniture in his living room.

Bluebell was wearing sunglasses and a set of gold chains. Indigo was smoking a cigar that was at least as long as he was. Silverthorne had a small diamond tiepin pierced through his left ear. St. Looie Blues had traded in his saxophone for a tiny music synthesizer. The others also displayed telltale signs of their recent excursion to the West Coast.

"How the hell did you get in here?" said Arthur.

"United Parcel got us to the front door," answered Royal Blue. "We took care of the rest. I hope you don't mind."

"I suppose not," said Arthur, setting down his bag. "You're looking . . . ah . . . well."

"We're *doing* well," said Royal Blue. "And we owe it all to you, Arthur."

"So you really managed to stop distribution of *Fantasia*?"

"Oh, *that*," said Bluebell with a contemptuous shrug. "We found out that we were meant for better things."

"Oh? I thought your goal was to destroy every last print of the film."

"That was before we learned to work their computer," answered Bluebell. "Arthur, do you know how much money that film makes year in and year out?"

"Lots," guessed Arthur.

" 'Lots' is an understatement," said Royal Blue. "The damned thing's a gold mine, Arthur—and there's a new generation of moviegoers every couple of years."

"Okay, so you didn't destroy the prints," said Arthur. "What *did* you do?"

"We bought a controlling interest in Disney!" said Bluebell proudly.

"You did *what*?"

"Disney," repeated Bluebell. "We own it now. We're going to be manufacturing Sugar Plum Fairy dolls, Sugar Plum Fairy T-shirts, Sugar Plum Fairy breakfast cereals . . ."

"Carnage and pillage are all very well in their place," explained Purpletone. "But *marketing*, Arthur—that's where the *real* power lies!"

"How did you manage to afford it?" asked Arthur curiously.

"We're not very good at dimensional quadrature," explained Royal Blue, "but we found that we have a real knack for computers. We simply manipulated the stock market—buying the New York City Ballet and all the rights to Balanchine's notes in the process—and when we had enough money, we sold Xerox short, took a straddle on Polaroid, and bought Disney on margin." He looked incredibly pleased with himself. "Nothing to it."

"And what about Tchaikovsky?"

"We can't stop people from listening," replied Bluebell, "but we now own a piece of every major recording company in America, England, and the Soviet Union. We'll have the distribution channels tied up in another three weeks' time." He paused. "Computers are *fun!*"

"So are you going back to Sugar Plum Fairyland now?" asked Arthur.

"Certainly not!" said Royal Blue. "Anyone can be a Sugar Plum Fairy. It takes a certain innate skill and nobility to be a successful corporate raider, to properly interpret price-earnings ratios and find hidden assets, to strike at just the proper moment and bring your enemy to his financial knees."

"I suppose it does."

"Especially when you're handicapped the way we are," continued Royal Blue. "We can't very well address corporate meetings, we can't use a telephone that's more than twenty inches above the floor, we can only travel in UPS packages . . ."

"We don't even have a mailing address," added Purpletone.

"The biggest problem, though," said Bluebell, "is that none of us has a social security number or a taxpayer I.D. That means that the Internal Revenue Service will try to impound all our assets at the end of the fiscal year."

"To say nothing of what the SEC will do," put in Silverthorne mournfully.

"You don't say," mused Arthur.

"We do say," replied Bluebell. "In fact, we just did."

"Then perhaps you'll be amenable to a suggestion . . ."

Three days later Arthur Crumm & Associates bought a seat on the New York Stock Exchange, and they added a seat on the AmEx within a month.

To this day nobody knows very much about them, except that they're a small, closely-held investment company, they turn a truly remarkable annual profit, and they recently expanded into Sugar Plum Fairy theme parks and motion picture production. In fact, it's rumored that they've signed Sylvester Stallone, Arnold Schwarzenegger, and Madonna to star in *Fantasia II*.

Winter's King

Jane Yolen

e was not born a king but the child of wandering players, slipping out ice-blue in the deepest part of winter, when the wind howled outside the little green caravan. The midwife pronounced him dead, her voice smoothly hiding her satisfaction. She had not wanted to be called to a birth on such a night.

But the father, who sang for pennies and smiles from strangers, grabbed the child from her and plunged him into a basin of lukewarm water, all the while singing a strange, fierce song in a tongue he did not really know.

Slowly the child turned pink in the water, as if breath were lent him by both the water and the song. He coughed once, and spit up a bit of rosy blood, then wailed a note that was a minor third higher than his father's last surprised tone.

Without taking time to swaddle the child, the father laid him dripping wet and kicking next to his wife on the caravan bed. As she lifted the babe to her breast, the woman smiled at her husband, a look that included both the man and the child but cut the midwife cold.

The old woman muttered something that was part curse, part fear, then more loudly said, "No good will come of this dead cold child. He shall thrive in winter but never in the warm and he shall think little of this world. I have heard of such before. They are called Winter's Kin."

The mother sat up in bed, careful not to disturb the child at her side.

"Then he shall be a Winter King, more than any of his kin or kind," she said. "But worry not, old woman, you shall be paid for the live child as well as the dead." She nodded to her husband who paid the midwife twice over from his meager pocket, six copper coins.

The midwife made the sign of horns over the money, but still she kept it and, wrapping her cloak tightly around her stout body and a scarf around her head, she walked out into the storm. Not twenty steps from the caravan, the wind tore the cloak from her and pulled tight the scarf about her neck. An icy branch broke from a tree and smashed in the side of her head. In the morning when she was found, she was frozen solid. The money she had clutched in her hand was gone.

The player was hanged for the murder and his wife left to mourn even as she nursed the child. Then she married quickly, for the shelter and the food. Her new man never liked the winter babe.

"He is a cold one," the husband said. "He hears voices in the wind," though it was he who was cold and who, when filled with drink, heard the dark counsel of unnamed gods who told him to beat his wife and abuse her son. The woman never complained, for she feared for her child. Yet strangely the child did not seem to care. He paid more attention to the sounds of the wind than the shouts of his stepfather, lending his own voice to the cries he alone could hear, though always a minor third above.

As the midwife had prophesied, in winter he was an active child, his eyes bright and quick to laugh. But once spring came, the buds in his cheeks faded even as the ones on the boughs grew big. In the summer and well into the fall, he was animated only when his mother told him tales of Winter's Kin, and though she made up the tales as only a player can, he knew the stories all to be true.

When the winter child was ten, his mother died of her brutal estate and the boy left into the howl of a storm, without either cloak or hat between him and the cold. Drunk, his ten-year father did not see him go. The boy did not go to escape the man's beatings; he went to his kin who called him from the wind. Bare-footed and bare-headed, he crossed the snows trying to catch up with the riders in the storm. He saw them clearly. They were clad in great white capes, the hoods lined with ermine; and when they turned to look at him, their eyes were wind-blue and the bones of their faces were thin and fine.

Long, long he trailed behind them, his tears turned to ice. He wept not for his dead mother, for it was she who had tied him to the world. He wept for himself and his feet, which were too small to follow after the fast-riding Winter's Kin.

A woodcutter found him that night and dragged him home, plunging him into a bath of lukewarm water and speaking in a strange tongue that even he, in all his wanderings, had never heard.

The boy turned pink in the water, as if life were returned to him by both the bathing and the prayer, but he did not thank the old man when he woke. Instead he turned his face to the window and wept, this time like any child, the tears falling like soft rain down his cheeks.

"Why do you weep?" the old man asked.

"For my mother and for the wind," the boy said. "And for what I cannot have."

The winter child stayed five years with the old woodcutter, going out each day with him to haul the kindling home. They always went into the woods to the south, a scraggly, ungraceful copse of second-growth trees, but never to the woods to the north.

"That is the great Ban Forest," the old man said. "All that lies therein belongs to the king."

"The king," the boy said, remembering his mother's tales. "And so I am."

"And so are we all in God's heaven," the old man said. "But here on earth I am a woodcutter and you are a foundling boy. The wood to the south be ours."

Though the boy paid attention to what the old man said in the spring and summer and fall, once winter arrived, he heard only the voices in the wind. Often the old man would find him standing nearly naked by the door and have to lead him back to the fire where the boy would sink down into a stupor and say nothing at all.

The old man tried to make light of such times, and would tell the boy tales while he warmed at the hearth. He told him of Mother Holle and her feather bed, of Godfather Death, and of the Singing Bone. He told him of the Flail of Heaven and the priest whose rod sprouted flowers because the Water Nix had a soul. But the boy had ears only for the voices in the wind, and what stories he heard there, he did not tell.

. . .

The old man died at the tag-end of their fifth winter and the boy left, without even folding the hands of the corpse. He walked into the southern copse for that was the way his feet knew. But the Winter Kin were not about.

The winds were gentle here, and spring had already softened the bitter brown branches to a muted rose. A yellow-green haze haloed the air and underfoot the muddy soil smelled moist and green and new.

The boy slumped to the ground and wept, not for the death of the woodcutter nor for his mother's death, but for the loss once more of his kin. He knew it would be a long time till winter came again.

And then, from far away, he heard a final wild burst of music. A stray strand of cold wind snapped under his nose as strong as a smelling bottle. His eyes opened wide and, without thinking, he stood.

Following the trail of song, as clear to him as cobbles on a city street, he moved towards the great Ban Forest where the heavy trees still shadowed over winter storms. Crossing the fresh new furze between the woods, he entered the old dark forest and wound around the tall, black trees, in and out of shadows, going as true north as a needle in a water-filled bowl. The path grew cold and the once-muddy ground gave way to frost.

At first all he saw was a mist, as white as if the hooves of horses had struck up dust from sheer ice. But when he blinked once and then twice, he saw coming toward him a great company of fair folk, some on steeds the color of clouds and some on steeds the color of snow. And he realized all at once that it was no mist he had seen but the breath of those great white stallions.

"My people," he cried at last. "My kin. My kind." And he tore off first his boots, then his trousers, and at last his shirt until he was free of the world and its possessions and could run toward the Winter Kin naked and unafraid.

On the first horse was a woman of unearthly beauty. Her hair was plaited in a hundred white braids and on her head was a crown of diamonds and moonstones. Her eyes were wind-blue and there was frost in her breath. Slowly she dismounted and commanded the stallion to be still. Then she took an ermine cape from across the saddle, holding it open to receive the boy.

"My king," she sang, "my own true love," and swaddled him in the cloud-white cloak.

He answered her, his voice a minor third lower than hers. "My queen, my own true love. I am come home."

When the king's foresters caught up to him, the feathered arrow was fast in his breast, but there was, surprisingly, no blood. He was lying, arms outstretched, like an angel in the snow.

"He was just a wild boy, just that lackwit, the one who brought home kindling with the old man," said one.

"Nevertheless, he was in the king's forest," said the other. "He knew better than that."

"Naked as a newborn," said the first. "But look!"

In the boy's left hand were three copper coins, three more in his right.

"Twice the number needed for the birthing of a babe," said the first forester.

"Just enough," said his companion, "to buy a wooden casket and a man to dig the grave."

And they carried the cold body out of the wood, heeding neither the music nor the voices singing wild and strange hosannas in the wind.

Götterdämmerung

Barry N. Malzberg

We are talking, essentially, about the need to preserve a sense of magic, of mystery. Explicitness is the enemy of reason, not its assistant. Wizardry is an honorable trade but it demands, no less than some of the metal trades, hard work and a sense of discipline. I have been at the profession long enough to contemplate this without irony, but with a certain disdain. None of this functions as a prologue to these confidences, it is simply a form of meditation.

I am talking of sitting on a high, bare yellow hill, smoke rising from my small quarters in the distance, the sun casting its fetching rays against this landscape, yellow on yellow. A dry time in a late season. The two elves, the dwarf and the giantess straggled up the elevation toward me, holding out their hands in homage. No gifts—I am known to be both jealous and capricious; the burnt offering trade is certainly not mine—but clearly an anxiety to please. They hovered before me at some respectful distance, then the older of the elves stepped forward.

—Greetings, he said. We come in peace and humility. Is that the proper formula?

—I don't know, I said. Where did the formulaic enter into this? Are you the spokesperson?

—We would prefer that, the dwarf said. He was pleasant-looking enough, not strikingly misshapen, generic features, the same description applying to all of them although there was a certain aggressiveness to the stance of the giantess which might have been threatening in other circumstances. Of course no wizard encounters "other circumstances." We live in a regulated way, surrounded by obeisance if not outright fawning.

—Of course, the dwarf went on, we could speak individually. But that would take too much time.

—Time is valuable, I agreed. It is our only coin. We must not expend it freely.

—And it would be consensual in any case, the dwarf said. So we will leave matters to Meyer here if you don't mind.

—I am Meyer, the larger elf said. My companion is Siegmund. The short fellow over here is Siegfried the dwarf, not to be confused, and Barbara. Barbara has not always been with us. We met only recently.

—In the valley, Barbara said. We shared backgrounds and history and since we have the same objective we decided to join forces.

—Of course, I said. But you appointed only one spokesperson.

A hint of reproof hung in the yellow air, embers against the falling sun. Meyer adjusted his cloak, glanced nervously at the others. —Of course, he said. You are right to bring us into line. Our time is limited and our need is great. We come to petition for help.

—Help, I said. Everyone needs help. I sit by this place in the light and the darkness, watching the tumult of the seasons and nothing, absolutely nothing happens except that now and then petitioners like yourselves come by seeking aid. That is my fate, of course, I added. I don't mean to indicate resentment. My function is wizardry just as yours is petition. But it does after a while begin to pall.

—Well, I can see that, Meyer said. I can understand well how that might have happened. Perhaps we should simply go away, then.

—Ask him the question, Meyer, the giantess said. Don't be intimidated. He may live in smoke and fire but he has to stoke the pots just like the rest of us. And I think the thunder makes him tremble.

—Doesn't she speak beautifully? Siegmund the elf said. Right away, in the valley, when she began to talk with us we knew that her taste for language was fetching. Really, what would we do without our language? I so admire those who can speak.

The giantess gave Siegmund a sweeping glance, then turned away. The dwarf, Siegfried, shook his head, causing his features to wobble in a most perilous fashion, and kicked at a pebble. —I knew this wouldn't work, he said. Come on, let's be on our way. Maybe we'll meet one of the Alberichts down there. I think we gave up too quickly, ascended too rapidly.

Meyer stared at me. —Do you see the problems we have? he said. It's not as if we have a *plan* or anything. We're just muddling through.

—Muddling away, Siegfried said. We meet a proper wizard and we won't let him speak. We straggle all the way up this mountain—

—I can't find the ring for you, I said.

They looked at me with a shared intentness of gaze, coming to a rapid attentiveness which warmed my spirit. There is something about a well-placed sentence which, like a properly cast spell, can induce a feeling of warmth for its own sake. To be taken for one thing and to demonstrate that one is quite another is a kind of pleasure I have long denied myself but sometimes, regardless, that arrogant need for response will seep through.

—The ring is at the bottom of the river, I said. It was pitched there many seasons ago and cannot be recovered. I am no more capable of raising the ring than I am of raising the dead. Or even reconceptualizing them. So that's the end of your interview, I fear. Really there's nothing more to be done.

—I told you, Barbara the giantess said disgustedly. She raised a foot to kick Meyer, then under my stark gaze seemed to reconsider the issue. Well I did, she said sullenly. I told them we would get no satisfaction here.

—Listen, Siegmund said, if you're so sure of this, if you understand everything already, why don't you just take a walk back through the valley, go to your castle? We didn't bring you here in the first place.

Siegfried fixed me with a dwarfish, piercing gaze. —Do you see the problem? he said. Here is the problem: we have turned to bickering, calumny and enmity. Surely if we were to recover the ring, this would pass and we would live in restored harmony and peace. How one's soul craves harmony! But you tell us that our course is fruitless. It is most discouraging.

—I know that it is hopeless, I said. The Alberichts were here not two sunsets past. We had a long discussion, the Alberichts and I, before the fires. They reported the permanent loss of the ring.

—That is what was rumored, Meyer said.

—Attempts were made at recovery, I said. Several Alberichts organized a diving party and washed themselves in the river, responding not to the powerful cries and mockery of the Rhinemaidens. They attempted desperately to recover the ring, having bitterly regretted its divestiture.

—No success, of course, Barbara said.

—None whatsoever, I said. They drowned. That is, four of the Alberichts drowned and a fifth was dragged to shore by his brothers in a state of unconsciousness. He has yet to recover, I was told, although now and then he pleads for the return of the ring. The Alberichts are as helpless as the rest of us, I said. I am afraid their powers have sunk into the river as well.

—They told you all of this? Siegfried said. They so readily admitted their helplessness?

—There are no secrets from a wizard, I said. Even in these difficult times at the end of chronology with the ring sunk deep in the river, the Alberichts on their expeditions of despair and search parties such as yourselves seeking in futility that which was already deemed lost. But enough of this, I said. I engage in banter to no real purpose. There is nothing that can be done for you, I fear, and so you must be on your way.

—I warned you, Barbara said. I told you that this was stupid and foolish. She kicked out at Siegfried. But no, you said. Go up and see the old man, he has many secrets. A day and a night on this hill, struggling toward mockery, that's the outcome.

—Did you have a better idea? Siegfried said, rubbing his ankle but making, I could well note, no threatening gesture in retaliation. You asked to accompany us on our mission.

—You see the problem, Meyer said to me. There is no accord, there is no harmony. We are bitter and discontent, surely the loss of the ring has driven us to this condition, but there is nothing that can be done.

—No, I agreed. There is nothing to be done. You fools and stragglers, I wanted to say, there was nothing to be done before you were born; we are living at the far end of a curse, we are enacting only that which has been foreordained. But that would have led to lectures on predestination and mortality which would have been far beyond their means.

—So you see, I said, standing, abandoning my crouch of confidentiality, lifting my garments and stepping back from them gracefully, there is really nothing more to be done. Perhaps there are some other Alberichts wandering around the territory. Maybe you can speak to them, see if they have any ideas. But I doubt that this would be at all possible.

—He's quite right, Barbara said, there's nothing to do but to go. I am going anyway, she said and turned, limped away. Even more imposing from the rear than front, she showed a certain humility, a broken aspect to her posture which rather touched me as she stomped away although, of course, I would never have revealed this to her or any of the others. We all stared with interest as she moved down the hill, becoming, more quickly than even I might have divined, a small object and then one which was barely visible. A hundred Alberichts could not have vanished as quickly or with more ignominy.

—I guess we'll all be on our way, Meyer said. You were our last hope, you know. We have no other ideas.

—And it's been a long, long journey, Siegfried said. You can't imagine how difficult the conditions have been. Now you take Siegmund here, you may think that his dwarfishness protects him from suffering or true passion but it's simply not so, he's had things to tell us—

—Come on, Meyer said. I don't think the wizard is interested in this. I know *I'm* not. I've heard quite enough of this and we still have a long way to go if we are to sleep away from the fires tonight. He inclined his head. Thank you for your trouble, he said.

—Not to mention, I said. If my powers were greater, it might have been different, but of course they are also part of the consequence here. Their destruction, I should say. Much has gone out of the world since the ring was lost.

—Well yes, Siegmund said, but we don't want to talk of that now, do we? He practiced a yawn, then turned, extended his hands. Let us leave, he said. She'll probably be down there waiting for us after all.

—Of course she will, Meyer said. She has absolutely nowhere to go.

—None of us do, Siegfried said, but in a distracted way, not really addressing anyone. They linked arms, showing somewhat more accord than they had on the way toward me—but this might only have been further evidence of newly crushed spirits—and hobbled away. As they passed into the swaddling light, I thought that one gave a suggestion of a wave but it was difficult to tell and then they were gone. It hardly mattered anyway.

I shrugged—another encounter gone—and went back to my quarters. Inside the smell of smoke was ebbing, time soon enough to throw another stick or three into the fire. Poised toadlike, their little eyes gleaming, the six Alberichts perched by the walls and stared at me, voiceless.

—I got rid of them, I said.

The Alberichts blinked, murmured, rubbed against one another.

—Simple, I said. They aren't even questioning anymore. They left in half the time that the last group did. Soon enough, they won't even ask questions. I'll just wave at them, shake my head and they'll go.

The Alberichts seemed to cackle. One chittered a question.

—Not yet, I said. It's not time.

They stared at me. I thought of the question of lost language and for a moment considered its replacement but decided that it was not time. It had been much easier, much less unpleasant with the Alberichts deprived of tongue and unable to speak.

—They'll go away soon enough, I said. But I think a few more groups will be coming through. It's a matter of purgation, that's all.

The Alberichts looked at me inquiringly. I strode over to the side, took a pair of sticks and lofted them toward the fire.

—Soon, I said, we'll go down to the river. We'll make our plans and go to the river together.

The Alberichts nodded with pleasure and anticipation. Loss of language does not mean loss of comprehension. To the contrary, it *heightens* comprehension as any good spellcaster will know. In that moment, then, it seemed that the Alberichts, just as I, understood everything.

—Mine, I said quietly. It will all be mine.

The Alberichts nodded.

—All mine, I said.

—No, a voice beyond the tent said firmly. And then through the opening, in postures of sudden menace and determination the four of them appeared, their elvish, dwarfish, gigantic features suffused with pleasure and witness.

—Not quite, Barbara said. I raised a hand, miming incantation.

She went to the pile in the corner and raised a stick.

—You see, she said. We have our own magic, old wizard.

Traitorously, the Alberichts giggled.

I think the situation has, perhaps, gotten away from me.

Down the River Road

Gregory Benford

The fairy tale is the primer from which the child learns
to read his mind in images.

—Bruno Bettelheim
The Uses of Enchantment

1. Going Ashore

The boy continued down the silver river in search of his father.

He crouched in his skiff, swaying with the rippling currents, and watched his trawling line. He had not eaten for two days. A fat yellow fish shimmered far down in the filmy water but would not bite.

Curiosity overcame hunger and he leaned over to see if the fish was nosing about his line. Instead of plump prey he saw himself, mirrored in a tin-grey metal current. But his image wore the cane hat he had lost overboard yesterday. He stared down into the trapped timeflow, which had kept pace with his skiff's downtime glide, and studied his optimistic gaze of yesterday—with smudged forehead and sprigs of greasy hair jutting around his big ears.

He edged back from the lip of the shallow-bottomed skiff. The liquid metal current was rising through the skin of water. It could sink him with a casual brush. Danger dried his mouth, tightened his throat.

Down through murky water he had glimpsed a slow churn of ivory radiance, mercury which shaped and roiled the broad, mud-streaked course. Treachery lurked in that metallic upwelling—oblong-shaped many-armers, electric vipers, fanged things that glided through the metal currents like broad-winged birds.

He lay still in the skiff bottom, hoping the time-dense flow would subside. A queasy temporal swell oozed through his gangly body, and to distract himself from the nausea he gazed up at the great spreading forest which hung overhead.

Patches of bare worldwall shimmered there, opulent with smoldering glows. The world was tubular, its sole great river a shiny snake that wound through bluffs and forests. Downriver, the vast bore of his circumscribed cosmos faded into mist. He could see a sizable city there beside a shimmering bend in the river. Behind him, uptime, he could make out the immense curve of the world and its rich hills until perspective warped and blurred them. He was tempted to take out his binoculars to see—

A thump against the skiff. Something heavy, moving.

He held his breath. Normally the skiff moved feather-light, responding to the rub and press of the air's very compression behind him as he voyaged down the silver river and thus accelerated through time.

Irregular patches of bare crust overhead gave forth smatterings of prickly light. He wished for a moment of darkness, to hide him. There was no sun here, and the boy had never seen a star to know what that word meant. Light came splintering down from the crust spots, like volcanoes of iridescence spattering the land on the opposite curve of the world-tube. He knew as well, only because his father had told him, that these shifting colors were the transmuted glow of monstrous collisions between unknown energies, distant flares vast and unknowable, the unfurling heritage of meaningless violence beyond human ken.

Something worried the water's surface.

He sat up and reached for his paddle and a skinny thing shot out of the water and snapped past his head. He ducked and slapped the tendril with his paddle. A knobby head with slitted yellow eyes heaved up from the wrinkled water. It smoked acrid green, out of its metal element, and struck at him again. He swung the paddle. It caught the tendril and sliced through.

The mercury-beast bleated and splashed and was gone. He dug into the water with the paddle—half its blade sheared cleanly off—and thrust hard. Splashing behind.

He labored into deeper water. The green fumes swirled away. When the currents calmed he veered toward shore. The big-jawed predator could snap him from the surface in an instant, crunch his skiff in two, if it could extend out of the low-running streams of silver-grey mercury and ruddy bromium. A turbulent swell had brought it up, and might again.

His arms burned and his breath rasped well before the prow ran aground. Hurriedly he splashed ashore, tugging a frayed rope. He got the skiff up onto a mud flat and into a copse and slid it far back to hide it among leafy branches.

Pondering and weak, he fetched forth some stringy dried blue meat to quiet the rumble in his stomach.

He peered overhead at the curved canopy of distant forest and patchy mud flats. These told him nothing of what he could expect here beside the river, of course, and he decided to explore a little. This was far down the river. He had fallen asleep last night again, sucked into slumber by a darkening of the world-tube, and might have drifted at a fair clip past Lord knew how many reefs and towns. The silent enormity of the river insulated a lonely skiff from the rhythms of land and made coasting downstream and downtime natural, silkily inevitable.

He walked upshore, into the silent press of time that felt at first like a mild summer's breeze but drained the energy of anyone who worked against it. As he went he eyed the profusion of stalks and trunks and tangled blue-green masses which crouched close to the river's edge. No signs of people. So he was unprepared for the man with a duckbill blunderbuss who stepped from behind a massive tree trunk and just grinned.

"What's the name?" the man asked, spitting first.

"John."

"Walking upriver?"

Better to skirt the question than to lie. "Looking for food."

"Find any?"

"Hardly had a chance to."

"Couldn'ta come far. Big storm just downstream from here." The man grinned broadly, showing brown teeth, lips thin and bloodless. "I saw it pull a man's arms off."

So he knew John couldn't have just strolled here from downstream. John said casually, "I walked down from the point, the one with the big old dead tree."

"I know that place, been there once. Plenty berries and footfruit there. Why come lookin' here?"

"I heard there's a big city this way."

"More like a town, kid. Me, I think you oughta stay out here in the wild with us."

"Who's 'us'?"

"Some fellas." The man's fixed grin soured at the edges.

"I got to be getting on, mister."

"This baby here says you got fresh business." He displayed the blunderbuss as though he had invented it.

"I got no money."

"Don't want or need money, boy. Your kind, my friends will sure enjoy seeing you."

He gestured with the blunderbuss for John to walk. John saw no easy way to get around the big weapon so he strode off, the man following at a cautious distance.

The blunderbuss was in fact the ornate fruit of a tree John had once seen. The weapons grew as hard pods on the slick-barked trees and had to be sawed off when they swelled to maturity. This one had a flange that opened into a gnarled ball and then flared further into the butt— all part of the living weapon, which if stuck butt-down in rich soil, with water and daylight, grew cartridges for the gun. From the size of the butt he guessed that this was a full-grown weapon and would carry plenty of shots.

He stumbled through a tangle of knife grasses, hearing the man snicker at his awkwardness, and then came to a pink clay path. Plainly this man planned to bring him to some kind of mean-spirited reception, and the boy had not a clue about what that could mean. Simple thieving, or a spot of buggery—these he had heard of and even witnessed.

But the man's rapt, hot-eyed gaze spoke of more. Something beyond a boy's world, from the unknown swamp of adulthood.

What should he do? His mind churned fruitlessly.

John's breath rasped and quickened as he took his time on the steepening path. Like most footways, this one moved nearly straight away from the river, and thus a traveler suffered neither the chilly press of uptime nor the nauseating slide of downtime. John judged the path would probably rise into the dry-brown foothills ahead. Insects hung and buzzed in the stillness of slumberous, sliding moments. A few bit.

He thought furiously. They passed through a verdant, hummocky field and then up ahead around a sharp bend the boy saw, just a few steps beyond, a deep shiny iron-grey stream that gurgled down toward the river, and a dead muskbat that lay in the gummy clay path.

A muskbat never smells grand and this one, at least a day dead, filled the air with a sharp reek.

John gave no sign, just held his breath. The stream murmured beside him. Its weak time-churn unsteadied his step only a little. A fallen

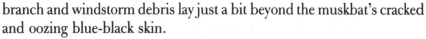

branch and windstorm debris lay just a bit beyond the muskbat's cracked and oozing blue-black skin.

He stepped straight over the muskbat and three steps more. As he turned the man breathed in the repulsive tang and his swarthy face contorted. The man drew back, foot in midair, and the blunderbuss wavered away.

John snatched up the branch. Without meaning to he sucked in the putrid fumes. He had to clench his throat tight to stop his stomach from betraying him. He leaped at the man. In midair he swung the branch, wood seeking wood, and felt a sharp jolt as he connected.

"Ah!" the man cried in pain. The blunderbuss sprang into the air and tumbled crazily into the stream—

—which dissolved the gun with a stinging hiss and explosive puff of fragrant orange steam. The man gaped at this, at John—and took a step back.

"Now you," John said because he could think of nothing else.

He got the words out at his lowest bass register. With a devouring metal rivulet nearby, any wrestling could bring disintegrating death in a flicker. John felt his knees turn to water, his heart jump into his throat.

The man fled. Scampered away with a little hoarse cry.

John blinked in surprise and then beat his own retreat, to escape the virulent muskbat fumes. He stopped at the edge of a viny tangle and looked back at the stream.

His chest filled with sudden pride. He had faced down a full-grown man. He!

Only later did he realize that the man was legitimately more frightened than John was—for he faced a wild-eyed boy of some muscle, ungainly but armed with a fair-sized club. So the man had prudently escaped, his dirty shirt-tail flapping like a harrying rebuke behind him.

2. Confusion Winds

John skirted away from the foothills, in case the swarthy man came looking with his friends. He headed downstream, marching until sleep overcame him. By keeping a good long distance from the river he hoped to avoid the time storm the man had mentioned—assuming it wasn't a lie.

The river was always within view from any fair-sized rise, since the land curved up toward the territories overhead. The sheen of clear water blended with the ruddy mud flats at this distance, so that John could barely pick out the dabs of silver and tin-grey that spoke of deadly undercurrents.

He had arisen and found some mealy brush fruit for breakfast and had set off again when he felt a prickling at the nape of his neck. A ripple passed by. It pinched his chest and stung his eyes. Hollow booms volleyed through the layered air.

He looked up. Across the misty expanse he could make out the far side of the world. It was a clotted terrain of hills and slumped valleys, thick with a rainbow's wonder of plant life, dappled lakes, snaky streams—all tributaries to the one great river. As he watched, the overhead arch compressed, like an accordion he had seen an old lady playing once—and then the squeezing struck him as well. Clutched his ribs, strained at his neck and ankles as though trying to pull him apart. Trees creaked, teetered, and one old black one crashed over nearby. He lay on moist, fragrant humus where he had fallen and watched the massive constriction of his entire world inch its way downstream, a compression wave passing and then relaxing, like the digesting spasm of a great beast. Strata groaned, rocks shattered. A final peal like a giant's hammer rolled over the leafy canopy.

He had only seen five ripples in all his life and this one was more unsettling, for as he watched it proceed on he saw through his binoculars for the first time the spires of the city, and saw one tumble in a glimmering instant as the great wave passed. Somehow he had thought of cities—or *towns,* as the man had said, a word strange to John—as grand places free of the rub of raw nature, invulnerable.

He moved on quickly. A purple radiance played among the ripe forest, shed by a big patch of raw worldwall which stretched beside a shiny lake, far across the world. Thoughts of the city possessed him, ideas of how to track his father, and so he forgot the time storm.

At first he felt a wrenching in the pit of his stomach. Then the humid air warped, perverting perspectives, and confusion rode the winds.

His feet refused to land where he directed them unless he kept constant attention, his narrowed eyes holding the errant limbs continually in view. Cordwood-heavy, his arms gained and lost weight as they swung. To turn his head without planning was to risk a fall. He labored on, panting. Hours oozed past. He ate, napped, kept on. The air sucked strength from muscles and sent itchy traceries playing on his skin.

The whispering tendrils of stupefaction left him as he angled toward the city. He sagged with fatigue. Three spires remained ahead, white-wash-bright, the most palatial place he had ever seen. Houses of pale polished wood were lined up neat and sure beside rock-roads laid arrow-straight with even the slate slabs cut square and true.

These streets thronged with more people than John could count. Ladies in finery stepping gingerly over horse dung, coarse frolickers lurching against walls, tradesmen elephantine and jolly, foul-witted quarrelers, prodigious braggarts, red-faced hawkers of everything from sweets to saws. All swarming like busybody insects and abuzz with talk.

To John it was like trying to take a drink from a waterfall. He wandered the gridded streets unnoticed, acutely conscious of his ragged clothes and slouch hat. He sought the one thing he did know, the river.

Along the big stone quay men loafed in the rising, insect-thronged heat. They slouched in split-bottomed chairs tilted back to the point of seeming dynamical impossibility, chins on chests, hats tipped down over drowsy eyes. A six-legged sow and her brood grunted by, doing a good business in droppings from split crates.

Beyond this slow scene lay the river, half-shadowed by the fitful radiance of three overhead worldwall patches, shining richly where the light struck it sure. John took off his pack and sat on a wharf railing and looked at the river's ceaseless undulation, broken by shards of raw silver which broke the surface, fumed, and were gone.

"Lookin' for work?"

The voice was rough. It belonged to a boy somewhat older than John but bigger, broad shoulders bursting his crosshatched shirt. But the eyes were dreamy, warm.

"Might be." He would need money here.

"Got some unloadin' to do. Never 'nuff hands." The young man held out a broad palm. They shook. "Name's Stan."

"Mine's John. Heavy stuff?"

"Moderate. We got droners to help."

Stan jabbed a thumb at a line of five slumped figures seated along the jetty. John had seen these before, only upriver they were called Zoms. They all sat the same way, legs sprawled out in front, arms slack, weight on the lower spine at a steep angle. No man could sit in that manner for long. Zoms didn't seem to mind. Just about anything seemed better than being dead.

"You new?" Stan asked, squatting down beside John and scribbling something on a clipboard with a pencil stub.

"Just came in."

"Raft?"

"Skiff. Landed up above that storm."

Stan whistled. "And walked around? Long way. That ripple knock you flat?"

"Tried to."

"Be a lotta trouble to get back to your skiff."

"I might just push on down."

"Really?" Stan brightened. "How far you come?"

"I don't know."

"Angel's Point? Rockport?"

"I heard of them. Saw Alberts but it was foggy."

"You're from *above* Rockport? And just a kid?"

"I'm older than I look," John said stiffly.

"You *do* have a funny accent."

John gritted his teeth. "So do you, to my ear."

"I thought, comin' this far downtime, you'd get sick, go crazy, or something." Stan seemed truly impressed, his eyes wide.

"I didn't just shoot down." That was a dumb mistake, even a boy knew that. "I stopped some to . . . explore."

"For what?"

John shifted uneasily. He shouldn't have said anything. The less people knew about you, the less they could use. "Treasure."

"Like hydrogen? Big market for hydrogen chunks here."

"No, more like—" John struggled to think of something that made sense. "Jewels. Ancient rubies and all."

"No foolin'? I've never seen any."

"They're rare. Left over from the olden lords and ladies."

Stan opened his mouth and stuck his tongue up into his front teeth in an expression of intense thought. "Uh . . . Who were *they*?"

"Primeval people. Ones from *waaay* uptime. They were so rich then, 'cause there were so few of them, that the sapphires and gold just dripped off their wrists and necks."

Wide-eyed now. "Earnest?"

"They had so much, it was like the dust in the road to them. Sometimes when they got bored, the ladies'd snatch up a whole gob of jewels, their very finest, all glittery and ripe, and they'd stick them all over some of those big hats they wore. Come a flood, people would drown and those jewel-fat hats would come downtime."

"Hats?" Open-mouthed wonder.

An airy wave of his hand. "Not the slouch hats we wear down here. I'm talkin' big boomer hats, made of, well, hydrogen itself."

"Hydro—" Stan stopped, a look of puzzlement washing across his face, and John saw that he had to cover that one.

"See, those prehistoric days, hydrogen was even lighter than it is to-day. So they wore it. The very finest of people weaved it into fancy vests and collars and hats."

A doubtful scowl. "I never saw anybody . . ."

"Well, see now, that's just the thing. My point exactly. Those olden ladies and gents, they wore out all the hydrogen. That's why it's worth so much today."

Stan's mouth made an awe-struck O. "That's wondrous, plain won-drous. I mean, I knew hydrogen was the lightest metal. Strongest, too. No puzzlement it's what every big contractor and engine-builder wants, only can't get. But"—he looked sharply at John—"how come you know?"

"How come a kid knows?" Might as well feed him back that remark. "Because uptime, we're closer to the archaic ages. We look out for those hydrogen hats that came down the river and washed up."

Stan frowned. "Then why'd you come down here?"

For an instant John had the sick feeling that he was caught out. The whole story was going to blow up on him. He would lose this job and go hungry tonight.

Then he blinked and said, "Uptime people already *got* the hats that came ashore there. It's the ones that got past them that I'm after."

"Aaahhh . . ." Stan liked this and at once began to shoot out questions about the grand hats and treasure hunting, how John did it, what he'd found, and so on. It was a relief when somebody called, "Induction ship!" and the sleepy quay came to life.

3. The Zom

The big white ship seemed to John to snap into existence, trim and sharp as it bore down upon them. It cut the river, curling water like a foamy shield, sending gobbets of iron-grey liquid metal spraying before it.

It was a three-decker with gingerbread railings and a pyramid-shaped pilot house perched atop. Large, thick disks dominated each side, humming loudly as it decelerated. Only these induction disks, which had to cast their field lines deep into the river and thrust the great boat forward, were untouched by the eternal habit of ornamentation. Curlicues trickled down each stanchion. Pillars had to be crowned with ancient scrollwork, the flybridge carried sculptures of succoring angels, davits and booms and mastheads wore stubby golden helmets.

Passengers lined the ornate railings as the boat slowed, foam leaped in the air, and backwash splashed about the stone quay. A whistle sounded eerily and deck hands threw across thick ropes.

Stan caught one and looped it expertly about a stay. "Come on!"

Crowds had coagulated from somewhere, seeming to condense out of the humidity onto the jetty and quay. A hubbub engulfed the induction ship. Crates and bales descended on crane cables. Wagons rumbled forth to take them and John found himself in a gang of Zoms, tugging and wrestling the bulky masses. Crowds yawped and hailed and bargained with vortex energy all around.

The Zoms followed Stan's orders sluggishly, their mouths popping open as they strained, drool running down onto their chests. These were corpses kindled back to life quite recently, and so still strong, though growing listless. Zoms were mostly men, since they were harvested for heavy manual labor. But a hefty woman labored next to John and between loads she put her hand on his leg, directly and simply, and then slipped her fingers around to cup his balls. John jerked away, her reek biting in his nostrils. Zoms hungered for life. Perhaps they knew that they would wither, dwindling into torpid befuddlement, within months. The heavy woman leered at him and felt his ass. He moved away from her, shivering.

And bumped into a shabby Zom man who turned sluggishly and mumbled, "John. John."

The boy peered into the filmed eyes and slack mouth. Parchment skin stretched over stark promontories of the wrecked face. Memories stirred. Some faint echo in the cheekbones? The sharp nose?

"John . . . Father . . ."

"No!" John cried.

"John . . . came here . . . time . . ." The Zom reached unsteadily for the boy's shoulder. It was in the tottering last stages of its second life, the black mysteries' energy now seeping from it.

"You're not my father! Get away."

The Zom gaped, blinked, reached again.

"No!" John pushed the Zom hard and it went down. It made no attempt to catch itself and landed in a sprawl of limbs. It lay inert, filmed eyes peering at the hazy other side of the world.

"Hey, it botherin' you?" Stan asked.

"Just, they just get to me, is all."

John studied the slack-jawed face and resolved that this Zom could not possibly be his father. There was really no resemblance at all, now that he took a close and objective scrutiny.

"Let it lay there," Stan said dismissively. "We got work to do."

The rest of the unloading John helped carry out without once looking toward the crumpled form. Ladies stepped gingerly over the Zom and a passing man kicked it, all without provoking reaction.

The labor was fast and hard, for the induction ship was already taking on its passengers. By the time John returned from a nearby warehouse where the first wagonload went, only ripples in the mud-streaked river showed that the ship had tarried there at all.

4. Mr. Preston

That day was long and hard, what with plenty of barrels and hogs-heads and wooden crates to unlash and sort out and stack in the crumbling stone warehouse. Stan was subagent for one of the big importation enterprises and had a steady run of jobs, so John was kept busy the rest of the day. The Zoms from the quay wore out quickly and Stan brought out another crew of them. John did not see the one that had collapsed and did not go looking for it in the musty rear of the warehouse where they were kept, either.

The laboring day ended as the big bare patch of worldwall overhead dimmed. This was a lucky occurrence, as people still preferred to sleep in darkness, and though there was no cycle of day and night here, a few hours of shadow were enough to set most into the slumber they needed. John had once seen a night that lasted several "days" so that folks began to openly speculate whether the illumination would ever return to the worldwall. When the sulphurous glow did return it waxed into stifling heat and piercing glare so ferocious that everyone regretted their earlier impatience for it.

Stan took John to his own boarding house and arranged for him, leaving just enough time for a bath of cold river water before supper.

John was amazed at the boarding table to see the rapid-fire putting away of victuals combined with fast talking, as though mouths were meant to chew and blab at the same time. Game hens roasted to golden brown appeared on an immense platter and were seized and devoured before they reached him, though Stan somehow managed to get two and shared. A skinny man with a goatee opposite John cared only for the amusements of his mouth, alternately chewing, joking and spitting none too accurately into a brass spittoon set beside him. Stan ate only with his knife, nonchalantly inserting the blade sometimes all the way into his mouth. John managed to get forkfuls of gummy beans and thick slabs of gamy meat into himself before dessert came flying by, a concoction featuring an island of hard nuts in a sea of cream which burst into flame when a man touched his cigar to it. Stan ate one and then contentedly sat back in his wicker chair, picking his teeth with a shiny pocket knife, an exhibition of casual bravery unparalleled in John's experience.

Afterward John wanted more than anything to sleep, but Stan enticed him into the hubbub streets. They ended up in a bar dominated for a time by an immense, well-lubricated woman whose tongue worked well in its socket, her eyes rolling as she sang a ballad John could not fathom. At the end of it she then fell with a crash to the floor and it took three men to carry her out. John could not decide whether this was part of the act or not, for it was more entertaining than the singing.

Stan thrust some dark beer upon him and artfully took that moment to pay John his day's wages, which of course made John seem a piker if he did not buy the next round, which came with unaccountable speed. He was halfway through that mug and thinking better of this evening, of this huge complex city, of his fine new friend Stan, and generally of the entire world itself, when he recalled how his own father had said that in their family one discarded a cork once pulled from a bottle, knowing with assurance that it would not be needed again.

This connection troubled him, but Stan relieved John's frown by stretching his legs out and sticking a sock-clad foot up. The sock had a face sewed on it so that Stan could jiggle his toes and make the face show anger, smile, even blink. All the while Stan carried on a funny conversation with the artistic foot. But this made John remember his first day at the orphanage, cold and bleak, when a tall boy had stuck his grey-socked foot from beneath some covers. John mistook it for a rat and threw his knife, skewering the foot. That had made him unpopular for some time around there.

He smiled at this and had another beer sip. Stan's face went pale. John felt a presence behind him.

Turning, he saw a tall man dressed in leather jacket and black pants, sporting a jaunty blue cap. No one but pilots could wear such a cap with its gold flashings across the bill.

"Mr.—Mr. Preston," Stan said.

"You gentlemen out for an evening? Not too busy to discuss business?"

Mr. Preston smiled with an austere good nature, as befitted a representative of the only unfettered and truly independent profession John knew. Lords found themselves hampered by parliaments, ministers knew the constraints of their parishioners, even schoolteachers in their awful power finally worked for towns.

But a silver river pilot knew *no* governance. A ship's captain could give a half dozen or so orders as the induction motors readied and she backed sluggishly into the stream, but as soon as the engines engaged, the captain's rule was overthrown. The pilot could then run the vessel exactly as he pleased, barking orders without consultation and beyond criticism by mere mortals.

Without asking, Mr. Preston yanked a chair from another of the raw hardwood tables which packed the bar, and smacked it down at the boys' table. "I heard you come from uptime—*way* uptime," he said to John.

"Uh, Stan told you?" John asked to get some time to think.

"He dropped a word, yes. Was he wrong?" Mr. Preston peered at John intently, his broad mouth tilted at an assessing angle beneath a bristly brown moustache.

"Nossir. Maybe he, uh, exaggerated, though."

"Said you'd been above Rockport."

"I caught sight of it in fog. That awful pearly kind that—"

"How far beyond?"

"Not much."

"Cairo?"

"I . . . yeah, I gave it wide berth."

"Describe it."

"Big place, grander than this town."

"You see the point? With the sand reef?"

"I didn't see any reef."

"Fair enough—there isn't any reef. What's the two-horned point like?"

"Foam whipping up in the air."

"Where's the foam go?"

"Shoots out of the river and arcs across to the other horn."

"You go under the arc?"

"Nossir. I stayed in the easy water close on the other shore."

"Smart. That arc's been there since I was a boy and nobody's lived who tried to shoot with the current under it."

"I heard that too."

"Who from?"

"Fellow upstream."

"How far upstream?"

Nobody ever lied to a pilot, but you could shave the truth some. John took a sip of the dark beer that was thick enough to make a second supper—as some in the bar seemed to be doing, loudly—and said with care, "The reach above Cairo. That's where I started."

Mr. Preston leaned forward and jutted out his long jaw shrewdly. "There's a big bar there, got to go by it easy. Sand, isn't it?"

"Nossir, it's black iron."

Mr. Preston sat back and signaled the barkeep—who had been hovering, wringing a dirty rag—for a round. "Right. A plug of it that gushed up from some terrible event in the river bottom. Books say a geyser of molten metal—not the cool ones which flow under the river—that geyser came fuming up through the worldwall itself."

"How can that be? What's outside the world?"

"Not for us to know, son."

"Please don't call me son, sir."

Mr. Preston's bushy eyebrows crowded together, momentarily puzzled at the quick, hard note that had come into John's voice, but then he waved his hand in an ample gesture and said, "Well, Mr. John, I am prepared to hire your services."

Stan was looking bug-eyed at this interchange. For two lowly freight musclers to be drinking with a pilot was like a damp river rat going to dinner at the mayor's. And this latest development—!

"Services?" Stan put in, unable to restrain himself any longer.

"Navigation. There've been five big time-squalls between here and Cairo since I was up that way. Now I got a commission to take the *Natchez* up that far and no sure way of knowing the river that far."

"I'm not sure I know the river all that well," John demurred, his mind still aswarm with scattershot thoughts.

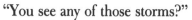

"You see any of those storms?"

"Two of them, yessir. From a distance, though."

"Only way to see one, I'd say," Stan said with forced jocularity. He was still stunned from the offer.

The pilot grimaced in agreement, an expression that told much of narrow escapes and lost friends. "You kept your skiff well clear?"

"I poled and rowed, both. Prob'ly just lucky with the currents, truth to tell."

"A time storm attracts ships according to their mass, see? Your rowing was most likely the cause of your salvation," the pilot said. "An induction ship, despite its power, must be more crafty. Its weight is its doom."

John sipped his strong beer and said, "I don't know as I want to go back up there, sir."

"I'll make it worth your while." The pilot squinted at him, as though trying to see something in John's face that he wasn't giving away. "I was hoping you might have business back up there."

Might have business. At once the Zom's face lurched into John's mind's-eye and he felt the barroom close about him, its suffocating air clotted with cigar smoke. The banks of blue fumes swirled amid the seeping yellow glow of filament bulbs which sprouted from the walls, each the size of a man's head with his hat on. John had kept his mind away from the memory until now but the weight of uncertainty again descended. He could not know if the Zom was his father unless he found it again, questioned it.

"Sir, I'm going to have to give you my reply tomorrow. I have to see to a certain matter right now."

The surprise in Stan's and Mr. Preston's faces was almost amusing. It increased when John stood, bootheels smacking the floorboards loudly from the drink he had put down. He nodded solemnly and without a word plunged into the darkness outside.

5. The Frozen Girl

Inky shapes still shifted in his mind as he knocked on the door of Mr. Preston's house. John still felt himself encased in the night.

It was a fitful morning, with grey light piercing a fog and sending traceries across the rooftops along the slumbering river. John could barely see the white picket fence framing Mr. Preston's yard. The pearly wisps blotted out detail beyond the brick walk which led to the house. This was a grand place, he had to admit, even in such diffuse light. It was porticoed in pale pine, the massive columns topped with flowery capitals. He rapped the iron door knocker again and instantly the brass doorknob turned, as if attached to the knocker. A dwarf answered, a mute servant, and led John along a carpeted hall.

He was unprepared for the grandiosity of a pilot's lodging, taking in with awe the mahogany furniture, a new electric lamp with yellow-paper shade, and an entire shelf of sound-sculptures. The dwarf retreated, gesturing at a yawning, tongueless mouth and showing the red servant tattoo on his shoulder to explain his silence.

A bounty of travel visions speckled the walls—*Above the Falls of Abraham, Volcanic Quest, Heart of Lightness, Struggle Against Destiny*—and many of literature, including the fanciful. John yearned to take the sheets and stroke them into luminosity, but as he reached for *Time Stream and World-Wrack* he heard heavy thumping footsteps and turned to find the pilot in full blue and gold uniform.

"I hope you have settled your other matter," Mr. Preston said severely.

Only now did John recall clearly his abrupt departure of the night before. The town beyond that raucous room had swallowed memory. He had made his way through narrow streets lined by rude buildings that seemed to lean out over the street, eclipsing the wan sky glow. The moist lanes near the river had been tangled and impossible to navigate without stumbling and stepping on sprawled forms, like bundles of clothing left for trash collection.

The masters of the Zoms left them where they lay, sure that they could not move without further feeding. John took hours to find the slack-jawed face he had seen on the quay, and then another long time before he was sure that the Zom was not merely in its lapsed state of rest. The thing had proved dead, limbs akimbo, stiffening into a hardened parody of a dance.

At morning the burly owner had come by, shrugged at the corpse, and thrown it into his wagon for disposal. John's questions about the Zom the big man brushed aside—he didn't know the names, no, nor where they came from, nor from what part of the river they hailed. And the last glimpse John had of that face had unsettled him further, as if in final death the Zom gave its last secret. There was a clear resemblance to his father, though John's memory from his early boyhood was shrouded by the rage, anguish and poverty of the intervening years.

So with fatigue in his bones but a fresh, iron resolve in his spine John made himself stand erect beside the oak mantelpiece and say to Mr. Preston, "I'll come, sir."

"Damn good! Here, you had breakfast?"

Cornmeal flapjacks and fritters, brought by the mistress of the house, quickly dominated John's attention while the pilot regaled him with lore and stories. John managed to keep the details of his long voyage down-river well-muddied, and was distracted from this task by Mr. Preston's collection of oddments, arrayed along the walls. There were crystals, odd-colored stones betraying volcanic abuse, a circlet of ancestral hair, five flint arrowheads from the fabled days, and some works of handicraft like dozens John had seen before. Beside these were bronze-framed, stiff images of addled-looking children, aged uncles and the like, all arranged awkwardly and in Sunday-suited best for their bout with immortality.

But these oddments were nothing compared with the large transparent cube that dominated the dining room table. It shed cold air and John took it to be ice, but as he ate he saw that no drops ran off the sleek flat sides. Within its blue-white glow small objects of art were suspended—a golden filigree, a jagged bit of quartz, two large insects with bristly feelers, and a miniature statue of a lovely young girl with red hair and a flowing white robe.

He had nearly finished inhaling the molasses-fattened flapjacks and slurping down a pot of coffee when he chanced to notice that one of the insect wings had lowered. Keeping an attentive ear to the pilot, who had launched into what appeared to be a four-volume oral autobiography in first draft, he watched and saw the girl spinning slowly about her right toe, the robe fetching up against her left leg and then gracefully playing out into a spinning disk of velvety delicacy.

By this time the insects had both flapped their transparent gossamer wings nearly through a quarter-stroke. They were both heading toward the girl. Their multifaceted eyes strobed and fidgeted with what to them must be an excited vigor, and to John was a torpid, ominous arabesque.

"Ah, the hunt," the pilot interrupted his soliloquy. "Beautiful, eh? I've been watching it for long enough to grow three beards."

"The girl, she's *alive*."

"Appears so. Though why she's so small, I cannot say."

"Where'd you get it?"

"Far downstream."

"I never saw such."

"Nor I. Indeed, I suspect, from the quality of the workmanship, that the girl is real."

"Real? But she's no bigger than my thumbnail."

"Some trick of the light makes her seem so to us, I reckon."

"And these bugs—"

"They're nearly her size, true. Maybe they're enlarged, the opposite of the trick with the girl."

"And if they aren't?"

"Then when they reach the girl they will have a merry time." The pilot grinned. "A week's pay packet, I just handed it over flat, to purchase this. That li'l golden trinket, it's revolving, too—see?"

Aghast, John felt a fresh wave of bitterly cold air waft from the cube of silent, slow time. He had an urge to smash the blue-white wedge of molasses-slow tempo, to release its wrenched epochs and imprisoning, collapsed perspectives. But this was the pilot's object, and such men understood the twists of time better than anyone. Perhaps it was right that these things belonged to them.

Still, he felt relief when he escaped from the dining room and emerged into the cloaking fog outdoors.

6. Going Upback

They were to boom out of the dock that very day. John had never known such awe as that instilled by his first moment, when he marched up the gangplank and set foot upon the already thrumming deck.

Never before had he done more than gaze in reverence and abject self-abasement at one of the induction ships as it parted the river with its razor-sharp prow. Now Mr. Preston greeted him with a curt nod, quite circumspect compared to the sprawl of the man's conversation at breakfast. With minor ceremony he received his employment papers. Other crew shook John's hand with something better than the cool indifference he knew they gave any and all passengers. The customers who paid the costs were of course held in the lowest regard of all those aboard, including the wipe-boys below. John could tell from the somewhat distant,

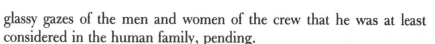

glassy gazes of the men and women of the crew that he was at least considered in the human family, pending.

"You been by that li'l flurry up ahead?" Mr. Preston asked him as they made their way up the three flights of external stairs to the pilot's nest.

"Nossir. I came ashore, stowed my skiff and walked round it."

"Ummm. Too bad. Think I'll nudge out across stream, keep some distance on it."

"Yessir."

The loading was finishing, the ship's barely restrained thirst for the river sending a strong strumming into the air. Freight spun off the wagons and flew aboard at the hands of jostling work gangs, mostly Zoms. Late passengers came dodging and scampering among the boxes and hogsheads awaiting loading. Wives carrying hat boxes and grocery knapsacks urged on sweaty husbands, who lugged carpetbags and yowling babies. Drays and baggage three-wheelers clattered over cobblestones and intersected each other's trajectories more often than seemed possible from the supposed laws of probability, sending cases and jars smashing. Profanity blued the air. Windlasses snapped into hatches, fore and aft.

John loved the turmoil and racket, the whiz and whir of earnest purpose. The bursar called, "All not goin', please to get themselfs ashore!" and last bells rang, and the thronged decks of the *Natchez* gushed their yammering burden onto the gangplanks—a running tide which a few last, late passengers fought. The stage-plank slid in and a tall man came running and tried to jump the distance. He got a purchase on the gunmetal side and a crewwoman hauled him up, but his back pocket opened and his wallet thunked into the river. The crowd ashore laughed and the woman had to stop the man from jumping in after it.

All this John watched from the elevated sanctity of the pilot's nest. It was an elegant place, glass in so many directions he had to count to be sure there were only four of the transparent walls. The Cap'n stood beside the pilot, both arrayed in their dark blue-gold uniforms, and an eerie whistle sounded. The orange flag ran up the jack-staff and the ship ceased its drift. Momentum surged through the deck and oily smoke belched from the three tall chimneys at the ship's midships.

The crowd along the quay called last-minute messages and cheered and the ship shot away from them, seeming to accelerate as it caught with induction fields the deep surge of metal beneath the waters. The town dwindled with bewildering speed, people on the quay turning into animated dolls that turned pinkish and mottled as John watched.

"The time flux," Mr. Preston answered John's frown. "I locked us onto her right off. We're seeing their images squeezed and warped."

Already the shore was dappled with reds and blues as time shifted and streamed about the ship, the slap and heave of currents resounding in deep bass notes that John felt through his big-heeled boots.

To fly across duration itself, to wrench away from the certainty of patient, single-minded time—John felt sour nausea grip his throat. Confusion swamped him as he felt their gut-deep accelerations—a quickening not in mere velocity but in the quantity which he knew governed the world but which no man could sense, the force of tangled space and time together. The firm deck went snake-slithery, thick air hummed and forked about him, the entire world took on a mottled complexion. His body fought for long, aching moments the urgent tows and tugs, his chest tight, bowels watery, knees feather-light—and then somehow his sinews found their equilibrium, without his conscious effort. He gulped in air and found it moist and savory.

"Steady." Mr. Preston had been eyeing him, he now saw. "I reckoned you'd come through, but can't be sure till it's done."

"What if I hadn't?"

The pilot shrugged. "Put you ashore next stop, nothing else for it."

"What about passengers?"

"It's easier down below. Up here, the tides are worse."

"Tides?" He studied the river's expanse, which looked table-flat from here.

"Not river tides—time-tides. Passengers with addled heads and stomachs can just lie down till we reach their getoff point. Most, anyway."

John had always figured that the job of a pilot was to keep his ship on the river, which was not a considerable feat, since it was so wide. Silently watching Mr. Preston trim and slip among the upwellings of rich brown mud, and then slide with liquid grace along a burnt-golden reef of bromium metal, he saw the dancer's nimbleness and ease that came from the whirling oak-spoked master wheel, the orchestrated animal mutter of the induction motors, the geometric craft of rudder and prow. To have this elegant gavotte interrupted was not merely an inconvenience, and dangerous, but an aesthetic atrocity.

This John learned when a trading scow came rushing down the wash-

board-rough main current and into the *Natchez*'s path. Rather than per-
turb his elegant course, Mr. Preston ran across the scow's two aft steering
oars. Scarcely had the snapping and crunching ceased than a volley of
gnarled profanity wafted up from the clutch of red faces shooting by to
starboard. Mr. Preston's face lit up with a positive joy, for here were fit
targets who could, unlike the *Natchez*'s crew, *talk back*.

Joy of joys! He snatched open the roller window and stuck his head
out and erupted back at the scow. And as the two ships separated and
the scowmen's maledictions grew fainter, Mr. Preston poured on both
volume and ferocity, calling upon gods and acts John had never heard
of. When Mr. Preston rolled the window shut on its spool the pilot was
emptied of malice, all tensions of the departure now well fled.

"My, sir, that was a good one," a voice said at John's elbow. It was
Stan, beaming with appreciation of the pungent profanity.

Not an opportune appearance. Mr. Preston skewered him with a glare.
"Deckhands with opinions? Nose to the planking, you!"

So it was hours before John learned why Stan was on the *Natchez* at
all, for Stan spent his time manicuring the already immaculate-looking
pilot's nest and then the iron stairs and pine gangways nearby. When
John found him slurping a steaming cup of blackbean in the rear galley
Stan waxed eloquent.

"*Treasure*, that's why I signed on. Deckhand pays next to nothin' and
the time-current made me sick a sec or two, but I'm going to stick it
out."

"Uh, treasure?"

"I'm already looking for those hydrogen hats. Nobody never spied any
this far downstream, so I figure you overshot, John, coming as far down
as us. They got to be above us, for sure."

John nodded and listened to Stan gush about the star sapphires and
fat rubies awaiting them and barely avoided laughing and giving it all
away. On the other hand, it had brought him a friend in a place he
found daunting.

"Too bad you had to give up your quest, though," Stan said slyly.

"What?" John was using a bowl of bluebeans to keep his mouth busy
and was brought up short by this odd remark.

"You overshot another way. That Zom was who you wanted to find.
Only you wanted the man in his first life, and that lies upstream."

How Stan could swallow whole the hydrogen hat story and yet put together the truth about John's father from little slivers was a confound-ment. John acknowledged this with a grunt and a begrudging nod, but cut off further talk.

He had learned early in his downstreaming not to allow others to indulge in yet another sentimental tale of a poor boy without a mother's love or a father's strong arm, heaved all unfriended upon the cold charity of a censorious world. That was not the truth of it and if he did tell them true they drew back in white-eyed horror.

7. Temporal Turbulence

The river's easy water lay close ashore. There the deep streams of bromium and mercury allowed the induction coils a firm grip, while the water current sped best in midstream. No vaporizing, hull-searing brom-ium streams broke surface here, so the watch was comparatively at ease.

Mr. Preston explained that the *Natchez* had to hug the bank, thus separating it from the downstreaming craft that lazed in the middle, harvesting the stiff current. John learned a few of the deft tricks for ne-gotiating the points, bends, bars, islands and reaches which encumbered the route. He resolved early that if he ever became a pilot he would stick to downtiming and leave the uptiming to those dead to caution.

But the time storm afflicted both types of craft.

Murmuring dark fell as they cut across river before the whorl of time that awaited. It rose siphon-like at midriver, whereas reports as recent as yesterday back in town had said it clung to the shore opposite where the *Natchez* now picked its way.

"Moving quick, it is," Mr. Preston said sternly at the wheel.

The whirling foam-white column dimpled and reddened the images of forest and plain above it. John stood to the corner of the pilot's nest and soon exhausted everything he could remember about seeing the storm days before, which proved of no use, for the tempest had grown and shaped itself into a twisted figure-eight knot that spewed black water and grey-metal fountains.

Rain pelted the pilot's-nest windows. The cyclone air sucked light from around them. Blue-black traceries made a fretwork above. Toward shore John saw the trees dim into spider-web outlines. Winds whipped and blasted at the *Natchez,* bending trees and turning up the pale un-derside of their leaves so that waves of color washed over the canopy.

Trees tossed their arms as if in panic and with a shriek one of the *Natchez*'s chimneys wrenched and split and the top half flopped down on the foredeck. Crew ran out to cut it free and toss it overboard. John saw Stan with them, sawing frantically as the wind blasted them nearly off their feet. Peals of profanity blossomed on lips, so close John could read them, but a gust whipped the words away.

This was no ordinary wind. It ripped and cut the air, warping images so that men laboring seemed to go in agonizing slow motion, then frantic speed, all the while stretched and yanked and pounded out of shape by invisible forces.

Then—*sssssttt!*—a vacuum hiss jerked a brilliant glory-filled radiance into the sky. An ethereal glow flooded the deck. Yet ashore lay in gloom. Treetops plunged and wrestled with imaginary antagonists. At midriver foam spouted.

Another *ssssstttt!* and a crash and the ship fell a full man's height, splashing itself into a bath of hot effervescence. In a fragment of a second the air got dark as sin and thunder rumbled across the sky like empty barrels rolling down stone stairs.

And then they were out, the gale was a scenic protuberance on a mild river again, and the pilot said, "Temporal turbulence was mild this go."

It did not seem so to John but he sat on a stool and got his breathing in order again.

When he saw Stan later the young man said, surprised, "Twist? Stretched legs? I never felt any such," and John understood that the shiftings and unsteadiness of both time and space were the province of an observer. But the truncated chimney, now being hastily restored by Stan and others in a full sweat, spoke of how real the waverings of time could be.

They cut across once more, skirting a big bar of aluminum that gleamed dully and could snatch the hull from an induction ship in a passing instant. This took the *Natchez* near the shore where John had left his skiff. With Mr. Preston's binoculars he searched the blue-green brush but could find no trace of it.

"Somebody *stole* it," he said, outraged.

"Or else ate it," the pilot said, smiling.

"I didn't grow that skiff, it's not alive. I sawed and hammered it into being."

"Maybe time ate it," was all the pilot would say.

The shore seemed watery and indeterminate, a blue-green emulsion.

As they beat their way upstream his respect for the pilot grew. No prominence would stick to its shape long enough for John to make up his mind what form it truly was. Hills dissolved as if they were butter mountains left on a dining room table during a warm Sunday afternoon.

Yet Mr. Preston somehow knew to make the *Natchez* waltz to starboard at some precise spot, else—he explained—the ship would have a grave misunderstanding with a snag that would rip them stem to stern in the time it took a man to yawn. The murky waste of water and slumbering metal laid traps for timeboaters of all keel depths.

Mr. Preston made her shave the head of an island where a small temporal vortex had just broken from the misty skin of the river, trimming it so close that trees banged and brushed the stern, nearly taking off a curious passenger—who hurriedly disembarked at their first stop, leaving his bag. He babbled something about haunted visions of headless women he had seen in the air. The crew guffawed and made faces. John joined them.

8. The Eating Ice

The vagaries of induction ships were of terrifying legend. Most folk who lived near the river—and many, indeed most, chose not to—reported seeing ships that winked into existence at a wharf, offloaded people and bags in a spilling hurry, and slipped away with motors whining, to vanish moments later by first narrowing, then becoming a door-thin wedge which sometimes rose up into the air before thinning into nothingness.

People who tried to keep pace with a ship felt a pressure like a massive unseen hand upon them. They tired, especially going upstream. Thus most lived within less than a day's walk of where they had been born. By straining effort a strong man or woman could take foot or horse into a distant town to find a price for a fresh crop, say, or purchase goods. Most preferred to let the induction ships ply their trade up and down, hauling bales of finespun, say, and returning with store-bought wonders ordered from a gaudy catalog.

Some, though, booked passage on the ships, as much for the ride as for the destination. The *Natchez*'s main rooms were well appointed with opulent armchairs and stuffed davenports, the doorways garnished with bone-white wooden filigree of fanciful patterns and famous scenes of

time-distortion. There was a technicolor symbolical mural of great pilots
in the main lounge, and in first-class cabins a porcelain doorknob and
a genuine full-wall image sheet which gave an artistic view when ca-
ressed. The public rooms featured curving ceilings touched up with
elegant gilt, and rainshower-style chandeliers of glittering glass-drops.
Day passengers could get down to shirt-sleeves and use a long row of
bowls in the barber shop, which also boasted public towels, stiff public
combs and fragrant public soap.

All this impressed John mightily. He had never, not even in the pilot's
own house, seen such opulence and finery. Passengers boarding from
the small, straggling, shabby hamlets along shore echoed his wide-eyed
reverence. Three days of cruising brought a certain bemused certitude
to him, though, so that he gazed at these scruffy travelers in their baggy
clothes with the same elevated scorn as the older crew.

Not that he inhabited the same celestial sphere as the pilot himself.
Mr. Preston's face wore lines earned by watching the immemorial clashes
of differing temporal potentials. His speech veered from elegant, educated downriver cadences, to slurred, folk-wise vernacular. Pilots boated
in eternity, and they knew it.

John was along for his passingly useful knowledge, not his skill. So
when the induction coils froze up he hustled below on sharply barked
command of the Cap'n, just as did Stan and the rest. Mr. Preston stayed
aloft, of course.

The vast engine room was a frenzy of shouted orders and shoving
bodies. The power that drove them uptime came separately from the
huge copper armature, which spun, when working properly, between
mammoth black iron magnets.

Normally, running into the river's past would suck great gouts of energy from the whirling metal. But in cross-cutting the river, snaking
through reefs and bromium upwellings, the pilot would sometimes end
up running at crosscurrent to the normal, and they would move for a
while upstream, as far as the normal water current was concerned, but
downstream and thus downtime, as the temporal contortions saw it.

There was no general sign of this, though John thought he glimpsed
far out in the river a huge, ghostly ship that flickered into being for a
mere shaved second. It had great fat towers belching grimy smoke, port-
holes brimming with violet light. A craft hovered in the air like a gar-
gantuan insect, vanes churning the mist above, as if it were a swollen
predator mosquito about to attack a metal whale.

Then—*ssstttpp!*—wind had whistled where the vision had floated, and a cry from below announced an all-hands.

Stan showed him the coated pipes and cables, already crusted a hand deep in hard, milk-white ice. Boilers nearby radiated intense heat into the room, but the time-coursing inside the pipes and cables sucked energy from them so quickly that the ice did not melt.

John and all other crew members fell to chipping and prying and hammering at the ice. It was solid stuff. A chunk fell off into John's hand and he momentarily saw the surface of a pipe that led directly into the interior of the induction motors. Though normally shiny copper, now the pipe was eerily black.

He stuck his nose in close to see and heard the *crack* of air itself freezing to the metal.

"Hey, get back!" a crewwoman shouted, yanking him away just as the entire gap he had opened snapped shut abruptly—air whooshing into the vacuum created, then freezing instantly itself, in turn sucking in more air.

Another man was not so fortunate, and froze three fingers rock-solid in a momentary crevice in the pipe ice. His cries scarcely turned a head as they all labored to break off and heat away the fast-growing white burden.

A cable sagged under its accumulating weight and snapped free. The high whine of electrical power waned when it did, and John felt real fear.

He had heard the tales of induction ships frozen full up this way, the infinite cold of inverse time sucking heat, life, air and self from them. The victim ships were found, temporally displaced years and miles from their presumed location, perpetual ivory icebergs adrift on the seemingly placid river.

John hacked and pried and at last sledge-hammered the ice. The frost groaned and shrugged and creaked as it swelled, like some living thing moaning with growing pains.

Across the engine room he heard another cry as a woman got her ankle caught by the snatching ice. Gales shrieked in to replace the condensing air. Voices of the crew rose in panic.

And the Cap'n's bellow rang above it all, giving orders—"Belay that! Lever it out, man, *heave* on that crowbar! Thomson, run there quick! Smash it, son!"

—and abruptly the howling winds faded, the ice ceased surging.

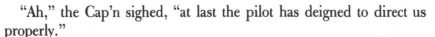

"Ah," the Cap'n sighed, "at last the pilot has deigned to direct us properly."

John took some offense at this, for no pilot ever could read the true vector of the time-current flux. Mr. Preston had brought them out of it, which should be fair enough.

There were awful tales of ships truly mispiloted. Of induction craft hurtling uptime out of control—solid iceberg ships, with deep-frozen crew screaming upstream toward the beginning of time. Of downriver runaways, white-hot streaks that exploded long before they could reach the legendary waterfall at the end of eternity.

But the Cap'n reflected on none of that. John learned then that the high station of a pilot implies harsh criticism at the slightest hint of imperfection.

9. Cairo

Casks and barrels and hogsheads blocked the quay but could not conceal from the pilot's nest the sprawling green beauty of the city.

Even the blocks of commercial warehousing sprouted verdant and spring-fresh from the soil. Cairo had perfected the fast-spreading art of growing itself from its own rich loam. This art was much easier than planting and raising trees, only to chop them down, slice them with band saws, plane them out and fashion them elaborately into planks, beams, joists, braces, girders, struts and dowels, all to make shelter.

Such easeful grace demanded a deep sort of knowing, of course. The folk of Cairo fathomed the double-twisted heart of living things.

The *Natchez* rang three bells as it docked. Uprivermen often had a woman in every port and the bells announced which Cap'n this was, so that the correct lady could come to welcome him—sometimes for only an hour or two layover, in his cabin, before departure for the next port uptime. The vagaries and moods of the time currents led to many a hasty assignation. But the Cap'n might enjoy another such succulent dalliance quite soon—if he were physically able.

A red-faced lady brushed by John on the gangplank as he went ashore. He gave her no notice as he contemplated the overnight here in the river's biggest city.

His head was crammed with lore he had learned in the pilot's nest, knowing that his challenge came next. At once he went to Cairo city hall and consulted the log of citizens. There was no notation concerning his father, but then it had been a forlorn hope anyway. His father was never one to let a piece of paper tag along behind like a dog, only to bite him later. John swallowed the disappointment and let his long-simmering anger supply him with fresh energy.

Stan caught up to him and together they patrolled the streets, Stan doing the talking and John striding with hands in pockets, bewitched by the sights.

The self-grown houses rose seamlessly from fruitful soil. Seed-crafters advertised with gaudy signs, some the new neon-piping sort which spelled out whole words in garish, jumpy brilliance—*Skillgrower, Houseraiser,* even *Custom Homeblossoms.*

They wandered through raucous bars, high-arched malls, viny factory-circles, and found them smoothly, effortlessly elegant, their atmospheres moist with fragrances which issued from their satiny woods. Women worked looms which grew directly from the damp earth. Stan asked one of these laboring ladies why they could not simply grow their clothes straight on the bush, and she laughed, replying, "Fashion changes much too quick for that, sir!" and then smothered a giggle at Stan's misshapen trousers and sagging jacket.

This put Stan of a mind to carouse, and soon John found himself strolling through a dimly lit street which reeked of, as Stan put it, "used beer."

The women who lounged in the doorways here were slatternly in their scarlet bodices and jet-black, ribbed corsets. John felt his face flush and recalled a time long ago, in the county school he had been forced to attend. They had made fun of him there simply because he was from the orphanage. The boys' athletic coach had given them all a sheet of special paper and a pen that wrote invisibly, with orders to draw a circle for each time they masturbated—"shaking hands with your best friend," he called it. The invisibility was to preclude discovery and embarrassment.

At the end of a month they had all brought the sheets in. The coach had hung them up in rows and darkened the classroom, then turned on a special lamp. Its violet glow revealed the circles, ranks upon ranks of them, to the suddenly silent boys. "This," the coach had said, "is the way God sees you. Your inner life."

The aim of all this displayed sin was to get the boys to cut down on their frequency, for lonely Onan's dissipation sapped the intellectual skills—or so the theory went. Instead, it led to endless boasting, after they had returned to daylight and each knew his own circle-count, and yet could claim the highest number present, which was one hundred and seven.

John had attained a mere eighty-six, somewhat cowed by the exercise itself, and felt that had he known the end in mind, could have pushed himself over a hundred, easy.

Now in Cairo, with women available for the first time in his life, he had every confidence in his ability, and only a fidgety tautness, but the women beckoning with lacquered leers and painted fingers and arched blue eyebrows somehow did not appeal. He felt that to do this here, while deeper matters troubled his mind, was not right. Stan made some fun of him for this and John reacted with surly swear-words, most fresh-learned from Mr. Preston.

Anger irked his stomach. He left Stan bargaining with a milk-skinned woman who advertised with red hair and hips that seemed as wide as the river, and made his way at random through the darkling city.

10. Zom Master

Labyrinths of inky geometry enclosed him. Passing conversations came to him muffled and softly discordant as he worked his way among the large commercial buildings near the docks. Here the jobbing trade waxed strong, together with foundries, machine shops, oil presses, flax mills and towering elevators for diverse crops, all springing from the intricately tailored lifecrafts known best in Cairo.

Not that such arts grew no blemishes. Slick yellow fungus coated the cobbled streets, slippery malignancies that sucked at John's heels, yearning to digest him. Trough-like gutters were awash in fetid fluids, some stagnant and brown-scummed, others running fast and as high as the thick curbstones.

Each building had a mighty cask, several stories high, grown out from the building itself and shooting stilt-roots down to support the great weight of rainwater it held. Never near the river was there enough topsoil to support wells. The passing veils of rain were all Cairo had, and as if to make this point, droplets began to form in the mist overhead and spatter John as he searched.

He descended into a lowland zone of the city, where the streets lay silent, with an empty Sunday aspect. But the wrought-iron symbology on the ramshackle buildings here told the reason. They made heavy, rugged ciphers and monograms, filled in with delicate cobwebs of baffling, intricate weave. John could make out in the gathering gloom the signs of Zom businesses, bearing the skulls and ribbed ornamentation.

It would be just his bad luck, of course, that the worldwall glow would ebb at just this time. The rain dribbled away, leaving a dank cold. He looked upward and saw that far overhead was a broad island of sandy waste, interrupting the worldwall, and so leaving this part of the city permanently darker. So they had decided to put the Zom industry here, in constant gloom.

He peed against a building, reasoning that it would help it to grow just like any plant, though he did modestly slip down a side alley to do it. So John was off the street when a squad of Zom women came by.

They shambled, chill-racked and yellow-faced, eyes playing about as if in addled wonder, and one saw John. She grinned, an awful rictus, and licked her lips and hoisted her skirt with one hand, gesturing with the other index finger, eyebrows raised. John was so transfixed he stopped urinating and stood there shock-still until finally the Zom shrugged and went on with the other miserables. His heart restarted again some time after and he put himself back in his pants.

Zoms were accepted as a necessity for their brute labor, he told himself, but still his breath came short, his chest grew tight and fluttery. Instinctively he reached up into the mellow, soft air and whispered his ritual words.

A long moment of nothing. Then he felt the reassuring grasp of an unseen hand clasping his own, shaking it firmly in reassurance. It was a callused workingman's hand, world-worn. He had felt it in moments of vexation since he was a young boy, since the day his father had left in blood and fire and his world had ended.

It had started that night. Somehow he had known that the spirit realm would understand that flame and hot fury, and so had simply reached up into the prickly spark-filled air of the burning house and had felt the firm fist that, sensing him, opened into a welcoming palm.

Years later, in another crisis, he had looked up to see what grasped him, and the hand was invisible, though he could feel it. But the air waxed gossamer-rich with crystalline motes—a manifestation, certainly. More sure than demons or *mana*.

The spirit hand gave him strength. Made freshly bold, he walked down a street of wavering oil lamps and searched out the Zom raiser.

The man was tall, in a stovepipe-thin charcoal suit. He sat in a spacious room, working at an ancient stone desk, scribbling on parchment. Along the walls were deep alcoves sunk into shadow.

"I'm looking for a, my father. I thought maybe—"

"Yes yes," the man said. "An old story. Go ahead, look."

This abruptness startled John so that it was some moments before he fully realized what he saw.

Grimy oil lamps cast dim yellow radiance across long rows of slanted boards, all bearing adult corpses. They were not shrouded, but wore work clothes, some mud-caked. John walked down the rows and peered into bloodless, rigid faces. In the alcoves were babes laid out in white shrouds.

All had the necessary ribbed ironwork cage about them. Pale revitalizing fluids coursed through tubes into their nostrils, pumped by separate hearts—bulbous, scarlet muscles attached at the ribs, pulsing. The fluids did their sluggish work down through the body, sending torpid waves washing from the sighing chest through the thick guts and into the trembling legs. Their charge expended, the fluids emerged a deep green from the rumps, and spilled into narrow troughs cut into the hardwood floor.

Amid echoing drips and splashes he returned to the stone desk, an island of luminosity in the cool, clammy silence. "He's not here."

"Not surprising. We move them on fast." The man's deep-sunken eyes gave nothing away.

"You raised anybody looks like me?"

"Got a name for him?"

John gave it. The sound of his father's name spoken full was itself enough to put John's teeth to grinding. The man studied a leather-bound ledger and said, "No, not in the records. Say, though, I recall something . . ."

John seized the Zom raiser by the shoulders. "What?"

"Leggo. Leggo, I say." He shied back and when John's hands left him he straightened himself the way a chicken shakes its feathers into order. "You damn fools come barging in here, you're always—"

"Tell me."

Something in John's voice made the man cease and study him for a long moment. "I was trying to recollect. You're all wrong, lookin' on the slabs for him. That name, it's in the trade somehow."

"Zom business?"

"Believe so. A supplier, if I 'member right."

John felt his throat tighten with memories. His father had worked now and then, always at jobs he picked up easily and let go of just the same. And always work that strayed to the shadowy side. "That would be right."

"He comes in here with a squad or so, every week or so."

"From where?"

"Gets them in the countryside, he says."

"That would fit."

The man picked up his quill pen and used it to turn the pages in a small volume of notes. John saw that he had only one arm. "Yeah, here. Zom master, license and all. You can see what he's rounded up lately, if you like," the man said without looking up.

"I can? How?"

"He's got a place where he holds them till he's got a goodly number. Then he brings them here for kindling up to strength."

"Where?"

"Last I heard, 'bout seven blocks over."

"Which way?"

"Annunciation and Poydras. Big long shed, tin roof."

John made his way through the rain-slicked streets, getting lost twice in his hurried confusion and slipping on something slimy he did not want to look at. He got to the low building as a figure came out the other end of it and something made him step back into the street and watch the man hurry away. He went inside and there was nobody there except five Zoms who lay on ready-racks, chilled down and with brass amulets covering their faces. A gathering sense of betrayal caught in his mouth and John trotted down the empty aisles where Zoms would labor in the day, the slanting grey light making every object ghostly and threatening.

He knew before he reached the end of it that the Zom raiser had played him for a fool all along, had maybe even recognized him somehow. While John was finding his way here the man had somehow sent word and now his father had slipped away.

He was not smarter, John reminded himself, but he was younger. He ran hard for some minutes through shrouded streets and caught a

glimpse of the same figure—running hard now, too, coat fluttering behind—as he came up into the open produce market.

The stalls yawned empty and the man ahead darted among them,
knowing better where he was going and gaining distance. John settled
in to run him down but then they burst out onto Galvez Street and up
it onto the ample docks. The man was going flat out. He ran down stone
steps to the riverside and leaped into a launch moored there. It was an
oddly shaped craft and the man worked frantically to start it.

John could hear the engines sputter and then rumble as he put on a
desperate surge, but the launch erupted away from the dock before he
could reach the stairs.

It sped off upriver, growling, and John saw with a souring taste in
his mouth what the vessel carried amidships, giving it the strange shape:
induction coils.

The man did not look back.

11. The Past is Labyrinth

Three deep, mellow bell notes floated off across the sublime skin of
the river and some moments later came wafting back, steepened into
treble and shortened in duration.

"Means we're getting close to the arc," Mr. Preston said.

John narrowed his eyes, searching the gloom before them. "Can't see
a thing."

"The bell notes get scrunched up by the time-wind, then bounced
back to us. Better guide than seeing the arcs, sometimes. They twist the
light, give you spaghetti pictures."

John would have preferred to watch the treacherous standing curves
of frothy water, for he had seen one smash a flatboat to splinters on his
trip down. A deep hush brooded upon the river. He felt a haunting sense
of isolation, remoteness from the bustle of Cairo, though they were only
hours beating upstream from it.

To starboard he could make out solid walls of dusky forest softening
into somber grey. Mr. Preston sounded the bells again and the steepened
echoes came, quicker and sharper this time.

Then the river seemed to open itself, revealing first the foaming feet
and then the marvelous high swoop of the arcs. Silently they churned

at their feet, sending waves to announce their power. Yet as the *Natchez* came up, holding tight to the opposite shore, the water was glass-smooth, with mercury breaking at midriver and sending spectral flags of glittering mist into an eerily still air.

This tranquility fractured. A wall of thunder shook the glass windows of the pilot's nest.

"Whoa!" Mr. Preston called and slammed on the power. The induction motors sent a shock through the decking.

"It look the way you seen it last?" Mr. Preston never took his eyes from the arcs, which were shimmering pink and blue now.

"Yessir, only the tall one, it had a bigger foot."

"You shoot down through here?"

"Nossir, stayed out by that sandbar."

"Damn right you were, too."

John had, in the chop and splash of it, been given no choice whatever, but he said nothing, just held on. The deck bucked, popped, complained.

"Eddy running here up the bank to past the point," Mr. Preston said, betraying some excitement despite himself. "Might get us through without we have to comb our hair afterward."

They went flying up the shore so close that twigs snapped off on the chimneys. Mist churned the air fever-pink and drumroll bass notes came up through John's boots. "Hold on for the surge!" Mr. Preston called, as if anyone wasn't already, and it hit.

The *Natchez* struck the vortex whorl plunging by near the point. It stretched clear across the river this time, an enormous mouth of mercury and bromium seething brown and silver together in smeared curves. The ship whirled around, John thought as his stomach lurched, like a favorite top his mother had given him, possessing the mysterious ability to stand so long as it spun.

This abstract memory lasted one breath and then water crashed over the pilot's nest and smashed in the aft window. The ship careened to port. Time-torques whipsawed the groaning timbers. An eddy seized her and crunched one of her chimneys into pathetic torn tin. Concussion clapped both John's ears and left his head ringing. Lightning-quick flashes of ruby radiance forked from the river and ran caressing over the upper decks. Shouts. Screams.

Athwart the current, then with it, the *Natchez* shot free of the howling whorl. Within a mere moment they brought up hard in the woods at

the next bend. Ordinarily this would have been an embarrassment for
a pilot, but as it came from passing uptime against the arcs, it was a
deliverance, a penalty, like a stingy tip left after a banquet.

In the lapsed quiet afterward they drummed upstream and John
watched the shoreline for signs he remembered, but mostly to find the
launch carrying the dark-clothed figure.

He did not tell anyone that, but Mr. Preston gave him sidewise study-
filled glances now and then. Stan, after the obligatory ragging of John
for having shied away from the women of easy virtue, kept pestering him
about finding hydrogen hats. So John spent long hours pretending,
watching beady-eyed the dense, uncut forest roll by.

To him the richness here was vaster than downriver, thicker and mysterious beyond ready expression. He had not the wit nor especially the
years to savor it fully; taste comes with age and is perhaps its only reward,
though some call the same thing wisdom.

He saw the great slow-working chains of cause and effect on the
river—forces which, though elusive in the redolent natural wealth, in
hard fact underpinned all the sweeping vistas, the realms of aery compass, and infinitesimal machineries of wood and leaf. The young must
make their way in a world which is an enormous puzzle, so he watched
the shifting hues quick-eyed, a student of the forever fluid, knowing that
the silver river might foam suddenly to suck him under or contrariwise
spew him aloft in a frothy geyser—all beautiful events, he supposed, but
they would leave him no less dead.

John kept lively advising Mr. Preston on reefs and bars. He inspected
the passing acres of lumber rafts, great pale platforms behind which the
launch could conceal itself. Likewise each bulky barge and the trading
scows which peddled from farm to farm, the peddler's family hanging
out washing on deck and kids calling hullos. So when Stan shouted up
from the passenger deck, "See that! Must be! Must be!" John felt a spur
of irritation at being distracted from his work.

Stan scampered aft and poled aboard some floating debris, then had
the temerity to carry it forward to the pilot's nest.

Mr. Preston scowled and looked to bite his moustache at the sight of
a mere deckhand intruding, but before John could shoo Stan out he saw
the flower-like grey thing Stan carried.

"It's a hat! A positive hat," Stan burbled. "Pure hydrogen—worth
plenty on its own, wager me—and lookee *here*."

Stan proudly displayed brooches and pins mounted into the gunmetal-grey thing, which to John's immense surprise surely did resemble a hat. It was nearly weightless yet hard and the jewels gleamed with inner radiance.

"And you led me straight on it, too, John, I'll not forget," Stan said. "I'll share out the proceeds, yessir."

"Uh, sure thing."

Mr. Preston's stormy face had turned mild as he studied the hat. "Never seen anything like *this*. *How* far upriver you say you come from?" He peered at John.

"Good bit further," was all John could say, for indeed that was so, but the shore already looked odd and contorted to him, as though his memory was warping.

That was nothing compared to the consternation he felt but could not give a hint of, for the hat story was total yarning—yet here was an actual, in-fact bejeweled hydrogen hat, worth many a month's pay.

His befuddlement got swept away soon enough by the twisty demands of the river. Under Mr. Preston he was coming to see that the face of the wedded water and metal was a wondrous book, one in a language dead to him before but now speaking cherished secrets. Every fresh point they rounded told a new tale. No page was empty. A passenger might be charmed by a churning dimple on its skin, but to a true riverman that was an italicized shout, announcing a wreak or reef of wrenching space-time vortex about to break through from the undercrust of world-wall.

Passengers went *ooh* and *aahhh* at the pretty pictures the silver river painted for them without reading a single word of the dark text it truly was. A lone log floating across the prow could be in truth a jack-jawed beast bent on dining upon the tasty wooden hull. A set of boiling, standing rings spoke of a whorl which could eat an entire induction disk.

Mr. Preston would sometimes muse out loud as they rounded a point and beheld a fresh vista, "That slanting brown mark—what you make of that? I'd say a bar of ground-up metal, dissolving now in the bromine current. See that slick place? Shoaling up now, be worse when we head back down. River's fishing for induction ships right there, you mark."

But mostly Mr. Preston asked John the questions, for the river perpetually tore itself down, danced over its own banks, made merry of memory. They saw a farmer had shoved down pilings to hold his ground, even set a crazy-rail fence atop it, only to have the blithe momentum strip and pry and overrun his fetters, break his handcuffs, and

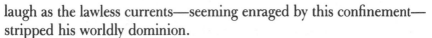

laugh as the lawless currents—seeming enraged by this confinement—stripped his worldly dominion.

Mr. Preston brought aboard a local "memory man" to help them through a set of neck-twisting oscillations, and the fellow displayed the affliction John had heard of but never witnessed. To remember everything meant that all events were of the same size.

The short, swarthy man sat in the pilot's nest and guided them well enough through the first two swaybacks, with reefs and snags galore, but on the third began to tell the history of the snaggle-toothed tree that had fallen in at the lee shore and so stopped them from using the close-pass there, and from that tree went on to the famous boiling summer which had scorched the tree, and from the summer to a minute rendition of the efforts of Farmer Finn, who had saved his crops by building a sluice-diverter of the river, to Finn's wife who run off with a preacher, only people *then* found out he was no preacher at all but in fact a *felon* escaped from some jail uptime, which suggested to the memory man the way laws had to be deformed here to accord with the passage back and forth in time of relatives and wives and husbands, which brought forth the scandal of the lady in a red dress who had taken on all the men at a dance once, hiking her skirts for each in turn plain as day, outside against the wall, and from there it was but a step to the intricate discussion of dance steps the memory man had learned (since he learned anything merely by seeing it once), complete with demonstrations, so that Mr. Preston had to yank the man's attention back to the veering river before it gutted them on an aluminum reef.

Within minutes, though, the memory man would drift into more tedious jaw about whatever strayed into view of his panoramic mind. Mr. Preston bore this for the swings and sways of those bends, and then put the memory man ashore with full pay. The man didn't seem to mind, and left still maundering on about great accidents of the past and where their survivors lived now and how they were doing.

John silently envied the man, though, for at least he did know exactly that one short portion of the river, whereas John's own memory betrayed him at each new rounding. Islands and bars arose from the water where none had been before, his mind told him. The river ran in new side-channels and had seemingly cut across headlands to forge fresh entries, thrusting aside monumental hillsides and carving away whatever misunderstandings had arisen with the spongy, pliant forest.

"This sure looks to be a horseshoe curve here. Remember it?" Mr.

Preston would ask, and John would peer through the misty wreaths which often wrapped the river, and shake his head.

On this particular one they hauled ashore, because a passenger thought he lived near here, though could not spot any landmark either, but wanted to try his own luck. John went ashore and slogged through brambles and sandy loam across the neck of the horseshoe, arriving well before the *Natchez* got there, coming hard-chuffing around the curve.

These branches and inlets lay in his past, yet despite their here-and-now solidity they had wriggled into new shapes, oddities of growth, even whole fresh porticoed master-houses. Slowly it dawned on John that none of this surprised Mr. Preston.

"Every time we go upriver, things lay different," Mr. Preston said, twirling a toothpick in his mouth as his only sign of agitation.

"Damnfire," John said, a new curse he had picked up and was proud to sport. "What use is a memory man, then?"

"Better than nothing, is all."

They were near to drawing all the water there was in the channel, a curious tide having sucked streamers up and into the clouds above. The hull caught and broke free and then snagged again, so Mr. Preston had to order the induction motors up to full, wrenching them off the world-wall bed of the river by sheer magnetic ferocity.

"Sure seems that way," John said. "Why'd you hire me as guide, then?"

"Your knowledge is for certain fresher than any I could find. And you're young enough, you don't think you know everything."

They were going slow, deck humming, riding on magnetic cushions that John thought of as bunched steel coils. Mr. Preston said that wasn't far wrong, only you couldn't feel or see the wires. They were more like the wrestling ghosts of spirit-world steel, he said.

"Sometimes a time-tide will come and cut a little gutter across a neck of land," Mr. Preston went on. "I saw one once while I was shipping downstream, no bigger than a garden path it was. Shimmered and snaked and snapped yellow fire. Now, there were handsome properties along that shore. But inland from there was a worthless old farm. When I came back uptime on the old *Reuben,* that li'l time-twist had cut a big course through. Diverted the whole damn river, it did. Shooting off crimson sparklers, still. That old farm was now smack on the river, prime land, worth ten times more. The big places that had been on the river stood inland. No ship could reach them."

"Lucky," John said.

Mr. Preston grinned. "Was it? Lot of people got mad, accused the family that owned the old farm of starting that time-wrinkle."

"How could they?"

"Who's to say? Is there a way to figure it? The past is labyrinth, truly. Give time a shove here, a tuck there? Anybody who knows how, sure don't talk about it."

12. Whorl

But John felt himself lost in a dense, impenetrable maze of riverways. Coming upstream against the time-pressure now refracted the very air.

Smooth and serene the majestic mud-streaked expanse had seemed as he drifted down obliviously in his skiff. Now the shore was morasses and canebrakes and even whole big plantations, the grand main houses beautiful in their ivory columns. He often gazed up at the world hanging overhead, lands of hazy mystery. A ripple passed, flexing the entire worldwall, and John felt suddenly that they all lived in the entrails of a great beast, an unknowable thing that visited the most awful of calamities upon mere humans by merely easing its bowels.

The whorl came upon them without warning. It burst through a channel of bromium, coiling like a blue-green serpent up into the shimmering air. A thunderclap banged into the pilot's nest and blew in two windows.

John saw it from the middeck where he was helping Stan and two men with some baling. The glass scroll window shattered but did not catch Mr. Preston in the face, so when John raced in the pilot was already bringing the *Natchez* about, clawing away from the swelling cloud-wrack.

The whorl soared, streamers breaking from it to split the sky with yellow forked lightning. John saw it hesitate at its high point, as if deciding whether to plunge on across the world itself and bury itself in the forest-wall hanging far overhead. Then it shook itself, vigorous with the strength of the newborn, and shot riverward.

The silver river seemed to yearn for this consummation, for it buoyed in up-sucking ardor and kissed the descending column. Instantly a foam of muddy water and a mist of metal soared through the time-whorl, writing a great inverted U that bubbled and frothed and steam-hissed amid more sharp thunder-cracks.

"Damn!" Mr. Preston cried. "That'll block us for sure."

John held tight to a stanchion. "Can't we shoot by—"

"It'll rip-tide us to pieces, we try that."

A blistering gale broke over the *Natchez*. "You figure it'll last long?"

"This big a one, you bet."

The *Natchez* beat steadily away from the whorl, which twisted and shuffled its water-feet around on the skin of the river. Mud and logs sucked up into it tumbled and seemed to break apart and come together again. In the midst of what looked like a water-wave John saw a log burst into orange flame. It turned in slow motion, streaming black smoke, and smacked full into the river.

Then he saw the launch. It had been across the river, probably hiding among some weeping willows. It broke out of there as the whorl lashed sidewise and John saw a dark figure at the helm. "Wait! Let's stay awhile, see if it—"

"Shut up, boy. We're running downtime."

Even the Cap'n could not overrule a pilot reversing course for safety. John stood frozen as the launch cut cross-river. Then he did not think any more but simply ran, down the iron stairs and pine gangway and then was in the water, flailing about him for a desperate moment and then striking for shore. Stan shouted behind him but he did not look around. The shore was pretty close and it lay near where the launch would end up, he estimated. But then he heard a whooshing boom, like a giant drawing its breath, and a funnel mouth of the whorl came skating on the choppy silver waters. It swooped with trainwreck malevolence down upon the *Natchez* and drew it up, elongating the decks like rubber stretched to its limit and then cracking—fracturing time with a rolling boom. A deckhand jumped overboard and his body stretched to translucent thinness.

The *Natchez* squeezed and contorted and obeyed the call of warping forces. It shot up the whorl-mouth. Time-tides wrenched and wracked it and then it was gone in a brilliant last pearly flash. The glare burned John's face.

John had no time to think or mourn. The mouth reeled, crackled and snaked and swept down upon him. He had time to gulp in air. Burning orange foam broke over him. Legs, arms—both stretched involuntarily, as though some God were playing with his strings—yet he was weightless. He knew he must be rising up the whorl but he felt a sickened, belly-opening vacancy of infinite falling. He struggled not to fill his lungs as the foam thronged at his skin, infested his nose, pried at his eyelids. *Don't breathe!* was all he could think as he prepared for the time-crushed impact his instincts told him was coming at the end of such a protracted fall.

He smacked hard. Bobbed to the surface. Paddled, gasping. Ignored the wave-wracked waters. Made the shore and flopped upon it.

13. Pursuit

He found the launch upstream, backed into a copse. It was hidden just the way he had done with his skiff and he smiled without humor.

A sweet dust of time blew high above the river and there was no sign of the whorl. Or of the *Natchez*.

John followed the boot tracks away from the launch. They led inland, so there was no time pressure to fight. His clothes dried out as he walked beneath a shimmering patch of burnt-gold worldwall that hung tantalizingly behind roiling clouds.

Inland the lush forest dribbled away into scrub desert. He realized his father might back around on him so he retraced his steps and erased signs of his passage from the water and onto safe stone. He avoided vegetation where possible and slid through bushes so that stems bent but did not break. This was crucial, for a broken stem cannot be fixed without careful cutting and even so, a sure reader of signs would catch it. Leaving stems or branches pointing the way you came was bad, too. They had to be gently urged back to a random pattern. He mussed up a scraped bush and tree so that it looked to be from an animal, from biting or itch-easing. Stealth spelled safety.

His head pounded with a mysterious headache that worked its way into his eyes. So much had happened but he put it aside, not thinking about Mr. Preston or Stan, just keeping on. It got dryer and a big-winged thing with teeth flapped overhead, eyeing him for possibilities. He flung a rock at it.

He wished for a blunderbuss tree, recalling the man who had threatened him with one of the awkward weapons. But a big fallen branch served to make a club after he stripped the bark away.

The boot tracks were steady, no heels dug in from haste. He had grown up well above here but knew the manner of empty spaces better than the rich riverland and so let his senses float out ahead of him. Once he reached up and the hand was there, shaking his with calm certainty.

Everything in the land fled from his footsteps. Lizards scattered into the nearest cracked rock. Four-winged quail hovered in shadow, hoping you'd take them for stones, but at the last moment they lost their nerve and burst into frantically flapping birds. Snakes evaporated, doves squeaked skyward, rabbits crazylegged away in a dead heat. Fox, midget mountain horn, coyote—they melted into legend, leaving only tracks and dung. The heart of the desert was pale sand, a field whose emptiness exposed life here for what it was: conjured out of nothingness, bound for it, too. Desert plants existed as exiles from each other, hoarding their circles of water collection done silently beneath the sand by single-minded roots. Vacancy was life. He had learned to think that way since his father left the burning house.

He caught a smell fetid and pestiferous and knew instantly that his father would be drawn to it. An upwelling—he worked his way around it by nose alone. But when he looked down into the bowl-like field he could see only sprawled dead. Cautiously he ventured out. Men in armor lay putrefying, faces puffed and lips bruised. Most were gutted, appearing to give birth to their own entrails.

The time-whorls sometimes did this, disgorging people or matter from times and places no one knew. What the induction ships did by laboring upstream a flick of space-time could accomplish in an instant. Sometimes carrion like this could still be saved for the Zom business.

John turned to merge again with the brush and there he was.

The face—angular, hollow-eyed, a familiar cut to the jawline and the downcurved mouth. John compared it with the last sharp image, the portrait framed in conflagration and carried now for a dozen immemorial years in his mind, taken out and studied every day. Yes. He was sure. The father.

"What do you want?" The voice was low and edged.

"Justice."

"Who are you?" The eyes showed skittering fear.

"You know me."

"In these places? Don't know *what* I know anymore. Nothing's regular. You've run me far uptime. Blew out the i-boat. Dunno what the hell this place even *is*. I—"

"You fled the house."

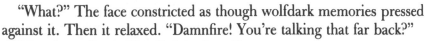

"What?" The face constricted as though wolfdark memories pressed against it. Then it relaxed. "Damnfire! You're talking that far back?"

"You know I am. She died in there."

A long silence. The man studied him as if looking for an edge, some advantage. Or was there some recognition? "Yes. Yes. All past now though. Listen, the family was finished."

"It will be when this is done."

The man squinted as clouds above parted and golden glare descended. John sensed his uncertainty and knew this was the moment and stepped forward quickly without thinking any more. He had been thinking over a decade and was tired of that.

The man's face flickered with sudden recognition and his mouth shaped a cry John was never to hear. He put up an arm and to John's surprise there was no weapon in it. John hesitated for only an instant. He swung the branch as a club, once, twice, three—and the man's head split open. Without saying another word.

14. The Whorehouse

He sat up from the blur of sleep and sucked in cloying, damp air, the reek of a room permanently perfumed. Utter blackness, which was unusual. For a long moment he could only remember the time-whorl and the *Natchez* and then the rest of it came back.

It had taken a day's work to fashion a raft from blown-down trees at the riverside—the legacy of the whorl, he reckoned—and lash it firmly. He had lain on the raft for days with a fatigue he could not explain. He had the man's clothes in a bundle and used it as a pillow but could not look at them beyond that. Fishing was poor and he was skeleton-thin by the time he saw the arcs above Cairo. He knew enough then to pole ashore, barely making it against the sharp reef-shaped current. Then he spent two days walking downstream, the time-pressure sickening him. He was eating leaves by the time he saw the distant church steeples of Cairo.

It had been hard to find any sort of job but with his belly full again he had thrown himself into it, getting two shifts of dock loader, sleeping and eating the rest of the time and not thinking much. He had saved his money and now after three weeks he had come and got this.

He sat up and ran his hands over the woman. She was better in the dark than to look at, all satin and black corset, garter belt and hose that made the creamy flesh somehow ripe to the point of near-rot. But he had been drawn to her in the big reception room downstairs. She had leaned on the upright piano and regarded him with sly, primeval eyes. He had refused the drink or entertainment normally due gentlemen callers, wanting to come upstairs and pay extra for the whole night. The first time should be really something special.

And it had indeed been fine. Like being seized by a great creature that had lived inside you all this time without your knowing, but now released, would never be put back.

He eased out from beneath the heavy quilt and lit an old brass oil lamp. The woman slept noisily, head back and mouth open, showing two missing teeth, through which whistled her moist sighs. An oddly urgent need made him pick up his scruffy knapsack and unlace its innermost compartment. He had carried all his valuables in it since his first days back in Cairo, out of a pervasive, floating insecurity. He usually worked with the sack on his back, afraid to even put it aside.

The papers were still there. Their reassuring official thickness he found pleasurable. Despite some blurring from John's immersion in the river, Mr. Preston's bold handwriting in his crew contract for the *Natchez* stood out, royal blue beneath the wavering liquid glow of the lamp.

People said the *Natchez* had not come back from its uptime voyage . . . not yet. Cairo dwelled so near the great timestorm arcs that its folks always spoke conditionally, ending their statements about events with *so far* and *seems to be* and *in the sweet by and by* and *we'll see.*

John paged through the crew papers, treasuring their solidity. Yesterday he had been coming back through the stockyards, from a hauling job, and had run into Stan on a plank-board sidewalk. Or at least the young man looked for all the world like Stan, with sandy hair and certain distracted gaze. But he stared blankly at John and disavowed ever being on the *Natchez* or uprivering at all. When John had started to tell of what had happened the young man had said irritably, "Well then, you shouldn't ought to have went!" and brushed by him.

John put back the papers and felt also deep in the pocket the wad of documents he had taken off his father. Probably time to look at them, he figured. As soon as the man had poured out his blood on the sand John had felt utter and profound release from the charge of over a decade, and had taken from the body only the papers and a leather belt.

There was little, mostly receipts and incidentals. But the dues book in the Pilots' Association was different, cardboard-thick and consequential. The straight columns showed dues paid right on time, the secretary's scribbled initials acknowledging them. John flipped forward to the front and found there in one single blistering instant not the name of his father at all, but that of himself.

The shock of it kept him rigid while the name itself, black ink set forth with a firm hand—a writing laborious and undeniable—loomed and oscillated in his gaze. Yet it was stone-solid, calling forth the sharp memories of that face in the desert, features lined and fearful but now completely and at last familiar.

The woman stirred and yawned, opened her large eyes. Slowly she smiled at the unmoving man who held scraps of paper and stared into nothing. With a thick-lipped smile as ancient as time she said languorously, "We got a right smart spell left, honey. Gobs of it. Honey? What you reaching up in the air for? Honey?"

Death and the Lady

Judith Tarr

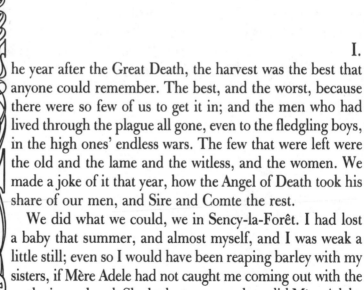

he year after the Great Death, the harvest was the best that anyone could remember. The best, and the worst, because there were so few of us to get it in; and the men who had lived through the plague all gone, even to the fledgling boys, in the high ones' endless wars. The few that were left were the old and the lame and the witless, and the women. We made a joke of it that year, how the Angel of Death took his share of our men, and Sire and Comte the rest.

We did what we could, we in Sency-la-Forêt. I had lost a baby that summer, and almost myself, and I was weak a little still; even so I would have been reaping barley with my sisters, if Mère Adele had not caught me coming out with the scythe in my hand. She had a tongue on her, did Mère Adele, and Saint Benedict's black habit did nothing to curb it. She took the scythe and kilted up her habit and went to work down the long rows, and I went where she told me, to mind the children.

There were more maybe than some had, if travelers' tales told the truth. Every house had lost its share to the black sickness, and in the manor by the little river the dark angel had taken everyone but the few who had the wits to run. So we were a lordless demesne as well as a manless one, a city of women, one of the nuns from the priory called us; she read books, and not all of them were scripture.

If I looked from where I sat under the May tree, I could see her in the field, binding sheaves where the reapers passed. There were children with her; my own Celine, just big enough to work, had her own sheaf to gather and bind. I had the littlest ones, the babies in their pen like odd sheep, and the weanlings for the moment in my lap and in a circle round me, while I told them a story. It was a very old story; I hardly needed to pay attention to it, but let my tongue run on and watched the reapers, and decided that I was going to claim my scythe back. Let Mère Adele look after the babies. I was bigger than she, and stronger, too.

I was growing quite angry inside myself, while I smiled at the children and made them laugh. Even Francha, who never made a sound, nor had since her family died around her, had a glint of laughter in her eye, though she looked down quickly. I reached to draw her into my lap. She was stiff, all bones and tremblings like a wild thing, but she did not run away as she would have once. After a while she laid her head on my breast.

That quieted my temper. I finished the story I was telling. As I opened my mouth to begin another, Francha went rigid in my arms. I tried to soothe her with hands and voice. She clawed her way about, not to escape, but to see what came behind me.

Sency is Sency-la-Forêt not for that it was woodland once, though that is true enough; nor for that wood surrounds it, closing in on the road to Sency-les-Champs and away beyond it into Normandy; but because of the trees that are its westward wall. People pass through Sency from north to south and back again. Sometimes, from north or south, they go eastward into Maine or Anjou. West they never go. East and south and north is wood, in part the Sire de Sency's if the Death had left any to claim that title, in part common ground for hunting and woodcutting and pig-grazing. West is Wood. Cursed, the priest said before he took fright at the Death and fled to Avranches. Bewitched, said the old women by the fire in the evenings. Enchanted, the young men used to say before they went away. Sometimes a young man would swear that he would go hunting in the Wood, or a young woman would say that she meant to scry out a lover in the well by the broken chapel. If any of them ever did it, he never talked of it, nor she; nor did people ask. The Wood was best not spoken of.

I sat with Francha stiff as a stick in my arms, and stared where she was staring, into the green gloom that was the Wood. There was someone on the edge of it. It could almost have been a traveler from south or east, worked round westward by a turning of the road or by the lure of the trees. We were a formidable enough town by then, with the palisade that

Messire Arnaud had built before he died, and no gate open but on the northward side.

Francha broke out of my arms. My Perrin, always the first to leap on anything that was new, bolted gleefully in Francha's wake. Half a breath more and they were all gone, the babies in their pen beginning to howl, and the reapers nearest pausing, some straightening to stare.

If I thought anything, I thought it later. That the Death was not so long gone. That the roads were full of wolves, two-legged nearly all of them, and deadly dangerous. That the Wood held things more deadly than any wolf, if even a tithe of the tales were true.

As I ran I thought of Perrin, and of Francha. I could have caught them easily, a season ago. Now the stitch caught me before I had run a furlong, doubled me up and made me curse. I ran in spite of it, but hobbling. I could see well enough. There was only one figure on the Wood's edge, standing very still before the onslaught of children. It was a woman. I did not know how I knew that. It was all in shapeless brown, hooded and faceless. It did not frighten our young at all. They had seen the Death. This was but a curiosity, a traveler on the road that no one traveled, a new thing to run after and shrill at and squabble over.

As the children parted like a flock of sheep and streamed around it, the figure bent. It straightened with one of the children in its arms. Francha, white and silent Francha who never spoke, who fled even from those she knew, clinging to this stranger as if she would never let go.

The reapers were leaving their reaping. Some moved slowly, weary or wary. Others came as fast as they were able. We trusted nothing in these days, but Sency had been quiet since the spring, when the Comte's man came to take our men away. Our woods protected us, and our prayers, too.

Still I was the first but for the children to come to the stranger. Her hood was deep but the light was on her. I saw a pale face, and big eyes in it, staring at me.

I said the first thing that came into my head. "Greetings to you, stranger, and God's blessing on you."

She made a sound that might have been laughter or a sob. But she said clearly enough, "Greetings and blessing, in God's name." She had a lady's voice, and a lady's accent, too, with a lilt in it that made me think of birds.

"Where are you from? Do you carry the sickness?"

The lady did not move at all. I was the one who started and spun about.

Mère Adele was noble born herself, though she never made much of it; she was as outspoken to the lord bishop as she was to any of us. She stood behind me now, hands on her ample hips, and fixed the stranger with a hard eye. "Well? Are you dumb, then?"

"Not mute," the lady said in her soft voice, "nor enemy either. I have no sickness in me."

"And how may we be sure of that?"

I sucked in a breath.

The lady spoke before I could, as sweetly as ever, and patient, with Francha's head buried in the hollow of her shoulder. I had been thinking that she might be a nun fled from her convent. If she was, I thought I knew why. No bride of the lord Christ would carry a man's child in her belly, swelling it under the coarse brown robe.

"You can never be certain," she said to Mère Adele, "not of a stranger; not in these times. I will take no more from you than a loaf, of your charity, and your blessing if you will give it."

"The loaf you may have," said Mère Adele. "The blessing I'll have to think on. If you fancy a bed for the night, there's straw in plenty to make one, and a reaper's dinner if you see fit to earn it."

"Even," the lady asked, "unblessed?"

Mère Adele was enjoying herself: I could see the glint in her eye. "Earn your dinner," she said, "and you'll get your blessing with it."

The lady bent her head, as gracious as a queen in a story. She murmured in Francha's ear. Francha's grip loosened on her neck. She set the child down in front of me—Francha all eyes and wordless reluctance—and followed Mère Adele through the field. None of the children went after her, even Perrin. They were meeker than I had ever seen them, and quieter; though they came to themselves soon enough, once I had them back under the May tree.

Her name, she said, was Lys. She offered no more than that, that night, sitting by the fire in the mown field, eating bread and cheese and drinking the ale that was all we had. In the day's heat she had taken off her hood and her outer robe and worked as the rest did, in a shift of fine linen that was almost new. She was bearing for a fact, two seasons gone,

I judged, and looking the bigger for that she was so thin. She had bones like a bird's, and skin so white one could see the tracks of veins beneath, and hair as black as her skin was white, hacked off as short as a nun's.

She was not that, she said. Swore to it and signed herself, lowering the lids over the great grey eyes. Have I said that she was beautiful? Oh, she was, like a white lily, with her sweet low voice and her long fair hands. Francha held her lap against all comers, but Perrin was bewitched, and Celine, and the rest of the children whose mothers had not herded them home.

"No nun," she said, "and a great sinner, who does penance for her sins in this long wandering."

We nodded round the fire. Pilgrimages we understood; and pilgrims, even noble ones, alone and afoot and tonsured, treading out the leagues of their salvation. Guillemette, who was pretty and very silly, sighed and clasped her hands to her breast. "How sad," she said, "and how brave, to leave your lord and your castle—for castle you had, surely, you are much too beautiful to be a plain man's wife—and go out on the long road."

"My lord is dead," the lady said.

Guillemette blinked. Her eyes were full of easy tears. "Oh, how terrible! Was it the war?"

"It was the plague," said Lys. "And that was six months ago now, by his daughter in my belly, and you may weep as you choose, but I have no tears left."

She sounded it: dry and quiet. No anger in her, but no softness either. In the silence she stood up. "If there is a bed for me, I will take it. In the morning I will go."

"Where?" That was Mère Adele, abrupt as always, and cutting to the heart of things.

Lys stood still. She was tall; taller in the firelight. "My vow takes me west," she said.

"But there is nothing in the west," said Mère Adele.

"But," said Lys, "there is a whole kingdom, leagues of it, from these marches to the sea."

"Ah," said Mère Adele, sharp and short. "That's not west, that's Armorica. West is nothing that a human creature should meddle with. If it's Armorica that you're aiming for, you'd best go south first, and then west, on the king's road."

"We have another name for that kingdom," said Lys, "where I was born." She shook herself; she sighed. "In the morning I will go."

. . .

She slept in the house I had come to when I married Claudel, in my
bed next to me with the children in a warm nest, Celine and Perrin and
Francha, and the cats wherever they found room. That was Francha's
doing, holding to her like grim death when she would have made her
bed in the nuns' barn, until my tongue spoke for me and offered her
what I had.

I did not sleep overmuch. Nor, I thought, did she. She was still all
the night long, coiled on her side with Francha in the hollow of her.
The children made their night-noises, the cats purred, Mamère Mondine snored in her bed by the fire. I listened to them, and to the lady's
silence. Claudel's absence was an ache still. It was worse tonight, with
this stranger in his place. My hand kept trying to creep toward the
warmth and the sound of her breathing, as if a touch could change her,
make her the one I wanted there. In the end I made a fist of it and
pinned it under my head, and squeezed my eyes shut, and willed the
dawn to come.

Dawn came and went, and another dawn, and Lys stayed. The sky
that had been so clear was turning grey. We needed every hand we had,
to get in the crops before the rain came. Even mine—Mère Adele
scowled at me as I took my place, but I stared her down. Lys took the
row beside me. No one said anything. We were all silent, that day and
the next, racing the rain.

The last of the barley went in the barn as the first drops fell. We stood
out in it, too tired and too shocked by the stopping of a race we had run
for so long, to do more than stare. Then someone grinned. Then someone else. Then the whole lot of us. We had done it, we, the women and
the children and the men too old or weak to fight. We had brought in
the harvest in Sency-la-Forêt.

That night we had a feast. Mère Adele's cook slaughtered an ox, and
the rest of us brought what we had or could gather. There was meat for
everyone, and a cake with honey in it, and apples from the orchards,
and even a little wine. We sat in the nuns' refectory and listened to the
rain on the roof, and ate till we were sated. Lame Bertrand had his pipe
and Raymonde her drum, and Guillemette had a voice like a linnet.
Some of the younger ones got up to dance. I saw how Pierre Allard was
looking at Guillemette, and he just old enough to tend his own sheep:
too young and small as he had been in the spring for the Comte's men

to take, but grown tall in the summer, and casting eyes at our pretty idiot as if he were a proper man.

I drank maybe more of the wine than was good for me. I danced, and people cheered: I had a neat foot even then, and Pierre Allard was light enough, and quick enough, to keep up with me.

It should have been Claudel dancing there. No great beauty, my Claudel, and not much taller than I, but he could dance like a leaf in the Wood; and sing, too, and laugh with me when I spun dizzy and breathless out of the dance. There was no one there to catch me and carry me away to a bed under the sky, or more likely on a night like this, in the barn among the cows, away from children and questions and eyes that pried.

I left soon after that, while the dancing was still in full whirl. The rain was steady, and not too cold. I was wet through soon enough, but it felt more pleasant than not. My feet knew the way in the black dark, along the path that followed the priory's wall, down to the river and then up again to a shadow in shadow and a scent of the midden that was mine and no one else's. There was light through a chink in the door: firelight, banked but not yet covered. Mamère Mondine nodded in front of it. She was blind and nearly deaf, but she smiled when I kissed her forehead. "Jeannette," she said. "Pretty Jeannette." And patted my hand that rested on her shoulder, and went back to her dreaming.

The children were abed, asleep. There was no larger figure with them. Francha's eyes gleamed at me in the light from the lamp. They were swollen and red; her cheeks were tracked with tears.

I started to speak. To say that Lys was coming, that she would be here soon, that she was still in the priory. But I could not find it in me to say it. She had eaten with us. She had been there when the children went out in a crowd, protesting loudly. When the dancing began, I had not seen her. I had thought, if I thought at all, that she had come here before me.

In the dark and the rain, a stranger could only too easily go astray. It was not far to the priory, a mile, maybe, but that was a good count of steps, and more than enough to be lost in.

What made me think of the Wood, I never knew. Her words to Mère Adele. My first sight of her on the Wood's edge. The simple strangeness of her, as I sat on the bed and tried to comfort Francha, and saw in the dimness the memory of her face. We had stories, we in Sency, of what lived in the Wood. Animals both familiar and strange, and shadows cast by no living thing, and paths that wound deep and deep, and yet ended

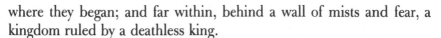

where they began; and far within, behind a wall of mists and fear, a kingdom ruled by a deathless king.

I shook myself hard. What was it to me that a wayward stranger had come, brought in our harvest, and gone away again? To Francha it was too much, and that I would not forgive. Whatever in the world had made our poor mute child fall so perfectly in love with the lady, it had done Francha no good, and likely much harm. She would not let me touch her now, scrambled to the far corner of the bed when I lay down and tried to draw her in, and huddled there for all that I dared do without waking the others. In the end I gave it up and closed my eyes. I was on the bed's edge. Francha was pressed against the wall. She would have to climb over me to escape.

One moment, it seemed, I was fretting over Francha. The next, the red cock was crowing, and I was staggering up, stumbling to the morning's duties. There was no sign of Lys. She had had no more than the clothes on her back; those were gone. She might never have been there at all.

I unlidded the fire and poked it up, and fed it carefully. I filled the pot and hung it over the flames. I milked the cow, I found two eggs in the nest that the black hen had thought so well hidden. I fed the pigs and scratched the old sow's back and promised her a day in the wood, if I could persuade Bertrand to take her out with his own herd. I fed Mamère Mondine her bowl of porridge with a little honey dripped in it, and a little more for each of the children. Perrin and Celine gobbled theirs and wanted more. Francha would not eat. When I tried to feed her as I had when I first took her in, she slapped the spoon out of my hand. The other children were delighted. So were the cats, who set to at once, licking porridge from the wall and the table and the floor.

I sighed and retrieved the spoon. Francha's face was locked shut. There would be no reasoning with her today, or, I suspected, for days hereafter. Inside myself I cursed this woman who had come, enchanted a poor broken child, and gone away without a word. And if Francha sickened over it, if she pined and died—as she well could, as she almost had before I took her—

I dipped the porridge back into the pot. I wiped the children's faces and Francha's hands. I did what needed doing. And all the while my anger grew.

The rain had gone away with the night. The last of the clouds blew away eastward, and the sun came up, warming the wet earth, raising

pillars and curtains of mist. The threshers would be at it soon, as should
I.

But I stood in my kitchen garden and looked over the hedge, and saw
the wall of grey and green that was the Wood. One of the cats wound
about my ankles. I gathered her up. She purred. "I know where the lady
went," I said. "She went west. She said she would. God protect her;
nothing else will, where she was going."

The cat's purring stopped. She raked my hand with her claws and
struggled free; hissed at me; and darted away round the midden.

I sucked my smarting hand. Celine ran out of the house, shrilling in
the tone I was doing my best to slap out of her: "Francha's crying again,
mama! Francha won't stop crying!"

What I was thinking of was quite mad. I should go inside, of course
I should, and do what I could to comfort Francha, and gather the children together, and go to the threshing.

I knelt in the dirt between the poles of beans, and took Celine by the
shoulders. She stopped her shrieking to stare at me. "Are you a big girl?"
I asked her.

She drew herself up. "I'm grown up," she said. "You know that,
mama."

"Can you look after Francha, then? And Perrin? And take them both
to Mère Adele?"

She frowned. "Won't you come, too?"

Too clever by half, was my Celine. "I have to do something else," I
said. "Can you do it, Celine? And tell Mère Adele that I'll be back as
soon as I can?"

Celine thought about it. I held my breath. Finally she nodded. "I'll
take Perrin and Francha to Mère Adele. And tell her you'll come back.
Then can I go play with Jeannot?"

"No," I said. Then: "Yes. Play with Jeannot. Stay with him till I come
back. Can you do that?"

She looked at me in perfect disgust. "Of course I can do that. I'm
grown up."

I bit my lips to keep from laughing. I kissed her once on each cheek
for each of the others, and once on the forehead for herself. "Go on," I
said. "Be quick."

She went. I stood up. In a little while I heard them go, Perrin declaring loudly that he was going to eat honeycakes with Mère Adele. I
went into the kitchen and filled a napkin with bread and cheese and
apples, and put the knife in, too, wrapped close in the cloth, and tied

it all in my kerchief. Mamère Mondine was asleep. She would be well enough till evening. If I was out longer, then Mère Adele would know to send someone. I kissed her and laid my cheek for a moment against her dry old one. She sighed but did not wake. I drew myself up and went back through the kitchen garden.

Our house is one of the last in the village. The garden wall is part of Messire Arnaud's palisade, though we train beans up over it, and I have a grapevine that almost prospers. Claudel had cut a door in it, which could have got us in trouble if Messire Arnaud had lived to find out about it; but milord was dead and his heirs far away, and our little postern was hidden well in vines within and brambles without.

I escaped with a scratch or six, but with most of my dignity intact. It was the last of the wine in me, I was sure, and anger for Francha's sake, and maybe a little honest worry, too. Lys had been a guest in my house. If any harm came to her, the guilt would fall on me.

And I had not gone outside the palisade, except to the fields, since Claudel went away. I wanted the sun on my face, no children tugging at my skirts, the memory of death far away. I was afraid of what I went to, of course I was; the Wood was a horror from my earliest memory. But it was hard to be properly terrified, walking the path under the first outriders of the trees, where the sun slanted down in long sheets, and the wind murmured in the leaves, and the birds sang sweet and unafraid. The path was thick with mould under my feet. The air was scented with green things, richer from the rain, with the deep earthy promise of mushrooms. I found a whole small field of them, and gathered as many as my apron would carry, but moving quickly through them and not lingering after.

By then Sency was well behind me and the trees were closing in. The path wound through them, neither broader nor narrower than before. I began to wonder if I should have gone to fetch the Allards' dog. I had company, it was true: the striped cat had followed me. She was more comfort than I might have expected.

The two of us went on. The scent of mushrooms was all around me like a charm to keep the devils out. I laughed at that. The sound fell soft amid the trees. Beeches turning gold with autumn. Oaks going bronze. Ash with its feathery leaves, thorn huddling in thickets. The birds were singing still, but the quiet was vast beneath.

The cat walked ahead of me now, tail up and elegantly curved. One would think that she had come this way before.

I had, longer ago than I liked to think. I had walked as I walked now, but without the warding of mushrooms, crossing myself, it seemed, at every turn of the path. I had taken that last, suddenly steep slope, and rounded the thicket—hedge, it might have been—of thorn, and come to the sunlit space. It had dazzled me then as it dazzled me now, so much light after the green gloom. I blinked to clear my eyes.

The chapel was as it had been when last I came to it. The two walls that stood; the one that was half fallen. The remnant of a porch, the arch of a gate, with the carving on it still, much blurred with age and weather. The upper arm of the cross had broken. The Lady who sat beneath it had lost her upraised hand, but the Child slept as ever in her lap, and her smile, even so worn, was sweet.

I crossed myself in front of her. No devils flapped shrieking through the broken roof. Nothing moved at all, except the cat, which picked its way delicately across the porch and vanished into the chapel.

My hands were cold. I shifted my grip on my bundle. I was hungry, suddenly, which made me want to laugh, or maybe to cry. My stomach lived in a time of its own; neither fear nor anger mattered in the least to it.

I would feed it soon enough. I gathered my courage and stepped under the arch, ducking my head though it was more than high enough: this was a holy place, though not, maybe, to the God I knew.

The pavement had been handsome once. It was dull and broken now. The altar was fallen. The font was whole, but blurred as was the carving on the gate. A spring bubbled into it and bubbled out again through channels in the wall. It was itself an odd thing, the stump of a great tree—oak, the stories said—lined with lead long stripped of its gilding, and carved with crosses. Here the roof was almost intact, giving shelter from the rain; or the ancient wood would long ago have crumbled into dust.

She was kneeling on the edge of the font, her dark head bent over it, her white hands clenched on its rim. I could not see the water. I did not want to see it. I could hear her, but she spoke no language I knew. Her tone was troubling enough: pure throttled desperation, pleading so strong that I lurched forward, hand outstretched. I stopped myself before I could touch her. If she was scrying her lover, then she was calling him up from the dead.

I shuddered. I made no sound, but she started and wheeled. Her face was white as death. Her eyes—

She lidded them. Her body eased by degrees. She did not seem surprised or angered, or anything but tired. "Jeannette," she said.

"You left," I said. "Francha cried all night."

Her face tightened. "I had to go."

"Here?"

She looked about. She might have laughed, maybe, if she had had the strength. "It was to be here first," she said. "Now it seems that it will be here last, and always. And never."

I looked at her.

She shook her head. "You don't understand. How can you?"

"I can try," I said. "I'm no lady, I grant you that, but I've wits enough for a peasant's brat."

"Of course you have." She seemed surprised. As if I had been doing the doubting, and not she. "Very well. I'll tell you. He won't let me back."

"He?"

"He," said Lys, pointing at the font. There was nothing in it but water. No face. No image of a lover that would be. "My lord of the Wood. The cold king."

I shivered. "We don't name him here."

"Wise," said Lys.

"He won't let you pass?" I asked. "Then go around. Go south, as Mère Adele told you. It's a long way, but it's safe, and it takes you west eventually."

"I don't want to go around," said Lys. "I want to go in."

"You're mad," I said.

"Yes," she said. "He won't let me in. I walked, you see. I passed this place. I went where the trees are old, old, and where the sun seldom comes, even at high noon. Little by little they closed in front of me. Then at last I could go no farther. *Go back,* the trees said to me. *Go back and let us be.*"

"You were wise to do it," I said.

"Mad," she said, "and wise." Her smile was crooked. "Oh, yes. So I came back to this place, which is the gate and the guard. And he spoke to me in the water. *Go back,* he said, as the trees had. I laughed at him. Had he no better word to offer me? *Only this,* he said. *The way is shut. If you would open it, if you can—then you may. It is not mine to do.*"

I looked at her. She was thinner than ever, the weight of her belly dragging her down. "Why?" I asked. "Why do you want to get in? It's madness there. Every story says so."

"So it is," Lys said. "That was why I left."

There was a silence. It rang.

"You don't look like a devil," I said. "Or a devil's minion."

She laughed. It was a sweet, awful sound. "But, my good woman, I am. I am everything that is black and terrible."

"You are about to drop where you stand." I got my arm around her before she did it, and sat her down on the font's rim. I could not help a glance at the water. It was still only water.

"We are going to rest," I said, "because I need it. And eat, because I'm hungry. Then we're going back to Sency."

"Not I," said Lys.

I paid her no mind. I untied my kerchief and spread out what I had, and put in a fistful of mushrooms, too; promising myself that I would stop when I went back, and fill my apron again. There was nothing to drink but water, but it would do. Lys would not drink from the font, but from the spring above it. I did as she did, to keep the peace. The cat came to share the cheese and a nibble or two of the bread. She turned up her nose at the mushrooms. "All the more for us," I said to her. She filliped her tail and went in search of better prey.

We ate without speaking. Lys was hungry: she ate as delicately and fiercely as a cat. A cat was what I thought of when I looked at her, a white she-cat who would not meet my eyes.

When we were done I gathered the crumbs in my skirt and went out to the porch and scattered them for the birds. I slanted an eye at the sun. A bit past noon. I had thought it would be later.

Lys came up behind me. Her step was soundless but her shadow fell cool across me, making me shiver.

"There is another reason," she said, "why I should stay and you should leave. My lord who is dead: he had a brother. That one lives, and hunts me."

I turned to face her.

"He wants me for what I am," she said, "and for what he thinks I can give him. For myself, too, maybe. A little. I tricked him in Rouen: cut my hair and put on a nun's habit and walked out peacefully in the abbess' train. He will have learned of that long since, and begun his tracking of me."

I shrugged. "What's one man in the whole of Normandy—or one woman, for the matter of that? Chance is he'll never find you."

"He'll find me," Lys said with quelling certainty.

"So let him." I shook my skirts one last time and stepped down off the porch.

I was not at all sure that she would follow. But when I came to the trees, she was behind me. "You don't know who he is. He'll come armed, Jeannette, and with his men at his back."

That gave me pause, but I was not about to let her see that. "We have walls," I said. "If he comes. Better he find you there than in a broken chapel, beating on a door that stays fast shut."

"Walls can break," said Lys.

"And doors?"

She did not answer that. Neither did she leave me.

After a while she asked it. "Why?"

"You're my guest," I said.

"Not once I left you."

"What does that have to do with it?"

She started to speak. Stopped. Started again. One word. "Francha."

"Francha." I let some of the anger show. "God knows why, God knows how, but she has decided that she belongs to you. You went off and left her. Her mother is dead, her father died on top of her; we found her so, mute as she is now, and he begun to rot." I could not see her, to know if she flinched. I hoped that she did. "I took her in. I coaxed her to eat, to face the world, to live. Then you came. She fixed the whole of herself on you. And you left her."

"I had no choice.'

"Of course you did," I said. "You had to have known that the way was shut. He exiled you, didn't he? your cold king."

"I exiled myself."

Her voice was stiff with pride. I snorted at it. "I believe you, you know. That you're one of Them. No one but a soulless thing would do what you did to Francha."

"Would a soulless thing go back? Would it admit that it had erred?"

"Have you done either?"

She seized my sleeve and spun me about. She was strong; her fingers were cruel, digging into my arm. She glared into my face.

I glared back. I was not afraid, not at all. Even when I saw her true. Cat, had I thought, back in the chapel? Cat, yes, and cat-eyed, and nothing human in her at all.

Except the voice, raw and roughened with anger. "Now you see. Now you know."

I crossed myself, to be safe. She did not go up in a cloud of smoke. I had not honestly expected her to. That was a cross she wore at her throat, glimmering under the robe. "So they're true," I said. "The stories."

"Some of them." She let me go. "He wants that, my lord Giscard. He wants the child I carry, that he thinks will be the making of his house."

"Then maybe you should face him," I said, "and call the lightnings down on him."

She looked as shocked as if I had done as much myself. "That is the Sin! How can you speak so lightly of it?"

"Sin?" I asked. "Among the soulless ones of the Wood?"

"We are as Christian as you," she said.

That was so improbable that it could only be true. I turned my back on her—not without a pricking in my nape—and went on down the path. In a little while she followed me.

II.

When the threshing was done and the granaries full, the apples in and the windfalls pressed for cider, my lone proud grapevine harvested and its fruit dried in the sun, and all of Sency made fast against a winter that had not yet come, a company of men rode up to our gate. We had been expecting them, Lys and I and Mère Adele, since the leaves began to fall. We kept a boy by the gate, most days, and shut and barred it at night. Weapons we had none of, except our scythes and our pruning hooks, and an ancient, rusted sword that the smith's widow had unearthed from the forge.

Pierre Allard was at the gate the day milord Giscard came, and Celine tagging after him as she too often did. It was she who came running to find me.

I was nearly there already. All that day Lys had been as twitchy as a cat. Suddenly in the middle of mending Francha's shirt, she sprang up and bolted. I nearly ran her down just past the well, where she stood rigid and staring, the needle still in one hand, and the shirt dangling from the other. I shook her hard.

She came to herself, a little. "If he sees me," she said, "if he knows I'm here . . ."

"So," I said. "You're a coward, then."

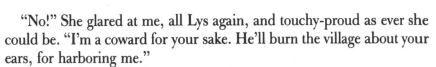

"No!" She glared at me, all Lys again, and touchy-proud as ever she could be. "I'm a coward for your sake. He'll burn the village about your ears, for harboring me."

"Not," I said, "if we have anything to say about it."

I tucked up my skirt and climbed the gate. Pierre was up there, and Mère Adele come from who knew where; it was a good long run from the priory, and she was barely breathing hard. She had her best wimple on, I noticed, and her jeweled cross. The sun struck dazzles on the stones, white and red and one as green as new grass. She greeted me with a grunt and Lys with a nod, but kept her eyes on the men below.

They were a pretty company. Much like the one that had taken Claudel away: men in grey mail with bright surcoats, and one with a banner—red, this, like blood, with something gold on it.

"Lion rampant," said Lys. She was still on the stair below the parapet. She could hardly have seen the banner. But she would know what it was. "Arms of Montsalvat."

The lord was in mail like his men. There was a mule behind him, with what I supposed was his armor on it. He rode a tall red horse, and he was tall himself, as far as I could tell. I was not so much above him, standing on the gate. He turned his face up to me. It was a surprising face, after all that I had heard. Younger, much, than I had expected, and shaven clean. Not that he would have much beard, I thought. His hair was barley-fair.

He smiled at me. His teeth were white and almost even. His eyes were pure guileless blue. "Now here's a handsome guardsman!" he said laughing, sweeping a bow in his high saddle. "Fair lady, will you have mercy on poor travelers, and let us into your bower?"

Mère Adele snorted. "I'd sooner let a bull in with the cows. Are you here to take what's left of our men? Or will you believe that we're drained dry?"

"That," said Lys behind, still on the stair, "was hardly wise."

"Let me judge that," said Mère Adele without turning. She folded her arms on the parapet and leaned over, for all the world like a goodwife at her window. "That's not a device from hereabouts," she said, cocking her head at the banner. "What interest has Montsalvat in poor Sency?"

"Why, none," said milord, still smiling. "Nor in your men, indeed, reverend lady. We're looking for one of our own who was lost to us. Maybe you've seen her? She would seem to be on pilgrimage."

"We see a pilgrim now and then," said Mère Adele. "This would be an old woman, then? With a boy to look after her, and a little dog, and a fat white mule?"

I struggled not to laugh. My lord Giscard—for that he was, no doubt of it—blinked his wide blue eyes and looked a perfect fool. "Why, no, madam, nothing so memorable. She is young, our cousin, and alone." He lowered his voice. "And not . . . not quite, if you understand me. She was my brother's mistress, you see. He died, and she went mad with grief, and ran away."

"Poor thing," said Mère Adele. Her tone lacked somewhat of sympathy.

"Oh," he said, and if he did not shed a tear, he wept quite adequately with his voice. "Oh, poor Alys! She was full of terrible fancies. We had to bind her lest she harm herself; but that only made her worse. Hardly had we let her go when she escaped."

"Commendable of you," said Mère Adele, "to care so much for a brother's kept woman that you'll cross the width of Normandy to find her. Unless she took somewhat of the family jewels with her?"

Lys hissed behind me. Mère Adele took no notice. Milord Giscard shook his head. "No. No, of course not! Her wits were all we lost, and those were hers to begin with."

"So," said Mère Adele. "Why do you want to find her?"

His eyes narrowed. He did not look so pretty now, or so much the fool. "She's here, then?"

"Yes, I am here." Lys came up beside me. She had lost a little of her thinness, living with us. The weight of the child did nothing to hamper her grace. Her hands cradled it, I noticed, below the parapet where he could not see. She looked down into his face. For a moment I thought that she would spit. "Where were you? I looked for you at Michaelmas, and here it's nigh All Hallows."

He looked somewhat disconcerted, but he answered readily enough. "There was trouble on the road," he said: "English, and Normans riding with them."

"You won," she said. It was not a question.

"We talked our way out of it." He studied her. "You look well."

"I am well," she said.

"The baby?"

"Well."

I saw the hunger in him then, a dark, yearning thing, so much at odds with his face that I shut my eyes against it. When I opened them again, it was gone. He was smiling. "Good news, my lady. Good news, indeed."

"She is not for you," said Lys, hard and cold and still.

"If it is a son, it is an heir to Montsalvat."

"It is a daughter," said Lys. "You know how I know it."

He did not move, but his men crossed themselves. "Even so," he said. "I loved my brother, too. Won't you share what is left of him?"

"You have his bones," said Lys, "and his tomb in Montsalvat."

"I think," said Mère Adele, cutting across this gentle, deadly colloquy, "that this were best discussed in walls. And not," she added as hope leaped in milord's face, "Sency's. St. Agnes' priory can house a noble guest. Let you go there, and we will follow."

He bowed and obeyed. We went down from the gate. But Mère Adele did not go at once to St. Agnes'. People had come to see what we were about. She sent them off on errands that she had given them long since: shoring up the walls, bringing in such of the animals as were still without, shutting Sency against, if need be, a siege.

"Not that I expect a fight," she said, "but with these gentry you never know." She turned to me. "You come." She did not need to turn to Lys. The lady would go whether she was bidden or no: it was written in every line of her.

It was also written in Francha, who was never far from her side. But she took the child's face in her long white hands, and said, "Go and wait for me. I'll come back."

One would hardly expect Francha to trust her, and yet the child did. She nodded gravely, not a flicker of resistance. Only acceptance, and adoration.

Not so Celine. In the end I bribed her with Pierre, and him with the promise of a raisin tart if he took her home and kept her there.

Mère Adele set a brisk pace to the priory, one which gave me no time to think about my frayed kerchief and my skirt with the stains around the hem and my bare feet. Of course milord would come when I had been setting out to clean the pigsty.

Lys stopped us at the priory's gate, came round to face us. The men had gone inside; we could hear them, horses clattering and snorting, deep voices muted in the cloister court. Lys spoke above it, softly, but with the edge which she had shown Messire Giscard. "Why?"

Mère Adele raised her brows.

Lys looked ready to shake her. "Why do you do so much for me?"

"You're our guest," said Mère Adele.

Lys threw back her head. I thought that she would laugh, or cry out. She did neither. She said, "This goes beyond plain hospitality. To chance a war for me."

"There will be no war," said Mère Adele. "Unless you're fool enough to start one." She set her hand on the lady's arm and set her tidily aside, and nodded to Sister Portress, who looked near to bursting with the excitement of it all, and went inside.

Messire Giscard had time for all the proper things, food and rest and washing if he wanted it. He took all three, while we waited, and I wished more than ever that I had stopped to change my dress. I brushed at the one I had, and one of the sisters lent me a clean kerchief. When they brought him in at last, I was as presentable as I could be.

Mère Adele's receiving room was an imposing place, long and wide with a vaulted ceiling, carved and painted and gilded, and a great stone hearth at the end of it. It was not her favored place to work in; that was the closet by her cell, bare and plain and foreign to pretension as the prioress herself. This was for overaweing strangers; and friends, too, for the matter of that. I hardly knew what to do with the chair she set me in, so big as it was, and carved everywhere, and with a cushion that must have been real silk—it was impossibly soft, like a kitten's ear. It let me tuck up my feet at least, though I was sorry for that when the servant let milord in, and I had to untangle myself and stand and try to bow and not fall over. Lys and Mère Adele sat as soon as milord did, which meant that I could sit, too: stiffly upright this time.

He was at his ease, of course. He knew about chairs, and gilded ceilings. He smiled at me—there was no mistaking it: I was somewhat to the side, so that he had to turn a little. I felt my cheeks grow hot.

"This lady I know," he said, turning his eyes away from me and fixing them on Lys. "And you, reverend prioress? And this charming demoiselle?"

Well, I thought. That cured my blush. Charming I was not, whatever else I was.

"I am Mère Adele," said Mère Adele, "and this is Jeannette Laclos of

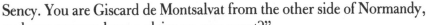

Sency. You are Giscard de Montsalvat from the other side of Normandy, and you say you have a claim on our guest?"

That took him properly aback. He was not used to such directness, maybe, in the courts that he had come from. But he had a quick wit, and a smooth tongue to go with it. "My claim is no more than I have said. She was my brother's lover. She carries his child. He wished to acknowledge it; he bound me before he died, to do all that I could on its behalf."

"For bastard seed?" asked Mère Adele. "I should think you'd be glad to see the last of her. Wasn't your brother the elder? And wouldn't her baby be his heir, if it were male, and she a wife?"

"She would never marry him," said Messire Giscard. "She was noble enough, she said, but exiled, and no dowry to her name."

"Then all the more cause for you to let her go. Why do you hunt her down? She's no thief, you say. What does she have that you want?"

He looked at his feet in their fine soft shoes. He was out of his reckoning, maybe. My stomach drew tight as I watched him. Men like that— big beautiful animals who had never known a moment's thirst or hunger except what they themselves chose, in war or in the chase; who had never been crossed, nor knew what to do when they were—such men were dangerous. One of them had met me in the wood before I married Claudel; and so Celine was a fair child, like the Norman who had sired her. A Norman very like this one, only not so pretty to look at. He had been gentle in his way. But he wanted me, and what he wanted, he took. He never asked my name. I never asked his.

This one had asked. It softened me—more than I liked to admit. Of course he did not care. He wanted to know his adversaries, that was all. If it had been the two of us under the trees and the blood rising in him, names would not have mattered.

Lys spoke, making me start; I was deep in myself. "He wants me," she said. "Somewhat for my beauty. More for what he thinks that I will give."

Messire Giscard smiled his easy smile. "So then, you tempt me. I'd hardly sin so far as to lust after my brother's woman. That is incest, and forbidden by holy Church." He crossed himself devoutly. "No, Mère Adele; beautiful she may be, but I swore a vow to my brother."

"You promised to let me go," said Lys.

"Poor lady," he said. "You were beside yourself with grief. What could I do but say yes to anything you said? I beg your pardon for the falsehood; I reckoned, truly, that it was needful. I never meant to cast you out."

"You never meant to set me free."

"Do you hate him that much?" asked Mère Adele.

Lys looked at her, and then at him. He was still smiling. Pretty, oh, so pretty, with the sun aslant on his bright hair, and his white teeth gleaming.

"Aymeric was never so fair," said Lys. "That was all given to his brother. He was a little frog-mouthed bandy-legged man, as swarthy as a Saracen, bad eyes and bad teeth and nothing about him that was beautiful. Except," she said, "he was. He would come into a room, and one would think, 'What an ugly little man!' Then he would smile, and nothing in the world would matter, except that he was happy. Everyone loved him. Even his enemies—they hated him with sincere respect, and admired him profoundly. I was his enemy, in the beginning. I was a hard proud cruel thing, exile by free choice from my own country, sworn to make my way in the world, myself alone and with no other. He—he wanted to protect me. 'You are a woman,' he said. As if that was all the reason he needed.

"I hated him for that. He was so certain, and so insufferable, mere mortal man before all that I was and had been. But he would not yield for aught that I could do, and in the end, like all the rest, I fell under his spell."

"Or he under yours," said Messire Giscard. "From the moment he saw you, he was bewitched."

"That was my face," said Lys, "and no more. The rest grew as I resisted him. He loved a fight, did Aymeric. We never surrendered, either of us. To the day he died he was determined to protect me, as was I to resist him."

Messire Giscard smiled, triumphant. "You see!" he said to Mère Adele. "Still she resists. And yet, am I not her sole kinsman in this world? Did not my brother entrust her to me? Shall I not carry out my promise that I made as he was dying?"

"She doesn't want you to," said Mère Adele.

"Ah," said Messire Giscard. "Bearing women—you know how they are. She's distraught; she grieves. As in truth she should. But she should be thinking too of the baby, and of her lover's wishes. He would never have allowed her to tramp on foot across the width of Normandy, looking for God knew what."

"Looking for my kin," said Lys. "I do have them, Giscard. One of them even is a king."

"What, the fairy king?" Giscard shook his head. "Mère Adele, if you'll believe it, she says that she's the elf-king's child."

"I am," said Lys, "his brother's daughter." And she looked it, just then, with her white wild face. "You can't shock them with that, Giscard, or hope to prove me mad. They know. They live on the edge of his Wood."

He leaned forward in his chair. All the brightness was gone, all the sweet false seeming. He was as hard and cold and cruel as she. "So," he said. "So, Alys. Tell them the rest. Tell them what you did that made my brother love you so."

"What, that I was his whore?"

I looked at her and shivered. No, he could not be so hard, or so cold, or so cruel. He was a human man. She . . .

She laughed. "That should be obvious to a blind man. Which these," she said, "are not. Neither blind, nor men, nor fools."

"Do they know what else you are?" He was almost standing over her. "Do they know that?"

"They could hardly avoid it," she said, "knowing whose kin I am."

"If they believe you. If they don't just humor the madwoman."

"We believe her," said Mère Adele. "Is that what you want? To burn her for a witch?"

He crossed himself. "Sweet saints, no!"

"No," said Lys. "He wants to use me. For what he thinks I am. For what he believes I can do."

"For what you *can* do," he said. "I saw you. Up on the hill at night, with stars in your hair. Dancing; and the moon came down and danced at your side. And he watched, and clapped his hands like a child." His face twisted. "*I* would never have been so simple. I would have wielded you like a sword."

Lys was beyond speech. Mère Adele spoke dryly in her silence. "I can see," she said, "why she might be reluctant to consent to it. Women are cursed enough by nature, weak and frail as all the wise men say they are; and made, it's said, for men's use and little else. Sometimes they don't take kindly to it. It's a flaw in them, I'm sure."

"But a flaw that can be mended," said Messire Giscard. "A firm hand, a touch of the spur—but some gentleness, too. That's what such a woman needs."

"It works for mares," said Mère Adele. She stood up. I had never seen her look as she did then, both smaller and larger than she was. Smaller, because he was so big. Larger, because she managed, one way and another, to tower over him. "We'll think on what you've said. You're welcome meanwhile to the hospitality of our priory. We do ask you, of your courtesy, to refrain from visiting the town. There's been sickness in it; it's not quite past."

He agreed readily: so readily that I was hard put not to laugh. He did not need to know that it was an autumn fever, a fret among the children, and nothing to endanger any but the weakest. Sickness, that year, spoke too clearly of the Death.

"That will hold him for a while," said Mère Adele when we were back in safety again: inside Sency's walls, under my new-thatched roof. People walking by could lift a corner of it and look in, but I was not afraid of that. Most were in their own houses, eating their dinner, or down in the tavern drinking it.

We had finished our own, made rich with a joint from a priory sheep. Perrin's face was shiny with the grease. Even Francha had eaten enough for once to keep a bird alive. She curled in her lady's lap, thumb in mouth, and drowsed, while we considered what to do.

"He won't go where there's sickness," Mère Adele said, "but I doubt he'll go away. He wants you badly."

Lys' mouth twisted. "He wants my witchcraft. No more and no less. If my body came with it—he'd not mind. But it's my power he wants; or what he fancies is my power."

"Why?" I asked. "To make himself lord of Normandy?"

"Oh, no," said Lys. "He'd never aim so high. Just to be a better lord in Montsalvat. Just that. If later it should be more—if his good angel should call him to greater glory—why then, would he be wise to refuse?"

"He'd burn for it," said Mère Adele. "And you with him. They're not gentle now with witches."

"Were they ever?" Lys combed Francha's hair with her fingers, smoothing out the tangles. "It's worse in the south, in Provence, where

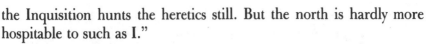

the Inquisition hunts the heretics still. But the north is hardly more hospitable to such as I."

"We're northerners," I said.

She glanced at me: a touch like a knife's edge. "You live on the edge of the Wood. That changes you."

I shrugged. "I don't feel different. Is the story true? That your king was a mortal king once, in the western kingdom?"

"He was never mortal," she said. "He was king of mortal men, yes, for a hundred years and more. But in the end he left. It was no mercy for his people, to be ruled by one who could never age nor die."

"No mercy for him, either," said Mère Adele, "to see them grow old and die." And when Lys looked at her with wide startled eyes: "No, I'm no wiser than I ought to be. I read a book, that's all. I wanted to know what the stories were. He swore a vow, they said, that he would go under the trees and never come out; not in this age of the world."

"Nor will he," Lys said, bitter. "Nor any who went in with him, nor any who was born thereafter. It's a wider realm than you can conceive of, and this world is but a corner of it; and yet it is a prison. I wanted this air, this sun, this earth. His vow—sworn before ever I was born—forbade me even to think of it."

"So of course you thought of it." Mère Adele sighed. "Young things never change."

"That is what he said," said Lys, so tight with anger that I could barely hear her. "That is exactly what he said."

"He let you go."

"How could he stop me? He knew what would happen. That the walls would close, once I'd opened them. That there'd be no going back."

"Did you want to?"

"Then," said Lys, "no. Now . . ." Her fingers knotted in Francha's curls. Carefully she unclenched them. "This is no world for the likes of me. It hates me, or fears me, or both together; it sees me as a thing, to use or to burn. Even you who took me in, who dare to be fond of me— you know how you could suffer for it. You will, you're as brave as that. But in the end you'd come to loathe me."

"Probably," said Mère Adele. "Possibly not. I doubt you'll be here long enough for that."

"I will not go back to Montsalvat," said Lys, each word shaped and cut in stone.

"You might not have a choice," Mère Adele said. "Unless you can think of a way to get rid of milord. We can hold him off for a while, but he has armed men, and horses. We have neither."

Lys lowered her head. "I know," she said. "Oh, I know."

"You know too much," I said. I was angry, suddenly; sick of all this talk. "Why don't you stop knowing and do? There are twenty men out there, and a man in front of them who wants a witch for a pet. Either give in to him now, before he kills somebody, or find a way to get him out. You can call down the moon, he said. Why not the lightning, too?"

"I can't kill," said Lys, so appalled that I knew it for truth. "I *can't* kill."

"You said that before," I said. "Is that all your witching is worth, then? To throw up your hands and surrender, and thank God you won't use what He gave you?"

"If He gave it," she said, "and not the Other."

"That's heresy," said Mère Adele, but not as if she cared about it. "I think you had better do some thinking. Playing the good Christian woman brought you where you are. He'll take you, child. Be sure of it. And make us pay for keeping you."

Lys stood up with Francha in her arms, sound asleep. She laid the child in the bed and covered her carefully, and kissed her. Then she turned. "Very well," she said. "I'll give myself up. I'll let him take me back to Montsalvat."

Mère Adele was up so fast, and moved so sudden, that I did not know what she had done till I heard the slap.

Lys stood with her hand to her cheek. I could see the red weal growing on the white skin. She looked perfectly, blankly shocked.

"Is that all you can do?" Mère Adele snapped at her. "Hide and cower and whine, and make great noises about fighting back, and give in at the drop of a threat?"

"What else can I do?" Lys snapped back.

"Think," said Mère Adele. And walked out.

It was a very quiet night. I surprised myself: I slept. I was even more surprised to wake and find Lys still there. She had been sitting by the fire when I went to sleep. She was sitting there still, but the cover was on the fire, and her knees were up as far as they would go with her belly so big, and she was rocking, back and forth, back and forth.

She came to herself quickly enough once I reached past her to lift the firelid; did the morning duties she had taken for her own, seemed no different than she ever had. But I had seen the tracks of tears on her face, that first moment, before she got up to fetch the pot.

When she straightened herself with her hands in the small of her back like any bearing woman since Mother Eve, I was ready to hear her say it. "I'm going to the priory."

I went with her. It was a grey morning, turning cold; there was a bite in the air. This time I had on my good dress and my best kerchief, and Claudel's woolen cloak. They were armor of a sort. Lys had her beauty and my blue mantle that I had woven for my wedding. She had a way of seeming almost ordinary—of looking less than she was. A glamour, Mère Adele called it. It was not on her this morning. She looked no more human than an angel on an altar.

Messire Giscard met us a little distance from the priory, up on his big horse with a handful of his men behind him. He smiled down at us. "A fair morning to you, fair ladies," he said.

We did not smile back. Lys kept on walking as if he had not been there. I was warier, and that was foolish: he saw me looking at him, and turned the full measure of his smile on me. "Will you ride with me, Jeannette Laclos? It's not far, I know, but Flambard would be glad to carry you."

I fixed my eyes on Lys and walked faster. The red horse walked beside me. I did not look up, though my nape crawled. In a moment—in just a moment—he would seize me and throw me across his saddle.

"Oh, come," he said in his light, princely voice. "I'm not as wicked a devil as that. If I do fancy you, and you are well worth a man's fancy—what can I do you but good? Wouldn't you like to live in a fine house and dress in silk?"

"And bear your bastards?" I asked him, still not looking at him. "Thank you, no. I gave that up six years ago Lent."

He laughed. "Pretty, and a sharp wit, too! You're a jewel in this midden."

I stopped short. "Sency is no man's dungheap!"

I was angry enough to dare a glance. He was not angry at all. He was grinning. "I like a woman with spirit," he said.

His horse, just then, snaked its head and tried to bite. I hit it as hard as I could. It veered off, shying, and its master cursing. I let myself laugh, once, before I greeted Sister Portress.

"I will go back with you," said Lys.

We were in Mère Adele's receiving room again, the four of us. This time he had his sergeant with him, whether to guard him or bear witness for him I did not know. The man stood behind his lord's chair and watched us, and said nothing, but what he thought of us was clear enough. We were mere weak women. We would never stand against his lord.

Lys sat with her hands in what was left of her lap, knotting and unknotting them. "I've done my thinking," she said. "I can do no more. I'll give you what you ask. I'll go back to Montsalvat."

I opened my mouth. But this was not my place to speak. Messire Giscard was openly delighted. Mère Adele had no expression at all. "You do mean this?" she asked.

"Yes," said Lys.

Messire Giscard showed her his warmest, sweetest face. "I'll see that you don't regret it," he said.

Lys raised her eyes to him. Her real eyes, not the ones people wanted to see. I heard the hiss of his breath. His sergeant made the sign of the horns, and quickly after, that of the cross.

She smiled. "That will do you no good, Raimbaut."

The sergeant flushed darkly. Lys turned the force of her eyes upon Giscard. "Yes, I will go back with you," she said. "I will be your witch. Your mistress, too, maybe, when my daughter is born; if you will have me. I am an exile, after all, and poor, and I have no kin in this world."

His joy was fading fast. Mine was not rising, not yet. But Lys had not surrendered. I saw it in her face; in the fierceness of her smile.

"But before I go," she said, "or you accept me, you should know what it is that you take."

"I know," he said a little sharply. "You are a witch. You won't grow old, or lose your beauty. Fire is your servant. The stars come down when you call."

"Men, too," she said, "if I wish."

For a moment I saw the naked greed. He covered it as children learn to do. "You can see what will be. Aymeric told me that."

"Did he?" Lys arched a brow. "He promised me he wouldn't."

"I coaxed it out of him," said Messire Giscard. "I'd guessed already, from things he said."

"He was never good at hiding anything," said Lys. "Yes, I have that gift."

"A very great one," he said, "and very terrible."

"You have the wits to understand that," said Lys. "Or you imagine that you do." She rose. The sergeant flinched. Messire Giscard sat still, but his eyes had narrowed. Lys came to stand in front of him. Her hand was on the swell of her belly, as if to protect it. "Let us make a bargain, my lord. I have agreed to yield to your will. But before you take me away, let me read your fate for you. Then if you are certain still that I am the making of your fortune, you may have me, and do with me as you will."

He saw the trap in it. So could I; and I was no lord's child. "A fine bargain," he said, "when all you need do is foretell my death, and so be rid of me."

"No," she said. "It's not your death I see. I'll tell you the truth, Giscard. My word on it."

"On the cross," he said.

She laid her hand on Mère Adele's cross and swore to it. Mère Adele did not say anything. She was waiting, as I was, to see what Lys would do.

She crossed herself; her lips moved in what could only be a prayer. Then she knelt in front of Giscard and took his hands in hers. I saw how he stiffened for a moment, as if to pull away. She held. He eased. She met his eyes. Again he made as if to resist; but she would not let him go.

My hands were fists. My heart was beating. There were no bolts of lightning, no clouds of brimstone. Only the slender big-bellied figure in my blue mantle, and the soft low voice.

She read his future for him. How he would ride out from Sency, and she behind. How they would go back to Rouen. How the war was raging there, and how it would rage for years out of count. How the Death would come back, and come back again. How he would fight in the war, and outlive the Death, and have great glory, with her at his side: ever young, ever beautiful, ever watchful for his advantage. "Always," she said. "Always I shall be with you, awake and asleep, in war and at peace, in your heart as in your mind, soul of your soul, indissolubly a part of you. Every breath you draw, every thought you think, every sight your eye lights upon—all these shall be mine. You will be chaste, Giscard, except for me; sinless, but that you love me. For nothing that you do shall go unknown to me. So we were, Aymeric and I, perfect in love as in amity. So shall we two be."

For a long while after she stopped speaking, none of us moved. Messire Giscard's lips were parted. Gaping, I would have said, in a man less good to look at.

Lys smiled with awful tenderness. "Will you have me, Giscard? Will you have the glory that I can give you?"

He wrenched free. The sweep of his arm sent her sprawling.

I leaped for him, veered, dropped beside her. She was doubled up, knotted round her center.

Laughing. Laughing like a mad thing. Laughing till she wept.

By the time she stopped, he was gone. She lay exhausted in my arms. My dress was soaked with her tears.

"Could you really have done it?" I asked her.

She nodded. She struggled to sit up. I helped her; gave her my kerchief to wipe her face.

"I can do it to you, too," she said. Her voice was raw. "I can hear everything, see it, feel it—every thought in every head. Every hope, dream, love, hate, fear, folly—everything." She clutched her head. *"Everything!"*

I held her and rocked her. I did not know why I was not afraid. Too far past it, I supposed. And she had lived with us since Michaelmas; if there was anything left to hide from her, then it was hidden deeper than I could hope to find.

She was crying again, deep racking sobs. "I was the best, my father said. Of all that are in the Wood, the strongest to shield, the clearest to see both how the walls were raised, and how to bring them down. None of us was better fit to walk among human folk. So I defied them all, brought down the ban, walked out of the Wood. And I could do it. I *could* live as the humans lived. But I could—not—die as they died. I could not." Her voice rose to a wail. "I wanted to die with Aymeric. And I could not even take sick!"

"Oh, hush." Mère Adele stood over us, hands on hips. She had gone out when Giscard took flight; now she was back, not an eyelash out of place, and no awe at all for the woman of the Wood. "If you had really wanted to cast yourself in your lover's grave, you would have found a way to do it. There's no more *can't* in killing yourself than in killing someone else. It's all *won't,* and a good fat measure of *pity-me.*"

Lys could have killed her then. Oh, easily. But I was glad for whatever it was that stopped her, *can't* or *won't* or plain astonishment.

She got to her feet with the first failing of grace that I had ever seen in her. Even her beauty was pinched and pale, too thin and too sharp and too odd.

Mère Adele regarded her with utter lack of sympathy. "You got rid of his lordship," she said, "and handily, too. He'll see the back of hell before he comes by Sency again. You do know, I suppose, that he could have sworn to bring the Inquisition down on us, and burn us all for what you did to him."

"No," said Lys. "He would not. I made sure of that."

"You—made—sure?"

Even Lys could wither in the face of Mère Adele's wrath. She raised her hands to her face, let them fall. "I made him do nothing but what he was best minded to do."

"You made him."

"Would you rather he came back with fire and sword?"

For a moment they faced one another, like fire and sword themselves. Mère Adele shook her head and sighed. "It's done. I can't say I want it undone. That's a wanting I'll pay dearly for in penance. You—maybe you've paid already. You never should have left your Wood."

"No," said Lys. "I don't think that. But that I've stayed too long— yes." Mère Adele started a little. Lys smiled a thin cold smile. "No, I'm not in your mind. It's written in your face. You want me gone."

"Not gone," said Mère Adele. "Gone home."

Lys closed her eyes. "Sweet saints, to be home—to live within those walls again—to be what I am, all that I am, where my own people are—" Her breath shuddered as she drew it in. "Don't you think I've tried? That's why I came here. To find the door. To break it down. To go back."

"You didn't try hard enough," said Mère Adele. "*Won't* again. Always *won't*."

"Not my *won't*," said Lys. "My king's."

"Yours," said Mère Adele, immovable. "I can read faces, too. Are they all as stubborn as you, where you come from?"

"No," said Lys. Her eyes opened. She drew herself up. "Some are worse."

"I doubt that," said Mère Adele. "You're welcome here. Don't ever doubt it. But this isn't your world. We aren't your kind. You said it yourself. You love us, and we die on you."

"You can't help it," said Lys.

Mère Adele laughed, which made Lys stare. "Go on, child. Go home. We're no better for you than you are for us."

Lys was mortally insulted. She was older than Mère Adele, maybe, and higher born. But she held her tongue. She bent her head in honest reverence. If not precisely in acceptance.

III.

The Wood was cold in the grey light of evening. No bird sang. No wind stirred the branches of the trees.

Lys had tried to slip away alone. She should have known better. This time it was not my fault, not entirely: I had followed Francha. So we stood on the porch of the ruined chapel, Francha with both arms about her waist, I simply facing her.

"If the walls can open at all," Lys said, careful and cold, "your mortal presence will assure that they stay shut."

I heard her, but I was not listening. "Are you going to leave Francha again?"

Lys frowned and looked down at the child who clung to her. "She can't go, even if I can get in."

"Why not?"

"She's human."

"She can't live in this world," I said. "She was barely doing it when you came. When you go, she'll die."

"We are forbidden—"

"You were forbidden to leave. But you did it."

Lys had her arms around Francha, almost as if she could not help it. She gathered the child up and held her. "Oh, God! If I could only be the hard cold creature that I pretend to be!"

"You're cold enough," I said, "and as heartless as a cat. But even a cat has its weaknesses."

Lys looked at me. "You should have been one of us."

I shivered. "Thank God He spared me that." I glanced at the sky. "You'd best do it if you're going to. Before it's dark."

Lys might have argued, but even she could not keep the sun from setting.

She did not go into the chapel as I had thought she would. She stood

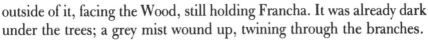

outside of it, facing the Wood, still holding Francha. It was already dark under the trees; a grey mist wound up, twining through the branches.

Lys' eyes opened wide. "It's open," she said. "The walls are down. But—"

"Stop talking," I said. My throat hurt. "Just go."

She stayed where she was. "It's a trap. Or a deception. The ban is clever; it knows what it is for."

Francha struggled in her arms. She let the child go. Francha slid down the curve of her, keeping a grip on her hand. Pulling her toward the Wood.

She looked into wide eyes as human as hers were not. "No, Francha. It's a trap."

Francha set her chin and leaned, putting all her weight into it. It was as loud as a shout. *Come!*

"Go," I said. "How will you know it's a trap till you've tried it? Go!"

Lys glared at me. "How can humans know—"

I said a word that shocked her into silence. While she wavered I pushed, and Francha pulled. Dragging her toward the thing she wanted most in the world.

Later it would hurt. Now I only wanted her gone. Before I gave in. Before I let her stay.

She was walking by herself now, if slowly. The trees were close. I could smell the mist, dank and cold, like the breath of the dead.

"No!" cried Lys, flinging up her hand.

Light flew from it. The mist withered and fled. The trees towered higher than any mortal trees, great pillars upholding a roof of gold.

The light shrank. The trees were trees again, but their leaves were golden still, pale in the evening. There was a path among them, glimmering faintly as it wound into the gloom. It would not be there long, I knew in my bones. I braced myself to drag her down it. What would happen if it closed while I was on it, I refused to think.

She set foot on it of her own will. Walked a step, two, three.

Turned.

Held out her hand. She was going. I had won that much. Now she offered me what I had made her take. The bright country. The people who knew no age nor sickness nor death. Escape. Freedom.

From what? I asked her inside myself. I would grow old no matter where I was.

"Let Francha have it," I said. "Maybe you can heal her; maybe she'll find a voice again. Maybe she'll learn to sing."

Lys did not lower her hand. She knew, damn her. How easily, how happily, I could take it.

My fists knotted in my skirt. "I was born on this earth. I will die on it."

Francha let go Lys' hand. She ran to me, hugged me tight. But not to hold. Not to stay. Her choice was made. Had been made at harvest time, on another edge of this Wood.

Lys looked as if she would speak. I willed her not to. She heard me, maybe; or she simply understood, as humans did, from the look on my face. She said nothing. Only looked, long and long.

The path was fading fast. She turned suddenly, swept Francha up, began to run. Down into the glimmering dark; down to a light that I could almost see. There were people there. Pale princes, pale queens. Pale king who was not cold at all. Almost—almost—I could see his grey eyes; how they smiled, not only at the prodigal come home, but at me, mere mortal flesh, alone beside a broken shrine.

I laughed painfully. She had my wedding cloak. What Claudel would say when he came back—

If he came back.

When, said a whisper in the Wood. A gift. A promise.

I turned my back on the shadow and the trees, and turned by face toward home: warmth and light, and my children's voices, and Mamère Mondine asleep by the fire. Above me as I walked, like a guard and a guide, rose a lone white star.

About the Authors

Poul and **Karen Anderson** have collaborated on a marriage and on several books including *The Unicorn Trade* and the four-part "King of Ys" saga. By himself, Poul Anderson is author of over eighty books of fantasy and science fiction, among them *A Midsummer Tempest* and *The Boat of a Million Years*.

One of the most acclaimed of all modern fantasists, **Peter S. Beagle** is the author of the urban romance *A Fine and Private Place* and the quest novel *The Last Unicorn*. His most recent novel is *The Folk of the Air*.

Astrophysicist **Gregory Benford** is best known for science fiction novels like *Great Sky River* and the Nebula-winning *Timescape*. He has collaborated with David Brin on *The Heart of the Comet* and most recently with Arthur C. Clarke on *Beyond the Fall of Night*.

Since 1959 **John Brunner** has been credited as one of science fiction's most prescient writers, tackling such issues as overpopulation in *Stand on Zanzibar*, ecological disaster in *The Sheep Look Up*, and the computer age in *The Shockwave Rider*. His notable fantasy tales include the five-story saga *The Compleat Traveller in Black*.

Emma Bull burst on the fantasy scene in 1986 with *War for the Oaks*, a tale of ancient magic and modern music set in contemporary Minneapolis. A leading light of modern urban fantasy, she is also the author of the science fiction novels *Falcon* and *Bone Dance*.

Charles de Lint received the William L. Crawford Award as best new fantasy writer in 1984 and has since lived up to that reputation with his highly regarded novels *Greenmantle*, *Svaha*, *Yarrow*, *Jack the Giant-Killer*, and *The Little Country*, an epic fantasy derived from his personal interest in Celtic folk music.

Stephen R. Donaldson endured forty-seven rejections before his unconventional fantasy saga *The Chronicles of Thomas Covenant: The Unbeliever* was published in 1977 to wide acclaim. Since then he has written three more novels of Thomas Covenant; the "Mordant's Need" duology; the stories collected in *Daughter of Regals and Other Tales*; and the first two volumes of his science fiction series "The Gap into Conflict."

With her husband Robert Silverberg, **Karen Haber** is co-editor of the *Universe* anthologies and author of *The Mutant Season*, the first novel of the "Fire in Winter" science fiction tetralogy.

One of science fiction's most incisive satirists, **Barry N. Malzberg** was awarded the first John W. Campbell Memorial Award for his 1972 novel *Beyond Apollo*. Among his works are *Herovit's World*, *Gather in the Hall of Planets*, and *Galaxies*, which together with his nonfiction collection *The Engines of the Night* offer some of the most astute criticism written about modern science fiction.

An electrical engineer employed by a private research and development company, **Dennis McKiernan** began writing in 1977 while recovering from an automobile accident. His work includes the "Iron Tower" trilogy, the "Silver Call" duology, and most recently the novel *Dragondoom*.

Patricia A. McKillip has described her first encounter with the work of J. R. R. Tolkien as "a revelation." She won the first World Fantasy Award for best novel in 1975 with *The Forgotten Beasts of Eld*, and followed this with her "Riddlemaster of Hed" trilogy. Her novel *The Sorceress and the Cygnet* has just been published.

Andre Norton is the author of more than 100 novels that blend science fiction and fantasy. Her "Witch World" series is credited with bridging the gap between young adult and adult fantasy and is considered a seminal influence on fantasy written in the post-Tolkien era.

Generally regarded as one of the funniest writers in fantasy, **Terry Pratchett** is the author of *The Colour of Magic, Mort, Sourcery, Equal Rites,* and *Pyramids*. With Neil Gaiman he has written *Good Omens*, the story of a funny thing that happened on the way to the Apocalypse.

Mike Resnick is one of the most highly praised science fiction writers of the last few years. His recent novels include *Santiago, The Dark Lady, Ivory, Paradise,* and the delightful alternate history fantasy *Bully!* His novelette "Kirinyaga" won the Hugo Award in 1989; another, "The Manamouki," won the same award in 1991.

Elizabeth Scarborough distilled her experiences as a nurse in Vietnam into the Nebula Award–winning novel *The Healer's War*. She is also the author of the four-part humorous fantasy series "The Songs from the Seashells Archives" as well as *Phantom Banjo*, the first book of her projected "Songkiller Saga."

Robert Silverberg's highly acclaimed fiction includes the science fiction novels *Dying Inside, A Time of Changes,* and *The Book of Skulls*; the "Lord Valentine" trilogy; and a retelling of Sumerian mythology in *Gilgamesh the King*.

Judith Tarr has a degree in classics from Cambridge University and a Ph.D. in Medieval Studies from Yale, both of which are evident in the historic detail of her "Hound and the Falcon" and "Avaryan Rising" trilogies. Elsewhere, she has written fantasy set in ancient Egypt in *A Wind in Cairo*, in the Dark Ages in *Ars Magica*, and in the Crusades in *Alamut* and *The Dagger and the Cross*.

History professor **Harry Turtledove** is best known for the four-part "Videssos" cycle and the "Tale of Krispos" series which includes *Krispos Rising* and *Krispos of Videssos*.

Folklorist and teacher **Jane Yolen** has authored more than 100 books for children, including *The Devil's Arithmetic* and *Owl Moon*. Her adult fantasies include *Cards of Grief; Sister Light, Sister Dark*; and *White Jenna*. She is a winner of the World Fantasy Award, the Daedalus Award, and the Christopher Medal, and has her own imprint, Jane Yolen Books, with Harcourt Brace Jovanovich.